On Death and Flying

Tim Martin

On Death and Flying

Text copyright ©2016 Timothy J. Martin

All Rights Reserved

ISBN-13: 978-1541313934

For Dawnya.

I'd still be stuck if it wasn't for you.

Since writing this book, I have spoken with an alarming number of people whose lives have been affected by child abuse. Not even a consideration in my childhood, the problem seems to be everywhere … and growing. Please don't turn a blind eye or deaf ear. Get up and do something.

PROLOGUE

I had just turned sixty. A big age.

Before sixty I had kept busy—too busy to think about dying. At sixty I had time to think about the end being closer than the beginning—a lot closer.

I found myself spending big chunks of my dwindling time, usually at three in the morning, thinking about my disappointing past. And no matter how much I thought about it, it just didn't get any better.

I couldn't imagine the end being good. It would just be *the end*.

So I wanted what most people want, I suppose, as they think about dying. I wanted to do something that would make up for all the things I regretted doing. And even more important, I wanted to do something that would make up for all the things I hadn't done.

I wanted to do something I knew, without a doubt, was right and good.

I decided to kill John and Scarlett Bradley.

Part 1 CHAPTER 1

John and Scarlett Bradley were awful people—awful in every way imaginable, and awful in some ways that were unimaginable.

They were doing a lot of illegal things; poaching, stealing, selling drugs. I could imagine all that. They had likely killed John's half-brother and moved into his house. I could even imagine that. But worst of all, they had children and they did bad things to them. That was the part I found unimaginable.

I didn't know them when this all got started. I wasn't sure I'd ever seen them. I probably had. It turned out they lived less than a mile from me. But not knowing someone living that close to you wasn't odd in North Idaho.

There were lots of people who didn't want to be known and you just let them be. You'd help them if they needed it, and they'd help you if you were stuck in the ditch, but you didn't go knocking on their doors.

John and Scarlett Bradley lived up off of Baldy Mountain Road on a dead-end stretch of dirt called Jesus Is My Redeemer Lane. How it got that name I didn't know, but I was certain they didn't have anything to do with it.

John had inherited the land and the house a decade earlier when his half-brother Travis Bradley, a building contractor, was killed at a work site. It had been a bizarre accident involving a framing nail gun wielded by … John Bradley.

Somehow a 16-penny nail had been driven into his half-brother's head, rather than into the stud on which John had been working. They were alone at the site when the tragedy occurred. With nothing beyond John Bradley's word to go on, the death was ruled accidental. A stupid accident for sure, but you can't prosecute a person for being stupid.

Apparently there was no other living family, so John and Scarlett moved out of their aging double-wide up in Boundary County and into the dead half-brother's house on Jesus Is My Redeemer Lane a few days after the funeral.

Sometime after that they started having babies—three little girls.

◆　◆　◆

I had not wanted a party for my sixtieth. It was the first of my birthdays that I had really thought about in terms of getting older … dying, I mean … and I didn't want to make it a bigger deal than it was already becoming in my head.

I was pretty proud that I was still in good shape. I could spend all day in the mountains hiking and fishing and not get very tired. I'd kept most of my hair, although it had turned white. I didn't take prescription drugs for my heart, or cholesterol, or high blood pressure, or heartburn, or anything. I had weighed pretty much the same since I was thirty. I was still quick on the uptake. I had gotten to the point I didn't have to be the smartest guy in the room.

People seemed to think I knew something valuable about business and communications. I had a few clients who were paying me to share that knowledge with them.

My wife Suzanne was a great partner—the smartest person I ever knew—and she wasn't afraid to piss me off by pushing back. It was pretty hard to appreciate when she did it, but in the long run she'd helped me look at things from a lot of different angles; a very good thing for me.

I lived on a mountain in North Idaho in a house I had built and it had a view to kill for. People told me I was lucky. All-in-all I couldn't complain … or I shouldn't have.

But sixty had some significance for me I couldn't shake. One of my grandfathers had died at sixty, and my dad had succumbed to cancer in the last year of his sixth decade. That kind of stuff gets to everybody at some level, whether you want it to or not.

My wife had always insisted that special birthdays, usually the ones with a zero, required a party. It could never have been a surprise so thank God we didn't have to go through all that drama. A group of friends came up to the house for food and drinks and games and talk. It had been months since I'd seen many of them.

My friends were many different ages. My closest friend, Steve Albright, who was working and missed the party, was in his mid-forties. My other friends ranged in age from thirty to nearly eighty. I got a kick out of the mixture of ideas and prejudices and futures and memories. And I appreciated people who were willing to learn something from others regardless of their age.

People have children a lot later than they used to, so our gatherings quite often included a gaggle of kids. I kind of liked that too, but I was usually relieved when they went home and the noise level dropped back down to what I was used to.

My birthday fell on a Saturday. It was the first really decent day after a long winter, and at almost fifty degrees we could stay outside in the sun, stand around a bonfire and have a drink.

It was at my party that I got the first installment of the John and Scarlett Bradley story, and what was going on just a short hike from my house.

I found myself alone by the fire ring, hearing that Beatle's birthday song in my head. The wood was damp and the fire was a little slow so the guests had gone down onto the back patio where the view was great and they didn't have to breathe a bunch of smoke. I could hear little kids squealing and playing.

I was fiddling with the fire when Ben Chandler eased up next to me, grinned and handed me a bottle of brown ale from a local brewer. "Here's a little present birthday boy," he said.

"Thanks," I said. "My favorite; how *did* you know?"

My friends knew I had a beer fridge in the garage. Most had brought something to drink and had stuck the stuff they wanted to keep cold out there without any prompting. They also knew they were welcome to help themselves. Ben had given me a bottle from my own stash. It was an on-going gag.

He took a long drink from his own brown bottle. "Happy birthday old man. So what words of wisdom do you have for the younger set?" Ben was in his early fifties. He didn't miss a chance to rub it in.

I said, "Oh, I guess I'd tell everybody they're going to die at some point so take advantage of the day; Carpe Diem."

We clinked bottles and drank, then stared silently into the struggling fire. The death subject usually had that effect on people and I regretted saying it.

Ben broke the silence, side-stepping the smoke that had swung around his way. "Yes, seize the day! It's kind of hard to maintain that thinking at our house right now," he said glumly. "Our new girls are in far worse shape than we had thought they were."

Huh, new girls? I didn't have any idea what he was talking about. I felt like an aging idiot.

Ben and his wife Jessica already had a bio-daughter, Cindy, and had adopted Lulu from Korea a couple of years earlier. Of all my friends' kids, they were my favorites.

I wasn't surprised they'd taken in more children, but was shocked I hadn't known. Ben and Jessica had huge hearts. Their place was a menagerie of cast off animals. They wanted to help every abused, put-to-pasture or homeless creature that came down the road.

I often wished I had half as much to give as they did.

These new girls, and whatever was going on with them, was obviously a big deal for Ben. I confessed my shortcomings as a friend and asked him to fill me in.

Ben gave me the story of John and Scarlett Bradley—the mistreatment and suspected molestation of their three daughters; Beth, Mary, and Dawn. How they had been taken away from the Bradleys by Idaho's Child and Family Services and placed as foster children with Ben and Jessica. "You cannot imagine how messed up these girls are," Ben went red in the face. I'd never seen that side of him. He was a big man, fit and muscular, but never imposing or threatening. He had my attention.

We heard the back door open, breaking his intensity. Ben's wife Jessica, glass of wine in hand, came out and walked up the short rock incline to join us. She was smart and determined. I always thought there was nothing Jess couldn't do.

I gave her a hug. "Hi Jess, really glad to see you. Been too long. Sounds like you've had a lot going on."

"Happy Birthday, Chip! You look pretty good for an old guy." Jessica was about the same age as her husband. They were good together. "Yeah, it's been quite a winter." She sipped her red wine. "Your wood's wet."

"My wood tarp's shot." I blinked in the smoke. "Maybe I'll get a new one for my birthday."

"I was just starting to tell Chip about the girls," Ben said, putting his arm through his wife's.

"Oh," she said, her voice going up a notch and her smile fading. "Oh Chip, the poor little things. I'm not sure you want to hear this."

Ben was silent, hard as granite. My friend replaced by a stranger with up-close, irrefutable knowledge of something unthinkable. The stricken stranger looked up over the house toward a spot on Baldy Mountain, then back at me. "You have no idea Chip. No idea."

How bad could it really be, I thought. "I'm here to listen," I said, forgetting about my other guests.

The Ben-stranger looked at Jess. She nodded.

"What would you say to a six-year-old girl who, after you read her a bedtime story and tucked her in, asks if she should suck your cock?"

NO. NO. NO! The horrible words coming from my friend's mouth were solid, grinding me between them, breaking me into useless pieces.

Ben and Jessica Chandler spent the next twenty minutes sobbing and unloading. I put up my armor and tried to get the rest of it to bounce off, but it was too late. It got through and stuck.

The Bradley girls had put Ben and Jess way off balance. They were sweet and cuddly one moment, hateful and striking out the next. Always watching—men in particular—with scared rabbit eyes.

The youngest, Beth, was blonde, pretty and the meanest person Ben had ever encountered. He was fearful she would hurt their animals, their other girls, or maybe even Jess.

Ben, sounding a long way off said, "They're afraid of me. They don't know what to do with Jess, but they're scared shitless of me."

Jess talked through angry sobs as she related how Dawn, the oldest and just eleven, held it all in during the day and screamed in her sleep all night—every night.

How do you convince an eleven-year-old girl that you're not going to come into her bed while she's sleeping and hurt her?" Ben lowered his chin onto his chest and sucked in a deep breath.

He went on to describe how the middle girl, Mary, was reclusive and tended to hurt herself if she thought she had done something wrong. "The other day she spilled a glass of juice at breakfast. She was so scared she grabbed a kitchen knife and locked herself in a closet. When we finally got her out, her arms were covered with blood."

I couldn't conceive of a nine-year-old so distraught that she'd cut herself.

Nobody in the Chandler house was sleeping. The entire family, even the animals, was acting strange, getting sick. There was the stultifying realization of how damaged the new girls really were, but Ben and Jess were determined to help no matter what it took.

"What about the parents, these Bradleys? What happened to them?" I saw murder in Ben's eyes before I finished asking.

"That's the part I just can't figure out," Ben said. "Those scumbags are still free. Nothing happened to them at all. They're running around loose up there." He pointed over the top of my house. "Probably less than a half mile from here."

"What, a half a mile from here?" How could I not have known?

"Yeah, up on Jesus Is My Redeemer Lane."

"Jesus! How can that be if the state took the girls away from them?" A few seconds ago I had lived in my safe, beautiful place where this horror wasn't even a possibility.

"I can't get a straight answer from anybody as to why they aren't in jail. I'd like to put a bullet in those sons of bitches' heads."

Jessica didn't interrupt. She stared grimly into the fire and sipped her wine.

And at that moment, I thought Ben would have done it and slept soundly.

At least until Dawn's screams woke him up.

◆ ◆ ◆

After the party I lay sleepless. I was looking at the time being projected in red up on the ceiling by my wife's elaborate clock. It also belched out surf and ocean sounds that actually were kind of pleasant. She got in, pulling the blue blanket up under her chin.

"Hope you had a happy birthday," Suzanne whispered. "You good?"

"Just a little restless from the excitement I guess," I whispered back.

She was warm and asleep almost as the words left my mouth; safe in our bed.

I thought about what Ben and Jessica Chandler had told me; the look of despair on their faces as they had told it. I thought about Cindy and Lulu, their original daughters, now witness to things no child should ever have to see.

I thought about the Bradley girls. During the party I had watched them running in my tiny backyard. Innocent, happy angels playing in sweet March sunshine—just down the road from where their beast parents still breathed, unpunished.

My safe little world had been broken into pieces. I felt a boiling wave of rage rise up and take over the dark bedroom.

◆ ◆ ◆

I proceeded to brood all the next day about the little girls and my friends—and what the Bradleys had gotten away with. I felt paralyzed; helpless and sick of everything and everyone. But down deep I knew it wasn't everyone ... it was me. When had I become this gutless shell, rooted to the ground, unable to act while everything went wrong around me?

That night I had a conversation that would change everything.

◆ ◆ ◆

When I moved to Sandpoint I joined the local chapter of Trout Unlimited. We were fly-fishermen working to improve trout habitat. I'd made some good friends there.

TU meetings were held on Mondays, but since St. Patrick's Day fell on a Monday and our president's name was O'Hara, we met a day early.

It was a typical March night. Drizzling cold that went through you—a good Sunday evening to be inside with friends. We talked about plans to improve Granite Creek, a little stream that ran into the east side of Lake Pend Oreille, the enormous alpine lake on which Sandpoint had been established in the 1880s.

We debated for an hour and a half about what it would take in money, manpower, and all the blah-blah-blah and political correctness that goes along with trying to get decisions made with a bunch of well-meaning volunteers. No decisions made; a regular meeting.

Afterward, a few of us went over to Skip's Pub for a beer. Skip's is the place in our tourist town for locals. It's full of old artifacts, old pictures and old friends. It feels and smells like a pub should; kind of old, but rich and full of character. Safe, I guess you might say.

I sat at a table with Steve Albright, the local fish and game officer, and my closest friend ever.

Steve was from Maine. He stood about five-foot-four, had a great wife, two cute daughters in high school, and had put a lot of tough people in jail.

If you haven't lived in North Idaho, you probably can't imagine the attitude some people have about being told when, where, or what they can hunt. When the freezer is empty, you go fill it. If there's a bear in the yard and it's starting to worry the wife, you shoot it. If a better elk rack than the one you got yesterday walks by, you may never get a better chance. Not the government's business.

And there was the poverty. It wasn't about low-paying jobs. There weren't *any* jobs. So a lot of these "hunting" activities weren't seen as illegal … just survival.

Through the years, as we got close, Steve had told me some pretty wild stories; true stuff about waiting on a remote logging road in the dark for guys with rifles to come packing out an elk quarter or dragging a bear shot out of season. And he'd busted more than one upstanding citizen with a load of drugs they'd just slipped down from Canada.

He never knew what he might be walking into and that's what he liked about his job.

This is an interesting guy, a person worth knowing. The kind of man you want to have on your side. Our level of trust was as high as it gets between a couple of men and I knew some things he really shouldn't have told anybody.

We were catching up. "So, how does it feel to be old and decrepit?" Steve laughed. "I hated to miss your party."

"We had the usual good time," I said. "The weather was perfect. Good company, good food. And it was especially nice not to have to put up with any crap from you."

"Sounds like a great way to celebrate going over the hill." He was still laughing. "You get a case of Depends or Viagra or anything useful?"

"Ha-Ha," I raised my voice to get over the music that had just started. "We all missed your quick wit."

On a Sunday night there weren't too many people in the Pub, but it was Open-Mic night so a bunch of the regulars were up on the little stage getting under way. They were making some pretty decent music.

Izzy Feldman, a heavy-set, forty-something guy with thinning red hair, a traditional Chinese herbalist and chiropractor when he wasn't singing rock and roll in Skip's

Pub, was at the microphone belting out *Blue Suede Shoes*, doing a pretty good Carl Perkins.

Steve and I listened to people we knew, or at least recognized, make music. We chatted and drank dark, heavy porter. We talked about fishing, rods and reels, and about some other friends, Ron and Jill, who hadn't been at the TU meeting that night. They were off in the Bahamas for their annual bonefishing trip.

"That damn Ron sure knows how to live, doesn't he?" Steve was saying. "He manages to make a living and still fishes more than anybody I ever met."

"Yeah, and he lives with a pretty good fisher person too," I said. Ron's girlfriend, Jill, could fish anywhere with anybody.

About 8:30 the rest of the TU guys started taking off. It was a school night.

Steve didn't give me the same cues about wanting to leave. When the door closed behind them he said, "I'm off tomorrow. Stay for another one?"

"Why not," I said, thinking I might get to hear another of his great stories.

I was right, I got a story. But it was not at all what I expected.

♦   ♦   ♦

Pub owner "Skip" Skipland swung by our table. "Hey Chip. Steve. You guys doin' OK here?"

"Bring us a couple more, if you would please, Skip." Steve pointed at our almost empty glasses.

Skip was a great publican; always there, always interested in what would make your visit to his place better. He didn't ask what we were drinking, he knew. And he had shown up before the story got started. I don't think he was listening, he just had the knack.

Steve suddenly looked pretty grim. "I need to get something off my chest, Chip. Do you mind?"

The look on my face must have been a doozy, because his serious demeanor vanished and he burst out laughing.

Skip returned with the pints, sat them on well-used cardboard coasters, swept up our empties and left us to our conversation.

"What's on your mind Steve?" I said. "You OK?"

Steve's grin vanished, "I shouldn't tell you this …"

When Steve preceded a story with that line, I paid close attention. We locked eyes in a visual handshake of confidence.

Steve kept going, "But I really want to—need to. Hell, I'm pretty busted up about something."

I got a knot in my stomach. I hoped like hell he wasn't having marital problems. I liked his wife, hated to see that happen to anybody, and his girls would be in it too.

"You and Bev OK?"

"No, I mean yes. Bev and I are great. The girls too. It's got nothing to do with them."

This tough guy, who put bad men with guns in jail, looked me in the eye and teared up. "This is something that happened at, uh … at work."

Now I was concerned about my friend, but I was fascinated too, hoping I wasn't looking like some kind of thrill seeker out for vicarious excitement.

He took a healthy swallow from his glass. "Where the hell do I start?"

"It doesn't matter Steve, just start," I said.

"I messed up. I've been doing what I do for more than twenty years, and I pulled a bonehead, rookie move. And now it's my fault some bad people got away with hurting some kids."

My guts tightened. The conversation I'd had with Ben and Jess the day before was blasting around in my head. "What happened?"

"Well, I was working on the east end of Baldy Road. You can't believe how many four-by-fours come tooling through there at one in the morning with a dead moose, tits up, lying in the bed …

"Anyway, I was up just past your turn off, it wasn't late, maybe nine o'clock or so, and I saw this truck coming. It turned onto Jesus Is My Redeemer Lane. I followed with my lights off just to see what he was up to. There's only one house up there; a guy named John Bradley owns it. You know him? A lot of people think he killed his step brother but they couldn't prove it …" Steve paused for a drink. The back of my neck danced and twitched.

"The sheriff had some interest in Bradley; and the Lane dead ends in his driveway, so that made me want to follow the truck too. Anyway, by the time I got there, the truck is already parked in front of the garage and the guy isn't in it. There were lights on, one on each side of the garage door. And I could see through the truck's back window. There wasn't anybody in the driver's seat, unless he was laying down, which some of these dumb asses would try. It's like he jumped out and ran."

"Holy shit." My mind was furiously blending Ben's story with what Steve was telling me.

"I sure as hell didn't want to get shot by some nervous asshole, but I didn't want to let this guy get away. It smelled funny, you know? So I walked up directly behind the truck where I could see him if he popped up. Nothing happened. I took a quick look in the bed; nothing there. I looked inside the cab; nothing in there either except a scoped rifle lying on the seat."

"What kind of rifle was it?" I don't know why that was important to me, but I had this movie image of an assault rifle with a night vision scope that I couldn't shake.

"Oh, some beat-to-shit old Savage bolt action, I think." Steve was gazing out the Pub's front window at the taillights drifting by. "I was standing there, trying to decide what to do, when there was a creak on the front porch. The door came open, somebody big ran inside, and then it slammed closed. It was a screen door on a spring. He must have been hiding in the shadows watching me." Steve rocked side to side in his chair, set his jaw. "Then I heard a little girl screaming ..."

"A little girl screaming?" I parroted back. My heart had gotten louder than the music. Its pounding and Steve's voice was all I could hear. Had that little girl been at my house yesterday afternoon?

"Yeah, screaming bloody murder. Then the screen door banged again and this little blond girl came running out. She ran down the steps and under the garage lights. I'm standing right there, like ten feet away, looking over the hood of the truck. She didn't have a stitch on; couldn't have been more than five or six. Ah man ..." Steve's eyes left the window and he started twisting his glass into the table. "Then this big fat guy comes running out after her. He's got this wide, studded leather belt looped in his hand. He's not wearing anything either."

I didn't want to hear any more. I hated what my imagination was doing with it. I could see myself standing in the driveway of a house at the end of Jesus Is My Redeemer Lane, every molecule capable of murder.

I worked my focus back to Steve. "Oh God, Steve, the guy was naked?"

"Yeah, and I lost it. I lost it! I extended my baton and the next thing I knew I had that sick son of a bitch laid out on the concrete in front of the garage, bleeding in about ten places. If the bastard's fat-assed wife hadn't come shrieking out of the house and pulled me off him, I think he might be dead right now. I almost wish I'd finished the job." He looked around, making sure he hadn't been too loud.

Nobody in Skip's seemed to be aware of what we were talking about.

"God Steve, who wouldn't have reacted like that? Was it Bradley?"

"Yeah, it was Bradley ... Then I did what I should have done in the first place. I cuffed him, left him bleeding on the concrete, went back to my truck and called in the troops."

There it was. Ben, Jess, the girls, Steve, and the Bradleys ... All tied together.

Steve sucked in and let out a huge shuddering breath. "When I attacked him, I ruined any possible chance of putting him away."

"Ah shit, Steve. Surely there's something ..." How could this be? Steve had seen this terrible thing going on and they just let this Bradley guy and his wife walk away?

"We went in, but we didn't find anything illegal inside the house. Not a thing. We hauled his ass in but the little girl wasn't talking. The wife is a psycho, screaming bitch who threatened to sue. It was his word against mine. We had to let him go.

"He probably could have had my job, or worse, I could have been the one locked up in the Pen down in Kuna. He could have sued the state for a million bucks. It was a cluster fuck. So that sick asshole and his wife got away with ... with ..." Steve choked.

My friend was withering; disappearing before my eyes.

"It's my fault and there's nothing I can do about it."

"What about the guy in the truck?" I said.

"Never saw him again. No idea who he was or what he was doing. The truck turned out to be registered to John and

Scarlett Bradley." Steve's hands were pressed flat on the table and there was enough quiet rage in his voice to make it quaver. "I really screwed up."

"What happened to the little girl?" I asked, even though I knew exactly what had happened to the little girl.

"There had been some suspicion about what was going on at that house. The Bradleys have two other daughters. The girls had missed a lot of school. There had been some bruises reported, strange behavior and that kind of stuff. Add that to what I saw, and the state was able to get all three of them out of there. At least that beautiful little girl ..." Steve had to stop again.

"I ... I just can't think about what that sick asshole and his wife were up to."

"Why didn't any of this come out?"

"The prosecutor kept it quiet and John Bradley obviously didn't want it out either. He and his wife ducked and covered."

"Steve, thank God you got those girls out. What if you hadn't been there at all? You may have saved their lives. Focus on that. I wish I'd done something that good just once in my own life."

I let that sink in before I asked, "What about you? You OK? Did you get in hot water with the state, or what?"

"Well, they weren't too pleased with me, but my boss understood and so did the sheriff. I think the prosecutor would have burned me if they hadn't intervened. I'm OK as long as I don't do anything stupid in the near future." He hung his head. "Don't know if I can ever forgive myself for the Bradleys going free. But, I did get those three girls out of there and that's got to be worth something."

"Damn right. It's worth a lot. Don't forget it," I said. "I don't know what I'd have done if I'd been there, but I have a feeling it wouldn't have been much different."

"But I've been trained to deal with this kind of stuff. It was just bad work on my part … bad work."

"Yeah, but you're a man and a person first. I wouldn't be sorry about that."

Steve looked me in the eye and gripped my hand over the table. "Thanks. Thanks for listening Chip."

I was glad he hadn't felt the need to mention how sensitive this all was. He had trusted me with something big; about as big as it gets. Steve and I held the handshake a little longer.

On the stage Izzy Feldman had moved on to *All Shook Up*. "Yeah, I'm all shook up …"

"Hey Skip!" I yelled across the bar, "Bring me the tab. The Game Warden and I are done."

◆　◆　◆

I walked across the street and got in my car, seething over the injustice and depravity of it all. Ben's and Jess's lives turned upside down. Steve, the best guy I knew, almost thrown in jail for doing what was unquestionably right.

How could anyone, worth anything, do nothing and let those animals, those fucking Bradleys, go unpunished? How could *I* live with that?

I didn't remember driving home—but there I was, parked in my garage; stomach churning, heart racing, looking in the rearview at the terrified old guy inside my shirt. He was thinking seriously about killing two people he'd never seen … and I was looking for the courage to let him do it.

Part 1 CHAPTER 2

I wasn't a Dead-Head, but the Grateful Dead started singing *Truckin'* somewhere inside my pillow. What a long, strange trip it's been ...

I listened to the music. My wife was there cuddled up next to me. The clock shot the red time onto the ceiling. And as always, when she slept and I couldn't, I drifted. Old memories jostled with each other for attention.

I was born in Lincoln County, Iowa in the very same hospital room in which my mother had been born twenty years earlier.

Mom and Dad had agreed my name should be Charles, after my paternal grandfather, but when the doctor came into the waiting room, Dad was passing the time playing poker. Doctor Carroll picked a blue chip up off the table, flipped it to my father and said something like, "You're the winner Keith. You got a big baby boy."

So, I was Charles 'Chip' Crandle from that minute on. I'd hated it as a kid, but I grew to like the story as an adult.

I started life with two great-grandparents, four grandparents, dozens of cousins, six pairs of aunts and uncles, and a sister. Another sister was added three years later. You couldn't turn around in Lincoln County without bumping into somebody I was related to.

I'd been born during the final decade of the small family farmer. When my parents drove me home from the hospital in their beat-up '49 Ford, our one-hundred-twenty-acre rented farm had chickens, hogs, milk cows, horses, oats, corn, beans, a huge garden, a windmill to pump water, corn cribs, a mammoth hay barn and a gravel road. Dad had a bunch of worn out machinery and there were still horse harnesses hanging in the barn.

By the time I left for Journalism school, eighteen years later, we owned five hundred acres. We raised hogs, corn, and soybeans. All the other crops and animals were gone. My dad had a new shed full of very expensive machinery, a new air-conditioned house, a new pick-up truck, and a Lincoln Continental he drove on the new highway in front of our house.

There had been so many generations of farmers in my family that they had no more idea of why they had chosen to farm than a duck knows why it flies south in the fall. I didn't seem to be from the same flock. My parents may have been disappointed about that, but they never let on and I flew in my own direction. Dad had asked me once, when I was a junior in high school, if I'd like to take over the farm. My answer was no. That's the last we ever spoke of it.

My parents were the most loving, forgiving, outwardly happy and quick-witted people I knew or have ever known. I was encouraged to try everything, and I was led to believe I could do anything I put my mind to.

My dad was always around. Farmers live where they work. We had breakfast, dinner (that's the noon meal on the farm), and supper together. He and Mom traded off putting me and my sisters to bed. Sometimes, when it was too hot to sleep in the house, we'd all lay on blankets in the yard and gaze while Dad pointed out the constellations.

From the beginning my dad made it possible for me to fly. He'd pick me up over his head and I would zoom around next to the ceiling, or under the trees and sky, banking and diving and soaring. I never crashed. His big strong hands held me up and I was weightless.

At some point, I don't remember exactly when, Dad wasn't necessary for my take-offs anymore. Effortlessly, I flew anywhere I wanted to go. At night I would just Peter Pan it right out the window, soaring across vast expanses of time and space. It was my secret. And it was the best part of being alive.

But I lost that magic. About the time I turned thirteen, I failed to stop a terrible thing from happening. My confidence eroded. And as I doubted my worth and abilities, my flights became fewer and farther between, only showing up when I was dead sure of what I was doing. Eventually I became certain of only two things; I would never make a difference and I would never fly again.

◆ ◆ ◆

My dad also helped me gain an appreciation for life and death and the fine line of time and circumstance that separates them.

I'd been given access to a .22 single-shot rifle when I was ten. I would spend hours holding stock still with that cocked rifle pointed at a hole in the foundation of the corn crib. Sooner or later a rat would poke its head out, black eyes searching for danger. I learned to stay cool, making that one little rifle shell count; dealing swift vengeance for stealing our corn.

Dad would pay me a dime for every rat I shot. I'd have done it for free, but those dimes made me feel valuable and able. It was exciting to be quiet and deadly. And it was a good thing that needed to be done. For something to live, something has to die. Not cruel. Not unjust. The rats ate our corn. The rats were subject to death. No questions. No regrets. No doubts.

Now I was wondering, could I get to that point with John and Scarlett Bradley?

◆ ◆ ◆

At 5:00 AM, my brain going a million miles an hour, things changed. I had a glimmer of hope that I could make a difference and fly again. Strange and morbid as it seemed, John and Scarlett Bradley might make it possible.

I dressed in the dark; put my pocket knife in my right pocket and my watch on my left wrist.

I hurried through a large bowl of AlphaBits, drank a big glass of orange juice, and carried a press-pot of coffee to my office; a room with a spectacular view in the lower level of the house.

My cell phone was lying in the middle of my desk, turned off. I had left it there on Saturday before the party started. It was an old-fashioned flip phone and I had it because I had to. I didn't text and I didn't tweet and I couldn't send e-mails from it. I sure as hell didn't answer it when I had guests.

I punched the power button and saw that I had some missed calls and voice mail. Thankfully, it was way too early to call anybody back so I got out my white board and markers.

I once had a wise old boss who was fond of saying, "Planning takes the doubt out of taking action."

How do you plan a murder?

◆   ◆   ◆

Sure, I'd plotted a few murders before; an ex-girlfriend, the ex-friend she ran away with, a couple of bosses, the jerk every neighborhood and office seem to have. I imagine we all think about it at some point. God, I hoped so or I was crazier than I thought. But those weren't really plans. It was just steam. Not ever a chance of really happening.

This was different. What I felt in my guts and my brain was *way* different.

As terrible as the thought of actually killing somebody had always been, somehow I was seriously considering it. No going back if you did it. Dead. Taking a life. Murderer!

I said it every way I could think of, trying to talk myself out of it, and still, I was setting up the white board and uncapping a marker … the power of my rage pulling me in.

My wise old boss came back. "Intentions only become actions with a plan." I couldn't consider doing it unless it could be done right. I needed to get past my emotions to be sure.

I wrote with a black marker.

Goal:

To be sure of something again. To do something unquestionably right and good. To fly again.

Strategies:

1. Kill John and Scarlett Bradley: Remove the possibility that they would ever hurt a child again.

2. They had to know it was me and why I was doing it: They needed to be aware I was killing them for what they had done and so they could never do it again. I was a stranger. This wasn't personal.

3. Make an impact that would encourage other people to act: Get the Bradley story out. Inspire other people to do what was right.

4. I would not do this in anger: I had to feel good and sure about who I was and what I'd done—after I killed them.

5. I wasn't going to prison: I would not be punished for doing something for the greater good. Afterward, I would have to escape. That would be another plan altogether.

I capped the marker and stepped away from the white board.

Things get real when you write them down. This wasn't just thoughts or self-talk. My heart hammered as I read the words. My forehead was cold and oily. One swipe of an eraser and it would all be gone; done with. I could walk away.

I uncapped a red marker, moved on to tactics.

Probably too early for this, but this is the part that everyone wants to get to—the execution.

I would shoot them. Shoot them dead with a large caliber handgun. I already had one in a box in my gun safe.

My initial thought was to kill them, together, inside their house where they'd done terrible things to their beautiful daughters. The Bradleys needed to be awake and aware of who was doing it and why. I wanted it to be fast and as painless as possible. Not complex. Detached.

To do that successfully I'd have to watch them and their house for a while. I could hike up there and scope it out. It was remote and I could probably watch them any time of the day.

I wondered what it would be like to watch somebody. What would it take to sneak into somebody's house? I'd never even thought of it before; never occurred to me. The idea made my heart pound again a little—OK, a lot.

I kept going on the plan. The stink of the dry-erase marker filled my office.

How do you influence a big audience? Media; broad-based, social, all of it. If you handled it right, you could get stuff out and viral in about an hour. I hoped my message would cause somebody else to do something that needed to be done. Not something as radical as what I was moving toward, but something they could feel sure about. I'd issue a release, a written statement after the Bradleys were dead; what I'd done, why I'd done it.

I went to the next point.

How could I keep emotion out of it and feel good about myself after killing somebody? Could I do this? Would I lose my nerve; take the easy way out as I had so often before? Would I feel bad? I wanted to think I could do it and not lose any sleep but …

I had to get to a place where I knew that the world would be better without them—like killing rats in the corn crib, no judgment, just necessary. I needed to be sure.

That got me through the toughest part; killing them. That only left the rest of my life to plan out.

How was I going to avoid getting caught? Showers with the guys was not in my file of acceptable endings. I had some time to figure that one out. I had a couple of ideas, but I still wanted to think it over for a while. No hurry.

Getaway: To Be Determined

I wrote down a couple of non-negotiables:

- No one else would get hurt in the process.
- No one else would be implicated or blamed.

I would need a budget. I had something like twenty-thousand dollars in my safe-deposit box. Seemed like more than enough.

Finally, when to do it? Things never got done without a deadline, but I had a lot to do and learn before I could write in a final date.

Deadline: To Be Determined.

The board was full. I stood back and looked at what I had written, hovering between past and future.

I was in my same office, with my same feet on my same carpet, breathing in the fumes from the same markers, as I gazed at the same whiteboard that had held countless plans— but the words were new, from some other universe. They held meaning only if I dared to take the terrifying steps they suggested.

I typed the whole thing into a word document, saved it to my desktop and wiped the board clean. Colored dust drifted in the sunlight of my office.

Enough thinking, I needed to get into action.

It would be a good day to shoot something.

Part 1 CHAPTER 3

I kept all my guns locked in a heavy steel gun safe. Except for my dad's old Remington shotgun; it was in the bedroom closet. I kept it there, loaded with double-ought buck, just in case. There are a lot of reasons to have a shotgun ready when you live up in the mountains and most of them have nothing to do with people.

The short baseball bat under the bed was what I had always thought I would use if it came down to a human intruder or me. I wanted to be sure I didn't come out of a dead sleep and accidentally kill the wrong person. I figured if I brained somebody with the bat I'd have a pretty good chance of knowing exactly who they were before I started swinging. But using it had always been dimly hypothetical; like life insurance.

I had collected quite a few firearms through the years; nothing big or too expensive. I had a shooting-gallery Winchester pump which had belonged to my grandfather Cleo, my first single shot rifle, and several pistols. They were all .22s—except the one I envisioned using for my plan.

That one was new, purchased a week ago on a whim; a Beretta PX4 .40 caliber with a twelve shot magazine. I saw it in the case and made the mistake of having the gun-counter guy let me play with it for five minutes.

So I took it home—told myself it was a birthday present. I hadn't even fired it yet. Funny how things show up when you need them.

The Beretta had only two possible purposes: Shooting at targets, which I had always enjoyed, and killing people.

I grabbed the Beretta, a box of ammo, and some ear plugs. I went out across the lower patio to the woods on the west side of the house and walked through the trees for a couple of hundred yards to a spot with a slope right behind it.

I emptied the box of cartridges into my coat pocket, dropped the clip out of the Beretta into my gloved hand and started loading it.

Forty-caliber pistol bullets are scary-looking things. I shuddered, imagining a copper-jacketed slug tearing through the air with such force that it would go right through a person—a gruesome thought.

I pushed twelve cartridges into the magazine and snapped it into the handle of the pistol; made sure the safety was on and chambered a round. The grip was fat and solid, filling my hand.

A cowboy theme song drifted into my head as two men faced each other on the Dodge City Street. TV in my childhood; gunfighters were kings, and the guys in the black hats always got what they had coming.

With the pistol in my hand I felt lethal, the way I used to feel waiting for a rat to stick its head out of the corn crib. I picked a ten-inch Ponderosa pine about fifteen feet away, raised the pistol, pushed the safety, and snapped off a quick shot. The report echoed off the surrounding mountains. No worries; gunfire was a common sound in my neighborhood.

The slug blasted a big chunk of bark off the tree. Not bad for a first, out-of-the-box shot. I grabbed the grip with both hands, took careful aim and squeezed. Dead center. I shot up the rest of the box, hitting what I wanted to hit, adjusting the sights a bit, and making sure the gun did what it was supposed to do. I wasn't planning on needing anything like twelve shots, but the two I was planning for had to work.

I picked up my spent brass, walked back to the house, tore down the pistol, cleaned and oiled it. As I locked the Beretta in the safe, the brass casings clicked in my pocket. I dumped them on my desk.

Blackened, empty holes stared up at me like accusing eyes. "What are you doing, Chip?"

◆ ◆ ◆

I went upstairs trying to shake the idea that the shell casings had been questioning me.

Coffee cures all. I stuck my cold cup in the microwave. It started beeping as my phone started vibrating; Ben Chandler. "Hey Ben, what's up? I don't talk to you for months and then twice in three days."

"Hey, I left you a couple of messages. Jess can't find her phone. She swore she had it when she got home from the party, but we can't find it. She thinks she may have left it out by your fire ring."

I didn't remember seeing it. "I'll go out right now and look around. I'll call Jess's number and see if the bushes ring."

"That would be great. I'm in town, if you find it give me a call and I'll run up. She's already in withdrawal."

Outside I punched in Jess's number and was rewarded by James Taylor singing *You've Got a Friend* from beneath one of the teak benches. I found the white phone, took a chance and touched two.

Ben's face came on the screen. He answered on the first ring.

"Hello dahhrrrling, I'm free this afternoon. Whadda you say?" I did my best Mae West, or was it Marlene Dietrich? One of those old timers with the great delivery.

"Sounds good," Ben said. "I hear you're not like all the other girls …"

I couldn't hold the woman's voice anymore and burst out laughing. "It was out by the fire ring, under a bench," I said. "Lucky it didn't get wet."

"Excellent," Ben sounded relieved. "Be up there in a few minutes."

"OK," I said. "Is it coffee or beer time?"

"Well, the phone is found. That's reason to celebrate," Ben laughed. "I think I left a couple of IPAs in your garage."

"Perfect," I said. "Somebody has to drink that crap. It's taking up valuable space in my fridge. See you in a few."

"Yep," Ben hung up.

I stuck Jess's phone in the pocket of my jacket.

I decided to police up the yard and see what other goodies might have had been left behind by Saturday's guests. I'd just gotten down to the patio, finding two cups and a beer bottle on the way, when James Taylor sang again.

I dug for the phone. No name came up, just a local number. The voice on the other end spat, "I'm gonna get my girls back you bitch … Sleep tight tonight." The phone went dead.

It could only have been Bradley. If the son of a bitch had been standing there, I would have split his head with a rock and fed him to the ravens without a second thought. No question. I would have done it and flown away in joy.

Anger and fear grew as I walked up to the garage. I fumbled the cap off a bottle of beer. The Bradley guy was crazy; a complete psycho. He would kill *me* without any plan and without any remorse at all. He'd just pull the trigger and move on. I'd never felt anything like that coming from anyone. And I'd never, ever, been so terrified.

And here came the other terrifying part—I was actually thinking of killing the voice on the other end of that phone. What the hell was I becoming?

This wasn't writing on a white board with colored markers, pretending to plan an advertising campaign. I was being spun by fear and hate and confusion and regret. I wanted to lie down, hug my wife, rewind the tape, and be isolated and safe on my mountain … where monsters didn't lurk up the hill.

I had to think. Get a handle on my emotions. I drank my beer and stewed.

Would I tell Ben about the call? What good would that do

besides scare them; which is what Bradley wanted, right? No. That didn't seem like the thing to do.

I checked Jess's phone. The last call was a Sandpoint prefix; a land line. I jotted the number down on my workbench then figured out how to clear the number from her phone.

A gleaming black Audi crunched up the gravel drive; looked like Ben had a new car.

I waved, relieved to see my friend's face and to have something good to center on. "Nice car!"

"Thanks, just picked it up. Had to have more room …" He pointed at my beer. "I see you couldn't wait for me."

"Hey, it's still my birthday for a couple more days." I handed him Jess's phone. "You better take this now so we don't forget."

He pushed some buttons, intent on the screen. "Don't see anything important," he said. "Maybe that's a lesson in itself huh?" He reached in the window and tossed the phone in the glove compartment.

The phone gone, I opened an IPA for Ben.

"So, show me the new wheels," I said.

Ben had good taste; great cars, nice house, his wife was a good choice too.

A dentist, Jess worked on kids' teeth exclusively and did a lot of it for free. If you knew her, you would have expected that.

Ben was a financial analyst of some sort. He got deep into the dealings of companies and how they got more value for their stock. Not my bag. I never even tried to understand it.

He had started working for a new company a few months back and it appeared he was doing very well. It seemed they could afford to do whatever they wanted, and now they had added three more kids to the family in one fell swoop. Not easy and not cheap either.

We walked around the Audi, a Q7 SUV. A gorgeous car and capable of working its way through the weather and the mud and the other stuff you had to be prepared to handle in North Idaho.

"Hop in," said Ben. "Let's take it for a drive. I think I'm gonna love this machine."

He insisted that I get behind the wheel. He jumped in the passenger seat, sat his bottle in the center cup holder and ran me through a check-list of where things were. I was surrounded by that wonderful new car smell—probably toxic—but there isn't anything like it. The seats were dark gray cowhide; soft and comfortable.

"Mmmm," I said "This seat has infinite position adjustment. It'll be great for long trips."

Ben said, "With my long legs and Jess's short ones, we need that. Check out the sound system." He reached over and snapped on the music. Aerosmith came out like they were playing live in the back seat. Steven Tyler was wailing right behind me: "Rag Doll livin' in a movie ..."

"What do you think?" Ben spoke up over the thumping bass line.

"Too nice for you." I sipped my Belgian beer. The car was nice. I relaxed into the leather.

"Probably, but life ain't fair," he said. "Let's take a drive." He turned the music down a bit.

With my seat figured out and adjusted, we took off. At Baldy Road he said, "Hang a left," pointing with the top of his beer bottle. "Let's go up instead of down."

That was a strange request. Above our house, Baldy was the domain of four-wheelers, monster pickups, mountain bikes, and the occasional lost tourist in a white rental car with a shredded tire.

He gave me a "just do it" look, jabbed a button and killed the radio.

"OK, you're the boss." I pulled out into the muddy road. I had to hold back a little; the thing would have jumped out from under me if I'd really punched it. I was grinning from ear-to-ear; a fun machine.

Ben was looking intently out the window to his right. We'd be passing Jesus Is My Redeemer Lane in a minute. It wasn't a coincidence.

"Slow down a little will you?" he said.

I wasn't going very fast anyway, too soft and muddy. I slowed to a crawl, drained the rest of my beer. The sign for Jesus Is My Redeemer Lane was coming up on the right.

"What are we doing Ben? This seems like a bad idea to me."

"I've never been up here and I just wanted to get it in my mind where these sick assholes are," he said. "That may sound weird, but I just want to know. I want to make everything that happened to my new girls real to me. I want to know where all that shit came down. Maybe it will help me help them. I don't know, probably crazy."

We both craned our necks, looking out Ben's window down the lane. It curved and disappeared back into the dense woods. No way you could see Bradleys' house without going up there.

"Shit," Ben said. "I thought we'd be able to see it from the road."

I caught movement in the rearview mirror. A jacked-up, red 4x4 Dodge pick-up came roaring up the hill behind us, its big square grill filling our back window.

I swung the wheel to the right, hit the gas, jerked over onto what little shoulder there was then jammed on the brakes to stay out of the steep ditch. The pickup braked hard, turned, and skidded up Jesus Is My Redeemer Lane just behind us. A beefy arm shot out of the driver's window, a pudgy finger flipping us off. The truck straightened out and disappeared around the curve; John Bradley going home.

"That had to have been that lousy son of a bitch! That was him, right there." This was the Ben I didn't know again. He strained against his seat belt. I thought he might jump out and give chase on foot.

Ben swung back around to look at me, knocking his bottle out of the cup holder into my lap, drowning my crotch and his new leather upholstery with bitter beer.

"Time to go home," I said. "We need to get this cleaned up right away or Jess will have your balls for breakfast, and she won't be too pleased with me either."

I backed into Jesus Is My Redeemer Lane and turned around to head home. Ben sat silent; eyes closed, the light gone out of him, radiating cold, dark malice and frustration. It felt like the windows of the Audi might blow out. I rolled mine down, let the air in, relieving the pressure and hoping my feelings would fly away before they mixed with his and drowned us both.

I hit the radio button. Steve Winwood wailed out of the back seat and The Low Spark of High-heeled Boys gave us another chance ...

◆   ◆   ◆

A few minutes later Ben and I were in my garage, cleaning and airing the beer smell out of the Audi. Most of it had soaked into my pants, so we thought he'd be able to keep the new car smell a while longer.

"I feel like a complete moron." Ben had a fresh bottle in his hand. "What the hell did I get so excited about? I knew what the deal was with the girls when we decided to help them. It's not like I can turn back the clock and wipe away what happened."

I threw a beer-soaked towel at him and said, "You're right. You can't do anything about it. Stay focused on the girls."

Ben caught the towel, this time keeping the beer inside his bottle. He sat on the wide step leading from the garage to the laundry room, nodding and sipping.

"Assholes like Bradley and his wife will eventually get what's coming to them. I really believe that." I hoped Ben was hearing me. "You go up there again, you'll just get into some kind of trouble. Keep him the bad guy. Those girls need *you* now."

"Yeah, I think if Bradley had stopped and hassled us I might have done something really stupid … satisfying, but stupid." Ben looked at me. "Glad you were with me buddy. Thanks for helping me clean up."

"Hell, I was more worried about my jeans than anything. I wouldn't want somebody to smell that cat piss on me and think I would really drink an IPA!"

We laughed, trying to let our brush with John Bradley fade, then dove into our own thoughts for a moment.

Ben, such a good guy who felt so wrong about the world right then. And me; feeling his pain, now understanding his frustration and the helplessness. Knowing I could not just let it go … planning my mission.

"Hey, I have a favor to ask." He rose from the step. "I've got a chance to go to Hawaii for a couple weeks on a work-related trip, sometime around the first part of May. I can take the whole family on the company's dime."

"What, you want me to come along and take care of Jess while you watch the kids?" I said seriously.

Ben gave me a stage scowl. "Asshole … No, I wondered if you would mind going by the house a couple of times while we're gone, just to check on things."

This was kind of a big deal. Ben didn't ask for help. Flattered, I said, "Sure, I'd be happy to. What do you want me to do?"

"Well, I've got a kid coming by every day to feed the

animals. If you could just check on his work. You grew up on a farm. You know what to look for." Ben, covering all his bases. "I don't want to embarrass the kid, or make him feel like I don't trust him, but two weeks is a long time."

I said, "No problem. Sounds like fun. Why don't I come over and walk through the chores with you before you go?"

"Sounds perfect," he said. "Man, look at the time. I better get Jess's phone back to her before she dies of a bad case of phantom ringing. I'll call you to do the walk around in the next few weeks." Ben hopped in his new car and disappeared down my driveway.

I turned to go back into the house and kicked his forgotten, half-full bottle across the garage and under my Land Rover. The bottle lay there spinning, spreading a circle of foam.

Sometimes it seemed that I just went from one mess to another.

◆ ◆ ◆

Emotions aren't good for making or executing plans, so I did what I usually did when I had to work something out—I kept moving. I cleaned up the beer and swept a bunch of winter grime and trash off the floor. Next thing I knew I was tidying up the whole garage.

I thought about the vile call on Jess's pretty white phone. Was it a bluff or was it possible that John Bradley would actually do something? I could still tell Ben. I could say I took the call and didn't want to worry them. No, that sounded lame. I didn't think I'd tell them.

I puttered around, straightening up my work bench, organizing cans of bolts and screws and nails. I saw the scrap of paper with the phone number from Jess's phone. I pulled out my own phone and tapped in the number. It rang eight times before a small voice said, "Hello?"

"Hello," I said. "Who is this?"

"Jamie Harris," the small voice said. "I was walking by and this phone was ringing."

"Hi Jamie, can you tell me where you are?" I said.

"It's just a dumb payphone by the Dairy Delight," Jamie Harris said.

"OK, thanks Jamie. I just dialed the wrong number I guess." I left Jamie standing at the telecommunications relic.

John Bradley had used the payphone for his threatening call—not stupid, just crazy. He made his call then drove home and flipped me off just because I was there.

What would a sick bastard like John Bradley do now? How do you put yourself inside the head of a freak like that? Thinking about it gave me a rush of revenge adrenalin, making my heart race and renewing my fear that I might act out of anger.

I walked around the house to the fire ring where I got a small blaze going and sat on a sun-warmed bench. I could see for miles down the Pend Oreille River. The water between the mountains looked like a ribbon of silver that somehow seemed higher than where I sat. How different than where I had grown up. And how lucky I felt to be sitting there with the sky and the river and the mountains spread out all around me. I thought about how much I did love it—and how wrong it was to have the Bradleys living there like maggots in an otherwise perfect apple.

Tom Petty, my favorite old rocker, sat down on the bench across from me, started singing: Well I won't back down …

Tom knew what was right.

I looked into my little fire, listened to Petty, and thought about everything.

◆   ◆   ◆

After high school, all my friends had gone on to college. Not one of us went back to be a farmer, or a small town whatever.

I had wanted to be Darren Stevens, the husband on the Bewitched television show. He was an advertising executive and, as far as I could tell, all he did was have fun and go to bed with Samantha, the gorgeous blond witch on whom I had a huge crush.

With that rock-solid motivation, I went to the University of Kansas and got my degree in journalism and advertising— people make choices for worse reasons than having a thing for a beautiful blond witch.

I expected to get a job right out of college, and with the help of my favorite professor, I did. I graduated, married Suzanne, and got a job all within six weeks. It was a different world in 1976.

After stints with a few ad agencies, I'd joined a Midwestern company where I stayed for twenty years. The company developed, grew and sold seed to farmers. It was a satisfying business to be a part of; profitable, pleasant, and honest. We were selling something people really needed. Seed turned into corn or soybeans and that turned into food or other products that, mostly, were necessities. I could get up in the morning, look in the mirror and feel sure that the things I did helped people. I liked it. And I liked the people I worked with. You pretty much knew where you stood with them.

None of us knew it at the time, but it was the end of an era.

When I started, people still said what they meant and did what they said. The lawyers and the accountants and the internet geeks hadn't screwed it all up yet. But, almost overnight, things began to change.

The business became more about the money and the

patents and the litigation and the shareholders and the few
getting ahead of the many. I rejected it and fought it and
succumbed to it all at the same time. After a huge chemical
company took us over, I hung around for a couple of years
and then took an early buy-out. I didn't like their greedy profit
motives, but I guess I was OK with having profit motives for
myself. Funny how things can gradually erode and you just
don't see it.

I walked away with a nice chunk of cash and became a
consultant. I hoped I could make a difference, and I wouldn't
have to play all the games that had taken over my work
world.

In a year I got restless. At forty-nine I decided I needed a
change; a change in just about everything. I took a couple of
trips to ski, fly-fish and scout out the West. The next thing I
knew I bought thirty acres of trees on the side of a mountain
just outside Sandpoint, Idaho. I sold everything in Iowa and
moved. I really didn't even think about it. I just decided to do
it and went.

I expect I shocked, maybe hurt, friends and family when I
just picked up and left. But on the other hand, I had a lot of
people say how much they envied my courage and the
freedom I must have felt. I found that kind of sad. Does it
really take that much courage to just do what you want to do?
Or was that their nice Iowa way of saying, "Are you out of
your fucking mind?"

I went for the fishing, and the coffee, and the mountains,
and the air and the remote wilderness feel of the place. But
most of all I went for the people and the chance to be without
a history.

I threw another handful of sticks on the fire and recalled
telling friends and family about my decision to move.
Skinheads and rednecks always seemed to come up. The Ruby
Ridge shoot-out had given the Idaho Panhandle a reputation

as being thick with encampments of survivalists and a hotbed of neo-Nazi nut cakes.

But it wasn't so ... mostly. There were some North Idaho racists, sure, but no more than anywhere else. Saying that North Idaho was full of Nazis was as stupid as Hollywood's portrayal of Iowa farmers as bib-overall-wearing rubes driving 1954 Chevrolet pickups.

What I discovered in Idaho was the most diverse group of attitudes I had ever encountered living together in such a small area. I chose Sandpoint because it was a live-and-let-live kind of place; a very peaceful, laid-back haven in which you could relax and just be.

At least it had been until I found out about the Bradleys.

◆　◆　◆

That night, looking at the red time projected on the ceiling, my wife quiet and warm next to me, I decided I would pay the Bradley house a visit the next morning. It felt like the right thing to do.

Then I flew around the room; just a bit, but it counted. I flew.

Part 1 CHAPTER 4

At 5:00 I got up and dressed in the dark. I put my pocket knife in my right pocket and my watch on my left wrist. I ate a large bowl of AlphaBits, drank the big glass of orange juice, and carried a press-pot of coffee to my office.

I spent a couple of hours checking my e-mail and schedules, making sure my consulting clients didn't have any pressing emergencies. Every week I spoke on the phone with several clients for an hour or two each.

Doing business with conference calls, e-mails, texts, tweets, video calls, and other forms of mobile communications—sometimes without ever actually seeing each other—created a tornado of misinformation for them. And worse, it never allowed people to disconnect from work. It made for loads of confusion and bent out of shape, highly-paid, overworked, sleep-deprived, never acknowledged business people.

My function was to mediate, referee, and give people space to think. I did my best to help them stay in touch, figure out what they really needed to do and to stay on the same page ... sort of.

They fought and scratched and cried and blew snot bubbles. I was fascinated by the whole thing, and my clients really appreciated having somebody to unload on. I felt like I was helping most days, but there wasn't ever going to be a cure. I was treating symptoms, distracting them so they wouldn't end up shooting themselves in their own virtual feet.

Things were quiet that day. My schedule was free for a walk to the Bradleys'.

◆   ◆   ◆

If I was going to kill them in their house, I would have to look it over carefully; inside and out. The guy was dangerous—crazy dangerous—and there was the wife too.

According to Steve Albright, Scarlett Bradley was just as bad and I had not seen her yet.

I grabbed my camouflage day pack and loaded it with gear I thought might come in handy. For some reason I felt the need to tell my wife I was going out. It wouldn't be a surprise to her; I walked alone a lot. Most mornings I just left, but I was jumpy just thinking about the Bradleys. I needed to have a touch with Suzanne to get myself centered some.

She was in her own space, gazing into the glow of her screen, working on a cup of herbal tea and gluten-free cinnamon toast. The toast looked like the end of a cedar one-by-six dipped in butter.

"Bye honey," I said. "I'm gonna take a little hike. Be back in two or three hours."

She looked up at me, not sure why I was checking in with her. "Sure, OK … doing something special?"

"Naw, just need to get outside."

"K, be careful," she said and looked back into the glow.

I stood for a minute, a whole minute, and took in her pretty profile, as she gazed intently at what she was doing. It would have been nice to just go back to our bed, but I had things I needed to get done. Maybe I'd get to cuddle with her later.

I went out the front door; a grey day, not raining yet.

I was a common enough sight on my neighborhood lane, no issue there. But once I got to the end of our lane and out to Baldy Road, I'd need to scoot across, get into the trees where I couldn't be seen. Then I'd cut through the woods to where I thought I'd find the Bradleys' house.

I had on waterproof hiking boots, a camo sweatshirt, a cap, and jeans. They would turn thorns and weren't easy to see in the woods. I had to admit, the idea of sneaking up there and looking around was raising my heart rate again.

I was crossing Baldy Road when I heard a vehicle coming.

I froze for a second—Guilty! I shook it off, sprinted through the far ditch and stood in the soft ground beneath a thick stand of cedars, terrified the driver would stop. An old Subaru wagon banged by.

Ha. The old hippy was picking his nose and singing, no idea I was watching him.

It was a thrilling game. Catching people unaware was cool. And this was the first time I would purposefully creep up on somebody. I'd watch their house, and them, and they'd never be the wiser—at least that's what I kept telling myself as I trudged.

The leaves were slick on the incline and I had trouble with my footing until I found a well-used game trail running along the hillside. Making my way carefully through the trees and brush, I kept an easy pace, quietly climbing northwest. I heard a couple of cars, obscured by the trees, going down Baldy.

Fats Domino crowded in next to me on the trail: I'm walkin', yes indeed …

I didn't imagine old Fats had ever been in the woods lumbering down a game trail. But I kept the beat, whisper-singing along with him until a white-tail deer snorted, bounded down the hill and disappeared across the road. I kept on tromping for another twenty minutes; feeling my way in.

A sharp horizontal line, something man-made, appeared through the trees. I hunkered down and made out the roof of a house. The fear of being caught snooping around rippled up my back.

I imagined Suzanne; "What on earth are you doing Chip?"

I had an answer. "Making sure. Just making sure. I gotta do this."

Somehow that helped. She left my head and my heart steadied.

Dense woods can turn you around. I had to be sure of where I was. I worked closer, got within seventy-five yards, keeping a good stand of trees between me and the house. I had no good reason to be there. People could take a very dim view of trespassing, and everybody up here had guns. I had no doubt that these particular people would use them.

I inched down a short slope and hid behind an old Ponderosa, three feet across, which had somehow escaped the loggers.

No movement or sound from the house. I settled down, unshouldered my pack and checked my watch; almost 8:00. The light filtering through the canopy was pretty good.

I dug around in my pack, found a brown paper bag, took some notes and sketched a rough image of the house. It was two stories with an open front porch stacked with junk. There were three windows on the second floor above the porch roof. Steps from the porch ran down to concrete in front of an attached two-car garage. The garage had one big overhead door with a light on each side. Under one of the lights, brass house numbers, 101.

I couldn't remember if Steve Albright had mentioned the address. I wrote it down on my paper bag.

The dirt driveway was full of big, deep, North Idaho potholes. The house was a dead end.

I'd have to follow the lane out around the curve to see how far it was to Baldy Mountain Road. I was guessing maybe a quarter of a mile. Everything I saw squared up with what Steve had told me about John Bradley's house.

I stuck the bag back in my pack and pulled out a small pair of Nikon binoculars. I glassed the front porch, saw a couple of red plastic coolers, a rotting overstuffed chair, part of an artificial Christmas tree, a bunch of shoes and boots, some cardboard boxes, several plastic gas cans and a tan-colored plastic dog hut. The name Adolf was scrawled above the hut's arched door in black spray paint.

Damn. Steve hadn't said anything about a dog, but they were standard issue in North Idaho. And out in the boonies, dog was synonymous with pit bull. That was something I had to know.

Next to the dog hut was a big screen door; wooden with a ripped up lower screen. The door also matched with Steve's story.

Nothing else to see, and with nobody shooting at me, I decided what the hell, I'd go check out the back of the house. I was gathering up my pack when I heard it coming—big, loud and right for me. Not sneaking. A pit bull making all kinds of noise, blasting through the trees to tear me up.

I lunged away, brush grabbing at legs and whipping my face. It was coming fast. Shit, I'd never outrun a dog. There, a tree! Get up that tree. Almost there! Please God. One more step.

Toe under a root, I went face-down hard. The wind out of me, gasping, flat on the ground, I laced my fingers over my neck, waiting for teeth ...

Something sailed right over my prone body and dashed away into the woods; stark white glowing against the brown of fallen leaves—a snowshoe rabbit, running like the devil was after him.

The devil struck between my shoulder blades; clawing, ripping my hands and then streaking away; a black blur through the trees.

A cat! A fucking little black house cat, beating his retreat around the back of the house—terrified of the killer in the woods ... me.

I put my face in the dirt; didn't know whether to laugh or shit my pants. Finally, I got enough strength in my legs to quiver back to my pack. I took a long drink of water, and wilted against the Ponderosa's rough bark, trying to get the adrenaline rush under control and hoping the damage to my old heart wasn't too bad.

There were four tiny cat scratches on the back of my right hand. I was pretty sure one might bleed—a little.

Some deadly commando; putting the sneak on a house, planning to shoot the psycho-owners, and I shit myself over a kitty chasing a bunny.

The woods spun. I leaned on the tree and took another drink. I looked back toward the house where the deadly cat had disappeared.

Enough ... time to go home Chip.

On the trail I had a feeling something was going to come racing up from behind and get me. It was the same butt-clenching, chilled feeling I got as a kid when I walked in the dark, alone, all the way from the barn to the house.

I didn't quite run.

◆　◆　◆

I came straight in the front door and gulped water from the kitchen faucet. Something in the drain smelled dead. My stomach turned over.

I shot out onto the deck, sucking in fresh air, leaning over the edge in a clammy, sour sweat; gagging. The watching game hadn't been fun. No fun at all. Maybe I wasn't cut out to do this. A breeze hit my damp skin and I shivered; the cold-blooded killer.

I went inside, laid down on the sitting-area sofa under an old blue afghan.

"That was pretty quick," my wife yelled out from her space.

"Yep," I mumbled.

She appeared, put her hand on my cheek. "You feelin' OK? You look a little green around the gills." She slid her palm across my jaw. It felt wonderful—soothing and safe. Maybe I'd never go up into the woods again. Maybe I'd just hold her for the next forty years.

"Yeah, I'm good. Probably just a little out of shape after sitting in front of the fire all winter." I fought back the urge to tell her everything. "Thanks for caring, doll. I appreciate you."

She kept her hand on my face for another second, looking in my eyes. "Maybe you should just take a nap. You'll feel better after." She gave me her little smile.

An hour later I woke up feeling some better, grabbed my pack off the kitchen floor and went down to my office. A lot of stuff to figure out. I peeled off my crusty tee-shirt, pulled on a clean one and put a fleece over it. The sun had swung around so I took a chair out on the patio where I sat, warm and sheltered, with a printed copy of my Bradley plan and a legal pad. Review time. What had I found out before I panicked and ran home?

I looked at the blank page, chewed on the end of my sharpie, thought about the black cat and the white rabbit. "Jesus Chip, how lame can you get?" My giggling fit went on for a bit. It helped. I wiped my eyes, took a deep breath and started writing.

• There was only one house up there. I still had no proof that it was the Bradleys'. But you have to make some assumptions in every planning situation. Who else's could it be?

• I had a pretty good idea that the Bradleys had a black cat. (The little fucker had scared a decade off my life). Big deal. So what?

• I knew what the front of the house looked like. I had a sketch in my pack.

• I knew how long it took to get up there on foot, and it was a pretty easy trip.

• I had a good idea of what the ground around the house was like. No surprises there.

• I hadn't seen anybody or heard anybody at 8:00 in the morning; probably already at work.

• I would have to get up there earlier.

I had learned something.

And then the part I was avoiding. I had also learned something about myself. I was not the tough guy I made myself out to be. I'd need some time to get used to … what was it … Risk or danger or terror? Saying I'd do it and actually doing it were two different things.

I looked down toward the river. The house number! So scared and sick, I'd forgotten about the house number. I went into my office, pulled my sketch and notes out of my pack. I got online and checked the name for the addressee at 101 Jesus Is My Redeemer Lane. John Bradley's name came up on my screen. OK, I knew something else for sure.

Making the list and finding the address made me feel a little more in control; ready to focus again. Then the phone buzzed in my pocket. I jerked and jumped. Ben Chandler.

"Hi Chip!"

I leaned back into my chair, thought of the normal thing to say. "Hey Ben, did we get busted or was the Audi clean as new when you got it home?"

"No problem," Ben laughed. "We got it all out. Jess loves it." Ben sounded like Ben was supposed to sound.

I said, "Well that's good news."

"Chip, I uh, I've got another favor to ask. I was wondering if maybe you could drive us over to the airport for the trip to Hawaii. I hate to have the car sitting there for a month. You could drive it while we're gone …"

I sat forward over my desk; John Bradley's address information still on the screen. Ben's voice and his obvious good mood were calming. The morning's scare seemed pretty silly all of a sudden. As I relaxed, something clicked in the planning part of my head.

"Did you say you'd be gone a month?"

"Well it looks like we may go for longer than I thought," Ben said. "From mid-April until around Mother's Day. Think you still want to check on things for us if we're gone that long?"

"You bet. Still sounds like fun. A couple more weeks won't make any difference to me." My stomach finally coming all the way out of its twist. "Is your company still paying for the whole thing?"

"Yeah, I'll be working half days on-site with a client," Ben said. "Phil Simmons, my new CEO, has a house we're going to stay in. It's a great deal."

Ben told me a few details about the CEO, a real character by the sound of it.

"Phil is a little quirky. He has a no-phones, no-computers rule for staying in the house. He insists that it remain completely digital-free, just the way it was when the house was built back in the late 1800s. The idea of getting away from phones, and TVs, and computers sounds like heaven to us. We're talking about just leaving our phones here."

"Sounds illegal to me, but wonderful," I laughed. I thought about a deadline and the decisions I was trying to make; forced myself back to the phone call.

"How 'bout if I come over a week from Friday, mid-morning? You can walk me through the chores and then you can treat me to a beer, if you promise not to dump it on me!"

"Yeah, OK," Ben said. "Come over, say around nine?"

"That's a deal. See you on the twenty-eighth about nine."

◆ ◆ ◆

I picked up my plan. Part of the answer to how I could escape had just arrived in the form of a beautiful black Audi Q7.

And the kill deadline had been set too; sometime between

the middle of April and Mother's Day.

It was falling together. A sliver of confidence. I'd have to suck it up, get sure.

I'd have to go back up to the Bradleys'.

Part 1 CHAPTER 5

I'm a creature of habit. I got up at the same time every day. I put the same knife in my pocket and the same watch on my wrist. I ate the same breakfast and drank the same brand of coffee; every single day. I was betting that most people were the same as me in that way; even the Bradleys.

Less than twenty-four hours after being scared out of the woods, I was going back. Start getting a handle on what the Bradleys did habitually; every day.

I was up the road and into the woods by about 6:00; just light enough to see through the trees. I was sweating; waiting for something to jump out of the shadows. Maybe I was looking for a reason to go home.

When I saw the Bradley house, I located the Ponderosa I'd hidden behind the day before and set up my observation post. Hunkering down, I pulled out my binoculars. A light came on upstairs in the center window. Somebody home this morning. My heart rate ticked up.

The light looked like it was on in the back of the house, just leaking out the front window. Down on the ground I saw a dark shape come around the garage onto the concrete pad; the cat again. Now I could see its white chest. Something got his attention and he slinked off into the woods. Nothing else moved; still no sign of a dog.

The sun popped over the ridge, breaking through spaces in the trees, throwing long shadows across the house and the yard. I checked my watch; almost 7:00.

My body was damp with nervous sweat, my mouth like chalk. I took a drink of water. A pocket squirrel started working in the tree above me. He scrambled around in constant, ultra-high-speed motion, chattering and dropping tree-junk on my head.

Then the torn screen door slammed. The squirrel vanished. I sloshed cold water over my camo sweatshirt, an icy trickle finding its way to my skin. The heart pounding got serious.

"Here kitty, kitty!" A woman's voice, shrill and grating, came sawing through the woods. "Adolf, where the hell are you? You little shit!"

Standing on the porch, a round woman in pink shapeless clothes, her hands on her wide, wide hips. I could see her belly above the porch railing, stretching pink sweat pants. My first glimpse of Scarlett Bradley.

"Adolf!" She bellowed. "Kitty, kitty, kitty. Come on, damn it. I have to go to work." She leaned on the porch rail. "Adolf! Damn cat anyway."

So Adolph wasn't a killer pit bull, but a black and white cat. North Idaho humor or just stupid?

The cat sauntered back around the corner of the house, stood in the front yard, and looked up at the pink blimp. Scarlett lowered her tone. I couldn't hear, but she was leaning over the rail having a one-sided conversation with the cat. Adolf ran up the steps onto the porch. The rotund woman opened the screen and lifted poor Adolf up and through the door with a well-aimed kick. She started into the house after him, turned suddenly and looked right at me. Right at me! Like she knew I was there all the time.

I froze, rigid against the tree. Scarlett walked over to the porch railing, plugged one nostril and expertly blew a big string of snot out of the other. She turned and disappeared inside.

I was vibrating—amazed that she hadn't drawn a big fat pink pistol and shot my head off. That was all the time I had to think about it. Two seconds later, the Bradleys' garage door went up.

I swung the binoculars. The image jittered in my shaking hands; John Bradley walking out of the open garage. Even at that distance I could feel something creepy and evil coming off him. He stood shirtless, fat and gross in a patch of light, his gut hanging over gray pants, man boobs jiggling as he scratched his ass. I thought of how much I liked sunlight and how a person like him shouldn't be allowed to stand in it. Sunshine was a purely good thing. He wrecked it.

I felt a new bloom of sweat form on the back of my neck and the palms of my hands. I thought about the hate foaming out of Jess's phone, "I'm gonna get my girls back you bitch. Sleep tight tonight."

His hand went to his pants pocket. He pulled a cigarette from a pack and lit it with a yellow plastic lighter. The smoke hung around him as he turned his face up to the sun, eyes closed, blowing smoke, enjoying the moment. What did he think about? What was going through his head as he stood there?

I enjoyed the same thing every day that I could—rare morning sun warming your bones on a cool, spring day—a simple, free, wonderful feeling; especially up in the mountains. How could a guy who did what he did feel anything like the joy I felt in such a moment? What had happened? Where had the wheels left the tracks?

I realized my new sweat had nothing to do with fear. The rage was back, boiling over at what Bradley was and what he had done to his children. It took me over. If I looked at him for another second, I'd have to run screaming down through the trees and tear him into pieces.

I took the binoculars away and leaned heavily on the tree, trying to find myself. A spider crawled past the toe of my boot. I raised my foot without even thinking. Smashing something, anything, was exactly what I wanted to do. But there had to be a better reason to kill something than a flash of rage. I lowered my boot and watched the spider scurry away. I was still me. I knew what was right and what was wrong.

I lifted the binoculars. John Bradley took one last drag on his cigarette, ground it out on the concrete and kicked the butt off into what passed for his front yard. He reached down into his pants, scratched, turned, and walked back into the garage.

It was quiet in the woods for a few minutes.

A car door broke the silence. An engine started and an old, black Toyota 4Runner backed out. I could see the pink woman wedged in behind the steering wheel as she rounded the curve and accelerated down toward town.

Another car door slammed and a rattling diesel roared to life. The red pickup came down the lane. I could see Bradley, elbow out the window, just as he had been the other day when Ben and I first saw him. At least he'd put a shirt on. He roared out of sight around the curve.

My black Casio read 7:35. I looked back toward the house. Something inside the house moved across the center window upstairs. Or it may have been a tree's shadow, a raven flying over, or a wisp of cloud. I was a little kid again, walking from the barn to the house in the dark. The sweat on my neck got very cold.

◆　◆　◆

Safe in my hot shower I tried to scrub off the fear and doubt.

When the Bradleys were abstract, unknown figures, I could coolly make my plan. Seeing them, and feeling the sick vibes that surrounded them, I felt the all-consuming rage that scared me down to my socks.

How could I keep that rage in check, but get it done? Get it over with before I just let it fade away as I'd done so many times in the past. I had to keep my resolve until I was ready … then carry out my plan because I was sure.

♦ ♦ ♦

A shave and clean clothes completed my makeover from killer to consultant. I hadn't talked to Suzanne yet that morning; probably still dreaming so I let her rest. My phone buzzed and vibrated across the top of my desk.

On the phone was a long-term client, Kyle Johansson. After three years, talking to me had become kind of a habit with him. Today he had something new.

"Chip, I have a friend who could use your help."

Seems the friend was having trouble with his employees; meaning Kyle's friend needed to unload.

"Oh? Tell me about it," I said. I wasn't sure what I'd do with a new client right then, but I had never turned down a new client in my life.

Kyle went on to tell me about Randal Cheatham and his employee retention business in Phoenix. He gave me the contact information then we chatted for a bit about weather and NCAA basketball, confirmed our next call and signed off.

I worked just about every day with people who were stuck in an easy, dismal life: work, money, kids, spouses, houses, status, stress, and death. All looking for the next thing that would make them happy for a little while. That was about it.

Now I had a chance to make sure I didn't end up like my clients. I stayed in my chair, brooding; the potential new client quickly replaced by murder planning.

I had a major hole to fill in my plan; the getaway.

There were only four roads out of Sandpoint, one for each direction of the compass. After I killed John and Scarlett—I was on a first name basis with them now—I didn't want to go hide out in the hills. But a guy on the road would be pretty easy to find until he got a few hours away. Canada was close. Maybe cross the border? How did that work anyway? Would a big guy in a red coat catch you and send you right back?

And what was my long-range plan? I'd kill them, and do all the rest of the stuff on my list, and get away, but then what? Movies never went into that. Killers just got away, or were killed, or thrown in jail. Prison scared me worse than anything … anything. I didn't want to get caught. But what would I do if I was?

Chip, you can't eat the elephant whole. You gotta take little bites.

I grabbed a cap and a jacket and headed outside, through the drizzle and past the fire ring to the wood pile. Splitting a nice piece of birch is one of the most satisfying things I know. There's a rhythm and a sound to it. Up, down, up, down, swing and split, lift and stack. The wood smells good, even on a damp day. Your muscles feel good and you get warmed up. You forget about trying so hard. I picked up the maul and settled into the rhythm. I began to feel sure about what I was planning.

I split birch and flew. I flew high and easy just like I used to.

It was like flying along a timeline in a textbook, only this wasn't a caveman-to-man-on-the-moon kind of timeline. It was a timeline of my life, illustrated with milestones: birth, school, deaths, loves, crises, child, pets, best days. Funny, I didn't see anything about jobs. But I saw the end—my end.

I wasn't going to be around too much longer. What would that be like? We all wonder about that, at one time or another, don't we? We spend most of our lives staying busy so we don't have to think about it.

I considered all the time I spent as a kid in the United Presbyterian Church, listening to the droning, and the singing, and the words spoken in unison by everyone as they stood in their suits and Sunday dresses. It was all aimed at answering what happened after you were dead, right? Isn't that what religion is really all about … croaking?

And nobody really knows what is going to happen; no one. Except the dead people and they aren't talking.

I wasn't sure what I believed about death. I knew what I'd like to think, but that's a wish, not a belief.

I supposed my mom and dad believed what I had heard in church. But we never really said anything about it to each other. Presbyterians believed in pre-determination. That meant we were going to do what we were going to do because God had a grand plan for all of us. I always thought that made for a good excuse to be a bum. Since it wasn't the individual person's fault, if you chose to be a bum, God had made you do it. You couldn't outsmart the system. You couldn't quite get your head around it.

My paternal grandmother had more faith in God, and in what was going to happen at the end, than the preacher and the choir combined. Death to her and Grandpa was a release from the toils of this world and a walk on a golden highway, or was that a yellow brick road? We're off to see the Wizard …

My mom's mother had gotten kind of creepy about religion and death after Grandpa died. She was saving it all up for when she would be reunited with him in the great beyond. And I hoped she was right about that because she wasted the rest of her life on earth moping around.

And then, flying along through my personal timeline, I got it.

My life had been vastly different than my father's, and his father's, and his father's and probably all my farming ancestors all the way back to the knuckle-dragging days in Mesopotamia or somewhere.

So if our lives were so different, why would any of us think that our deaths might all be the same? Maybe we choose our post-death just the same way we chose how we lived our lives. Why the hell not?

It's just as good a doctrine as thinking anybody who doesn't believe the way you do is going to burn for all eternity in some fiery pit.

It was all getting too heavy.

Tom Petty's wonderfully mundane, nasal voice came burning through over that big, low-end coil of the electric guitar, with the acoustic guitar strums on top like whipped cream: Yeah runnin' down a dream …

I looked down at myself standing by the woodpile and chose my post-death to be flying through the clouds with my cape streaming out straight behind me … until the next better thing came along.

I split wood for three hours; flying and working out the end of the plan.

◆   ◆   ◆

The first part of the week I put the Bradleys on the back burner while I stayed busy with the everyday stuff that business people believe is important: Who said what about whom? What did that *really* mean? Why was I left out? How come they make more than me? And how come I'm not appreciated? Earth-shaking stuff like that.

Then I had a call with somebody who had just gotten a cancer diagnosis. "Wow," he said. "My daughter just started college. Seems like she was in kindergarten just yesterday. What the hell did I do with the last fifteen years?" All of a sudden, today got a hell of a lot more important.

And it happened over and over and over. Life moved toward endings, but nobody really thought about it until their ending was right on top of them.

I found myself thinking about .40 caliber bullets during some of those client calls. Not fair to my clients, but I was going to do something worthwhile with the time I had left.

I also stayed busy with the new client referral. After some cyber-tag, I set up a meeting in Arizona with Randal Cheatham. I'd go down there on the first of April.

The rest of my mornings that week I'd hustle off to the Bradleys' in time to see them go. Then I'd come back to my office in plenty of time for everything else I had to do.

The Bradley visits got different. Now I realized how easy it was for me to be scared out of my wits. When your brain is screaming *run* it's pretty hard to calmly stay with a plan. And then there was the rage …

I tried to follow the advice I'd been giving to clients for years. Keep it simple. Know what you can control and what you can't. Watch the house for a few days. Find out what the Bradleys' morning schedule was, nothing more.

I got there about 6:00. At 6:30 lights would come on. At 7:30 I would hear the garage door go up. Then the black 4Runner, Scarlett at the wheel, would leave, followed by John in his red truck. Down the road they would go. They were like clockwork, predictable even in their trailing cigarette smoke and subwoofer thumps.

After they were gone, I would wait around for an hour or so. They never came back. And nobody ever came up to visit. I got confident about the Bradleys' morning schedule.

It looked like catching them asleep, a couple of hours before they got up, would be the deal. I'd surprise them in bed. Shine a light in their eyes—like shooting sparrows with a BB gun in the barn. Maybe it would be easier to do it in the dark.

Part 1 CHAPTER 6

Ben and Jess Chandler, and their five little girls, lived about fifteen miles east of my house; a nice spot right on the Pack River.

Their acreage was covered with pens and a multitude of outbuildings and barns that housed just about every kind of barnyard animal you could imagine and some fairly unusual critters too: alpacas, pot-bellied pigs, an ostrich, llamas, and loads of peacocks, pheasants and other exotic birds.

They had a nice home. Ben had always said he built too much house, but I suspected it had become pretty crowded recently.

I pulled into the Chandler's drive around 9:00. Ben met me by my car.

He was clad in blue jeans, a green fleece pullover and knee-high black gum boots covered with mud and manure. Ben never wore a cap. He had a great head of curly black hair. So, unlike some of us, his scalp was never in danger of getting burned. And I think he liked to show off his mane too … couldn't blame him.

I jumped out of the Subaru. "Hey man, great day to be outside!"

"Yeah, we picked the right day. Been a pretty good spring, huh?" Ben said it with an easy grin.

I popped the hatch and pulled out my old green rubber boots.

Ben didn't hold back, "I'd have been so disappointed if you hadn't brought your Iowa pig farmer boots!"

"Yep, by crackie, us hog boys love our green boots," I said. "Hmm, what's that stuff I see on your boots? That alpaca or ostrich?"

"Could be some of both, or none of neither," Ben laughed again. "I can't keep my shit straight!"

"Well, can't fault you much there," I laughed back.

"How 'bout a cup before we go out to the pens?" Ben nodded toward the house.

We made the walk around to the back, dropped our boots by the door, and climbed upstairs to the kitchen.

"It's nice to have the place to myself for a while," he said, fixing the coffee. "Spring break and the girls are all in town."

Just off the kitchen, in the family room, two big dogs, two terrier types, and a couple of extra-large limp cats lounged together on an area rug. They were enjoying the warm morning. Snores and contented breathing emitted from the group; one happy, furry family. The well-used room was a gigantic wreck of toys, books, kid's clothes, a treadmill, scattered DVDs, comfortable furniture, and a huge TV.

I looked across the pet pile, out the window toward the river. Nice view. I wondered about the fishing. Ben was not a fisherman so I'd never asked. Maybe someday I'd get around to trying his spot.

"Aren't they a bunch?" Ben said, pointing his chin toward the sleeping animals. "I've never seen dogs and cats so comfortable together."

It *was* odd. It was as if the universal rules of cat and dog behavior were suspended at the Chandler's place.

The orange cat seemed to know we were talking about him. He rolled over on his back and stretched out, pushing with his back feet against a hundred-and-twenty-pound golden retriever mix. The touch started a chain reaction and the whole pile stretched and squirmed before settling back into a rhythmic, snoring pile of contentment.

A fifth dog, its black muzzle tinged with grey, slept alone under the electric keyboard on the other side of the room.

"What's up with Finster?" I asked. "He anti-social or what?"

"Oh, he's getting so he'd just rather not put up with the rest of 'em anymore," Ben said, a sad look in his eye. "Fraid

Finster won't be with us too much longer. He's starting to have trouble getting up and down the stairs. Poor old guy … If I ever get in that shape will you just pull the plug for me?"

I gave him a long look. Guys say that stuff, but I always wondered if they really mean it. "You serious?" I said.

"Yeah, I guess I am," he said. "You ever think about that? I mean, my dad died when he was 68, and it wasn't pretty. I doubt he'd go through all that chemo and stuff if he'd had it to do over. I have a feeling he would have lived as long and certainly better if he'd just done nothing. When it got too bad he'd have figured out how to go out on his own terms."

Ben looked over at Finster, chasing rabbits in his sleep. "That would be the way to go. Do what you need to do and then just go."

I felt like Ben was somehow looking a little too deep into my own thoughts. "Yeah, I do think about that. I agree. It shouldn't be just hanging on at the end."

A beep from the kitchen said Ben's coffee was done. He poured us each a cup, black and strong. I thought how good a cigarette would be. It had been twenty-five years, but it sounded pretty damn good. Walk out on the deck, drink coffee, look at the river and have a smoke.

Ben startled me out of my nicotine-lust dream, a hard edge in his voice that hadn't been there a second ago.

"Somebody is harassing us, making threatening phone calls and putting obscene stuff in our mailbox in the middle of the night." Finster got up off his rug, came in and looked up at Ben. Dogs know stuff. Old dogs know a lot of stuff.

"Gotta be that fucking John and Scarlett Bradley." Ben laid his hand on the dog's head. Finster leaned in, held Ben against his shoulder "Jess is pretty scared, pissed too, but pretty scared. I've told the cops, but they can't … or won't do anything. Almost seems like they're afraid of it."

I kept my face neutral, making sure I didn't give away what I knew from Steve Albright. "What are you going to do?" I asked, hoping he wasn't thinking of .40 caliber pistol bullets.

"Don't know yet. I mean, what are my options anyway? Just drive up there and kill both of 'em? I could confront them, but what the hell good would that do? They'd know they were scaring us. I won't give them that. But the guy is crazy. I don't know what he might do. You throw his wife into the mix and it'd be double crazy!"

I looked at Ben and thought; throw Chip into the mix and it might get triple crazy.

"God Ben, you don't want to hurt anybody. You'd have to live with it and the kids and Jess would too. You gotta be careful, be watchful, but let the right people handle it." So easy to give good advice when you weren't going to follow it yourself.

"Yeah, that's the logical approach, but there isn't anybody handling it. I'd like to stomp that son of a bitch and his wife into the ground. The world would be a better place for it. I might be a better man for it too. Shit!" Ben clutched his coffee cup, frustration almost overcoming him.

"You can say it, but don't go any further," I said. "Stay cool. You've got Hawaii coming up."

"Yeah, we'll be completely out of touch for almost a month." Ben looked at Finster who rolled his eyes up. My friend laid his hand back on the old dog's head. "Do you think those fuckers would come over here and mess with the animals or tear the place up?"

I didn't even think before I said, "How 'bout I just stay here a few nights while you're gone? Fresh tracks in and out of the driveway, lights on in different places. Some activity to let people know somebody is around."

"Well ... I hadn't really thought about that." Ben wanted me to do it, but didn't want to ask.

"I don't suppose *you'd* do it for *me*, would you?" I said.

Ben looked at the dog. Finster looked at me.

I was locked in for some guard duty at the Chandler Ranch.

Ben and I stepped back into our boots. I could smell the manure on his. "That smell kinda reminds me of home," I said.

Ben just grinned as we walked off toward the animal pens.

The Chandlers had a special set of piles where they composted animal waste. They were experimenting with the various types, of which they had a global cross-section, to determine what made for best yields in their vegetable gardens. They were having fun with their shitty little experiment.

Ben started to tell me about the kid who would be doing the chores. "Our neighbor's kid, John James, will be over here every day checking on things. He'll be keeping the stalls and the lots cleaned up and doing the composting." Ben was trying to be serious, but he had to grin because we were standing almost knee deep in mud and shit and I was laughing my ass off at the whole thing.

"OK. Dr. Turdwad, I'll check the piles and make sure they're increasing. I guess we'll just have to trust that he's getting the percentages and types blended correctly."

"Don't worry, the kid knows his shit. And I'm not shitting you. You're my favorite turd."

Two grown men at our best ... still in fourth grade.

"Well, I can see if he doesn't do it he'll be in deep doo-doo. Up shit creek without a paddle, S.O.L.!"

Ben held up his hands in surrender. "No shit Sherlock."

With the shit handled, we moved on to the other end of the animals; feed.

We walked toward a thirty-by-thirty-foot feed and hay shed. You could get from the feed shed to the pens along lanes that ran out like spokes on a wheel. Each pen had a watering system that kept fresh, clean water available. The chore kid would have no trouble doing his job. Checking up on him would be a breeze.

I stood outside the Alpaca pen; odd creatures, but cute in anyone's book. They were curious, stretching over the fence, checking out my pockets and nuzzling my fingers and ears.

"Careful!" Ben said. "That brown one bites."

That was about the time the brown one's lips closed around my left ear. I jumped away, startling the animal. I touched my ear expecting to find blood; nothing there but some green-tinged spit.

"Still got your ear?" Ben was laughing. "Sorry Chip … couldn't resist. They don't have teeth on the top. Can't really bite."

"Ha Ha," I said. "I think you owe me a beer."

"That I can do," he said.

Jess and the girls pulled in. The dogs came storming out through the dog door to greet them. Chaos. Ben's girls, all with smiles on their faces, piled out of the Audi and swarmed us with hugs.

He walked the little girls over to the closest pen where the pot-bellied pigs were sunning themselves. The dogs milled around, grinning.

Jess came over and gave me a hug. It felt like she needed it.

"How's the new sister act coming along?" I wanted to be interested, but didn't want to pry.

"Peaks and valleys, valleys and peaks," she murmured. The kids were within earshot so she continued in a low voice.

"More valleys than peaks right now; lots of adjustment. Cindy and Lulu are being great, but it's pretty tough having three new bodies in your space. And nights are long with loads of ghosts to deal with. I'm hoping that Hawaii will help put some of it away. God, I hope so Chip." She lowered her chin, closed her eyes tight.

I thought for just a second she was going to cry. What would I do if the tears came?

The conversation spiraled into an unloading. Ben had found a doll hidden in the barn, mutilated in graphic, sexual ways. Money was gone from Jess's purse. A large, often-used kitchen knife had vanished. Nobody was getting much sleep.

Ben left the girls by the fence and came over. "This looks like a pretty serious conversation. We were on our way for a beer before we got sidetracked, still interested?"

I looked at Jess; she nodded to let me know she was OK. I wasn't so sure, but didn't know what else to do.

"A beer sounds great," I said.

Jess and the girls were tossing hay to a horse and laughing as we walked away.

Ben said, "I've got something in the house I want to show you."

Ben's beer fridge was downstairs by his office. We drank in silence for a long minute, just enjoying the quiet. Ben broke the stillness. "I'm going to give you the combination to my gun safe."

I met his gaze. What was he saying? 'You want to be ready to shoot somebody if they show up while we're gone?' or maybe he was saying, 'Would you please shoot the bastards for me while I'm gone.' Or maybe I was reading way too much into everything.

His gun safe was a nice big one. He spun the red dial. "10-22-10, my grandfather's birthday." Lots of guns and ammo inside; he grabbed a battered old .12 gauge pump shotgun.

"This was my dad's. He shot a ton of quail with it." He handed it to me and I racked back the slide, looked in the empty chamber.

"Here's a box of double-ought buck," he said, pointing to a little flat box on the top shelf. "There's some bird shot here too." Ben put the short shotgun back in its spot and locked up the safe.

He didn't say anything else as we carried our beers up the stairs to the kitchen.

Through the window over the sink I could see Jess pushing a cart full of hay, smallest girl in tow.

Ben said, "We'll be leaving the eighteenth. Flight's at eight AM so plan on us picking you up about five. Sound good?"

"Yeah, it all sounds good, except one thing."

"Oh, what's that?" Ben leaned against the counter and tipped up his beer.

Finster came sauntering into the room, leaned up against Ben. The dog's thick tail beat a slow knock, knock, knock on a cupboard door.

"Is there more of this good beer in the house, or will I have to bring my own?"

Part 1 CHAPTER 7

I had just stepped out of the shower when my cell phone buzzed; Ron Holden. A call from Ron meant fishing—one of my main reasons for moving to North Idaho. The warm day must have made some bugs hatch somewhere. He was the man who knew.

He knew how many cubic-feet-per-second were flowing down every major river within a four-hour drive of Sandpoint. He knew where the fish would be and how long a drift boat would take to get from point A to point B. He also knew what bugs were hatching and had thousands of flies in his boxes to match the hatch.

A beautiful, pure fisherman, I counted myself lucky to sit in a boat with him a few times each year.

I flipped open the phone. "Hi Ron, what's shakin'? How was the bonefishing?"

"Fantastic. I'll tell you about it tomorrow. We're heading to the St. Joe. Wanna come? It's supposed to be mostly sunny and sixty. The fish will be UP!" Ron always sounded excited on the phone.

I had no plans for the weekend. "When do we leave?" I said.

"Seven AM, my house, you, me and Jill." Ron couldn't wait. He fished at least seventy-five days every year, and he was as excited about the last trip as the first.

"OK, see you in the morning." I punched off, dried off, slipped into some sweats and hit the couch with Suzanne to watch a movie.

"Gonna go fishing with Ron and Jill tomorrow up at the Joe," I said, getting sleepy. "OK with you?"

"You know it is," she said. "You always have a great time with those two. How old is he now?"

"Umm, I guess he's sixty-nine. Yeah he's nine years older than me, or at least he will be this summer some time."

"Well, make sure you at least offer to row, even if you know he won't let you."

When I woke up, the movie credits were playing and Suzanne was gone. I shut off the TV and stumbled upstairs to bed.

As I looked at the time on the ceiling, I thought I must have been making progress on cooling my attitude about the Bradleys. Who ever thought I'd take a fishing break in the middle of plotting a murder?

◆   ◆   ◆

Ron's drift boat sailed along behind his pickup so nicely that you hardly knew it was there. At Coeur d'Alene we headed east on I-90, then took the exit to St. Maries and were in our waders and putting the boat into the St. Joe River by 10:30. A shuttle service was already on the way to our take out point, several miles downriver, with Ron's truck and trailer.

It was time for Ron's boat launching ceremony. Out came the silver flask. He held it high as we stood soaking our wader boots soft in the edge of the St. Joe.

"May the fishing gods smile on us today, and may we always be thankful for our friends, the fish and this river!" Ron took a good pull on the flask, let out an "AHHH!" and handed it to Jill. She followed suit, then passed the flask to me. I wasn't much of a booze drinker, but a sip before the launch was good luck so …

"OK friends, let's go fishing!" Ron jumped in the center seat. Jill plopped down in the front. I pushed us out into the current and got situated in the rear.

Easing out into the flow was always a favorite part of the trip for me. Anything was possible. Rivers are never the same two days, or two hours, or even two minutes in a row.

"I feel good!" I sang.

"Knew that I would!" Ron chimed in.

"Da, Da, Da, Da, Da Da Daaaa!" Jill was the band.

The music filled the boat as I cast a squala fly toward a fishy-looking cut in the bank.

The sun was out and the air was still. The river ran high and fast; power right under our feet to be wary of. Mountains rose on each side, three or four-thousand-footers, mostly covered with evergreens and the occasional stand of birch still waiting to leaf out. In close to the river were expanses of low wet ground with willows and cottonwoods that ran away to the mountains.

Trout do not live in ugly places. And I have never met a person in pursuit of trout that did not appreciate where they were pursing them.

We settled into our steady rhythm of casting and retrieving, alert and watching for the telltale silver flash of a fish, ready to set the hook and feel that magical thrumming in our bones and muscles.

Fifteen minutes later a sixteen-inch cutthroat came sliding up and sucked in Jill's fly. It was not the slashing, blasting fight of mid-summer, but that wonderful spring drift-up-and-eat-it-while-you-watch thing. It took willpower and skill not to jerk the fly away before the fish had it.

Jill had the knack. Her rod bent in a lovely arc as the trout went deep. Ron let the anchor drop, stopping the boat in the middle of the swollen river. Jill patiently brought the fat cutty up to Ron's net.

He grinned a first-fish-of-the-day grin. The fish lay in the shallow net glinting brown, purple, silver, green, yellow, and the slash of red down under the gills. "Purdy, purdy fish!" he said. Satisfied that we had gotten a good look, he dipped the net back in the river and turned it gently over. The fish flicked and sped away.

"Skunk's out of the boat," Ron said. A couple of minutes later a twin of Jill's fish took my squala.

Two fish landed early. It had the makings of a great day.

◆ ◆ ◆

About 1:00 we pulled over on a gravel bar for lunch.

"Ron," I said, around a mouthful of ham and cheese, "Wasn't it around here that you drowned?"

"Yeah, that's right," he said. "See that big cottonwood down there with the raven in it? There's a good lunch spot right there when the water's down in the summer. That's where I went in after the boat." Ron munched on chips and swigged an IPA—even the old guys were drinking it.

"Tell me about it again, would you?" I'd heard this story probably ten times. But I needed to hear it again.

Ron gave me an are-you-sure look; then began. "This was oh … twelve years ago. I had just gotten this boat. I went over to Billings to pick it up then I pulled it back and camped here on the Joe that night. Guy Ross was with me; you remember Guy … He's been gone, oh what Jill, six or seven years now?"

Jill agreed, "Mm hmm."

"Guy and I took off from Calder pretty early. We caught some good fish and hit that gravel bar down there for lunch. We beached the boat and were sitting on a big log just sunning and eating when Guy jumps up and says, 'Good God Ron, your boat's going down the river!'

"I guess I hadn't tied it up well enough. It had gotten out into the current. I saw it drifting away and I just went right in after it. I didn't even think. I stepped off a ledge and shipped water into my waders. It must have been ten feet deep. The current caught me and took me out to the middle, just like that. I came back up, just my chin above the water, but my damn waders filled full and I couldn't float. I went back under again and again. The current kept moving me down the river. Every now and then I'd feel the bottom and push up and get another little shot of air, but I was losing my strength fast."

"God," I said, "I can't think of anything that scares me more."

"You know," Ron said, "You'd think that, and maybe I was really scared at some point. If I was, I don't remember. I was thinking how stupid I was for going after the boat. Somebody would have stopped it or found it and the boat would have been fine. About the seventh or eighth time I went under I said to myself, well Ron, you're not gonna come up again. I thought about all the stuff I'd done. But you know what I thought about most? The stuff I still wanted to do. And there was a lot of it.

"Then I started dreaming or something. I saw my dad and mom, my little brother who got killed in '61 sledding up on the Pine Street Hill, and my grandparents. And they all looked really happy, and it was like they were dancing or something. I never saw a light or any of that, just more like a space where the mood and the place were the same thing. Sounds weird, I know, but it was like dancing around in happiness. I was pretty much ready to stay there."

Ron seemed to be there, in that place, as he told the story.

"Well, there was another group in boats down around the next bend. They saw my empty boat and went for it. The story I got later was that one guy saw my hair swirling around in the water or they wouldn't have known I was there at all."

Jill reached over, gave Ron's white pony tail a little tug and said, "We're never gonna cut that off are we?"

"No way baby," Ron smiled at her.

"They got me out on a gravel bar. There's a lodge and a cafe down a few turns. It's closed now. Somebody went and called 9-1-1. Life Flight came and flew me out. I woke up in the hospital. Doctor said I had been dead. Those guys had gotten me going again and the paramedic in the chopper got me stabilized." Ron stopped, looked into the same river that had almost killed him.

"They were from out of state somewhere, the guys who saved me. They were in a car wreck going home on I-90 the next day. All five of 'em were killed. I never met or talked to any of them."

"God, all of 'em? What would you have said? "

"Well," he paused. "Do what you gotta do *now*. Nothing like dying to make you realize you gotta live on purpose. Believe me, I've tried like hell to make every minute count since then. I like food more. I drink good wine. I don't have to have a lot of stuff. I worry less, and I try to give people a lot more space to be who they are." Ron held his beer bottle up in a salute toward the current. "This river could swallow you in the next minute and it most likely isn't going to spit you back out like it did me."

Ron had said it before, but this was the first time I really got it.

The rest of the day fell off as far as the fishing was concerned. We caught a few, but the wind got stronger as the afternoon wore on. At 5:00 we reached our take-out. Thirty-five minutes later we were back on the road.

The truck cab warmed up. Ron and Jill discussed the downfall of the free world as a result of Republican greed. I drifted off to sleep thinking of life and death and how little control we had over any of it.

I soared in my dream; flying with somebody high over a wide-open plain, happy and free and weightless.

Part 1 CHAPTER 8

On Monday, I got out the Beretta and turned some chicken noodle soup cans into sharp lace. My aim and confidence in the new pistol was dead on.

This time when I looked at a handful of empty .40 caliber brass, they didn't look back.

I packed and spent the rest of the day getting ready for my new business trip to Phoenix.

◆   ◆   ◆

Randal Cheatham suggested we meet at his house. A limo got me there, and then we sat out by the pool for most of our all-day meeting.

Randal's company, Retention Specialists, Inc. (RSI) was in the business of helping clients design employee retention programs that pretty much trapped people in their jobs. The whiz-kids at RSI tweaked programs and systems deep inside client organizations. That meant his people were on site with those clients for years on end with the meter running, and he charged a lot. Cheatham had three hundred employees and only about twenty worked in the home office. The rest lived and worked all over the world.

He had the same sorts of issues with his employees that everybody did. They couldn't seem to get along with each other, and of course there is always that *one* guy.

No matter how great your team, there is the asshole that gets handed off and promoted again and again because even the boss is afraid of them. In RSI's case, that one guy's name was Eugene Triska. He rubbed everybody the wrong way. Randal said, "I can't fire Eugene, he makes us—meaning Randal—too much money. I'd like to see the whole team get along better. I'm fed up with the bitching."

So I signed up Randal and his management team for a year of coaching. My trip was a success.

Part 1 CHAPTER 9

When April came to North Idaho and the clouds set in, a guy could get really down in the dumps. Some people would sit in front of a "happy light" that was supposed to put vitamin D in your system and make you feel good. I tried it. I didn't feel any better.

My way to beat the North Idaho blues was to get outside and move, even if it was raining. I had a built-in excuse for going out into the woods now. I had to know more about the layout of the Bradleys' house, what was in it, and the ground surrounding it.

On April 2, I looked out at a white wall of mist and clouds and put a camouflage Gortex rain suit over my fleece. I considered strapping on the Beretta, but that just seemed like asking for trouble.

The woods were coming out of winter. The birds were moving around. As I hiked, a raven flew right over me, up above the tops of the trees. I could hear the swish-whoosh, swish-whoosh of its big black wings as it checked me out. Up ahead I heard the pterodactyl voice of a Pileated woodpecker. They were big too, but shy. I didn't catch a glimpse.

I thought about how free the birds seemed. Free of the earth, and the mud, and the burning legs it took to work your way up a mountainside. They flew above it all; effortless and unthinking.

Tom Petty piped up: Learning to fly, but I ain't got wings … I thought I knew what Tom was talking about.

Then it got quiet; getting close to the Bradleys'. The floor of the forest was wet and still. The light was flat and dead like a black and white movie. I worked on not making any sound; melting in.

I saw the square of light through the trees. Then I smelled the smoke. It's funny how far and fast the smell of smoke will travel in dead, damp air. I had no doubt about what kind of smoke it was. Reefer this early in the morning?

I moved slowly and easily, staying as loose as I could, working around behind the house. At maybe fifty yards out, I found a low spot where I could lie in the leaves and raise my binoculars over the edge without exposing myself. It gave me a clear shot, through their parked-out back yard, at the deck where two men stood against the rail passing a joint back and forth.

One was unmistakably John Bradley. The guy was a freak about not wearing a shirt. Forty degrees and he's out on the deck in only his pants.

I'd had a crazy cousin once who ran around outside all winter in Iowa in a tee-shirt. He'd been shot dead by the cops, on the side of the road, more than twenty years ago when he'd brandished a gun during a drunken confrontation.

I guessed there must have been something about body chemistry and brain function; gray matter floating in bad broth, the mixture a little too rich or something. Bradley obviously had something funky percolating through *his* pipes.

My binoculars brought him right up close. When I saw him, there was a little pop of my pores opening up and the sweat started again.

I put the Nikons on the other guy. He looked like one of the trees had jumped out of the ground and gone up for a little morning doobie with Bradley. A seven-foot-tall white guy with a shaved head. His yards and yards of legs were inside brown duck work pants, a red plaid flannel shirt tucked into them. He had on logger's boots. He'd be hard to miss anywhere.

The two men talked and smoked. I couldn't make out what they were saying. Not joking around. Just talking and smoking.

They finished up and John went through the sliding patio door. The light went on and I could see kitchen cabinets. The Tree Man ducked in under the door and sat down, dwarfing a cheap-looking round table. Bradley went out of my line of sight.

Scarlett arrived a couple seconds later. She must have had a closet full of pink clothes. It was a little bit startling that early in the morning to see that pink vision; big hair, cigarette in her mouth, Big Gulp travel mug in her hand.

She said something to Tree Man, then moved across the room and booted Adolf out onto the deck. I heard the whump of the door shutting. Scarlett stood looking out through the glass; *right at me.*

It freaked me out. I froze. I hadn't been moving much anyway, but I felt like her eyes were locked right onto mine. Maybe I was like an old cartoon and my eyes were magnified and bugging out of the lenses of the binoculars.

I pictured her screaming bloody murder and the Tree Man chasing me down in the woods, whipping a chain saw out of his pocket and cutting me up into bite-sized pieces.

Then Scarlett turned back to the kitchen, a pink draft horse clopping past Tree Man, and went out of sight.

I checked my watch; 7:18. I looked back at the kitchen; now all three of them were standing there. John had put a shirt on, thank God. They talked for a minute and then disappeared.

A few seconds later, both rigs left.

Adolf moved off the deck, probably thinking about several blissful hours without getting kicked around by the pink Clydesdale.

I pulled down below the edge of my spy spot. Two vehicles had left but what about Tree Man?

The slider opened. The bald giant stooped and came out wearing a camo poncho. In the poncho he looked even bigger.

Like a covered wagon with a shiny head and three-day's growth of black beard.

He drank coffee, watching the cat stalk something. Adolf sprang. A little brown bird jumped off the ground, beating for altitude. The cat followed it up, knocking feathers away, but coming down empty-handed. The bird landed, safe in the top of a Hemlock, and looked down at the house, the cat, the Tree Man and me.

Tree Man's voice rumbled across the yard like thunder, "Nice try cat. No birdy for breakfast this morning," he laughed. No joy there. More like he was pulling the cat's whiskers. Poor old Adolf didn't seem to have any real friends.

Then Tree came off the deck; coming at me. I pulled down from the edge. If I ran, he'd have me for sure. I curled up in a ball and tried to melt into the leaves and brush.

It got dark. A cloud moved over, dropping a solid sheet of rain that turned into graupel. The hard and soft moisture made a lot of racket in the trees. I had no idea where Tree was. I held my knees close to my chest and prayed … or something. The cloud moved on.

I lay there and saw a thousand horrible deaths before I heard a cell phone beep, footsteps on the deck, and the slider open and close.

I didn't look. I rolled over and beat it down into the gully, sucked through the mud and rotting leaves, and cut up the hill. I hunkered down, trying to get control of the pounding behind my eyes.

The damn slider opened again. Tree walked straight off the deck, pulled the poncho aside and took a leak on the warm spot where I'd been lying a minute before. I realized I was holding my breath.

He turned, walked across the spongy yard, through an opening in the trees and headed west up the mountain.

I had some giant roaming around out in the woods, doing

God knows what. He probably had a gun and a knife and a chainsaw and a shovel with which to bury my dismembered body.

Drink some water. Eat something. Think. Don't run. He can't know you're here.

I was pretty sure Tree Man wasn't going to show up behind me. There was another drainage between him and me, and he'd left like he was on a mission.

It was 8:00. Lots of people were just getting their day started. I'd already had a vigorous hike and died twice.

I peeled off my jacket and stuffed it in my pack, left the rain pants on to protect my butt. I hadn't panicked. It had been close, but I hadn't run home to mama. Maybe I was getting better at this.

I leaned on a tree, visualized my plan; ticking off decisions made and yet to be made.

I'd kill them. They would know why. I'd get the story to the media. I'd take Ben's car and drive away. Ben and all his girls would never have to worry about the Bradleys again. I wouldn't be in jail. I wouldn't have hurt anybody that didn't deserve it. I would end well. It all felt right.

Behind me water was running, gurgling just a little bit on the way to Carr Creek. I thought about the Chandlers with all the girls in Hawaii, the Beretta and the wicked .40 caliber bullets, my lovely wife on a blue blanket with her eyes closed.

◆ ◆ ◆

A big shadow covered me—yards of legs in brown duck pants. A big fist holding something that flashed in the light, plunging toward my chest. I jumped up. He jumped after me, swinging and knocking a puff of something from my side. He came down empty-handed and sank into the boggy, rotting forest floor as I flew away, higher and higher. A little bird floated by my head, looking at me with one dark shiny eye as we glided effortlessly above everything else in the world. There was music, but I couldn't quite make out what it was. It was right there tickling at me, just out of reach. It had a nice steady beat. Plat! Plat! Plat! Plat!

I startled awake as rain thudded on my cap and shoulders. My jacket was in my pack. Now I was good and wet. The wind blew hard for about two freezing minutes, and then went dead still as the sun came out again. Tree Man emerged from the woods and strode across the ratty yard. This time I wasn't dreaming.

Up on the deck, the giant pulled his poncho off revealing a big, camouflage frame pack, loaded and bulging. He unshouldered the pack, shook the wet poncho out and carried his gear inside. The glass door had become a big mirror, reflecting green and brown images of the yard and woods.

A couple of minutes later a four-wheeler or motorcycle headed west, up over the mountain toward the little town of Priest River.

Who the hell was he? And what the hell was he doing with the Bradleys? I didn't know, but what I did know was that I was going to get the hell out of there while the getting was good.

Part 1 CHAPTER 10

I was lying in bed, drifting, listening to Suzanne sleep. I could picture her serene face. It made me feel warm and good—but I ruined it by letting something from a long time ago creep in.

The spring of 1967, I lost a big chunk of the I-can-do-anything faith I'd always had. It was April and it had been beautiful in Iowa.

The men; Dad, Grandpa, and my uncle Harold, were all in the field when I got home from school. It was a warm balmy day, perfect for planting corn. Those are the days farmers live for; another beginning.

Dad had asked me to go on squinty patrol. I headed toward the back of the farm with a little silver can of peanuts coated with some kind of deadly pink dust. The idea was to walk around the fence lines, find ground-squirrel holes, and put three or four of the poisoned peanuts deep down inside. You wanted to kill the squintys before they dug up and ate the expensive seed corn.

I had been admonished by Dad in the sternest terms that if a hog or dog or cat got hold of a peanut, it would die. He trusted me with a can full of sure death.

I also had my single-shot, lever-action .22 over my shoulder. I'd gotten it the summer before with twenty dollars of my own money—after gazing at it for months through the window of the Gambles Hardware store. I'd already knocked off a variety of game and I was looking forward to trying my skill on a tiny, fast-moving squinty.

The ground along the fence row was black and freshly worked into a wonderfully mellow state; the smell of the warm earth was joy. I left shallow tracks as I searched for recently dug holes.

Below me, Grandpa was pulling the disk in the forty-acre field farthest from the house. In the field above me, my uncle was planting corn. Dad was off doing the hog chores; taking care of the money-makers.

Grandpa saw me and waved as he drove the green 4020 John Deere tractor back and forth, the disk with the harrow raising a dust cloud behind. I waved back.

The 4020 was a big, open diesel tractor. You sat in the yellow padded seat and leaned on the fender as you looked back at the implement you were pulling. The wind and the sun and the rain and the cold all hit you right in the face when you drove it. It was the best tractor of its day, and if you were a seventh-grader you were proud that your farm had one. It had a distinctive throaty bellow. On a quiet night during field work, lying in your bed, you could hear them for miles. Thirty years later there would be a lot of deaf old farmers because of it.

I watched as Grandpa reached the end of his round. He pushed the hand throttle on the steering column up, slowed, raised the disk out of the ground, stepped hard on his right wheel brake pedal, spun the steering wheel, swinging the disk and harrow just inches from the fence, and dropped the disk back into the ground. A puff of black smoke belched up from the pipe, and the tractor roared ahead again.

He'd done it thousands of times, smooth and flowing, never missing a beat, carving lines in the field, arrow straight from fence to fence, doing what he had been born to do.

I spotted a fresh squinty hole and blew out a sharp whistle. The *little bastard* (my dad's term) poked his buff-colored head out of the Oreo-sized hole and looked at me. I eased the rifle up, thumbed back the hammer, and drew a deep breath to steady my aim …

The 4020's engine noise changed. The low, powerful roar went to a tortured, high-pitched whine. It was running wide open, but it wasn't pulling. It wasn't in gear. Something wrong.

The yellow, six-foot-tall wheels had stopped turning. Something wrong.

Grandpa there in the seat, looking up at the sky. Something wrong!

My rifle, still cocked, went in the dirt. Pink poison peanuts spilled out on the black ground. Hands on top of a fencepost, feet up and over the barbed wire, landing in the bean stubble. Running, shouting, "Grandpa! Grandpa!" Soft earth; slipping and stumbling. Stupid feet mired down, slow and heavy.

The monstrous sound of the tractor's engine blaring louder and louder as I closed the gap.

"Grandpa!" He sat still, unmoving. His head and shoulders thrown back over the seat, fine white hair hanging toward the ground, arms flung out on either side of the bright yellow arm rests.

I could get there. I could save him. I would save him!

I reached the tractor. The roaring of the diesel engine shattered the air. I jumped to the steel step and vaulted onto the open platform, straddling Grandpa's left leg. His face, eyes closed, slack, covered with field dust. False teeth, perfect white and pink, jutting out of his mouth. I yanked up on the throttle and the horrific wailing of the tractor's engine dropped to idle. His cap lay in the powder-dust on the tractor dash, covering the gauges.

My mind thudded, grasping. Time slowed.

He'd had several heart attacks. Ash-faced, lying in the back seat of my uncle's car, he'd winked at me before being rushed to the hospital. My mom had given me a bottle of pop and left me with Great Aunt Minnie who had smelled like old flowers and sweat.

Now Grandpa was on the tractor and we were alone. I stuffed his cap in the back pocket of my jeans; his fake teeth went in my shirt pocket. He would be OK. I would save him. I could do this. I was sure. Not scared. Not panicked. I felt calm, in perfect control. I grew taller over him.

"Grandpa, can you hear me? Can you hear me?" I hammered him hard on the chest. Once, twice, three times; dull thuds with my fist, the shock traveling up my arm. "Grandpa!" Nothing.

Had to get him home.

I put my butt against his belly and chest; had to keep him on. I pushed in the clutch, got the tractor moving, and raised the disk up out of the ground, the sharp round blades riding above the soybean stubble. The tractor bellowed in my ears, belched black smoke in my eyes as I opened the throttle.

I steered with my left hand, held him in the seat with my right, crushing his cigarettes against his chest. I stood between his feet, holding on as the tractor bucked across the field—afraid I'd hit a big hole or a high spot and he would bounce off and go under a wheel. He was limp and heavy; so hard to keep him on the seat, his arms and head flopping with every jolt.

Several hundred yards ahead I could see Uncle Harold standing at the corn planter filling the seed boxes from yellow and white bags. His hand came up, visoring his eyes. Something wrong.

I roared up, my uncle on the steel platform with me before the tractor stopped rolling. He didn't speak. He grabbed my grandpa by the front of his denim work coat, hauled him over the back axle and laid him flat on the bare ground.

"I'll go get Dad!" The little Ford tractor hooked to the corn planter was running. I jumped on, stuck it in gear and made for the barn.

Dad rounded the corner of the barn in my uncle's red Chevy pickup. I saw his eyes widen. Something wrong.

He skidded to a stop on the dry dirt lane. I pointed through the dust, back the way I had come. "Grandpa had a heart attack!"

Dad flew.

I went the other direction for the house and the phone on the kitchen wall. I gave the operator all our names and doctor Carroll's. She would relay it all to the Lincoln County Hospital. I hung up. The holes in the dial of the black phone stared, and the house made empty sounds.

The red pickup skidded to a stop on the gravel drive. Dad driving, Uncle Harold crying, my grandpa propped up between them.

"I called the doctor. They know you're coming," I said it to my dad, not wanting to look at my uncle's tears, and trying not to see how grey and dead Grandpa looked.

They raced away, sliding in the gravel as they turned onto the county road.

I was left there alone.

♦ ♦ ♦

Grandpa died.

Nothing I had done had made any difference. One of the things I did may have made it all worse.

They drove to the doctor's office. The doctor wasn't there. He was at the hospital waiting for them to arrive.

I can't imagine what Dad and Uncle Harold had gone through on that long drive—my grandpa limp between them—speeding up to the office only to find Dr. Carroll not there. Driving to the hospital; seeing the worst in the face of our family doctor. Precious time wasted … My fault.

They drove home, alone together, where we were all waiting for the news.

They said, "He was dead in the field of a massive heart attack." His fifth, and last, as it turned out.

They said, "Thank God he got the tractor out of gear before he died or he might have gone under the disk."

They said, "Be happy it was quick and he was doing something he wanted to be doing."

They said, "That's tough for a thirteen-year-old boy to find his grandpa dead in the field like that."

They said, "Keep an eye on Chip. That could screw him up."

◆ ◆ ◆

The funeral was a big one. Grandpa's family had lived in Lincoln County since before the Civil War. The place was crawling with cousins and friends.

The casket was open. All the well-wishers filed past and looked down at him, lying there in that grey steel box. I wouldn't do it. It was the end. He was dead and I didn't want to look at him.

My grandpa's brother, Great Uncle Matt, said to me, "I'm glad there was a good man like you around when your grandpa needed him."

I thought it was a load of crap. I thought I would save him and I didn't. It was a gyp. It wasn't fair. It didn't happen that way in the movies. I hadn't made any difference at all.

What Grandpa needed was not to have smoked two packs of Camels a day for forty years. I couldn't do anything about that.

My dad and mom didn't offer any explanations. They had their own struggles to deal with, I guess.

At sixty Grandpa was dead. Before he died, I had been sure I could do anything.

Part 1 CHAPTER 11

Saturday.

I was thinking about Tree Man. He was complicating things, confusing my thinking. This was supposed to be about getting rid of the Bradleys … doing the right thing. I had to get a handle on it before I lost sight of what I had set out to do.

On Sunday, I waded around in the Priest River, up high by the lake, thinking a little fishing would get my mojo working.

I didn't catch any fish and I didn't fly either.

◆   ◆   ◆

Monday morning I was in a new spot in front of the Bradleys' house by 6:00. From there I could see Baldy Mountain Road *and* the house. This was the day I was going to go inside.

Adolph strolled around to the front porch at 7:27. He ran up on the porch and the screen door slammed. Somebody must have let him in.

A couple of minutes later Scarlett backed out of the garage, followed by John in the pickup. Tree Man sat hunched in the passenger's seat, his big pumpkin head knocking up against the roof.

I sat still, listening as they headed down Baldy toward town. The three people I knew about were gone.

I sat for another minute. "OK Chip, if you're gonna do this, now is the time." I was talking to myself and I didn't care. I dropped my day pack by a rock where I knew I could easily find it and started toward the house.

I felt guilty or scared or angry or something. Whatever it was, it was something different. It was exciting and sickening at the same time. I almost turned and ran back. I could still stop this whole deal and nobody would know but me.

Then I'd be twice as screwed up … wouldn't I?

No, I was going in.

I followed the curve in the lane, zig-zagging around pot holes, still talking, "Please don't let there be somebody else in that God-damned house watching me trudge up the drive."

So what if there is? I'm just out walking and wanted to meet the neighbors. No law against that. The light coming out of the front window kept whispering in my ear, trying to make me think there was somebody in there.

Did the curtain move? Tension wound me tight.

I walked across the concrete pad in front of the garage door and climbed the few steps onto the junk-strewn porch. Adolf was waiting for me. Scarlett hadn't let him inside after all. He wasn't a bad looking cat. They kicked him around, but he *was* getting fed. He gave me that wary what-the-hell-are-you-doing-on-MY-porch look that cats are so fond of.

"Hey Adolf, what's shaking?" I said. "Is there anybody else left inside the house today?"

Adolf wasn't talking, but he must have decided I was alright because he came over and rubbed on my shin and wrapped his tail around my calf.

I walked past the junk. The cat drifted over to the plastic dog igloo and went inside, dropping onto a pile of filthy, hair-covered rags.

I rapped hard on the edge of the torn-up screen door. Nothing happened. I banged harder; nothing.

The screen's spring twanged taught and the metal entry door swung in with a little push. Huh, I thought it would be locked. I stuck my head inside the house, waiting for the shot, or the ball bat to swing. "Anybody home?"

The steps to the second floor were across the entry hall. Adolf bolted past me, shot up the stairs. "Shit!"

I stood and listened. This was it. Go in or run.

I didn't hear a sound. With my hip holding the screen door open, I pulled four plastic Walmart bags from my pocket, put two over each of my boots.

I yelled again. "Hello, it's your neighbor! Anybody home?"

Nothing.

I stepped across the threshold.

Greasy food, cigarette smoke, old carpet and used cat litter. It was a damp wall of stink. Under my feet, cheap, filthy tile which might have been beige under the grime. Why had I worried about leaving tracks? Next to the door, a pile of muddy shoes and boots; women's, men's, and a lonely pair of very small pink tennis shoes. Tree Man's camo poncho hung limply on a peg above the sour-smelling pile.

I listened hard. The place felt empty and dead.

The staircase in front of me was open to the living room on the left. On the right was a solid wall separating the steps from the dining room. The steps were covered in matted green shag carpeting. A shaded window at the top leaked some light onto the upper landing.

The living room was a tumble of worn out furniture smashed flat by heavy bodies. In front of the ruined couch a coffee table hid under beer cans, dirty glasses, a couple of porn magazines, and several overflowing ashtrays. I couldn't remember seeing an ashtray inside a house for years.

In the dining room, a plastic brass chandelier hung from loose ceiling wires over a table stacked with crap. A dirty path, worn into the hardwood floor, led into the kitchen.

I froze and listened again, guts in knots. "Hey! Anybody home? There's a stray dog outside, wondered if it's yours?"

Still nobody.

I paused at the bottom of the stairs. The damn cat had gone up there. I'd have to go get him. Going up, counting steps … at six I shuddered. Something about being at eye-level with the upper floor made me clench. Thirteen steps up and I was standing in an oppressive hallway. The hall and railing wrapped around the stair opening.

The place reeked of dirty sheets, mildewed towels and sweaty socks. Gross pigs living in a gross pig sty.

The walls of the landing and the hall around the staircase were covered in some kind of ratty faded-out wallpaper; the carpet thick with litter, fuzz and oily stains.

To my right, the bathroom. It had been painted a light color ... once. Blue toilet and blue tub coated in grunge.

There were three more doors in the L-shaped hall. I walked across the hall and pushed open a door; the master pig sty. A mess of dirty clothes. A sagging, greasy-bed with a tangled floral spread. His-and-her night stands littered with filmy glasses and pill bottles. Mismatched reading lamps on the stands, probably so they could proof-read their dissertations before turning in. Across the room, a pair of sliding doors hung askew revealing a shallow closet jammed full; the hanger rod sway-backed under its load of pink clothes.

There was actually a sort of order to the room. John's side; drab and earth-toned, dirty piles of Wal-Mart clothing, and Scarlett's; dingy pink piles of sweat pants and knit stuff that could stretch ... a lot. Wasn't hard to figure out which sides of the bed they slept on.

I went to John's side and pulled open the drawer on the night stand. It was full of junk; some .25 caliber pistol cartridges and loose 12 gauge shot shells. A 12 gauge was on the floor under the bed. There was brass and red plastic peeking out of the loading port. I lifted the mattress; nothing but hair and crumbs and a plastic cap from a tube of something.

Scarlett's side was just junk; nothing dangerous there. She'd let John do the shooting.

I went to the window, looked out through streaked glass. I could see where Tree Man had disappeared into the woods in his poncho.

Before I went out the door I had another look at the bedroom. What kinds of awful shit had gone on in here between the pink and the brown goal lines?

I went back out into the hall.

The next room had an unused smell, more like dust than anything else. It looked like they hadn't touched it since moving in. The old sheet they'd hung over the window had fallen on the floor, surrounded by dead fly carcasses. I could see Jesus Is My Redeemer Lane snaking south. I closed the door tight behind me.

Dead ahead of me was the last door. It hung open a few inches but not enough to see inside. It felt like something was in there. Nothing I could put my finger on, just some kind of presence.

A compressor motor clicked and whirred to life downstairs; the refrigerator kicking on. Probably keeping old John's caviar and capers chilled to perfection.

Gripping the railing with my left hand, I gently moved the door with the fingertips of my right. It whiskered open over pinkish carpeting revealing pink walls and white trim, dim light coming in the window over the porch roof.

I felt movement in there. Whoever it was would be looking over the railing at me as I went down. They'd have a clear shot. I could hear the pistol cocking. The bullet would come through the top of my cap as I hit the fifth step.

Adolf came out the door and rubbed up against my ankle, purring. The little bastard had done it to me again.

It was a cheap scare, but effective. I almost went to my knees. I held on to the doorknob for a few seconds, fought off the heebie-jeebies, and went into the room.

Adolph jumped up on a single bed, curled into a ball and watched.

There were three single beds. Thumb-tacked to the princess-pink walls were posters of Hello Kitty, Disney Princesses, and some prissy-looking teenage kid.

Two of the beds were end-to-end and rumpled, spanning the entire east wall. The one Adolf had chosen was on the front wall. Its pink and white lacey spread and dust ruffle was exactly square, oddly military.

There was a pair of brown Carhartt work pants next to a pair of enormous logger's boots, half again as big as my size 10 hikers. Tree Man. It looked like he would continue to complicate things.

Another shotgun, the twin to the one in the master, was under the end-to-end beds. Two shotguns. Three crazies. And just me. I went back out in the hall thinking I had been inside the house way too long. But I needed to see the rest of it.

"Here kitty, kitty."

Adolph came out. I swung the door back in place and he followed me down the stairs, through the dining room and into the kitchen.

The sink was piled high. If there was a square inch of counter space not buried under stacks of trash and dishes I couldn't see it. All four burners of the stove were covered by encrusted, blackened pans. On the other side of the room a long hallway stretched toward a closed door.

The cat and I moved down the hall past a scungy half-bath, and into a pass-through laundry room; drab dirty clothes and giant pink wads all over the floor.

The closed door had to be to the garage. Last closed room. Last spot for somebody to hide. "Hello, anybody there? Hello, I'm your neighbor. Anybody there?"

Adolf rubbed on my leg and purred. He had asthma or something. His purring had a clicking wheeze as he breathed in. Other than the cat's respiratory issues, I didn't hear a thing.

In the garage I was met by a draft of cold damp air tinged with gasoline, mold, wet cardboard and dead mouse. There was one dim bulb in the center of the ceiling next to the garage door opener.

The vague light, coming through the cobwebs, created skinny, undulating shadows. Their patterns lengthened and contracted as the curtain of webs wavered in the draft.

Chilled, I crept across the cracked, oil-stained concrete toward the front of the garage.

In spite of all the rest of the shit they piled along the walls and in the middle of the floor, the Bradleys fit two large vehicles and a four-wheeler into the space.

The four-wheeler, a big powerful one, crouched next to a jumbled wall of junk that ran up to the ceiling. I made out three small bikes, a yard cart, a push lawnmower, scores of sagging boxes, and the top half of an artificial Christmas tree.

And two pale, naked legs with dull red toenails pointing up toward the ceiling, dancing in the strobe shadows—a big yellow screwdriver handle jutted out from pubic hair.

Psycho music screeched in my head. I tore through the garage and back down the hall, the cat just ahead of me, into the horrible stinking kitchen.

Then the garage door was going up; the vibrations running through the floor of the house, up my legs and clenching my ass. The sound of a rattling diesel engine roared in as the door opener finished its work.

I went for the slider, got tangled up with Adolf and slammed into the glass with the flats of both hands leaving sweaty smears in the center. I grabbed the handle and pulled. Locked! Why the hell would they lock the back door and not the front?

The diesel's roar died. Quiet now out in the garage. I fumbled with the lock, how the hell did it work? Got it. Slid the door open; leapt out onto the deck and slid the glass shut.

The slam of one and then the other truck door inside the garage; two people.

I began my turn to escape from the deck. I was going to make it. Then I saw him.

Adolf starred out at me through the glass, standing inside on hind legs, his front paws on the slider a couple of feet below my sweaty hand prints.

I racked the door open six inches. Adolf shot out as I heard the garage door going down.

No time to run down the steps, I stepped once to my left and hugged the house siding. Men in the kitchen. Their voices making low noise. Footsteps coming. The slider clicked and moved in its track.

In two long strides I was over the rail, rolling in the wet grass, slithering under the deck, pulling myself along in the dank muck; low crawling away from the edge toward the dark, un-seeable center.

I lay there on my back, gasping, looking up through the bright spaces between the planks at strips of the two men standing over me.

"A couple more trips and we'll have it all moved. Then we can relax a little and get the last of it sold." It was John Bradley. A lighter flicked. I smelled tobacco smoke.

"Yeah, I figure a couple more will do it." Tree's voice was so large and low I could feel the mud underneath the deck vibrating. His huge feet were right over my face. Grit scraped out of his boots, falling into my eyes.

I blinked away the sand, could see part of Bradley's face, smoke billowed out as he talked. "By the middle of May we'll have it all moved out and then we'll just disappear. The cops won't have a clue."

"Yeah," Tree grumbled. "I'm tired of always hiding out. Be good to go someplace warm and walk down the street like a real person. Get away from you and your fat-ass old lady … maybe get laid."

"Tell you what asshole," Bradley wasn't laughing, "We get this thing done and you're the last person on earth I want to see again."

One of them snapped his cigarette butt out into the wet yard where it hit with a hiss.

"Don't fuck around with me on this. You can't get that stuff out of here without me, and unfortunately, I need your end too." Tree was a man to be believed; at least I believed him. "Just hang loose for a few more weeks and then we'll be out of each other's hair. We both stand to lose too much to fuck it up now."

Another cigarette butt landed in the wet grass. They didn't say another word. They scraped across the deck, peppering me with more mud and sand; worked the slider and went inside.

They'd either said too much or too little. I didn't know what they had up there in the woods that they were selling, or moving, or whatever the parlance was. Drugs came to mind of course, but there was a lot of black market stuff these days: weed, ammo, cigarettes, guns, mushrooms. There was rumor of a couple of pretty good moonshiners up on Baldy someplace too.

It didn't matter. It was illegal, whatever it was, and only a few weeks before they planned to disappear. I laid there a while trying to get the grit out of my eyes and hoping I could move out before I pissed my pants. I checked my watch. I'd been in the house about an hour before I crawled under the deck.

Adolf, the cause of my discomfort, stood below the edge of the deck and gave me the now-what-are-you-going-to-do look.

There was something fairly big and hairy over against the house foundation ... Dead raccoon, its rotted face locked in an eternal snarl. Dead under there for a long time and who would ever know?

I lay for another hour-and-a-half, listening to the rumble of Tree Man and John Bradley from the kitchen. I'd never taken a whiz lying down ... I had to piss so bad it was all I could think of. Then the garage door went up and the truck left.

I crawled through the slick mud and rot, reaching the edge of the yard just as the slider rolled open again. Footsteps right above me followed by a stream of urine splashing in the grass. Did the guy ever piss inside?

Ten agonizing minutes later, I heard the four-wheeler leave. I rolled over and low crawled out as fast as my stiff sixty-year-old body would take me and relieved myself right there.

I hustled around front, stayed in the trees and went to retrieve my backpack. It was gone. I could see the spot where it had mashed down the wet leaves. But the pack was gone. I felt like crying. I just wanted to go home to a hot shower and a long nap with Suzanne. I leaned up against a rock and hugged my shoulders. What the hell was I doing out here anyway? And now Bradley or Tree Man had my pack and my stuff.

Was my name in there? Probably ... Yes, sure it was. I'd taken a Sharpie and written my name in it when I bought it. Back then I wasn't some stealth commando planning to kill a couple people.

Shit, they'd come and kill me in my sleep.

"You looking for this?" The voice behind me was familiar and deep.

Part 1 CHAPTER 12

"Jeez Chip, what the heck are you doing running around up here by this scumbag's place?" My favorite Fish and Game officer, Steve Albright, with my backpack in his chunky hands.

"God Steve, you scared the bejeezus out of me." I didn't have a story. I got to my feet, grinning stupidly. I could have kissed him. "I was just out hiking around, hadn't ever been down to the end of the lane. I guess my curiosity got the better of me."

"Yeah, so why'd you leave your pack lying here?" Lawman Steve could smell a lie.

"Uh, just got tired of carrying it …"

Steve shook his head. Not buying any of it. "How'd you get covered in mud?" He scanned me head to toe.

The muck from under John Bradley's deck was all over me. "Oh, uh, I tripped on a root and went right down. Lucky it was so soft. I really did a face plant."

Steve kept shaking his head. "Chip, after what I told you the other night, I'd think this is about the last place you'd want to come snooping around. These are bad, bad people. They're capable of about anything. You know how easy it is to just disappear up here?"

I did. And I'd thought about that. But I wasn't going to tell *him* that. "Gosh, Steve," I put on the Iowa farm boy talk. "Guess I just kind of found myself up here, and I didn't see anybody around so I was just seeing what was back here." I hated to lie. "You're right, pretty stupid."

Then it occurred to me, "What are *you* doing up here?"

Steve wasn't any better prepared with a story than I was. "I'm just looking around a little … Damn it Chip! If it got back to my boss there'd be hell to pay. I'm on a short rope as it is."

Steve danced from one foot to the other, swinging my pack back and forth.

He was busted. So was I.

"OK, if you're supposed to stay away, why are you up here stealing people's packs?" I had him; off-setting penalties.

Steve set his jaw. "I'll never feel good about myself, maybe about anything, until John Bradley is in jail. I don't care what the county prosecutor says, I know what Bradley is and I'm gonna put the son-of-a-bitch away."

I felt so bad for my friend. But I would square the whole deal soon enough. Steve, Ben, Jess, the girls, even me; we'd all win. It struck me, standing there in the trees, that the Bradleys would probably be better off too.

Steve and I continued in hushed tones, the way you speak when you're in the woods and you don't want to scare everything away; or when you're afraid a bad guy might hear you and come out of the bushes and kill you with a dull ax.

"Let's get the hell out of here before somebody sees you, or us, or something," I said. "Where's your truck?"

He told me it was about a mile down Baldy, stashed in an out-of-sight spot used by poachers, underage drinkers, and apparently game wardens.

"Tell you what," I said. "My house for a cup of coffee, then I'll drive you down. Save you the walk."

"OK." Steve held out my pack. "But I'm not carrying this for you."

◆   ◆   ◆

We had coffee and avoided talking about the Bradleys; at least until I got Steve back to his truck. He hopped out of my Subaru, slid in his truck and rolled down the window for some parting words.

"Did you see anything up there?" Steve asked. "I heard a four-wheeler goosing up the hill. Saw the fresh tracks in the lane. Didn't see 'em though."

"All I saw was a cat and a bunch of junk on the porch," I lied. "Didn't see the four-wheeler, but I heard it and decided to split. Came back for my pack and there you were."

"I don't know what you're *really* up to, but please don't play around up there!" Not a suggestion; an order.

"OK, OK," I lied. "You got my attention. That was my first and last trip."

"For some reason, I have the feeling you're not telling me the whole story." Steve fired up his engine. "But I don't think you'd be stupid enough to go up there again ... Right?" He pulled out, easing down Baldy, his arm out the window waving goodbye, looking at me in the rearview.

I sat in my car and waved back, trying to decide if I was smarter or stupider than Steve thought.

Part 1 CHAPTER 13

A day off was in order. I needed to clear out my head, and I needed to get rid of the trash that was piling up at the house too. With three full garbage bags in the back of the car and my laptop in the passenger seat, I headed into town.

In Sandpoint, if you're not one of the dump-it-in-the-ditch-in-the-middle-of-the-night crowd, you take your trash to the County Dumping Station. It's a big gravel lot surrounded by a chain-link fence, has a dozen dumpsters, a couple of recycling bins, and some pallets stacked with castoff electronic equipment.

There's a shack inside the gate. An attendant comes out to make sure you have a sticker on your window. It's all clean and well managed. Not a bad system.

But I don't go there only to dump the trash. I go there to visit Free Stuff.

Free Stuff is a set of open wooden shelves with a roof and a big hand-painted sign that says… Free Stuff. It's where people leave the stuff that is too good to throw away; one man's junk is another man's treasure. I'd scored a great pair of insulated coveralls there, and the kettle on my woodstove was also a Free Stuff gold nugget.

After being cleared at the shack, I slung my bags into dumpster #2 then did the mandatory Free Stuff drive-by.

This being garage clean-out season, the shelves were loaded. Power tools, baby stuff, lidless pans, the permanent stack of books and magazines, two white trash bags of clothes, an electric bread maker … And a naked, baby-sized, flesh-colored plastic doll; headless, its legs and red toenails pointing up toward the underside of the tin roof.

I closed my eyes and drove away, a little too fast, to Bevans Brothers Coffee House.

Being around people gave me energy, necessary to keep my brain going and my will to live intact. After my under-the-deck experience, being caught by Steve, and the image of the legs and the screwdriver dancing in my head, my favorite coffee spot was just what I needed.

Bevans Brothers is in an old grain elevator in the middle of Sandpoint. It has concrete floors, a low ceiling covered with burlap coffee bags, and all the other clutter you see in non-corporate coffee houses.

The place has great coffee roasted on site, a living rainbow assortment of attitudes and lifestyles, and decent food … except the gluten-free objects passing as baked goods.

Nothing there matches: the chairs and the tables, the cups and saucers, the forks and the spoons, or the customers. But that lack of uniformity makes the place better.

It's a perfect microcosm of the town. A living snapshot of the main reason I moved to Sandpoint.

At one table: Caucasian twenty-something Rastafarians, dreadlocks, the colors of Jamaica, sandals, Apple laptops. The only people eating the ghastly organic, gluten-free, imposter food.

At the next table: three thirty-something men in button-downs and dress slacks, shoes with lots of rubber on the toes, smart phones in their hands talking in even tones about interest rates. Bagel eaters.

Over by the north windows, the cowboys: well-worn boots, Wranglers, big belts, plaid shirts and Stetsons tilted back a bit so they can easily look you in the eye, in their fifties and on up. Doughnuts.

At the long narrow table, the real estate clutch: women and a couple of guys, expensive jeans, high-tech jackets, senseless shoes. Car keys, cell phones, three-ring-binders. Mid-twenties to gray hair. Consuming everything.

At a small table by the south windows, the drawing group: retired, loose shapeless sweaters, jeans spotted with paint, ancient canvas shoes, equal men to women; sketching. Never eat anything; tea drinkers.

At the stop-sign-shaped table near the bulk coffee rack, the knitters: six women and a guy, knitting, spinning yarn, yacking. Homemade clothes, backless clogs, grey ponytails. Big, flat cookies.

Finally, the group that fascinated me most. Farthest from the door at a big round table covered with newspapers, the Conspiracy Theory Group: pretty old, five or six guys and one sexless woman, thin hair, beards, a couple of big mustaches, a cheesy leather outback hat, army surplus fatigues, combat boots and glowing black laptops. Breakfast burritos; lots of 'em, all day.

And sprinkled in the seams, rounding it all out: couples in running clothes, gays, lesbians, single mothers, truck drivers, merchants, CPAs, cops, construction workers, tourists, lawyers; and high school kids, free for a period, trying out their new coffee-drinking muscles.

I walked through the door about 9:30, perfect mid-morning coffee time with the whole gang. I was greeted by a few people I knew, but I didn't see any close friends. That was fine. I needed people not conversation.

I got my usual big mug of the brew of the day, Ethiopian something. The newest in a long line of baristas served it up with a smile. I dropped my change in the tip jar.

I landed a small table in the middle where I could listen without being obvious.

The knitting octagon was talking about the merits of various types of outhouses. Not helpful.

The artists' table; drawing not talking.

The Conspiracy Theory Group was, as usual, having a lively discussion. It was perfect. Energy radiated.

There had been a tornado in Nebraska. The twister had killed people and ripped up a lot of property—way too early for a tornado, had to be a plot to get the National Guard in there.

My battery was getting charged. My head was clearing.

In an uncharacteristic fit of logic, one of the group read tornado stats from her laptop. "There were 811 confirmed tornadoes in the States last year. They began as early as January and ended in December. April is early, but it happens pretty often. The highest percentage of tornadoes occurs in Oklahoma in May."

The leather-hatted guy pounded the table, "Only if you believe the government's statistics!"

And they were off; veering away from twisters and into the evils of the federal government snooping into the lives of private citizens.

I'd heard that part before, but the tornado stats, now that was interesting.

I fired up my laptop. There was loads of info, pictures, videos and data regarding tornadoes. The only thing predictable was that they would occur in Oklahoma, in May, and they would be monsters.

If you got in front of a twister out in Tornado Alley, you went underground. Or you learned how to fly.

◆ ◆ ◆

In the Safeway, with my shopping list, I headed for the AlphaBits.

There was Jessica Chandler. She looked bad; the walking wounded, five little girls in tow, two carts overflowing and a third half-full. She saw me, turned away, hoping I hadn't seen her. Very odd ... I was already blundering down the aisle, bent on breakfast cereal; too late to make a graceful U-turn.

"Hi Chip." An embarrassed half smile, split lip, puffy green skin peeking out from under her sunglasses.

"Jess ... hi girls," I said, pulling up to their procession with my empty cart.

"Takes a lot to keep this crowd going," she said, pointing to her cart and the two being pushed by daughters. Her voice trembled and fell off. She was spent, used up and hurt.

"You ... you OK?" I stammered.

A tight grip on the cart; two tears quickly wiped away. "Guess I'm just tired. Sorry ..."

I wanted to hug her. Let her cry. "What happened to your eye? Angry Alpaca?" The joke hung there ... Stupid.

She looked back at the girls, lowered her voice, "It was an accident. Dawn was having a bad dream."

"God, Jess. I'm sorry." Not the place to take this conversation any further. "Well, I better keep after it. Say hey to Ben." I began to move.

She got her little wagon train moving, "Bye Chip."

◆   ◆   ◆

In the checkout line I swiped my Club Card; it didn't take. I swiped it again; didn't take.

The cashier looked at me. "Wanna just give me your phone number?"

"That card hates me." I gave him my number.

He rang up my little pile of groceries, "OK, now swipe your credit card."

I swiped my credit card. It didn't take. The guy rolled his eyes, grabbed the card.

As I unloaded the groceries at home, I realized I had forgotten the AlphaBits.

◆   ◆   ◆

My phone rang at 5:30 the next morning. It was Randal Cheatham, the new client in Phoenix. I had the feeling he was one of those guys who sent e-mails at 3:00 AM and expected an immediate reply.

"I wondered if you might have a few days free next week." He was pleasant enough.

I spent the rest of the morning making arrangements to be in Salt Lake City, Monday through Thursday of the next week. Randal was going to bring his team together for an executive meeting. I would facilitate.

I'd be back in plenty of time to get Ben and Jess and the girls to the Spokane Airport on Friday.

Part 1 CHAPTER 14

For my second look inside the Bradley house, I was going to be in and out in half an hour.

I needed to get familiar with where things were. Get calm enough to think through how I would eventually do what I needed to do.

Both Bradley vehicles left right on time, Scarlett in her 4Runner, John in his truck with Tree Man riding shotgun. I checked my watch, started timing my thirty minutes.

On the porch I beat on the door hard. "Hello! Hello! Anybody home?" The screen door spring twanged and screeched as I stretched it tight and opened the inner door. "Anybody home?" I hoped I yelled it like a friendly neighbor. All quiet.

First, check out Tree's room. Figure out if he was living there full-time and what I was going to do about it if he was.

I ran up the thirteen steps. I hit the top and spun left around the newel post, ran down the hall and went into the pink bedroom.

It smelled like a bear and there was a pile of dirty, giant clothes. Tree was living in the pink room for sure. Something under the mattress of the ultra-neat bed was poking the spread out; hadn't been there before. I stuck my hand in, four or five flat objects … DVD cases. I took one out; no markings, sealed shut with tape. I stuck it in my pack, smoothed the bedspread.

Something in the clothes pile caught my eye; a triangle of light reflecting from the back pocket of filthy dungarees. Another DVD case; this one wasn't sealed. Inside, covering the disc, was a computer-printed color photo; folded and grainy. Only part of the image was visible, but it was clear enough. Three naked sisters: Dawn, Mary and little Beth stared out at me. I snapped it closed and jammed the thing back into Tree Man's pocket.

Then I ran.

Down the stairs, through the kitchen, out across the deck and into the woods.

All the way home.

I was a mess. Thank God Suzanne had not met me at the door. I dropped my pack, shed my clothes, and stood in the shower with my eyes closed.

I couldn't get rid of the horrible image. Partly obscured behind the naked girls had been a very large man, a huge bald head jutted above a leather mask. Tree Man.

Killing three people would be harder than two. Two of them slept in the same room. Just go in there, wake them up, and bang-bang. Not easy, but simple.

Now there was a sick giant sleeping down the hall who would have to fit into my plan.

◆   ◆   ◆

For some reason, I slept very well that night. Maybe I just needed to float away and not think about what a rotten place the world can be. I hit the pillow, whispered a good night to my wife, and was away, flying.

I flew higher and farther than I had since I was a little kid. I went up, up, up and a little bird flew beside my head. It's black eye regarding me calmly as if it was accustomed to gliding around in my company. Not exhilarating so much as just easy and sure.

◆   ◆   ◆

In the morning I poured AlphaBits into a bowl, but couldn't eat. Sitting on the couch in my office, I opened my pack.

The sealed DVD case I'd taken from under the mattress in the pink room was right on top. I broke the tape along the edge with my thumbnail, choked back my revulsion, and opened it.

The same sickening image was folded up in there. Barely able to think, I unfolded the photo and crushed it into a wad before it could drive me out of my mind. Not just Tree Man and the girls; there were two other naked bodies … John and Scarlett Bradley.

A DVD sat in the case exposed; BETH written in neat, black letters across its silver face.

I knew what it was. I didn't want to touch the thing. I snapped the case shut and sat vibrating with rage.

Tree Man and the Bradleys; I'd brought them into my house. I would not share this place with monsters.

I gathered up their filth, walked onto the patio, lifted the lid on my grill. Sitting on the wire grate was lighter fluid and a long-barreled butane lighter. I doused the photo and the case, pulled the lighter's trigger; a click and nothing else.

"Whatcha doing down there, barbeque for breakfast?" Suzanne, uncharacteristically upright before 8:00 AM, stood above me on the deck, my body shielding the grill's contents from her view.

The color I could feel rising up out of my collar and igniting my ears had to be telling her I was up to something.

"Yeah," I said, putting the can of fluid down on the grate and pulling the lid closed. "I was afraid this lighter was empty. Thought I'd check it out before our first barbeque." A lame response, but the best I could muster.

I turned toward my wife held up the lighter and pulled the trigger. A nice yellow flame burst out. "Look, it still has a few shots left," I said.

"Yeah, that's great," she said from on high. "I guess you were worried for nothing; as usual." Suzanne disappeared into the house.

Why was I burning it anyway? It was unquestionable proof. What was I thinking?

I carried the filthy, oily, rubbish back inside. The photo was a melting mess of bleeding ink and fumes. But I had the DVD, that would be enough. The case had kept most of the starter fluid off.

After I washed it in the bathroom sink, the disc went in an envelope and under the Beretta's box in the gun safe. I sealed the DVD case and the soggy photo in a bag with all the normal stuff from the bathroom waste basket. Then I looked at my white hair in the mirror, smelled the lingering fumes, and threw up in the toilet.

I worked at calming down all the way to the Dumping Station. Approved for entry by the old hippie lady at the shack, I tossed the bathroom trash bag into an empty dumpster. The DVD case and the reeking photo would soon be underneath tons of other garbage in the landfill north of town. It was like I'd buried a piece of the Bradleys—a little piece, but it was something real.

Habit took over and I checked out Free Stuff. A yellow-edged magazine caught my eye. Its cover showed a man and a truck in the middle of a highway with a tornado bearing down on them. I grabbed it and tossed it in the front seat.

Bevans Brothers was full—the regulars and a few diehard skiers from out of town who would downhill until the rocks started banging up their skis.

At my favorite eavesdropping table I opened the doughy Free Stuff magazine. The cover story was about a famous storm chaser. He and his crew were trying to outrun a multi-funnel storm in Oklahoma. Sadly, it killed all of them. One of them was just gone; never found.

I flipped the magazine closed and tuned into the room. The members of the Conspiracy Theorist Group were in full mushroom-cloud mode. We should make sure we all had our guns and ammo ready when the Commie troops started pouring down through Alaska into Canada and then right into our laps. It was coming, sure-as-hell, and this time it wasn't just a rumor. Nosireebob.

I looked over at the real estate bunch. California skiers had money to spend. Life was good.

The Rastafarians looked stoned, and their kids were just like all kids; making too much noise and spreading germs.

The knitters and spinners kept on making clothes out of animal hair.

I wondered what they all would think in a couple of weeks after the shots were fired up on Jesus Is My Redeemer Lane.

Part 1 CHAPTER 15

Sunday. Time to meet Randal Cheatham in Utah.

I laid my black Casio and my pocket knife on the front right-hand corner of my nightstand. I put four days-worth of stuff in my bag; business casual, that's what Randal had said.

The last thing on my list was to check in with Ben Chandler. "Just making sure nothing has changed for Friday's trip to the airport." I propped my feet up on the old coffee table in my office. "I've got a meeting in Salt Lake for a few days."

"Yeah, no, nothing's changed. Hawaii's on." Ben was distracted, multi-tasking.

"OK then. I'll see you and the girls Friday morning at five."

I hung up and put on my grandpa's old Bulova self-winder, then double checked to be sure I didn't bring along anything the TSA would take away from me at the airport.

◆   ◆   ◆

I got on the plane and got absorbed in my book.

A very attractive, slender woman about fifty years old sat in the seat next to me, buckled in, opened her book and didn't say a word all the way to Salt Lake City.

In the check-in line at the Marriott, I was surprised to see her again.

"Hello," she said. She had great eyes and the intelligent look that makes women attractive, especially as they get older.

"Hello," I said. "Hope you don't think I'm a jerk because I didn't say hi on the plane."

"Oh, not at all," she laughed. "Nothing's worse than sitting next to a talker. I can't stand it when somebody wants to tell me about their first-ever plane ride … God!"

I liked this woman. She stepped up to the front desk and said, "Checking in. Jackie VerMeer with RSI."

Jackie was the CFO of Retention Specialists, Inc.; I'd seen her name on the list Randal Cheatham had sent.

She turned from the desk, flashed a promising smile and said, "Well, nice to meet you. Maybe I'll see you on another plane someday."

◆   ◆   ◆

At room 1204 I had pushed the key-card in the slot for the third time without success and was saying, "son of a bitch," just as the door to room 1203 swung open behind me.

Jackie VerMeer came bopping out wearing a nice pair of jeans, a very soft-looking, plum-colored sweater and expensive shoes. "Temper, temper," she scolded. "Having trouble?"

"Well, yeah. These things don't like me." Heat coming off my face.

"Maybe you just need to leave it in a little longer," she said. Then she closed her eyes and tucked her chin onto her chest. Now the heat was coming off *her* face and I burst out laughing.

"Uh, maybe I better just keep walking," she was laughing too, moving off down the hall.

I jabbed the card in the slot and let it sit there. The little light went green and the lock clicked. "You were right," I said over my shoulder toward her retreating figure. She didn't say a word, just kept walking away, held a slender hand above her head giving me the queen's wave.

I met Randal Cheatham in the hotel restaurant where we talked through a rough agenda for the next day. "Just see if you can make them behave," he said.

◆   ◆   ◆

The RSI meeting was in the Pine Room. Lunch would be in the Spruce Room, which was between Fir and Cedar.

Despite the forest theme, the meeting room was the same as they all are: white suspended ceilings, a gaudy chandelier in the center, recessed lights down the sides projecting harsh, man-made light that makes it hard to think, shitty stacking chairs, ugly carpet, tepid coffee, stale air, metal water pitchers sweating on plastic coasters.

And to think I could have been lying under a deck having sand kicked in my face.

I got there first; 7:00 AM for an 8:00 o'clock start.

The first RSI person to arrive was Eugene Triska. He looked like your average tired, fifty-something business guy: khaki chinos, starched blue button-down, long-toed oxfords, and a good head of sandy-gray hair.

At 7:15 he came straight across the threshold with his hand extended toward me, a big forced grin on his face. He should have had a sign on his chest that said; I'm full of shit.

"Hello, you must be the coach guy," he said. "You ready to meet this bunch of flatheads? Wait till you meet Dave, that son of a bitch …"

In-A-Gadda-Da-Vida thumped in his pocket. He punched his phone and said, "Fuck it all Murry, I'll have to call you back," and he was out the door and down the hall.

Next was Jackie VerMeer. She looked great. I had a feeling she looked great when she woke up. She wore a charcoal-gray suit with a cream-colored silk blouse. Great shoes too … really great. She was ready to go, and more than a little surprised to see me standing by the conference table drinking my fifth cup of coffee.

"Well, the man from the plane who doesn't introduce himself to strangers," she said, striding through the door. "Chip Crandle, I presume?" She shook my hand firmly. "You have any more trouble with that door lock?" She said it in a low, husky voice; probably so no one could hear, but maybe because she just liked to have fun.

I blushed like an eighth-grader and felt something jumping around in my gut. It was not unlike the feeling I'd had when I saw Adolph the cat up against the glass slider in John Bradley's kitchen, only it was swinging the adrenalin meter into the green zone.

I shook off my distraction. "Nope, I think I got the old in and out figured out," I said, in my version of her husky voice.

She met my look and blushed back.

I shifted gears. "Grab some coffee and a roll?"

The rest of the crowd straggled in. They all looked tired. They all were cranky. A couple of them looked more than a little hungover. All of 'em ready for a fight. The energy in the room built like a storm coming as they gathered.

Dave, the North American Sales VP, looked at his watch and said, "Well that's par for the course. We break our asses to get here and our fearless leader hasn't even come down yet."

Randal popped in at about 8:45; leading by example …

And the rest of the day went straight to hell.

Randal sat, hands flat on the table, with his eyes closed. He reminded me of my dad standing in the barn watching a hail storm coming across the prairie in July. The corn's up, the hail's coming down. All you can do is wait and clean up the damage later.

I asked that they turn off their laptops, tablets and phones. At some point shortly after that, a phone buzzed. Eugene got twitchy and bug-eyed and his phone came out. Then they all followed suit and turned everything back on.

I was in charge of executive daycare, making them take turns and showing a modicum of decency toward each other. We were doomed to failure from the start because they hadn't asked for any of it. They liked to fight.

Thankfully, Randal shut it all down at 6:00 PM. "Meet in the lobby in one hour. We've got reservations at 7:30." He said it and walked out.

At the elevator, I felt somebody follow me in. I looked down at Jackie VerMeer's shoes; four hundred bucks, easy. I hadn't seen a pair of shoes like that on anybody, ever, in Sandpoint.

I kind of missed that style. Some days I missed wearing suits and smoking cigarettes in a nice wood-paneled office; before the lawyers, the IRS, the computer geeks, and the HR snarks took all the fun out of being in business.

She kicked off her shoes and put them inside her bag. "They look great, but taking them off sure feels good," She smiled, flexed her toes.

"Well, style has its price," I said as we got out on twelve.

We both opened our room doors on the first try. I said over my shoulder, "I'll have to race you next time."

"OK," she said. "What does the winner get?"

"Uh, well, maybe a drink?" The heat was crawling up my neck again. She had that effect on me.

"MMMM, well, unless we think of something better …" She lifted one beautiful eyebrow, padded into her room and dropped her bag, holding the door open with one shoeless foot. "See you in the lobby in a few."

I walked through my door and fell onto the bed. Except for the teenage tingle that Jackie was giving me, it had been a useless, wasted day. And I certainly wasn't going to act on anything with Ms. VerMeer. No, I was too old a dog to go down that road. I flopped over, channel surfing, paused on the Weather Channel. They were busy.

A highly made-up young woman in front of footage of a huge, black rotating cloud was saying, "Tornados were reported in ten states yesterday. Dr. Bruce Davis of the severe storm prediction center in Norman, Oklahoma thinks this spring may be shaping up to be a long and devastating one. Hello Dr. Davis."

Her image was replaced by a middle-aged man with a

mop of brown hair and black-framed glasses. "For the next few days severe weather will persist from the Great Lakes to the Gulf. There will be tornados. Conditions indicate this may be the beginning of a long and severe tornado season, especially here in Tornado Alley."

The universe seemed to be cooperating with my plan.

◆ ◆ ◆

Dinner was not what I'd expected in Salt Lake City.

We were met at the door by a beautiful, dark woman in a sari. She obviously knew Randal, greeting him with kisses on each cheek. We were seated in pairs at a long table, with a waiter assigned to each pair.

I decided the quiet approach would be best. Listen, learn and stay in record mode.

Six bottles of wine arrived; three red, three white. Apparently I was in the middle of an RSI family tradition.

Randal stood and raised his glass. "Here's to a great year and a great bunch of people." Glasses were clinked all around and the table erupted into laughter and conversation. Nothing about business was discussed for the next three hours as we ate and drank.

It was tremendous and expensive. The restaurant owner knew something about making the whole thing come together in food and experience. Randal knew what he was doing too. It was a pay-off; a shut-up-and-do-your-work bribe.

The conversation went in more directions than I would have guessed. Nancy, the project director, started talking about the future of mankind in a world that never slept, or allowed for mistakes. They all agreed that it had to stop somewhere—but none of them would be the first to hang up their phones or stop answering e-mails twenty-four-hours a day.

The North American Sales VP, Dave, said, "You want the money? You have to be on, twenty-four seven!"

I found myself breaking my silence, "So what do you get up in the morning excited about?"

"Making money," he said. "You do that, all the rest of it is possible. I like my Porsche!" Dave was sure.

Eugene Triska chimed in, not wanting to let Dave have the final say on anything. "I like making clients see the right way to do things. That's what they hire us for right? They fight and bitch and moan about being told what to do, but I love it when the light finally comes on and they see how fucked up they are!"

There was a beat of silence. I thought maybe I was being set-up for a big laugh. But no, Triska meant it.

He reminded me of the kid in my sixth-grade class who was always the first to finish tests and last to be picked for the team. Jerks for parents, born to be a jerk, no clue he was one. Eugene was that guy.

Randal added his thoughts. "For me it's the people. I have such a good team. You have that, the money follows ... then you get happy."

Jackie took a breath and shifted in her chair next to me. "I don't think it's a stretch to say we make life better for people. When systems work and business is easier, that's a good thing. People pay for it. And, I happen to like expensive shoes."

She held her glass high and said, "Here's to my next pair of Prada's!"

"To Jackie's shoes!" the whole crowd joined in the toast.

Jackie's knee was pressing against mine just a bit, and I really liked it.

Sinatra sang over trombones: And the way you look tonight ...

Then Randal was signaling, time to go back to the hotel. "Tomorrow we'll meet in the lobby at eight. Wear casual clothes. Don't bring your laptops or your bags. And Jackie, wear some running shoes that you don't mind getting a little dirty—if you have such things."

♦   ♦   ♦

Back at the hotel, most of the group went to the bar.

Jackie and I were alone on the elevator again. I leaned against the wall, wishing I was back in North Idaho listening to my wife snore. At the same time I wished Jackie would wrap her arms around me and say something like, "Wouldn't it be great to be close to someone for a while and forget about everything else?"

I shot a glance at her. She was staring down at her famous shoes. Was she thinking the same thing as me, or was she in Neiman Marcus trying on her next pair of happiness?

"Caught you looking," she said. "So what's your scene man?" She took on a '60s hippie tone when she said it.

The elevator dinged. We started down the hall.

"My scene?" I wanted to say something good, something important.

God, if you only knew half of my scene. I just turned sixty and I need something bigger. I want to feel like I did something that matters. I can see the end. It's right out there now, and I don't want to claw and scratch hanging onto the edge. I want to jump off clean. I've decided to kill some horrible people and then fly away. You are exciting. Maybe you are my last glimmer of that. I think you're smart and beautiful and I think I could tell you the truth. Sell your shoes. Stand naked on a beach somewhere. Find somebody to kill, or love. Do something; just don't wait.

But I didn't say that. I turned to Jackie. Her eyes were green, and she closed them and turned her face up. I brushed her nose with mine.

"I have to get some sleep," I said. I stabbed the card in the lock, got a green light and went through the door of 1204 to a king-sized bed with far too many pillows.

◆ ◆ ◆

I woke up in Salt Lake City at the same time I did at home.

The night before, I hadn't said what I might have said to Jackie, but I also didn't do what I might have done, and for that I was thankful. The idea of what might have been would always be perfect now. And I wouldn't have any angst.

I went down to breakfast. Randal was there eating a huge pile of eggs, bacon, potatoes, and toast. It smelled great. It was early enough that the food hadn't been sitting around too long.

"Pull up a chair," he said. "I'm just getting started."

I stuck with my normal cereal and juice and coffee.

Randal filled me in on the day ahead. He had arranged for the group to have a challenge course competition. He laid a team roster on the table in front of me.

Team Blue: Randal, Jackie, Tom, Eugene, Dave and me. Team Red: Glenn, Tim, Duane, Nancy, Chris and Elmer.

I hoped that Jackie and I would be OK. My question was answered when she plopped down with a bagel and a cup of coffee.

"Morning!" she chimed. "It looks like it's gonna be a beautiful day." She smiled at me and meant it. For a moment I thought she might ruffle my hair. I felt more alive than I had just a couple of minutes before.

We met the rest of the RSI crowd in the lobby; all glued to their phones.

Randal herded us out to a short bus. During the ride, he handed out huge t-shirts with TEAM RED and TEAM BLUE printed across the chest, and disclaimer forms from the challenge course.

We pulled the shirts over what we already had on, looking like a bunch of kids playing dress up in our dads' clothes.

Next was the election of captains. Randal disqualified himself. Jackie was the unanimous choice for team Blue. Duane came out on top for Red.

At our destination, a very fit looking kid about twenty-five years old met us under the trees in the gravel parking lot. "Hi, I'm Remington."

Perfect. He probably had a girlfriend named Sagebrush and a dog named Yosemite.

Remington kept firing. "Today we're going to put you through a competition that will require you to work together to solve problems and get safely and quickly through the course. The team with the combination of best time and the least penalty points wins."

He then described in great detail all the safety rules, helmet rules, ropes rules, blah, blah, blah, while we stood in the shade shivering, wishing we'd peed before he started.

"Please give all your phones to me. There will be no electronic devices on the course."

The phone junkies looked like they'd been hit between the eyes with an axe handle. Elmer took his out and sent one last text before going cold turkey. I suspected Dave had a hide-out phone in a holster on his ankle. He finished his call and held his phone out to Remington. "Take good care of that," he scowled.

Remington walked us a quarter of a mile on a bark-covered path through tall conifers to the course start.

Our team won the coin toss. We had to figure out how to get a bucket full of ice water across a rope bridge fifty feet long and about six feet off the ground. Time to get across and amount of water in the bucket on the other end counted toward winning.

Going first was not an advantage. It wasn't pretty. At the other end of the bridge we stood, teeth chattering, our blue t-shirts dark with frigid water.

With the lessons learned from watching us, Team Red not only beat our time getting across the rope bridge, but got there with most of their water safely in the bucket. They laid on the trash talk.

"Little cold there U-Gene?" Nancy taunted. "You guys look pretty soggy around the edges!"

"Hey Dave!" Tim shouted from the next platform, "Blues is lose, man!"

Dave flipped Tim off. Eugene, not to be outdone, said, "It ain't over till the fat lady sings NAN-CEE!"

The Red Team's captain, Duane, came over to Jackie. "Nice try Jackie. I thought your idea was good. I'd have tried that first too."

Remington, stopwatch and clipboard in hand, announced, "Red, you lead. You're up first this time."

Station two was a series of logs, set like stumps in the ground at various heights that formed a path to the platform on the other side. We had to carry a dozen loose eggs across.

This time we got to watch the Red Team flounder. Their elaborate egg passing scheme started well enough but ended in a tangle of arms, legs, shoe soles, and broken eggs right in the middle of the course. God it was funny. They broke 'em all—the whole dozen.

Team Blue went berserk.

"Looks like you finally came out of your shell, Chris!" Dave was all over him.

Nancy was one big, slimy, egg mess. No hiding. She had to take the heat. "Fried or scrambled Nan-cee?" Eugene reveled.

"OK Blue, you're up!" Remington cut off the talk, but was giggling with the rest of us.

Our team finished with all the eggs intact and, according to Remington, in near record time.

Eugene Triska was ecstatic. He danced. He did a one man wave. "We take the lead!" he proclaimed to the tops of the trees. "I'm winning!"

We went through four more stations that had varying degrees of difficulty; depending on how you felt about being up off the ground twenty feet on a swing, or falling into waist-deep fifty-degree water.

The trash talk kept up, the teams were running neck and neck and it seemed that everyone was having a pretty good time. I had to admit, the people were working pretty well together.

We reached the next to last station. It was any team's game. Team Blue would go first.

"This is the most difficult station on the course," Remington said, as both teams circled around him. "You will have to rely on each other to get across that rope up there." He pointed at two ropes stretched between two trees, forty feet above us. One rope to hold onto, the other to walk across. There was a platform at each end with a rope ladder for getting up and down.

"You'll be in a harness and perfectly safe, but you'll have to get your whole team across, two at a time, and then back down on the ground to finish." Remington paused as if trying to remember something. "Oh, and every other one of you will be blindfolded."

"Oh shit, I hate heights," Dave groaned. "No way I'm goin' up there blindfolded. No way."

"Man up you sorry son of a bitch," Eugene glowered at Dave. "Don't puss out on me now. You been talking big all day. You're not going to lose this for me."

I shot a look at Randal and then at Jackie. Neither one of them said a word. Tom stared at his feet.

Eugene moved up close, right in Dave's face. "How 'bout it big man, you gonna start something, and then take a hike, or are you gonna stick around and finish for a change?"

I thought Dave was going to tear Eugene's head off right there.

"OK, asshole," Dave hissed in Eugene's face. "I'm in. But you're wearing the blindfold and I'm leading you across." Dave wasn't backing down. They were nose to nose. Nobody was blinking or breathing.

"OK by me, fuck-stick. Let's go!" Eugene spat.

For a few seconds I could have kicked the shit out of Eugene Triska. Rage, as if John Bradley was standing there next to me in a blue tee-shirt.

Triska reappeared and I told myself, "He's just who he is. Rancid son of a bitch, but you can't cure it all."

"Dave, you don't have to go up if it bothers you," Jackie had shaken off the spell.

"I know that," Dave said, never taking his eyes off Eugene. "I'm going. Teamwork and leadership, right?"

"You sure?" Randal had waited until Dave couldn't possibly back out before giving him the option.

"Jackie, what's the strategy?" Randal asked; keeping his eyes fixed on Dave.

"It's Dave and me," Eugene blurted.

"You good with that Dave?" Jackie asked.

Dave just nodded.

"OK, the pairs for the crossing will be Randal and Tom, Eugene and Dave, Chip and me. Each pair will decide who leads and who wears the blindfold. We'll go in the order I just named." Jackie, team captain, spelled it out clearly.

"So last night I kind of left you hanging," I said in a low tone. "Think maybe I should be the one to wear the blindfold?" I hoped she didn't think it was any kind of a joke.

"I might just leave you standing out on a rope," she said; then the smile came.

"I'll take that chance," I said.

Randal and then Tom climbed the rope ladder, no easy feat in itself, up to the platform where Remington waited.

Leon Russell; white face, black eyes, top hat, banging on the piano: I'm up on the tight rope ... One side's hate, and one is hope ...

I looked up at my team members. This seemed dangerous to me now. The competition had juiced people up. Winning seemed to be the only thing that mattered.

Randal and Tom had struggled up over the edge of the platform in their tight safety harnesses. Remington had given them a hand up and they stood on the tiny platform forty feet above us, just enough room for three good-sized men. Remington got them securely hooked up to the lines.

Tom eased off the perch, gripping the overhead line, standing sideways on the bottom strand. I could see the line running across under his feet between his heels and his toes. He grinned down at me, enjoying the adventure.

Once Tom was in place, Remington directed Randal off the platform. The kid reached out and wrapped a blindfold around Randal's head.

"OK. You guys all set?" Remington barked it out.

They both gave a thumbs up.

Remington made himself heard, "Take it slow. Tom, you have to tell Randal what's up and give him plenty of time at the other end. I'll be there to help you get off the line and back on the ground. You are tied onto the lines, you cannot fall. OK, you're on your own."

He came down the rope ladder, making it look so easy. Then he walked to the base of the second tree, went up that rope ladder, like a cat, and was in place at the other end of the rope bridge—all before Randal and Tom had gone three feet.

They were taking it slow. Tom talking Randal steadily across, sliding their hands along the top rope, safety harnesses riding up into their crotches.

They arrived safely to our cheers; and encouragement from the Red Team as well.

Remington pulled Tom onto the platform. He talked Randal in a little closer and took the blindfold off. Randal looked down at us, stuck his tongue out and went up on the platform where the instructor unhooked them from the ropes.

"Someone from the Blue Team grab the bottom of the rope ladder and steady it," Remington commanded. Jackie went to the base of the ladder.

When they all were safe on the ground, Remington slapped them on the back.

"That was very well done. Great teamwork and trust there! Never seen it done better." Tom and Randal beamed.

Remington looked over at Eugene and Dave, who had already moved under the first platform, and loudly said, "So you two must be going next?"

Eugene started up the rope ladder saying, "Let's go."

Dave was green, but steadied the rope ladder and looked up at Eugene who seemed remarkably able as he climbed.

"Hold up gentlemen," Remington shouted. He was moving. "Let me get up there first!"

Eugene didn't hear or didn't want to. He was already up several rungs. Remington went past Jackie and me fast.

"Hey dipshit!" Dave hollered up the ladder. "You're supposed let the guy get up there first!"

"Stop sir!" Remington was running.

Eugene was going up. Nobody was going to stop him.

"Please! Stop NOW!" Remington was frantic.

"Triska, you stupid prick!" Dave was incredulous. "What the hell are you trying to prove?"

Both teams turned their faces up, yelling at Eugene.

Eugene Triska never looked down or gave any indication he heard what was going on. He reached the platform, threw a hand up on the edge and pulled himself up and over. He stood looking down at us with a big shit-eating grin on his face.

"That's how you do it guys," he yelled down at us. "Now if I had a teammate that was worth a shit …"

Remington was half-way up, climbing fast.

Eugene peered down at the climbing instructor, gave him a mocking look, thrust his hand in his pocket, took a step back … and plummeted to the ground. A sharp crack ran away through the trees, replaced by a lull of disbelief and dead, stunned silence. Then we all heard it; In-A-Gadda-Da-Vida playing from Eugene's pocket, the one with his hand still jammed in it.

Eugene Triska, his neck broken when he hit the ground, had died to answer his phone

The thing I remember most, besides the horrible angle of his head, was his look of complete surprise. His eyes were wide open, eyebrows arched; astounded that someone so important had died for something so incredibly trivial.

We spent the next four hours waiting around while a deputy talked to everybody. My turn came last. After the deputy established who I was, he asked me a lot of specific questions about the accident. He ended with, "Watching somebody die is a tough thing. I'm sorry you had to see Mr. Triska fall. What made him go up there like that, do you think?"

"I think he just wanted to win. He took a wrong step and now he's dead." I didn't say, Eugene thought it was more important to answer a fucking phone than to take care of his life. It was all pointless—stupid and pointless.

◆   ◆   ◆

We crawled onto the short bus and silently rode.

At the hotel, Randal gathered us outside under the awning. "Tomorrow morning we'll have to sit down and make sure we can keep the wheels on … now that Eugene is, uh … gone. We'll meet in the same room at eight o'clock. Make arrangements for flying out tomorrow after lunch." He looked down at his feet, nothing else to say.

I fell in with the rest of the group going to the elevators. Jackie went to the back with me. She was leaning against my left shoulder until the last RSIer, Tom, got off. Then she sobbed until the doors opened again on twelve. I walked her to 1203, took her card and stuck it in the lock; red light. She snuffled, took the card from me and popped the lock on the first try.

"You're such a putz," she said, smiling through the tears running down her dirty face.

"And you're a mess, Ms. VerMeer."

"Good night Chip." She tucked a strand of hair behind her ear and then closed the door behind her.

"Good night, Jackie."

After a long, hot shower, I laid down on the crisp sheets. I couldn't forget how much I had hated Eugene for those few seconds on the ropes course. And then he was dead. I hardly knew the guy yet I felt like I'd somehow played a role in his death—like I had that kind of power. Maybe I did. Maybe I didn't. But one thing was sure. Emotion wouldn't have anything to do with the deaths I was planning. There wouldn't be anything accidental or pointless about them.

Part 1 CHAPTER 16

On the plane back to Spokane I thought about death. And how death must always seem sudden to the person it's happening to. Eugene Triska had been walking around for fifty-two years. And now he wasn't. Just like that. He zigged when he should have zagged. No great plan. It just happened. The sun came up the next day, the planes flew, the brief hole Eugene left behind closed up, and the business went on.

He'd been a pain in the ass to the RSI people. He'd probably been a pain in the ass since the day he took his first step. Maybe he knew it, or maybe he didn't. Maybe he meant to do something about it … but he fell. Too late now.

An obscure song started in my head: Cell phones ringin' in the pockets of the dead …

I wanted to get home and carry out my plan. But more than that, I wanted to get home and talk to Suzanne. At that moment I missed her as much as I ever had.

◆　◆　◆

On the drive home from the airport, I gave Ben a call. Maybe talking to him would get me refocused.

"Hey Chip, I thought you were out of touch until tomorrow morning some time," he said.

"I'm back a day early. One of the guys at the meeting got killed."

"Holy shit! He got killed?"

"Yeah, he fell out of a tree while we were on a challenge course doing team-building stuff."

I gave him the whole story—except the Jackie VerMeer parts.

"Man … Man," Ben sighed. "That's just unbelievable."

I moved off the Eugene story, "All set to head out to Hawaii?"

"I wish we were going tomorrow. Just like to get going.

Get out of here."

"What's up?" I asked. "You sound even more stressed."

"Awww, somebody put a dead cat in our mailbox last night. I'm just glad I found it before one of the girls did."

"You think it was …?"

"Had to be," Ben's voice went fierce. "I'm going to have to do something about it. But right now I just want to run away from home and catch a break."

"You're right. Things will be better when you get back."

"God, I hope so. Nights with the girls are bad enough. We don't need this other creepy shit going on … Hey, I gotta go. Don't be in bed when we get there Friday!"

"That'll be the day!" I said.

Ben was gone.

I was almost home when my phone rang.

"Hey Chip!" my favorite game warden, Steve Albright. "I haven't heard from you for a while. Just checking in. I'm headed down south to a meeting. You behaving yourself?"

"Oh, yeah, I just got back from a business trip to Salt Lake City. I'll have to tell you all about it sometime."

"Not taking any hikes where you don't belong?"

"Not me pal. How 'bout you? Keeping things in perspective?"

"I'm very cool," he said. "I'll give you a call in a week or so, I'm gonna lose my signal. Take care, my friend."

"Bye Steve." I sent the words to silence as Steve went behind a mountain somewhere.

I pulled into my garage and pictured him driving down Interstate 90 in his green uniform—and I flashed to another uniform, and a smashed white car, and a blue blanket spread on concrete in the sun—something else from a long time ago. I closed my eyes against the memory. I wouldn't let myself go there. I couldn't.

Suzanne's smiling face appeared in the doorway. "Hey

fella, seen any good looking sixty-year-old guys around here?"

She was just what I needed.

◆   ◆   ◆

Thursday morning I had my pocket knife and watch back where they belonged. It was sort of comforting, especially after what had happened in Utah. Silly, I suppose.

I went back to 101 Jesus Is My Redeemer Lane to have one more look around. Tree Man had something important going on in the woods. I needed to know what it was so there wouldn't be any surprises when the time came.

I hit a good pace on the trail. A raven flew over, elegant and low. Swoosh-whoosh, swoosh-whoosh; wings beating through the air as he fixed his intelligent eyes on me. Tree frogs were singing everywhere in the woods.

At the expected time, out came the pink blob in the black SUV followed by the red pickup. John smoked and drove—alone.

Fuck-it-all, where was Tree Man?

The answer came about ten seconds later.

The four-wheeler fired up and came blasting down the lane. Tree was hunched over the handlebars, backpack strapped in place. He went up Baldy. His noise faded into the trees.

OK Chip, suck it up and go. Nobody can sneak up on you when they're riding a four-wheeler.

I went around to the back of the house. Up on the deck, I looked into the horrid kitchen. Nothing had changed.

I looked down at my feet on the deck's planks and thought about John and Tree scraping crud into my eyes. What had Tree said? "Just hang loose for a few more weeks and we'll be out of each other's hair. If we don't, we both stand to lose a lot." What had that meant?

I looked over at the opening in the edge of the woods, the path Tree had taken to get the backpack that day in the rain. It wasn't hard to find if you were looking for it.

I followed it north and west. The white peak of Baldy Mountain loomed a couple thousand feet above me.

Tree had been taking care not to walk exactly the same course. But the boots he wore made a distinctive print, and the sheer size of his feet left no doubt about who had made the tracks.

I wound through the trees, jittery and tight, no idea what to expect. I'd gone maybe half a mile when the tracks stopped at an outcropping of salt-and-pepper granite.

There wasn't anything unusual about running up against a wall of granite, they were everywhere. This was a big one, towering over me by thirty feet.

I circled it, intent on finding another sign of Tree's course. A pocket squirrel let me know I was intruding. He filled the air with chatter, knocking pine cones onto the rock. One rolled down the round face of a big boulder and disappeared under a ledge. There was something about that rock. Nature tilts things in certain ways. This one didn't fit.

I got closer. The boulder had been moved frequently. In the damp ground at its base, carefully covered with pine straw, were huge unmistakable tracks.

I raked back the mat of brown needles. The bare soil was one big waffle pattern. There was a low, packed spot, almost a trench, where the rock had been rolled back and forth to cover and expose an undercut at the base of the wall.

I couldn't imagine the strength it had taken to move a four-foot-tall boulder. Building our house I'd moved a lot of rocks with a skid-steer loader. It didn't take a big one to weigh a ton.

I pushed on it for about a second. Stupid. I knew I'd never budge the damn thing, amazed even a monster like Tree Man could move it.

Whatever was behind the rock, it was a cinch that John Bradley couldn't get to it without Tree's help.

I crawled around for a couple of minutes, trying to get a look behind the boulder without success. No way to tell what was behind the damn thing. I moved around the wall away from the path, un-wrapped a granola bar and drank coffee out of my little thermos.

Did it really matter if I didn't know what was behind there? What if there were more pictures and videos? What if there were other kids—or bodies—hidden behind the boulder?

I imagined a series of increasingly grisly, twisted scenarios that explained Tree's work in the woods.

I could have just asked him. He was ten yards away, coming around the rock wall.

The squirrel had spotted him and raised holy hell. I melted into the rocks.

Tree Man picked up a baseball-sized rock, chucked it. "Shut your hole!" he rumbled.

The squirrel knew when he was out-matched and split for higher ground.

I felt exposed, completely alone. Like the dead raccoon under the deck. Who would know?

Tree lifted a twelve-foot-long pole from a fissure in the wall then placed a sharp, wedge-shaped rock near the base of the boulder. With the pole over the wedge and under the boulder he pulled down. The damn thing rolled a few inches. He repeated the process eleven times.

Tree got down on his belly, crawled in behind the rock and disappeared. The wall had swallowed the giant whole.

I sat still and waited. About five long minutes later he came out, head first, pushing a big camo backpack. He got fully out, moved the pack to the side, turned and slipped back inside the rock. Two minutes later he was back, pushing another identical pack into the sun.

He grabbed the pole and had the boulder back in place in half the time it had taken him to move it away. He jammed his lever into its hiding place and stuck his fulcrum rock under the ledge next to it.

Tree leaned against the granite wall. The smell of his cigarette making me realize how close I was to him, and how far I was from any help.

After an eternity of waiting, he ground out the butt. Then he picked up one of the backpacks and stepped toward me. Ten steps and I'd be a bug under one of his boots. He took three more—and dropped out of sight into a cleft in the rocks.

There was rustling and then he popped back out; without the pack.

He went to the other one, strapped it on, and set off walking around the curved rock face, back down in the direction of the house.

It had taken me about twenty-five minutes to walk up there. If Tree was going to the house, and then coming back for the hidden pack, I had less than an hour before he would show up again.

I moved down into the cleft. No pack to be seen. He'd only been in there for a few seconds. What had he done with it? I searched in and around the rocks; nothing. I poked around in a pile of brush and leaves; not there. I went on through to the other side. Maybe if I came in the same way he had, I'd be able to see it. I scrambled up out of the crack and turned to have a look. There was a gleam nine feet up the wall on a rock shelf.

How was I gonna get the damn thing down? And if I got it down I'd have to put it back. A four-foot step ladder would have been handy.

I ran up by the boulder and pulled Tree's pole out of its hiding place. It was a stripped cedar tree, knobby enough to be climbable. I carried it down into the rock cleft, leaned it up against the edge of the shelf. Shinnying up, I put my elbows on the ledge and found nubs on the pole that would hold my feet. Not bad for an old guy, Chip.

The pack had a simple flap held in place by two buckle-down straps. I tested the weight; heavy. If I knocked if off the shelf, I'd never get it back up there. I wrestled it up on end. My make-shift ladder was tricky, it wobbled and tipped as I snapped open the buckles.

The pack held a black plastic garbage bag, closed with a red and white twist tie. Holding on with one hand, I untwisted the tie and carefully laid it on the rock shelf, shifting to get a better look.

My right foot slipped off the branch stub, my knee raked down the pole, both feet scrambling for a hold. I clutched on, whacking my elbow on the ledge, but regained my footing. I raised myself back up. My knee was skinned, shin probably bloody, elbow throbbing; I'd heal later.

I shot a look at my watch; fifteen minutes till Tree time.

Luckily, the pack had stayed balanced on end and the twist tie still lay on the rock shelf. I opened the bag. A foul odor hit me; liver or meat or something dead …

I had expected DVDs or photos or flash-drives or maybe square packages of white powder. Instead, it was packed with small plastic bags of varying sizes, tied with twist ties. Each held some kind of powder, a collage of earth-toned colors; dozens, maybe a hundred of them.

I picked a small one out. The stuff inside was the color of dried peas. The twist tie had a tag on it; like when you buy bulk goods at the super market. There were characters written on it; Chinese maybe. What the hell was it?

I stuck the little bag in my pocket and checked my watch. No time to waste. I put it back like Tree had left it—looked good to me. The pole went back in its hiding place. I scooted back to my day pack. No sign of the giant, and I was going to keep it that way.

I angled down through the woods and popped out onto Baldy Road less than a hundred feet from my lane. Chip the human compass.

I put the smelly plastic bag in my desk drawer, went in the bathroom and scrubbed my hands hard. No telling what the stuff was and what it might do to me if it got on my skin. I wondered if my hand wasn't going a little numb …

I went to do a little research, find out what I was dealing with. I was the least drug savvy person I knew. I'd smoked a total of three joints in college and decided I didn't like the stuff. Online I didn't find anything that gave me a hint of what was in the bag. I was astounded at how many ways there were to screw yourself up, but the green powder didn't seem to be one of them.

I put the bag of dust on top of the envelope holding Tree Man's DVD and locked my gun safe.

I took a little nap on the couch. Suzanne was standing there when I woke up. We opened a bottle of wine and spent the rest of a very pleasant afternoon sunning on the deck, watching marmots chase each other around the meadow.

Part 1 CHAPTER 17

I woke up at 3:30, lay there and practiced flying; a good session. I zoomed around the room and got right up against the ceiling where the whiz-bang clock projected the time on my chest like a digital tattoo. Next thing I knew it was 4:00. I landed, had breakfast and got ready to go.

Knowing Ben, he'd be there at 5:15 and then we'd speed all the way to the airport.

At 4:59 I padded back to the bedroom. My wife was doing her deep breathing, not-quite-a-snore routine, the blue blanket pulled up under her chin. I put my cheek on hers. "Ben and Jess will be here soon," I whispered.

"Uh-huh," she said, warm and languid in her sleep. No idea I was there or talking to her. I hoped she was flying somewhere too.

"I'll see you later. Love you doll." I smoothed Suzanne's blanket and kissed her on the end of her perfect nose.

At 5:20, Ben pulled up in front of the garage. A small trailer loaded with luggage was hitched behind the car.

I could tell by the expression on Ben's face it would not be a good morning to give him a hard time. So of course, that's what I did. "Wow, looks like the Joad's are hittin' the road for California." I put on my best geezer voice.

Ben leaned his forehead on the steering wheel and closed his eyes. "Come on, Chip. We're running late as it is!"

Jess gave me a tired smile. The swelling and discoloration around her eye was fading. The mental strain looked worse. She settled into her seat, not saying a word.

"Maybe Cindy can sit on your lap," Ben said. "It will be a little crowded."

I lifted the sleeping girl and slid into the Audi. Under the glare of the dome-light a white scalp glowed. One girl's hair, crudely chopped off, a pale head showing scabby nicks and bald spots.

Ben turned to meet my eyes. Mary got hold of the scissors and a razor," he murmured.

The first ten minutes of the ride were painful and silent. When we hit the pavement there was an audible sigh of relief from the adults and a kind of unconscious relaxation coming off the girls. Nobody had said anything. We picked up speed.

Ben perked up a bit. "We're on our way and in eight hours we'll be in heat, and salt air, with palm trees and the sound of surf."

We all pictured that bliss for a moment, saying nothing.

When the silence got to be too much, I tried to keep it light. "What's the first thing you're going to do when you get to Hawaii?"

"Get in the ocean," a little voice from one of the girls in the back said. "I've never been in the ocean."

"Me too." Cindy snuggled in under my chin, very warm. Talking in her sleep.

The girls had bathed with some kind of baby soap. I was surrounded by that innocent smell. Nothing bad had happened there in that space; new and clean. Those girls needed that. They'd find more of it in Hawaii.

And they'd find a lot more of it when they got back.

♦ ♦ ♦

An hour later, driving through Coeur d'Alene, Ben flashed a look in the mirror at me.

"I thought of one more thing Chip; when you go over to the house, if you'd have a look in the mailbox. I stopped the mail, but you never know ..."

He hadn't told Jess about the dead cat. I gave his eyes in the mirror a knowing look. "No problem Ben."

We crossed the river into Washington. Ben said, "I e-mailed you an itinerary."

"I printed it off and it's on my desk. Your flight gets in at 2:07 on the eleventh." I didn't say I'll have to figure out who is going to pick you up because by then I'll be gone.

"If something blows up, handle it. We're going to detox and rebuild." Ben truly smiled.

Jess handed me her phone, said, "It's off. Just leave it in the kitchen will you Chip?"

"Sure." I said. "I'll put it next to my empty beer bottles."

I looked at the phone; heard John Bradley's voice, "I'm gonna get my girls back you bitch ..." I felt sure about my plan.

Ben laughed as we pulled up to the curb at the airport. "The Joad's have arrived! OK girls, wake up! Let's start unloading."

It took fifteen minutes to get it all onto the curb. All the noses were counted and the check-in had begun.

I leaned on the Audi, looking at the chaos. "Ben, is your insurance all paid up? I might get a wild hair and take this thing out for a high-speed joy ride."

"You mess up my car and insurance will be the least of your worries," Jess said, trying to keep the girls in line.

"Have you girls flown before?" I asked.

Still groggy the girls just stared at me.

"You're going to love it," I said.

Ben handed me his phone and winked. "Thanks Chip. See you on the eleventh."

I kissed them all, even Ben, goodbye.

◆ ◆ ◆

On the way back through Spokane, I stopped by Trader Joe's for a good supply of what I like to call "road eats." Groceries in the back, I drove the Audi toward Coeur d' Alene on I-90.

Aretha Franklin came on the oldies station. I cranked the super sound system up.

"R-E-S-P-E-C-T … find out what it means to me."

I looked down at the speedometer. I was doing ninety, very smooth, miles an hour. Whoa. I'd have to watch that.

My phone buzzed in my pocket. I hated it when the damn thing went off while I was driving. I almost just let it go. But I thought maybe Ben had forgotten to tell me something.

It was Ron Holden, fisherman par excellence.

"Hey Chip, gonna be a nice weekend." Ron and Jill would be in a boat and he was asking me along. "Heading up to the Joe; gonna get rooms at the old railroad barracks. Stay Saturday and Sunday nights. We'll be back in time for a late dinner on Monday. You in?" He laughed.

His laugh was a gift I always opened with joy.

Why not? I thought. Why not? "Sounds great."

We worked out the rest of the details.

◆   ◆   ◆

Next stop Shepherd's, my favorite outdoor store. It was local and had everything. The trick was finding where they put it—a treasure hunt on every visit.

Through Shepherd's door was every good outdoor-gear smell you could imagine: canvas, leather, rubber, gun-oil, Hoppe's #9 solvent, varnish, and a hint of dogs thrown in. A wonderful place.

I was looking for a light, the kind you wear on your head. I found exactly the right one. You could stick it into your pocket, whip it out, and put it on your noggin in about two seconds. It had two settings, bright white and night-vision red. I suspected the red wouldn't be much good outside, but it would be great inside a small room—like a bedroom. And it was hands free; a key selling point.

I went over to Firearms for .40 caliber pistol cartridges. The price was astounding, but I wanted to do a little more practice. I also decided on a black tactical holster that clipped onto your belt.

In Camping, I grabbed a red bottle of stove fuel, and then I cut over to Shoes.

They had some raggedy-looking canvas loafer things hanging on a rack. The sign shouted, These Aren't Shoes! They're Sandals! I tried a pair. They felt great; light and quiet—very quiet. I dropped a pair in my cart.

At check-out, a tiny girl with a buzz cut and the Colt Revolver logo tattooed on the top of her right breast rang it all up and dropped it in a plastic bag with a drawstring.

"Have a nice day." Bored; probably would rather have been out shooting something.

I sped toward home, music up, thinking of camping and driving and death and flying.

◆ ◆ ◆

I was really ticking things off my planning list. Budget was next.

I'd been stashing extra cash in my safe-deposit box for ten years. The cash had accumulated, coming from selling extra junk and some guns that were gathering dust in my safe. And a client, in the middle of a divorce, had paid me in cash for a meeting I'd facilitated. I'd saved it for a rainy day.

Looked like it was going to rain on the Bradleys and Tree Man.

I parked on a side street in Sandpoint, took the stuff I'd bought at Shepherd's out of the bag and stuck the bag in my jacket pocket. Nobody saw me get out of the Audi.

I walked three blocks to the North Idaho State Bank. I got a free cup of coffee from the air pot, signed my name on the little card, produced the key, and was escorted into the vault by a scrubbed young woman in Mennonite clothes. She smiled and left me in a private, booth-sized room.

The safe-deposit box was crammed with my life-time of seemingly important stuff: the will, car titles, insurance documents, jewelry, some old coins, a blue poker chip worn smooth, and twenty-two thousand in cash. I stuck the poker chip in my pocket. The cash went into the Shepherd's bag. The rest of the stuff was just stuff. I left it.

The girl slid the box back into its steel home, turned both brass keys in the locks. We left the vault. The stainless-steel bars snapped shut behind me like a stab; a punctuation mark. Get it done. Get away. Keep Chip out of jail. No surprises.

I walked around the block, made sure nobody I knew saw me get in the Audi, tossed the money bag on the floor and headed home.

Rain fell.

Ann Peebles growled out of the radio: "I can`t stand the rain …"

A hit in 1973 … when I was sure who I was. Things had changed; I felt like I was sitting on the other side of the car, watching somebody I used to know drive Ben's Audi.

◆   ◆   ◆

I stashed the twenty-two thousand beside the DVD and the bag of what-ever-it-was. My gun safe was getting pretty full of secrets, and now it smelled like dead meat to boot.

I went to bed that night with a million thoughts careening around in my head: What ifs and why didn't I's, plans to finish, and what thens …?

I was going fishing the next day. My last chance to be with Ron and Jill, and I needed the river too.

I flew next to an osprey that night. We snatched fat, wiggling fish out of the water. We killed 'em and ate 'em raw. It didn't ruffle our feathers a bit.

◆　◆　◆

I was up the next morning, everything the same as usual, except for the smooth, blue poker chip. My dad had started carrying the chip the day he named me. It had ridden in his pocket for more than forty years. Now it was in mine.

My Rover sat in the driveway with my fishing gear inside. I didn't need the UPS guy or a neighbor to see the Audi, so when I'd gotten home the night before I had put it in the garage where the Land Rover normally lived. Ben's trailer was tucked in the woods about thirty yards from my garage. I'd take it back when I checked on his chore kid.

Suzanne met me in the laundry room as I had come in from parking the Audi. "That's a nice car," she'd said.

"I figured I'd keep Ben's car inside until I get it back to him. Hate to see it get hailed on."

"Sounds like a good idea." She followed me through the kitchen into the sitting area.

We sat on the couch together. I filled her in on the fishing trip, where we would go, when we'd be back. "Wanna go?" I asked, knowing I wouldn't see her there.

"Naw, too much chance I'd catch a fish." She had grinned—the great eyes and the smile that always got me. "I'd just be a drag."

"No, you wouldn't."

She had given me a kiss on the mouth, then a knowing look. "Be careful Chip. I don't want anything to happen to you."

◆　◆　◆

Ron and Jill were waiting for me in his driveway. My stuff went in the truck and we took off.

On the other side of the Long Bridge, we pulled into a gas station with an awning and four sets of pumps.

My turn to buy, I jabbed my card into the pump's reader. Nothing. I turned the card over and jabbed it in again. Didn't take. Three more tries before Ron took it away from me and made it work.

I left Ron and Jill laughing and filling his truck while I ran inside to use the john and get myself a pack of little powdered sugar doughnuts.

The john was clean, the paper towel dispenser was full, and it worked.

I grabbed the doughnuts, and then laid them on the counter for the guy to ring up. Young guy, nice enough, wearing a navy blue uniform shirt. "Tony" in red thread on his white, oval-shaped name patch.

"Find everything OK?" Tony said.

That was the scene inside the station.

Outside, a guy in a green monster 4x4 pick-up pulled away from one of the pumps with the gas pumping, and the nozzle and the hose still stuck in his tank. The hose was supposed to disconnect. It didn't.

Boom.

A spout of flame gushed up under the white awning, curling back down toward the people and the cars and the other gas pumps.

Ron had finished filling up and he and Jill were just pulling out from under the awning when the thing erupted like Vesuvius. He jammed down on the accelerator and got clear.

Burning paint gave off black smoke. Fluorescent bulbs exploded. A plastic trash can sagged toward the concrete. Two more trucks lurched out and got safely away.

That left one tourist and his white rental car near the geyser of burning gasoline. He was running around in circles with his hands clapped over his ears.

A big guy in jeans, boots, and a well-worn Carhartt coat ran in under there, put the tourist in a hammerlock and pulled him, screaming obscenities, from under the smoking roof. The tourist bucked and struggled. The big guy just held onto him.

The rental car had a hose and nozzle still sticking out of its tank—a two-ton Molotov cocktail ready to blow.

Inside, Tony, the counter guy, heard an alarm go off. He turned and saw the eruption of flame. Without hesitation, he handed me my doughnuts, vaulted over the counter, caught his toe on the edge and did a face plant on the concrete floor next to a tub of iced energy drinks.

I rolled him over, his nose gushing, broken for sure.

"Knell swwiiintch. By the iccce freezner." He was struggling to his feet. Tough kid. "knill swiiintch." He pointed toward the entrance.

I shot out the door. The heat off the awning was searing. Acrid smoke from burning plastic in the back of my throat. I saw the kill switch mounted on the wall, hinged open the Plexiglas box and jammed the heel of my hand on the big red button.

The gushing flame stopped as fast as it had burst, leaving a smoking, creaking, melting mess. It didn't look like anyone had been hurt and no cars had been incinerated. The whole thing had lasted about fifteen seconds.

The white rental sat there through all of it, meter racking up gallons and dollars and cents, until the kill switch stopped it exactly at $48.00. It was a miracle.

The tourist now realized what had happened. He was apologizing and thanking the big guy in the Carhartt coat. A clueless, round woman in jeans and white shoes, with a little yappy dog on a leash, came out from behind the station with a sixty-four-ounce fountain drink and a party-sized bag of chips.

"Jesus Leon!" she shrieked, "What in God's name are you doing out here?"

Tourist Leon just looked at her; blink, blink, blink. The big guy looked at her too, briefly considered putting *her* in a hammerlock, then kicked his Harley alive and took off toward Sandpoint.

The poor guy in the over-sized green pickup with the gas pump attached to it, still sat behind the wheel. He looked straight ahead, his door open a few inches, left elbow out the window, left foot in a black boot, dangling down between the door and the running board. Too embarrassed to get out, I guessed.

Tony walked under the smoking awning, nose bleeding profusely, surveying the damage. He pulled the hose from the white rental car and stuck it into the holder on the pump, screwed the tank lid back down tight. He pulled a blue paper towel from a dispenser and pressed it to his nose.

Then he walked out to the monster truck and swung the door open.

"Are you alri …" Tony never got it finished. The driver toppled sideways. Tony tried to catch him, but the driver went thump, right onto the concrete. He looked pretty dead from where I was standing.

Ron and Jill came over. He had his hands in the back pockets of his jeans. "That guy is a goner," he said. Ron could say that and not make it sound like a line from a stupid movie. He looked hard at me, "You alright? I about shit my pants when that gas went up."

Sirens and lights were coming across the Long Bridge; the sound blasting over the water and echoing off the mountains.

"I'm good," I said. "But my doughnuts may never recover." I opened my left hand to reveal a wad of cellophane and powdered sugar doughnuts.

I started laughing; couldn't help it. Jill cracked up and Ron just shook his head, kept his hands in his pockets and rocked back and forth on his heels and toes.

An hour and a half later we were done talking to the cops. The body had been taken away. The fire department had gone. Tony had been taken away to have his nose set. The gas-station manager had driven up and locked the doors.

I sat in the back seat of Ron's truck feeling bad about making a joke about doughnuts while the guy was lying there dead next to a smoking awning.

Ron said, "That guy didn't look old enough to be dropping dead like that. And that tourist should be a crispy critter. What an idiot."

Jill said, "Yeah, if that biker dude hadn't dragged him out of there who knows what might have happened? You just never know who's gonna step up and be the hero do you?"

"Hero?" I said. "You think the biker was a hero?"

"Sure he was," Jill said. "He just as easy could have jumped on his bike and split. He ran back under there to get that moron."

"Huh," Ron leaned over the steering wheel. "I don't think he was a hero, he just did what anybody would do, don'tcha think?"

"I don't know," I said. "You gotta feel good about how most of the people acted there. I felt the worst for the kid behind the counter. He busted his nose and had a guy fall dead at his feet. Not the Saturday he'd planned ..."

I was getting groggy. The adrenalin had burned out. Alone in the back seat, I had room to spread out and the sun was warm. I just slid right out the window and flew alongside the truck.

The hero biker pulled up behind us. Next to him, on another hog, was the tourist. He had on a gold leather football helmet and a big grin on his face. He'd left the woman, and the dog, and the white rental cars behind and was hitting the road to do something on his own. The next emergency he'd figure out by himself.

I flew back beside them and he pumped his fist. Then I peeled away and flew up into the trees that covered the mountains. They were sequoias, cathedrals two hundred feet tall. I flew up to the top of the tallest one. There was Eugene Triska, with the world at his feet, talking on his phone. "Fuck-stick!" he said. And then he fell; turning end over end, heels and head, heels and head, still talking on the phone, not realizing he had stepped off the top of a two-thousand-year-old tree.

I swooped down after him screaming, "Eugene, Eugene!" He fell and fell, never hit the ground. He would be falling forever, talking on the phone about nothing.

It was almost noon when we got into Calder. Ron went in the general store and arranged for a shuttle. I stumbled out of the truck, bleary eyed and a little dizzy from my flight.

"Morning sunshine; you were sawing logs pretty good back there," Jill said. "Glad Ron was driving. I took a little nap myself. Too much excitement for old people, I guess."

Rather than put the boat in the river right away, we broke out the beer, chips, and the sandwiches. We enjoyed the sun on our backs and the sound of the river sliding by.

"It's good to be alive," Ron said. "Good to be here with you guys, and the river, and the fish."

That day, having seen what we had seen, Ron's toast was somehow truer.

◆   ◆   ◆

We had three great days on the river. Sixty degree weather, hardly any wind. The blue winged olives were hatching. The cutthroats were taking them, as Ron said, "With great enthusiasm."

I was in the zone. I caught every fish I meant to catch. I could feel them coming up before they hit my flies. I didn't miss a strike. It was as perfect a trip as I ever had.

We took the boat out of the river about 4:00 on Monday afternoon. Jill was packing gear in the back of the truck, and Ron and I were tying the boat down on the trailer. Ron looked at me and cocked his head just a little.

"What's up with you Chip?"

"That's a funny question," I said. Ron could be spooky with that second-chance-at-life intuition of his.

"You got a different look in your eye. And you're making things happen without trying."

He was right. He knew it.

"I guess maybe I've figured out what you've been telling me all this time about … well … life," I said. "I saw that guy die Saturday, and I didn't tell you, but I saw a guy die last Wednesday too. It has taken sixty years, but I've finally decided what I'm about."

"Well, I'm glad." Ron had a look of absolute peace. "You're going somewhere aren't you?"

"Yeah, I am. This is gonna be my last trip with you my friend."

"I thought so," he said. "And Chip, you're a good angler."

We pulled the boat back to Sandpoint, mostly lost in our own thoughts.

I hugged Ron and Jill in their driveway and said, "Goodbye."

Part 1 CHAPTER 18

The 22nd of April, the sun was up at 5:30. It was forty degrees and damp. I started a fire in the ring. It was like camping; only I had a good bed, a kitchen, a hot shower, and a coffee maker about twenty-five feet away—the best of everything.

The Chandlers had been in Hawaii for four days. It was time to check up on things and get Ben's trailer out of my woods. I didn't see a soul as I drove. The radio was playing Motown.

Papa was a rolling stone … I sang along with the Temptations, and Smokey, and Marvin Gaye all the way out to Ben's.

The indestructible mailbox sat across the road from his driveway. For years, local kids had targeted his mailbox with all manner of missiles hurled from cars as they careened by. Ben's answer was a cast iron box, surrounding another steel box, on top of a steel pipe, set in concrete. It had taken some heavy, direct hits and still stood unfazed. The armored monstrosity was just below shoulder level out the window of the Land Rover. I gingerly opened the steel door a crack. Just an empty mailbox.

I wound down his long drive. There was an old, faded Mustang II parked up against the garage. It wasn't cool; made when Ford had forgotten what a Mustang was supposed to be. It had to belong to the chore kid.

The Chandler's pack of dogs came boiling up out of the back yard and raised hell for a few seconds before they figured out who I was. Finster minced his way up the hill. He seemed to be doing OK, just slowing down, sore in the hips, not wanting to put up with any puppy-crap. I understood that.

A couple of the younger, terrier-sized dogs stayed with

me. The rest of the group retired to the back. With the little dogs in the lead, I drove the Rover and trailer up the access lane to the feed shed. A head popped out around the shed's corner, with a "who the hell is this?" look on its face.

I didn't want to scare him so I gave a yell, "You must be John. I'm Chip Crandle, Ben's friend."

A wiry kid wearing cowboy duds and a gray hoodie emerged. A maroon stocking cap with a load of straw jutting up out of it was down over his ears. Kind of a hip-hop, hop-a-long look. He was covered with chaff. His face said something was up; something not in his job description.

"Uh hi," he said, slapping the straw off his jeans. "Ben said you'd be here. I'm John, uh, J.J. actually."

"Hi J.J.," I said. "I'm going to back Ben's trailer into the shed and check on the house and stuff." It felt pretty awkward. The dogs, used to seeing the kid, ignored him and got busy smelling and marking my tires. I got out and left the engine running.

J.J. shot a look back toward the shed.

"Everything OK?" I knew something was out of whack.

"Uh, yeah, uh ... fine." J.J. shifted side to side.

I started to walk toward the big sliding door. Rustling noises came from the shed.

"Uh, sir, uh could I talk to you for a minute?" He jammed his hands deep in his jean pockets and gave me a pleading look.

Sir used in a barnyard context, meant somebody was looking for pre-forgiveness.

"What's up?" I said, trying not to laugh as I walked toward him.

"Well, you see I ..." The poor kid looked like his eyes would explode and his stocking cap would ignite if any more blood got pumped into his face.

"Tell you what J.J., why don't I go check on the house first and I'll come back out and put the trailer in the shed when you're finished with your, ah, *barn chores.*"

"Oh, yeah, that would be great." Teenage relief; a monumental thing.

At the house, I laid Ben's phone on the kitchen counter. I held Jess's; thought about turning it on and checking for messages. Be better if there wasn't anything disturbing waiting for her. I let it go and slipped the phone back in my pocket.

There was a bottle of nice Chianti on the counter with a yellow sticky note: CHIP, DRINK ME.

On the fridge: CHIP, OPEN ME.

I stood with the door open, laughing out loud. There were notes everywhere: MORE BEER IN THE FRIDGE DOWNSTAIRS, LASAGNA and SALAD, YOUR DINNER WHEN YOU STAY, PERFECT WITH CHIANTI, MAKE YOURSELF AT HOME BUT DO YOUR OWN DISHES—I'M NOT YOUR MOTHER!

Jess had been her old self sometime before she left.

I checked out the rest of the house.

The dogs were using the downstairs mud room as their kennel. The bowls were full of food and water. The lights were off, the toilets flushed. It looked like J.J. was doing his job.

I stepped out onto Ben's patio. The river rolled past only a few yards below, making some great high-water noise. A fish broke the surface. It rose steadily. I was happy. Just to watch it was enough. I headed back inside, past the pile of dogs and cats sleeping blissfully in the yard.

I spun the red dial, 10-22-10, popped Ben's gun safe open. I was after the Wingmaster 12 gauge and the shells. I fed in one green shell; the double-ought buckshot. It held nine .32 caliber pellets; fucking deadly. Then I slid in the birdshot; three red-colored shells. Death up close, painful at a distance. I jacked one of the red shells into the chamber.

I was tempted to root around in the safe a little bit and have a look. Ben wouldn't have cared, but I figured I better get back out, get the trailer parked, and see what J.J. was up to. I put the shotgun next to the couch on my way out.

I felt good, walked to the barn with Jr. Walker: I said shotgun ... shoot 'em 'for they run now ...

J.J. and an equally wiry teenage girl were breaking hay bales for the horses.

"Hey, I'm back," I said it as low as I could. I didn't want to startle them or the four horses that were milling around.

"Oh hi," J.J. said. "This is my friend Bobbi McGee."

I wish I had been cool enough to just go with it and say, "Hi." But I must have had a look on my face the girl had seen a million times.

"Yes, I know," she said, rolling her eyes. "People your age always get it. My folks think it's pretty funny."

She was a doll. Red hair, freckles, about five-foot-two, huge blue eyes and dressed in tight jeans and other horse-lover attire. She picked up a hay bale that had to weigh nearly as much as she did, and broke it in front of a tall, sorrel mare. The mare put her forehead on Bobbi's shoulder, gave her a push of gratitude.

"You're welcome Sadie," the girl said, regaining her balance and running her hand down the horse's neck.

"You look like you know your way around horses," I said.

She looked grateful that I hadn't sung a line of the song. "Yeah, I love them; been around them all my life."

We spent the next couple of hours feeding stock and just enjoying the day. J.J. and Bobbi were good kids. They actually talked face-to-face. They seemed valuable to each other. It was nice to be around them.

I could feel them thinking of the future—huge potential, an expanse of seemingly unlimited time. They were dreaming about what lay before them and all the things they might do together.

I envied their time and their youth and their beauty, but not the hard knocks that would be required to finally realize what they could do with it all.

I wished I could say something valuable, something that would save them a decade or two of touching the hot stove and getting burned—but I knew I couldn't, not on purpose anyway. They'd go about it the same way I had, with blistered fingers.

I finally broke the spell. "J.J. can you give me a hand with the trailer?"

We left Bobbi standing at the fence. J.J. went to the shed and slid back the big door. I backed the trailer in. J.J. had it unhooked and sitting on its jack by the time I walked back.

"I guess Bobbi and I will take off. We'll be back tomorrow afternoon."

"You guys are doing a great job." I didn't mention that I planned to stay the night at Ben's.

We said goodbye. Bobbi gave me a strong cowgirl hug. She was rock solid. I felt a little tired and sad. Young girls can do that to us old guys.

I gave in to the song. I heard Kristofferson's version in my head: Freedom's just another word …

I dropped my overnight bag on the carpet next to the 12 gauge and picked up the shotgun. The Wingmaster had been around for a long time, a lot of character but well cared for. Why had I gotten it out first thing and laid it next to where I'd be sleeping that night? Was I trying to make something happen?

Ron had said, "You're making things happen without trying …"

The sunshine and the river drew me back outside. I sat in the grass, watched the water, and wished I had a cigarette.

Merrily, merrily, merrily, merrily, life is but a dream … As I sat, smoking an imaginary cigarette, humming one of the truest songs about life ever written, a fish rose on the opposite bank.

I rolled over in the grass and looked up at the blue, blue sky. A dark shape shadowed my face, blocking the sun.

"Hi Finster," I said. "Did you see that fish, boy? Wasn't he a beaut?"

Finster grinned at me and licked my cheek; two old dogs, no worries, lying by the river on a warm April day.

Around 3:00, almost two hours later, I came to. Finster was snoring, warm beside me, but the ground was leaching dampness up through my clothes. I got up, put my car in Ben's garage for the night and retired to the kitchen where I heated up the lasagna and garlic bread and poured a glass of Chianti.

Turner Classics was showing World War II movies all afternoon and through the night. Van Johnson in a frozen fox-hole, scrambling eggs in his steel helmet during the Battle of the Bulge. I ate Jess's most excellent pasta with too much bread, and drank more Chianti than I meant to.

It was dark when that movie ended. I couldn't believe my luck. *The Dirty Dozen* came on which would be followed by *Kelly's Heroes*. And Telly Savalas was in both of them. Who loves ya baby? I was thirteen again.

An hour into *Kelly's Heroes*, I heard the noise outside; not loud, but it was different, didn't fit. The dogs heard it too and went bellowing out of the basement like the hounds of hell.

Shoes on, shotgun in hand, then out the mudroom door. I rounded the corner of the house blind. I'd been staring at the TV for hours, night vision completely shot. I gazed into the dark, trying to make out anything that didn't belong.

The silhouette of a jacked-up pickup sitting way down the driveway materialized. I couldn't make out the color or the make, but I had a pretty good guess. The dogs had halted at the end of the concrete by the garage, howling and growling.

I skirted around the dogs and hugged the board fence running along the driveway. Something sounded like a chain scraping on a pipe, a high-pitched metallic clinking sound then the scream of a rusty hinge; somebody opening the pen gates.

Then, someone coming down the drive toward me. Slow footsteps. A tall figure. He walked closer. I raised the shotgun, whispered, "Stop. Stop there." He never even slowed. I snapped off the safety, kept my finger out of the trigger guard. Do this on purpose. He kept coming; steady, slow, deliberate. The guy looked huge.

"Stop," I croaked.

He took two more steps. I could hear his boots on the gravel. I leaned in and put the shotgun against my cheek. My finger went inside the guard, putting some pressure on the cold trigger.

I said it louder, "Stop. I've got a shotgun aimed at your head ..." Right at his big, basketball-sized head. Curly hair ... not right ... something wrong.

The Alpaca strolled up, took my ear between its soft lips and gummed it. My heart felt like it would pound itself clean out of my chest.

Done spitting in my ear, he strolled away.

I grabbed onto the fence. Stars were spinning around my vision. I had come so close ...

Another noise snapped in the dark.

Three pigs ran past, grunting with each step. Then horses coming at a trot. I gripped the fence, straining to see as they went by. I hung on, getting myself together, willing my night vision to improve.

Something dark ran down the drive from the house. It shot past, disappeared into the open side of the feed shed. A ferocious growling tore the air and a scream—a human scream—followed by two echoing reports and bright flashes through the window.

A round form on two legs ran; cut across a pen, headed for the end of the driveway and the dark shape of the pickup.

"Go! Go!" a man shouted. "Go!"

The pickup's brake lights flashed and a diesel engine clattered to life.

The fat guy had a funny gait, but he could move pretty well. He went over the board fence, dashing for the truck. A door opened, the dome light flashed on and off, too fast to see who was at the wheel. Maybe pink?

The truck roared away, lightless, out toward the road. A terrific noise out there; then the truck roared on, out to the blacktop and away west.

The dogs up at the house were going berserk; their insane howling blaring through my head, making it hard to sort out what had just happened.

I had leveled the shotgun on the guy. It was dark, I couldn't see, maybe I could have knocked him down, maybe killed him. But that wasn't my plan. And he'd had a gun. That wasn't part of my plan either. And I hadn't known for sure who it was. Too damn many maybes!

I clicked the safety on, leaned the Wingmaster up against the fence.

Afraid to look in the shed, I willed my block feet to the door. Dark as pitch, the smell of blood in the air. I found the switch. A row of bulbs blazed on, filling the shed with horrible, clear light.

Finster.

I wrapped the old dog in a tarp from the shed. I couldn't bear to leave him there alone. I cried as I did it. I cried as if it were my dad, or my wife, or my son, or my grandfather.

I cried and wished I'd shot that fat son of a bitch. I wished

I'd knocked him down and then kept shooting until I had torn him to pieces. I would have left him for the pigs.

I went to all the pens and hooked open all the gates.

Then I carried Finster up to the Rover.

I remembered the shotgun, still leaning unfired on the fence. I took it inside, shucked the shells, wiped it down and put it back in its spot. Ben would never know I had taken it out.

After a long hot shower and a couple of beers, I fell asleep on the Chandler's couch.

I flew with my dad, and my grandpa, and my wife, a little boy, and Finster. I remember thinking that dogs looked funny when they flew; their lips and ears flapping away in the breeze.

We all flew together over a never-ending field of wheat under a dark moody sky, sharing thoughts that were important to us. I woke up feeling fine; a little sad, but fine.

Every one of the animals was in its pen. They came back during the night to the familiar comfort. I wasn't too surprised. Well, I was a little surprised at the pigs, but they were there, hoping J.J. and Bobbi would show up soon with more grub.

There was a lot of blood on the dirt in the feed shed. I got a spade and dug up the bloody area, turned it over and tamped it back down. It would pass a pretty close examination. There was also a trail of blood out the door. Finster had not gone down without a fight—he'd taken a piece out of the fat man.

I followed the blood trail all the way to where the truck had been parked. Across the road, Ben's indestructible mailbox was smashed, no match for a four-wheel drive truck, a red one by the look of the paint left on the torn wreckage. I was betting there was a beat-to-shit Dodge pickup parked at 101 Jesus Is My Redeemer Lane and that the floor mat on the passenger side had to be pretty bloody. Score one for the good guys.

I wasn't sure what time J.J. and Bobbi McGee would show up, but I didn't want to be there when they did.

Busted flat in Baton Rouge ... Janis Joplin's raspy voice was perfect that cold clear morning.

I wrote a note for the kids:

J.J. and Bobbi,

I decided that Finster would like to stay at my house for a while. He's fine. I guess us old dogs like to stick together. I'll be back in the next few days. Hope I get to see you again.

Your friend,
Chip

I tacked the note to the feed shed door and split for home.

The rest of the day was spent brooding about what I could have done, what I should have done, and what I had done. I was pretty worn out by all the ups and downs so I napped on the couch in my office until it got dark. Suzanne came down and we sat and talked with the lights off for a couple of hours.

Later that evening, after Suzanne had floated off to sleep, I sang Amazing Grace and buried Finster next to a big rock in my meadow. While I was at it, I threw Jessica Chandler's white phone in with him.

Part 1 CHAPTER 19

At 7:31 the garage door came up. Scarlett's black 4Runner came out. John sat in the passenger seat. That was new.

Then the red pickup came out with Tree driving. The Dodge looked like somebody had tried to part its hair right down the middle. The big chrome grill was stove in. The hood was buckled where something solid—like a steel mailbox— had crashed into its front edge. Bradley had killed Finster, no doubt.

I'd had him in my sights. I hadn't pulled the trigger. Now I had even more reason to follow my plan through to the end.

I turned the knob on my binoculars. Four camouflage packs riding in the back snapped into focus. The mangled truck rounded the corner and clattered down Baldy toward town.

They must have been keen to get something done fast or Tree never would have driven the truck in that shape; especially if they thought anyone had seen it out at Ben's.

Where the hell were they going? And since when did Tree Man have driving rights?

◆　◆　◆

Back in my office, I pulled the bag of green dust out of the gun safe. It sat on the desk in front of me; a couple of ounces of something illegal. I still had no idea what it could be.

"Whatcha got there?" My wife appeared in the doorway drinking some weird-smelling herbal tea. "Looks like something Izzy Feldman would sell in his shop," she said.

She'd startled me. I hadn't expected her just then. "What?"

My wife had always hated to repeat herself ... "I *said*," she emphasized it, "That green powder looks like something you might see at Izzy Feldman's place; you know, our local chiropractor and traditional-Chinese-herbalist? What is that stuff anyway?"

"I *know* who Izzy Feldman is, I just didn't hear you," I said, not wanting to be mad, but firing back anyway. "I don't know what this stuff is. I found it in the woods when I was hiking."

That wasn't really a lie. I just happened to be spying on the deviant giant who left it there. "You think it's some kind of tea or something?"

My wife took a big slurp from her cup. She picked the bag up off the coffee table and rolled the powder inside around a little bit. "Huh, I don't think its tea of any kind. And it doesn't "feel" like it came from a plant either."

How she could say it didn't "feel" like it came from a plant was a mystery to me. But if she said it, it was probably right.

Then she held the bag up to her nose. "God, it smells like liver or gizzards or something." The vegetarian in her was revolted. She put it down. "Maybe somebody's old Chinese take-out that's been in the woods for twenty-five years?" She laughed. "What the heck made you bring it home?" A gleam in her eye; still pushing my buttons.

Good question. What had made me bring the damn thing home? "Oh, you know, I just don't like to see trash in my woods."

"Well, I can't fault you for being you," she said. "Maybe take it down to Izzy's place, see if he knows? Might be kind of fun. You've never been in there."

"You know how I feel about that witch doctor stuff." In my estimation there was a lot of voodoo and quackery going on in Sandpoint and I wasn't going to participate in it. But she had a point; why hadn't I thought of that? Maybe Feldman could tell me what the dust was.

"OK," I said to my wife. "I'm going down to Feldman's right now. Can I pick up a shrunken head or some unicorn urine for you while I'm there? Maybe some dried eye of newt?"

"Ha, Ha," she said, "Actually, ask him about Mullein. There's a bunch growing in the meadow and I heard someplace that it will cure anything." She drifted away up the stairs.

I picked up the mystery bag, headed for Izzy's.

Sellin' little bottles of … Love Potion #9 …

Driving, with the little bag of dust on the passenger-side floor of the Subaru, I felt like the cops were going to bust out of the woods and throw me in jail on serious drug charges before I got a mile down the road.

Feldman's shop was in an old church… over on Church Street. You had to love Sandpoint's founding fathers.

There was a 4'X 8' hand-painted sign between two posts in the yard out front.

IZZY FELDMAN
CHIROPRACTOR
TRADITIONAL CHINESE HERBALIST
9:00 AM - 4:00 PM MON-FRI
Walk-ins Welcome
Visa, Master Card, Sorry no American Express

I was guessing Feldman's shop had been Presbyterian or Methodist a hundred years before. I wondered if God cared that the once Christian church was now a witch's lair.

I walked through red double doors, painted with Chinese characters, into what had been the sanctuary. The place smelled like my idea of a back street Hong Kong apothecary; dead stuff, old plants, mint, copper, alcohol and tea.

The ceiling was high, maybe twenty feet; original, cracked and crumbling. Light angled down through an arched stained glass window creating a dull spray of color in dust motes and drifting fibers from exotic plants.

Church pews had been replaced by long tables and rows of shelves covered with bottles and bags, boxes and jars. They all had labels with Chinese characters or spidery hand-written English descriptions.

There were shadowy forms suspended in opaque liquid, and powders and granules of every color. Dried forms hung from heavy wires suspended between uprights. I expected to see dead birds, or at least some animal heads and snakes hanging there, but it mostly looked like weeds and flowers.

There didn't seem to be anybody around.

I peeked in a side door. There was an elderly exam table with a long strip of white paper down its center and some cabinets. The back-cracker's operation theatre; just relax … this won't hurt a bit …

I tried another door. This one opened into a hallway with a thick oriental carpet runner and several doors down one side. The doors were solid wood on the bottom and clear glass on the top. A frosted number was etched into the center of each window; the old Sunday-school rooms.

Voices came from somewhere down the corridor. One was big and deep. The other was softer and mellower; probably Izzy Feldman and a patient.

I walked toward the voices. The wooden floor gave and creaked through the carpet under my feet.

I looked in Room #1. The place was posh; a living room full of leather furniture and sophisticated electronics. So Izzy not only had his office there, he lived in the church too. Room #2 was a beautiful walnut-appointed office with a lot of original art on the walls. Looked like the chiropractor lived pretty well. Room #3 had become a kitchen; stainless steel, granite and cherry; high-end, very nice.

The big deep voice made the hallway vibrate around me. I took one slow step on the carpet runner to look through the glass past the #4.

Tree Man's immense back was toward me as he unloaded familiar bags from a camo backpack. He spread dozens of little plastic sacks out in rows on the long table in front of him.

I leaned close to the hinge side of the door where I could still see him and not be seen myself.

The voice on the other side of Tree said, "Hurry up. Feldman will be back any minute and I want to have this ready when he gets here."

I was lying under the deck again listening to John Bradley and Tree Man talk hate.

Tree Man stooped to lift more bags out of the pack and there were John Bradley's pig eyes looking toward me through the glass of door #4.

"Why don't you get off your ass and help me if you're in such a hurry!" Tree Man's irritated words vibrated under the door. He was putting bags into groups by color. "You fat, lazy son of a bitch. I wish that dog had ripped off your balls instead of just trying to eat your leg."

As he straightened up, Tree's bulk had obscured Bradley again, but I could picture him slouching against the table, arms folded over his gut, telling Tree what to do.

"Look," Bradley said. "I can barely walk." He hobbled into view beside the table. "The doc put twenty-eight stitches in my leg this morning. It hurts like hell. Give me a break."

"I'd like to give you a break …" Tree had emptied the backpack and dropped it on the floor with three others. "What the hell did you two idiots think you were doing out there? We're just about done with this deal and you decide to go raise hell with those people? You're just fucking stupid."

"They stole my girls. They're gonna pay for that! Them and that fuckin' game warden." Bradley was shouting now. "They got no clue about what I'm gonna do to all of 'em. Maybe I'll start by warming up on you right now!"

Bradley pulled a little black automatic out of the back pocket of his jeans and jabbed it at Tree Man. It looked like a toy pointed at the giant, but at three feet, in the right place, it might have done the job.

Tree didn't twitch. "Put that thing back in your pocket. Let's get this deal done so we can be rid of one another."

Tree Man's voice was more powerful than John's rage. Bradley folded in on himself and wilted. His arm came down. He thumbed the safety on the pistol and jammed it back in his jeans.

"God, I'm tired," he said. "My knee hurts." He pulled a bottle from a pocket, threw pills in his mouth and swallowed them dry.

A noise echoed from the front of the church.

I turned, scooted back down the carpet runner to door #3 and slipped into the kitchen as the door from the sanctuary opened and the hallway floor boards started creaking toward me. Room #1 ... Room #2 ... Room #3 ... A foot away from me the footsteps stopped. The doorknob beside my left elbow jiggled and the door moved inward ...

Tree Man's seismic voice rose through the wall, followed by a retort from John Bradley.

Door #3 pulled back shut. The footsteps creaked on.

"Gentlemen! Gentlemen! Good to see you!" Izzy Feldman had arrived.

Tree and Bradley went quiet.

I could hear Izzy clearly. He must have left door #4 open when he went in.

There was only one way out of the kitchen. I pulled door #3 open a couple of inches.

"We've got the stuff," John Bradley said. "You won't find this much bear gallbladder, of this quality, anywhere else, at any price."

Bear gallbladder? I hoped I hadn't snorted or made a

sound. Bear gallbladder?

"Let's take a look," Izzy said. "This is pretty impressive."

"As always, it's all wild black bear. No bear farm stuff. Killed in the wild and dried-fresh," John Bradley sounded like he was hawking fish at the Pike Place Market in Seattle. "It's marked, sorted by color, and weighed out by the ounce. Your labels are in place, just as you requested."

"The last batch was superb," Feldman said. "My buyers were very pleased."

The room went quiet for what seemed like a long, long time. This whole deal was freaking me out. It wasn't about porno or drugs at all. The scumbags were poaching bears, killing hundreds of them for their gallbladders. I'd heard stories of the Chinese using bile and other animal parts as aphrodisiacs and virility potions. And Izzy Feldman! How many times had I seen him singing on the stage at Skip's? Steve Albright hadn't known how close he was to this when it all went bad that night in the Bradleys' driveway.

"This is what we agreed to," Izzy said. "Your money is there, next to the door, two-and-a-half-million dollars."

I tried not to make a sound. Holy shit! Two-and-a-half-million?

John Bradley spoke up. "You're getting a hell of a deal Feldman. The shit on this table is worth a lot more than that. I still don't know how I let you talk me into this."

I heard scraping and steps as the men in room #4 moved around. I pictured them with aluminum briefcases full of cash.

Feldman spoke again. "What about more frozen whole ones? My buyers will take all you can provide, three-thousand per. And paws? You must have more paws. The demand is high right now and I could go fifteen-hundred each."

Bradley said, "We've got at least thirty-two bladders in the freezer at my house. And a couple dozen paws too."

Tree spoke up, "I make that at one-hundred and thirty-two thousand. And we've got another hundred ounces of dust too. You'll pay full price this time ..."

Apparently Tree was a mathematics whiz when it came to adding up the price of bear organs.

Izzy said, "Yes, full price. I'll have the money ready on Monday. Let's meet here at nine-thirty. That work for you gentlemen?"

"Good for us," said Bradley.

"That's a deal then. I've got a very nice bottle of forty-year-old scotch in the kitchen. Not too early for you is it?"

I heard them shifting around. I shot out door #3, trying to run silently down the long hall and out to the sanctuary—I wouldn't make it.

John Bradley would shoot me in the back with his ugly little automatic.

I got to door #2—turned around and walked back the way I had come; a patient looking for the doctor.

Izzy Feldman came out of room #4. He was looking back over his shoulder at Bradley. Tree Man followed carrying a couple of bulging orange trash bags. I was a surprise. Feldman turned, stopped dead with a funny, questioning look in his eye. Bradley ran into him and Tree finished the Three Stooge's routine, nearly knocking the two guys in front down.

"Uh, may I help you?" Feldman recovered nicely.

"Yes, I'm having some trouble with my back. I must have slept on it funny or something. I didn't see anybody out front so ..." I hoped I looked clueless, instead of scared shitless.

"Well, I'd be glad to have a look at you right now." The Chiropractor emerged and the bear poaching, black market son of a bitch receded. I wondered why he bothered to keep doing the chiropractor thing. He'd just been talking about millions of dollars and now he was going to come crack my back for seventy-five bucks?

Feldman looked back at his two business associates. They

looked at me like they would just as soon have buried me in the basement.

"If you gentlemen wouldn't mind waiting in the kitchen for just a few minutes …" Izzy was smooth.

John limped through the kitchen door. Tree shot me a murderous look before he ducked under the doorframe, hauling the bags that held two-and-a-half million bucks.

"Now, let me show you to the examination room and we'll have you feeling better in just a couple of minutes."

Feldman lit a stick of incense under a red porcelain Buddha on a table in the corner. He had me sit on the end of the exam table. The white paper crinkled and crackled under my butt.

"What's bothering you, mister ah …?"

Bothering me? Well you're in business with a couple of complete sickos dealing in illegal animal parts, poaching, child porn, and a bunch of other stuff I don't even want to know about. And now I'm stuck in a room with you and I'll bet I have to take my clothes off. That's bothering me a lot.

What I said was, "Crandle, Chip Crandle. It's down in my lower back. I just woke up with it. My wife recommended that I come in. I don't usually see chiropractors."

"OK Chip, take off your jacket and shirt and your pants, and lay down on your stomach there."

I knew it.

He went over to a little white sink and washed his hands, then stuck them under a blow dryer thing on the wall. Nice touch, hot hands.

I got out of my clothes, hung 'em on an old hall tree. I was going to have to let this creep touch me. Touch me on my naked skin. I went to the table and lay down on my stomach. The white paper was stiff and cold. I shivered as I waited.

He walked up behind me. "OK," he said, laying his hand on my spine just above the elastic of my underwear. His hand was warm, but the sensation was like cold electricity running down between my legs to my toes. I had a death grip on the edges of the table.

"Chip, you're pretty tense. Just relax. I can feel a couple of spots that are really out of line. You always this tight?" He spoke in soft tones. Probably used to calming people down before he broke their spines and ground them into natural remedy ingredients.

"I don't know," I said. "Probably not. Just a little nervous about doing this. My wife's the chiropractor person."

"Well, I hope you'll feel that way too when we're done. Now take a deep breath, then let it out and relax as much as you can." He put both hands on the small of my back—ready to break me.

I took a deep breath and let it out. POW, he pushed down hard with both hands. The guy was strong. There was an audible crack and then a couple of smaller ones. Then he moved up a little and hit it hard again. SNAP!

"You were really out of place right there," Feldman said. "You'll be a lot better now. Go home and put some ice on that and don't do anything strenuous for the rest of the day. You'll be tired tonight. Have your wife rub this on your back later." He handed me a white tube of something that I hoped didn't contain bear guts.

He stepped away from the table to wash his hands again.

I sat up on the end of the table. My back actually felt pretty good. Maybe I was just relieved to be alive. It didn't last. My little plastic bag of green powder was lying on the floor next to the carved wooden feet of Izzy Feldman's antique hall tree.

Feldman had his back to me, stooped over the sink. I sprang from the table took two strides to the hall tree, knocked my jacket off and over the bag on the floor. As the chiropractor turned, I gathered my pants and stepped into them.

"You must be in a hurry to get home," Feldman remarked. "Most people lie there awhile and let things settle in a bit."

"I think my back feels better already." I slipped into my shirt, glad to be covered. "It will be hard to admit that to my wife. By the way, what do you know about Mullein?"

"Mullein? You mean like the weed that grows all over the place around here?" He cocked his curly red head at me.

"Yeah, I hear it heals everything."

"I dunno, gives me a rash when I pull it out of the yard. I should probably see you again, say Monday next?" Feldman was booking up a pretty busy Monday for himself.

"Late Monday morning would work for me." I didn't expect to see Izzy Feldman ever again. Let alone have him lay his hands on me.

"I have time around 11:30."

"Great."

"If you don't mind, I need to get back with my guests."

Great … Fine … OK … Let me out of here. "Sure, I can show myself out."

His damp hand shook mine and Dr. Feldman slipped out the door to drink forty-year-old scotch with his buddies, Tree Man and John Bradley.

♦ ♦ ♦

It seemed like a long drive home. I parked the Outback in the garage and woke up on the sofa in my office about 4:00 PM; grouchy, hungry, and cold. But my back felt great.

My wife came drifting down the steps. "So what did you find out?"

I grouched at her, "I just woke up. Can I eat something before we talk about it?"

She stuck her tongue out at me.

I snacked. The food helped.

"OK, lemme tell you what Izzy Feldman said about that green stuff in the bag. He didn't know what it was," I lied. "I think he was a little afraid to touch it. Said I should take it to the cops or just flush it."

"Huh," she said. "And what *are* you going to do with it?"

"I was thinking maybe I'd give it to Steve Albright. He might know what it is."

"Good plan. What did Feldman say about Mullein?"

"Well he says Mullein gives him a rash. He'd recommend bear gallbladder paste instead."

"Really? What's it supposed to do for you?"

"Gives you an erection," I said.

"Perfect," she said, "I've never had one of those."

Suzanne had always been able to make me laugh.

◆   ◆   ◆

I put my bag of bear gallbladder in the safe and took out my plan; a load of information to process.

Bear parts, not porno—at least not in this deal. That didn't really have any bearing on the goals of my plan, but it nagged me. Where were all the bear parts coming from? John Bradley had said there was a freezer full at his house. I hadn't found any freezers; that was a big detail. What else had I missed?

Damn. Looked like another visit inside the Bradleys'.

And other concerns whirled through my head, dragging me off task. Would Bradley visit Ben's house again? Were J.J. and Bobbi McGee in danger?

Steve Albright. I thought about him some. Steve could take care of himself without me gumming up the works. I'd stay out of Steve's way.

What about Izzy Feldman? How did he fit into my plan, if at all?

This was Thursday the 24th. They were going to do the final deal in just four days, on Monday, April 28. That put *my* deadline in crystal-clear focus.

And how come my back felt so much better than it ever had? I didn't even know I had a problem.

I was in bed early. Suzanne was busy somewhere else.

If you could wish in your sleep, I would have wished I was still awake.

Part 1 CHAPTER 20

I had an old, bad dream. It had been a long time, but it had a way of showing up when I was stressed out or under the gun in some way.

It was about my dad—my understanding, calm father and source of my flying.

Dad and I were hunting on our farm. In front of us were my two dogs, red and shining, slipping through the weeds and the brush, their noses to the ground in search of pheasants. One of the dogs went into a slow-motion creep and locked into a point. The second dog honored the point, freezing ten feet behind the first.

My dad walked up to flush the bird, only now he wasn't walking in an autumn field. He was emaciated, gray-green and dying, lying in a hospital bed in the living room of our farmhouse.

"Are you ready to shoot?" he rasped, throat dry from morphine. "Are you ready to shoot? There he goes! Why didn't you shoot? You let him fly away. What were you waiting for? Didn't you see the dog pointing? Why didn't you shoot?"

He was yelling at me. Not at all like him.

And then he lifted off out of the bed and flew away into the sky that had replaced the ceiling. And the room wasn't there anymore, just the autumn field and the two dogs and me. And both dogs looked at me, as they did when you missed a shot. That accusing look. I could hear them thinking why didn't you shoot? What were you waiting for? Now he's flown away! You'll never get another chance. He's gone! Why didn't you pull the trigger?

I woke up cold and sweaty in twisted sheets, 3:27AM glowing hell-red on the ceiling.

I thought about my dad. How he'd died. And how I had done nothing to help him live; only stood by as he melted away. And in the end, praying with my mom and sisters that he would die and end all the suffering.

The hunting part of my dream had come from a real day. A day twenty years ago when he had told me he was afraid. It was opening day of pheasant season, a beautiful October day. We'd shot our limit and were back at the house cleaning the birds in the yard when, without any buildup Dad said, "I've been pissing blood for a month, Chip … and I'm pretty scared."

I had looked at his face. He wasn't scared; he was terrified. "Well, have you talked to your doctor?" What was it Dad was asking me for?

"He says it's nothing to worry about, just an infection or something. But he's this new doctor. Doc Carroll died you know." Dad was showing me something I didn't want to see; fear, uncertainty, a reverse in who was in charge. A reverse I was not ready to even think about, let alone take on right then while I stood in the autumn sun with blood all over my hands.

"What do you think I should do?" Dad said.

"Well it sounds like the doctor doesn't think it's anything to worry about." That was it. I wasn't the dad. I wasn't in charge. I wasn't supposed to make decisions for my father. I was supposed to fly around while he held me up.

The new doctor was wrong. It *had* been something to worry about … Something to *really* worry about.

I had done the easy thing, which was nothing, and said, "Don't worry." I hadn't said, "Let's go to another doctor right away. Right now. Let's get your ass in the car and go now! Let's don't be afraid. Let's *do* something. Shoot already."

But I hadn't said that and I hadn't done anything except finish cleaning the birds and wash my hands. Then I got in my car and went home. Nothing to worry about. Let's not ruin our day. See you later. Love you lots.

It had been cancer, bladder cancer. The first doctor had missed it. By the time Dad and Mom went to the next doctor it had spread.

He had surgery and chemotherapy and radiation. And then he had a bag full of piss hanging off his side and he weighed about half his normal weight. And in the end, I shot him full of morphine and changed his diapers and emptied his bag and listened to him rave as the cancer went into his brain.

And I prayed that he would die because he was suffering and I had not done all I could do. I had done the least I could do.

And then *he* flew away. And I knew that I had missed. No, I hadn't missed. I had not even taken a shot. And he had flown away forever.

The blue poker chip was lying on my night stand next to the bed. Dad had carried it in his pocket from the day I was born until the day he crawled into the hospital bed and didn't get out again. I had found it in the drawer of the over-bed table after they took his body away.

Part 1 CHAPTER 21

At 5:00 I got up. I put Dad and the poker chip in my pocket. I was going to *do* something this time. I was going to take the shot.

I sat closer to their house than usual. Rain threatened. Something was happening on the Bradleys' front porch.

Bloated, pink rage burst out through the door, stumbled over Adolph and cursed. The cat shot down the steps. Scarlett screamed, brandishing a big kitchen knife. "Come back here you little shit and I'll cut you into pieces!"

She was insanely furious, ripping at the air with the knife, shrieking. Unintelligible obscenities bouncing off my mountains. She hacked at the porch rail with the knife.

John came out wearing only boxer shorts. Jiggling, he hobbled in circles, overturning the dog hut, throwing boxes and trash into the front yard, screaming at Scarlett. "Where the fuck is it? What could he have done with it? You were supposed to keep an eye on the son of a bitch!"

"Me?" She screamed back. "You're blaming me? Get real John. You fucked this whole thing up beyond belief. You went too far, too fast. He …"

John shouted her down, and it all ran together in a flood of curses and wails. He stayed in his tantrum, kicking and hurling trash. Scarlett whirled the knife in wild arcs as they screamed. She leaned in. He took a wobbly step back, hands out in front. She was going to kill him while I watched.

Scarlett yelled, "We'll never find …" The rain came down hard, drowning the mountains along with her words.

The downpour did something. It was like they ran out of gas. They slumped. The rain hammered. They stood in the trash staring at each other.

Through the deluge, I saw Scarlett lay the knife on the railing and put her hands behind her husband's head. She put her forehead on his, saying something. He patted her on her horse's ass, and they went back inside—Crazy love.

◆   ◆   ◆

Something big had happened ... Something bad. I shuddered to think what bad in their sick world would look like.

At 7:32 both vehicles left. It seemed strange that they kept going to work. Looked like they intended to keep things looking normal then just disappear.

I came back to what *I* intended to do—find the missing freezer. One hitch, where was Tree Man?

Maybe he was up at the cave. Maybe he was sleeping up in the pink room. Maybe he was sitting at the kitchen table counting stacks of cash, smoking a doobie.

I moved around to the back of the house. I sat for half an hour in the rain. Nobody at the table. No lights in the kitchen. Nothing moving.

I returned to my starting point out front. Scarlett had been within a heartbeat of using the knife on John. What the hell had happened?

Through the binoculars I saw Adolf trot up onto the porch. The clouds moved over and the sun came out hot, steam rising from the lane.

That house was empty. No life. I knew it.

I made my way to the porch. Scarlett's knife, more than a foot long, lay there in a pink-tinged puddle on the white railing, forgotten in her touching moment with John.

As I went through the door, the new smell hit me like a punch—ammonia and Pine Sol, fresh and toxic. A dead feeling permeated everything, punctuated by the harsh antiseptic fumes.

The entryway was scrubbed. The shoe pile gone. All the clothes on the hooks gone. The filthy path across the dining room to the kitchen was scrubbed raw. The clean floor continued into the kitchen. What the hell?

I stood in the doorway thinking. The kitchen freezer. Had I ever opened it? It couldn't be that simple, could it? How much space did a bear gallbladder take up? And what about the paws?

Forgotten food, vodka, and two inches of white fuzz. Their kitchen freezer was gross but not full of bear parts. I swung open the lower door. A wall of reeking bottles and cartons. Something wrong … No beer. Not a single one. And there were sour empties all over the house.

I looked down the hall toward the garage. The floor looked damp all the way to the door. I stood in the laundry and looked at the door. The terrible garage with its terrible dead legs. My heart was convulsing and my guts felt like water. I hated what was on the other side of that damn door, didn't ever want to see it again.

Screw it. I went through.

The light was already on. The shadows were the same, flowing and undulating so the whole space danced and gyrated. But things had been moved. The cracked, uneven floor had been power washed. Cold damp air thick with Pine Sol.

At the far side of the garage, the four-wheeler crouched like a spider in its regular spot. The front of the garage was still piled to the ceiling with the same junk.

The legs were still there. Pale, dead and washed out; except for the yellow of the screwdriver handle protruding from the pubic hair. I move toward them, counting each step.

A mannequin's legs. Pubic hair scrawled in dark magic marker on slick plastic. A cheap Halloween house of horror's trick and it had scared me right down to my bones.

I felt relief and anguish. And then I felt stupid.

It was right there. Right next to the plastic legs; a refrigerator-freezer, cardboard colored, probably forty years old, covered with boxes and magazines and an old sleeping bag.

I opened the bottom door first. The dim light illuminated beer; a ton of cheap, canned, see-through beer. I swung the top door. It was stacked with little pint-sized Ziplocs, purple stuff inside. I turned one over in my hand. Everybody in North Idaho had huckleberries in their freezer, even the child molesting, bear poaching, murderers.

Damn.

I leaned on some plastic storage bins stacked next to the fridge, and the whole wall of junk rolled smoothly away.

I had to admit it was pretty ingenious. The junk pile was constructed on a rolling platform. I grabbed hold of the plastic legs and pulled. The junk sculpture rolled right out onto the garage floor where the red truck usually sat.

In the exposed wall behind the junk was a pocket door. I slid it. I was looking at a stainless steel door with heavy hinges and a long, chrome handle. The wet clean floor ran right up to it.

John Bradley's freezer.

With my hand on the cold handle, I told myself, "Whatever you find, it will only add to your resolve. Killing them is the right thing."

The heavy door swung open, immersing me in a rush of icy fog. Harsh ceiling lights went on, everything colorless inside the frozen cell.

I went dead cold. Foggy shapes loomed in the narrow space. At the far end, dim in the frozen cloud, sat two rows of something large on the floor. It was twelve feet to the back. I stepped in, my rain-damp jacket and pants crackled, freezing around me. Blinded by its fog, I held my breath.

Along the left-hand wall, bundles on shelves. I lifted loose butcher's paper and long black claws in coarse, dark hair jutted out. I made out rows of containers with something round and dark inside.

My teeth chattered and my jaw ached with cold and tension.

I made my way to the back of the space where eight large forms waited. Four were big trash bags, red or orange, bulging with soft shapes, closed tight. In front of the bags, at my feet, were four familiar backpacks, standing on bottoms stained dark.

I pulled at the frozen edge of a pack's cover flap.

A frozen tangle of fingers tumbled onto the floor. Stark white bone ends, ringed in dark tissue. I sucked in frigid air, searing my lungs. Stumbling, my knee slammed into the pack. It toppled, ejecting another blackened wad of bones and meat onto the floor. A huge, bald head—a ragged black hole where the nose had been—rolled free, stopping against the knot of severed fingers.

My bare hand stuck to the wall. I fought to stand, the freezer filling with my breath's fog. The frozen room expanded and then closed in, crushing me, forcing the horror on the floor up into my face.

Flying or falling? My fingers pressed hard against my screams. I had to get out.

No, Stop. Breathe. You're here. You can't go back. You wanted it. You found it. Take the shot.

I wrestled the pack upright. I can't describe picking up Tree Man's frozen head, but I did it. And the nose. And the clumps of icy fingers.

I backed out, shut the door behind me, slid the pocket door, turned the catch, and rolled the junk back in place.

I went out to the deck, trying to pull it all into focus. What the hell had they done to him before they dragged him in there ... and why? And what the hell were they going to do with what was left of him now?

The sun helped me think. I would never know why they'd tortured and maimed him. But I did know this; the Bradleys had removed the Tree Man complication for me.

My resolve to kill them was stronger. The only thing worse than the hell in the freezer, would be letting them live.

I had risen off the deck, ready to go home, when I saw the tracks leading into the woods. The path to the cave looked like a herd of cows had been driven up it. I walked without thinking. Something irresistible ran my feet, drawing me up the path.

The stone was rolled back. Tree's pole was thrown haphazardly by the opening. There were footprints everywhere; Tree's, a man's and a woman's, running under and around every nook and cranny.

I snapped my new headlamp tight around my forehead and squirmed into the passageway I'd seen Tree crawl in and out of. It was man-made, maybe thirty inches wide, about fifteen feet long, disappearing into a dark space. Somebody, a long time ago, had chipped it out of the solid rock.

I wormed through on elbows, feet trailing on the rock floor. At the other end was an airless, ten-by-ten-foot chamber. There were wire restaurant shelves along one wall and a few empty pint-sized plastic bags and twist ties were scattered on the floor.

An old meat and death smell lingered. My light fought the gloom. Some kind of drawings or paintings on the dim ceiling. But then the cold rock won, it closed in, smothering what little courage I had. I slithered out, never so grateful for sunlight, gulping the miraculous fresh air.

I drank water and looked toward the slit where I had found Tree Man's pack. A glint of metal nine feet up on the rock shelf restored my nerve. It was a pack, hidden in plain sight. John and Scarlett had missed it.

Standing on Tree's pole, I maneuvered the pack to the edge. The thing was wet and heavy, sixty or seventy pounds easy. Tree had probably tossed it up there like a sack lunch, but my average, sixty-year-old body had a little trouble balancing on the nubs of a cedar pole while trying to lower it. After a struggle I just let it drop.

There were no dark stains on this one and there couldn't be anything worse than what I had seen in the freezer. I pulled back the flap.

Two bags of powder and three DVDs. The rest of the pack was stuffed with cash.

◆   ◆   ◆

I was back on my patio wriggling out of my hiking gear when Suzanne appeared on the deck right above me.

"Hey, you went on a long one this morning."

"Yeah, had a good hike, once the rain quit," I said, setting the pack on the concrete. "I guess I kind of lost track of time."

"I think we better talk," she said. "I'll be right down."

I hurried for my office. My daypack went on top and the money-filled backpack went quickly in the kneehole under my desk. Emptying it would have to wait.

My wife was there, beside the couch. "Chip," she gave me her knowing look. "There anything going on you'd like to tell me about?"

"Nope," I shot back without hesitation. "Everything is good."

"You sure?" Her eyes locked onto mine.

"Positive." I didn't blink.

She gave me a tender kiss. "As long as you're sure ... that's what matters ... Love you."

"Me too."

I held her close. I was there with the best person I knew—holding on.

◆   ◆   ◆

Opening Tree Man's pack was a little like Christmas, and a little like an open casket funeral. Both things you remember for very different reasons.

The bags of dust were two different colors, and they had the little twist tie labels in Chinese, just like the one already in my gun safe.

The three DVDs had probably spent some time under the mattress in the pink room.

I dumped what was left in the pack out across my desk. If all the bundles of hundred-dollar bills were the same, it was two-and-half-million dollars.

Tree Man hadn't talked. Killing him hadn't been just crazy; it had been greedy and crazy.

I put the cash back in the pack and sat it at the end of my leather couch. Hidden in plain sight.

The DVDs and the bags of dust joined their mates in the gun safe.

◆   ◆   ◆

I wrote two letters that day; one to Steve Albright and one for Ben Chandler.

I capped off my day by putting together a short media release and a list of gear for my trip. A few more things to do, but the wheels of execution were really in motion.

That night, exhausted, I slept—flying with a camo parachute on my back. As I flew over Sandpoint, I pulled the rip cord. The top popped open and I was dropping hundred-dollar bills in a big green cloud.

I could see people's upturned faces and they waved and laughed and grabbed bills out of the air as I spread joy. Finally, the money was all gone and a black bear tumbled out, followed by Tree Man's head. They fell, spinning down, growing smaller as they got closer to an olive-colored house in the woods. I could smell it from ten thousand feet. The bear and Tree's head disappeared down the chimney and the house disintegrated into a Pine Sol cloud. I flew east toward the rising sun.

Part 1 CHAPTER 22

Saturday. I had only a couple of days left to get ready.

I started ticking things off my list and piling them in the middle of the garage.

I looked at my fishing gear out of habit, I guess. This wasn't going to be a fishing trip.

I packed some necessities: atlas; I still liked hard copy maps, binoculars, travel mug, sunglasses, wet wipes and a tool kit. These I put within easy reach inside the Audi.

I needed bottled water and coffee, made a mental note to get a pound of Bevans Brothers ground beans when I was in town.

Money; I had the money from the safe-deposit box in my gun safe. And now I had a *little* extra cash supplied by Tree Man. I hadn't decided about that yet.

My phone buzzed; Steve Albright. "Hey, hope it's not too early," he said.

"I'm just sitting on the edge of the bed waiting for you to call," I laughed a bit. It was comforting to know he was OK. I had seen what John Bradley did to people he didn't like.

His voice got a little more serious. "I been thinking about you, wanted to check in again and make sure everything's alright."

"Steve, everything is OK. I've been fishing and working and it's all good. I guess I haven't told you about one of my clients getting killed in Salt Lake City. That's been bothering me some." If Steve was getting any funny vibes, maybe Eugene Triska could be my excuse.

"No kidding?" Steve sighed into the phone. "Well you never know which day it's going to be, do you?" Steve was matter of fact. He'd been there.

"That's for sure," I said. "Hey, can you meet me for a beer at Skip's tomorrow? I can tell you the whole story, and I have something I need to give you."

"Yeah?" Steve had a question in his voice. "What time, and what have you got that I need?"

"How 'bout seven?" I asked. "We should have the place to ourselves that time on a Sunday."

"OK, seven at Skip's. What's the mystery?" He said.

"No mystery. I found something in the woods I think will interest you. It's just easier to show it to you than explain it." I hoped he wouldn't press me anymore.

"OK buddy. You got my interest up. I gotta run. See you then."

I closed the phone and looked around the garage. Just a couple more things. The duct tape and Ziploc bags went on the front seat.

I spent the rest of the morning remembering how to do a media blitz, and most of the afternoon checking freight train schedules and weather reports and road construction zones for the Great Plains.

The backpack sat mute at the end of the couch. What was I gonna do with two-and-a-half-million bucks?

◆   ◆   ◆

I coasted past Ben's destroyed mailbox. One more thing Ben would have to deal with when they got back.

A chorus of howls and barking welcomed me. I rolled around in the yard with them for a few minutes—the little dogs running figure eights around the group, huge grins on their faces and tongues hitting their ears as they peeled out, flipping grass up in their wakes.

Then everybody stopped and sat down. The cats came over too, taking their time, on their own schedule.

I addressed them like a leader talking to a pack of cub scouts. "Well guys, this is it. You know Finster isn't coming back." They all acknowledged that in one way or another. One of the terriers let a tear roll down his cheek. The cats looked indifferent, but I knew they didn't really mean it.

"You behave and be good to those little girls and Ben and Jess. They're gonna need your help when they get back." They all gave me the thumbs up ... Even the cats.

I walked out to the feed shed; neat as a pin. All the animals were happy, fed, and had nothing to complain about. J.J. and Bobbi McGee were just alright with me.

Congas started playing. I was singing as I walked, "J.J. is just alright with me and Bobbi is just alright, oh yeah," all the way back to the house.

All was well there too. I was glad I knew these wonderful people who gave so much. I grabbed one of my beers out of Ben's fridge.

The dogs started raising hell out front; somebody pulling in.

Through the side windows at the front door, I saw the black 4Runner sitting behind my Land Rover. There was a pink blob behind the wheel.

John Bradley was limping up the walk as all four dogs circled him. He couldn't fool them. He just smelled bad.

No time to get into the gun safe. I threw open the door, said, "Hello, can I help you?"

I wasn't what he had been expecting. He stopped dead in his tracks. He didn't recognize me from the hallway in Izzy Feldman's office ... different context.

I'd never been this close—never been face-to-face with him. He smelled bad to me too. His little porker eyes were red around the rims and his hair was greasy. He hadn't shaved in a couple of days. His yellowed tee-shirt was stretched around his gut and over his boobs. The discolored bandage on his knee needed to be changed.

The dog pack split up. Half of them had John under control. The little guys went to keep an eye on Scarlett. I seriously doubted she would try to get out.

"Uh, do you live here?" Bradley was perplexed.

No, he wasn't perplexed. His eyes didn't look right. He was tripping on something.

"No, I'm just living here while the owners are away. My name's ... ah ... Tree. What can I do for you?" Tree? Where had that come from? I was babbling over my thumping pulse.

"You guys go lay down now," I said to the dogs. They knew I wasn't serious. They kept up a moving, distracting presence. The largest, Peter, had a low rumbling growl going the whole time; one eye on me, one eye on Bradley.

John kept glancing down and behind at the dogs. "Oh, uh, we're lost, yeah, we're lost. Which way do we go to get back to Highway 200?" He swayed a little; bad knee, bad brain, bad guy.

"Well, you just go out to the road and hang a left. About two miles to 200," I said. "The river makes the roads angle out here, not hard to lose track of where you are." Especially if you're a complete asshole full of oxycodone.

His eyes shifted side to side, thinking. He took a deep suck of air, fumbled with the waistband of his shorts, let out a big blow of stinking breath.

He turned, flip-flops clacking on his heels, and hobbled very carefully through the hostile dogs back to the 4Runner. I could see the grip and hammer end of a pistol jutting up out of the waistband of his shorts. He'd come ready to do something bad. I hadn't been a part of the plan. Confused, he was running away.

The dogs brought the volume up a couple more notches as he slammed the car door. Scarlett missed what was left of the mailbox on the way out.

The dogs had regrouped. Peter was addressing his troops, congratulating them on a job well done. I took out a handful of Milk Bones. They devoured the treats and were humming and snoring in their pile within ten minutes.

The cats hadn't shown up. I expect they were watching from some higher place.

I took a little overnight bag out of the Rover and went back in for a final night at Ben's.

◆   ◆   ◆

After some of Jess's wonderful red beans and rice, *She Wore a Yellow Ribbon* came on; John Wayne as Captain Nelson Brittles. I leaned Ben's loaded shotgun against the arm of the couch, hoped I wouldn't be disturbed.

I woke the next morning with a sour, un-brushed taste in my mouth. Ben Hur was on so I made myself some breakfast and stayed around until after 8:00.

Ben's shotgun went back in the safe.

I gave the Chandler dogs one last round of treats, watched a fish rising in the river, and took off for town.

Sunday morning, Beatles hour on the radio:

We're on our way home ... We're going home ...

◆   ◆   ◆

In Safeway, I found the stuff on my list and a few more things you always buy when you're going camping: string cheese, cookies, candy bars, oranges, a bag of little carrots, some peanuts in the shell, and red licorice.

Self-checkout wasn't busy. I swiped my credit card; wouldn't take. A blue-haired woman, eighty-five if she was a day, came over, rolled her eyes, took my card and swiped it for me.

◆   ◆   ◆

The only regulars at Bevans Brothers were the CTGers. Conspiracy knows no Sabbath.

Big mustache was leading them in a lively discussion on the relative merits of Christians versus Muslims and why our country's policies regarding both were dead wrong.

I stepped up to the counter. The barista of the moment; a pale, skinny guy with a black tee-shirt printed with skulls and a pink disc in each earlobe the size of a quarter asked me what I wanted.

"I'll take a pound of Big Sky Blend," I said. "Could you grind that coarse for me please?"

"You got it," he said. "Just take me a couple of minutes."

While the grinder was buzzing, I walked over to the Conspiracy table. They were in a rare moment of silence.

"How's the weather in Oklahoma?" I said.

"Not so great," was the answer from the Director of Weather Conspiracy. "The forecasts call for the worst tornado season ever, and it's all because of the change in our climate due to the overflights of the spy satellites."

I started to laugh, and caught myself when I remembered who I was talking to. "Really, worst season ever predicted?"

"And now they've got the drones out there too which is really unsettling things." The Director was getting warmed up. "Be glad we live up here where it's almost still a free country."

"You got that right," I said.

"Your coffee's ready dude," the barista held up a brown bag. "You want a little cup for the road? I recommend the Columbian Los Lobos."

"Sounds great." I was getting more comfortable with trying new things. Coffee in hand I headed for the door.

Izzy Feldman came through, almost spilling my coffee in the process. "Sorry! Oh, hello ... it's Chip isn't it? How's the back doing?" He wore brand new, high-end technical clothes. His fleece pullover's logo said, "I cost four hundred bucks," his trousers and boots the same.

"Uh, my back is feeling really good," I said. "You made a believer out of me. I've told my best friend to come pay you a visit."

"Well, that's great." He clapped a cold hand on my shoulder. A heavy gold Rolex glimmered on his wrist. "I'll see you tomorrow."

I had to concentrate hard not to shrink away.

Feldman held the door and I went out.

Part 1 CHAPTER 23

Except for the coolers, my clothes and my computer bag, the car was packed and ready. On the passenger-side floor was a large manila envelope; fifty thousand dollars in it. More than I had planned on but I had it so why run short?

Time to get the letter I'd written to Steve Albright ready.

April 27

Dear Steve,

> If my plans have gone well, John and Scarlett Bradley are dead. Maybe they'll get another chance to get it right. If so, I did everybody, including them, a favor.

> I think you will understand what I have done. I don't expect you to condone it.

> All I can see now is an end, and I want it to be on my terms. It's time for me to get something done right.

> The DVDs in this envelope involve the Bradleys' daughters. I could not bring myself to look at them, but I'm sure they're horrible. I'm sorry to pass them on. I am giving them to you so you can prove how sick and evil John and Scarlett were. You didn't deserve the way you were treated and I hope these may help you set things right. You should have no doubt that you did the right thing.

> There is a photo inside each case. You will recognize the Bradley girls and John and Scarlett. There is also a man, I don't know his name, who I believe is the person you followed to the Bradleys' the night this all started. The Bradleys murdered him. You will find what's left of him in a walk-in freezer in the Bradleys' garage. The door to the freezer is hidden behind the junk next to the brown refrigerator.

On Friday there was a bunch of bear parts being stored there. I believe the bags in this envelope contain powdered bear gallbladders. You'll know more about that than I do. These are only a small sample of what I saw.

The dead guy and the Bradleys have been selling the bear parts to Izzy Feldman, the chiropractor. He's got some kind of Asia connection for it all. He doesn't know I have found him out. But after he learns that I've killed the Bradleys, he may run.

About half a mile northwest of the Bradleys' house, you will find a rocky outcropping. Look for a path fifty feet west of the Bradleys' back deck in the edge of the woods. It will lead you to a cave in the outcropping. This cave was used for storing the bear parts as well. I couldn't find anything there on Friday, but you may have better luck with real forensic help.

That's it. I did it. I wanted to do something exactly right before I went away. And I have.

You're a good man Steve. I have been lucky to know you. I hope you can feel something of the same thing about me. Please, let this take the demon of John Bradley off your back.

I have also done this for Ben Chandler, his wife and his daughters. The Bradley girls are living with them now. They deserve a new start in a better world. I know this will be a better world when the Bradleys can no longer stand in the same sunshine as good people.

I think I'll know you again,

Chip

P.S.

Ben and Jessica and the girls are in Hawaii and unreachable. They're going to need a ride home from the airport on Mother's Day at 2:00 PM. They have a lot of luggage. Ben has a trailer at his house. Take that with you. You and Ben should get to know each other better.

I put the letter, the DVDs and the bags in a padded envelope then overwrapped it with a couple layers of packing tape. It would take a knife to get it open.

I got the Beretta loaded, stuck it in the holster, put the whole thing in the side drawer of my desk. My cap, hiking boots, jacket, and day-pack were on the couch.

Done in the basement, I went upstairs and packed a week's worth of clothes and personal stuff in a blue duffle.

I kept out a pair of dark jeans and a green tee-shirt.

Time for another goodbye.

◆　◆　◆

I felt nervous all the way to town. I wanted to say the right things to Steve, without saying too much.

At Skip's, Steve was already sitting at a table.

Skip, publican deluxe, was there at my elbow. "You guys eating, or drinking, or both I hope? Pretty slow tonight."

Steve looked up, "I'll have an order of garlic fries and a porter."

"Black and Tan," I said, sitting down. "I'll have the fries too."

Skip said, "You got it" and went toward the kitchen.

Steve asked, "What's going on?"

"Oh, you know … It sure has been warm … great for hiking … been catching some good fish." The small talk was going to make me scream. I wanted to say something with weight.

Skip brought our beers. "Your fries will be out in just a minute."

Steve and I did a silent toast; clinked and sipped.

Then I opened a door I hadn't meant to. "Steve, this is pretty heavy, but I been thinking about it. Maybe turning sixty has something to do with it. What do you think happens to you when you die?"

"Wow," he said. "That *is* pretty heavy. You really want an answer?"

"Yeah, I do. I wish more people would talk about it."

"Well, I think there is God. I don't know what God is—energy or something. Everything is part of it. We come and go. But I don't think there's some kind of hell or heaven. I think that's just people making stuff up. Trying to be in control of something they're afraid of." Steve drained half of his porter; nervous work discussing the question of the ages. "So I think heaven and hell are probably more what you put yourself through while you're here than anything after you die."

"So you think if you're satisfied with your life, you're in heaven?" The pub owner, hands full, was heading our way.

"Yeah, something like that. You gotta follow your heart and be who you're supposed to be."

"Fries!" Skip dropped the baskets full of fat steak fries smothered in cheese and garlic in front of us and headed for the bar.

I looked back at Steve. "So, what happens to you if you kill somebody?"

"Why ... do you think I killed somebody?" Steve dropped his voice.

"No. Not asking about you," I said. "I just wondered what you thought. If you kill somebody can you be happy with yourself? Can you be in heaven?"

He didn't hesitate. "You kill somebody who deserves it, damn right. No question. Heaven is if you're sure."

"So who gets to decide who deserves it?"

"You thinking about anybody in particular now, Chip?" He ate a fry, his gaze never left mine.

"You mean the decider or the deserver?" I ate a fry out of my basket.

"I think we both know who I'm talking about," Steve said.

This was going exactly where I *hadn't* wanted it to.

"Well, it can't be the guy who made these fries 'cause they are fuckin' great!" I said.

"Asshole," Steve said and grinned.

We talked about anything and everything for the next two hours, but the subject of killing somebody never came up again.

Steve didn't ask me about what I wanted to show him. He'd let me bring it up when I was ready.

At 9:00 I said, "Hey, I gotta go. I got something for you out in the car."

I settled up for the beers and the fries. "Skip," I said, "You run a great pub. Thanks for everything."

Skipland said, "Uh, Chip … I think when you die you get to sit in a good pub, with a good friend, and eat and drink whatever you want." He winked and said, "See you around."

Steve and I walked across the street to my car. I grabbed the padded envelope off the back seat. "Steve, this is for you." I held it in both hands in front of me. "One thing before I give it to you. You have to promise you won't open it until tomorrow."

"What the hell Chip?" Steve looked at the tape-encrusted package. "What's it for?"

"No questions." I fixed him with a look. "Tell me you won't open it until tomorrow, or I'm not giving it to you."

"OK, I won't open it until tomorrow." He was irritated, didn't like the secrecy. "Any special time, any special place …

like behind the cemetery outhouse while I'm swinging a dead cat?"

"Yeah, glad you asked. You'll know when to open it. Wait until you know. Don't get out of bed at 12:01 and open it. At some point during the day, you'll absolutely know."

He took the package out of my hands and weighed it in his own. "That's all you're gonna tell me?"

"Let's just call it a ticket to heaven. Thanks Steve. I love you man." I hugged him; the first time ever.

Steve grabbed me and bear-hugged back, the envelope crinkling in his hand.

He turned, went back across the street and disappeared down the alley behind the Pub.

I laid out some clothes and was in bed by 10:00, hoping to get a few hours sleep before it all came together.

◆　◆　◆

I stared at the ceiling, watching the red numbers change, running through my plan and the timing; and all the things that could go wrong.

I went through a zillion permutations of everything that John and Scarlett might do. But I always came back to what I was sure of; they were greedy, they were lazy, and they were rotten enough to poach bears, rape kids and murder people for money. They wouldn't miss an easy payday when all they had to do was show up with the stuff tomorrow at 9:00 at Izzy Feldman's. And besides, they were two-and-a-half million short.

I stopped thinking about what could go wrong, went back to staring at the ceiling; 10:42 PM.

Then, I let myself start thinking about the car wreck. It filled my head, taking away all my thoughts about John and Scarlett, and what I would be doing in a few hours.

There was a blue blanket spread out in the sun on the pavement—and broken glass, broken bodies, shrieking metal, and burning gas all over my bedroom.

◆   ◆   ◆

It had been my turn to drive the Suburban. It was big enough to pull the U-Haul with all his stuff in it and we'd put all the last minute loose junk in laundry baskets in the back with our luggage.

They were both in his old white Toyota; me following.

Taking turns with the driving gave us all a good chance to have time with one another, and to really talk for the three solid days it took to get from Iowa to his first real job in Southern California.

It had happened on day three. We were almost there. I had let a couple of cars get between us, but I sat up high in the Suburban and could see his white car up ahead in the traffic.

I hadn't seen the van come across the median. I'd only seen the debris flying and the two cars in front of me swerving. One went left, the other went right. I came to a sliding, jarring halt in the median, trying to make sense of what had happened.

A red van sitting in the left lane was facing the wrong way, smoking, accordioned to half its normal length.

I was running, then starring through the passenger window. The driver was screaming; maybe thirty-five, red hair, pinned by the steering wheel; blood spraying out of his mouth, eyes wild. "So sorry! So sorry! Go check on them! Go check on them!" Blood bubbles on his lips.

On the other side of his van, through his window, I could see the buckled hood of a small white car sticking up into the sky.

I ran around the front of the van to the white car. It didn't look like his Toyota anymore. The windshield looked as if bricks had been thrown into it. I saw her behind the wheel; her head lying back on the headrest, looking up at the inside of the white roof.

He was lying across the gear shift, his head in her lap. I couldn't get her door open. No point in trying his. I got in the back door on her side, laid my hand on her forehead. She moaned, unable to see me through bludgeoned eyes, her lovely nose crushed.

I leaned between the seats to check on him; he wasn't moving. There was no blood and the seatbelt held his body in the seat. He had on shorts and his legs, twisted at impossible angles, looked like purple rubber tubes, not legs at all. The dash was pushed inward. A pair of black-framed sunglasses—his sunglasses—stuck in the center of the shattered windshield. His eyes were closed, his face a misshapen, flattened version of the one I had smiled at over breakfast that morning.

My eyes went back to her. She tried to lift her head. Her crushed lips were moving. No words.

"Don't worry, Suzanne, I'll get you both out. You're going to be OK." I may have been yelling. I may have been whispering. I may have been thinking. I may have been there two minutes or an hour.

From somewhere a Smoky Bear hat appeared. The eyes under the hat looked in the open door at me as I talked to her.

"Are you OK, sir?"

"Yeah, I'm OK. I was following them. But they're both hurt bad."

"Yes, I'm afraid they are. Just keep talking to them. There's a life flight on the way. Just keep talking to them. It should be here very soon."

Then the hat was gone.

I talked to him. "We'll be alright. We'll get to San Diego and get all the stuff unloaded into your apartment. "Maybe we'll get to see where you work before we go back home."

He was silent. She tried to move and moaned every couple of seconds.

"I'm not going to let you go to sleep. You stay here with me and when the helicopter gets here we'll have a ride. It'll be here soon and it will be OK. Don't go to sleep on me, OK? You hear me? Don't go to sleep on me."

I kept that up for an eternity. Smoke from somewhere burned in my nostrils.

An EMT van blasted up the median. Two teams got out. One went to the red van. The second team came to us.

A young woman in a blue uniform came in through the door opposite me. A young guy, the same uniform, stood at the door I had come through.

"I was following them. I didn't see them get hit. She's moving and trying to talk. He hasn't moved and his legs are badly broken."

"You're doing fine." This came from the young woman, now kneeling amid the junk on the back seat with me. She was taking pulses. Put needles in their arms and had IV tubes hooked to them in just a few seconds.

"Here, hold these above them," she said firmly, handing me the two bags. "Hang in there. We're going to have to do some work to get them out." She and the other blue uniform disappeared.

I spent the next forty-eight minutes in the back seat while they cut the car apart around us.

They covered all three of us with heavy padded blankets. A beefy guy with a helmet and a clear plastic face shield said, "OK. I want you to stay with them." He put a pad over my head. "I don't want to get any hot metal on you. Stay still."

I crouched under the blankets alone with them, holding the bags.

The shriek of the blade cutting the metal was deafening. At last the noise stopped. Someone lifted the blanket. Both front doors were gone, the windshield posts and part of the roof had been cut away. The passenger-side dash had been crudely chopped off.

She was lifted out of the front seat. Someone took her IV bag from me. She moved and moaned. They laid her on a blue blanket, spread out in the sun, on the concrete. She was stripped to the waist, lying there in the road. Round white monitor pads were stuck to her torso; wires ran to a machine being monitored by the young woman in the blue uniform. I wanted them to cover her up.

He was still in the front seat. His feet trapped in the twisted metal. They pulled the blanket back over my face and the scream of the saw cutting through the metal started again. They took the blankets away and lifted him from the car. Someone took his IV bag away from me. They laid him on a blue blanket spread out in the sun. And they put another blue blanket over his torso and face. I wanted them to uncover him.

Black boots with blue uniform pants above them walked around him as he slept there on the concrete of I-15 in the warm California sun.

"OK," the young man in the blue uniform said. "You can get out now. You did great ... just great."

As I got out of the car a helicopter came in, blasting dust into the air as it landed astride the white center line.

My wife died lying on that blue blanket. The guy in the red van, an epileptic, died when they pulled the steering wheel out of his chest. My son had died traveling to his first job, his life barely started.

I hadn't done anything but sit in the back seat of his car talking to myself.

◆   ◆   ◆

I looked at the red time on the ceiling of my bedroom—
11:30 PM. I'd lost some time, but I wasn't dreaming ... only
remembering.

The memory could never go away. But I had, at last, said
goodbye.

Sleeping was out of the question. I got up and made the
empty bed. I unplugged the clock. The time on the ceiling
disappeared.

I put on the clothes I had laid out, stuck my pocket knife
in my right pocket, the poker chip in my left, put my watch on
and went out to the kitchen.

No music. No Suzanne. Just the sound of an empty house
and me.

I made coffee and ate my AlphaBits. I stuck the bowl and
the spoon in the dishwasher, along with my favorite coffee
cup, started it up.

I poured the rest of the coffee into my stainless steel travel
mug and went down to my office. I checked my daypack; all
the usual stuff plus the floppy brown sandal-loafers.

I took the pistol out of the drawer. It felt important. The
Beretta's clip was full. The chamber was empty; safe. I clipped
the nylon holster onto the right side of my belt and slid the
weapon into it. It wasn't very heavy, but I was very aware it
was there.

I pulled on my camo jacket and cap, stepped out onto the
patio with my boots and pack.

The concrete was cold and hard under my wool socks.
The air was chilled and still. The stars were deafeningly
bright. I could see their gleam reflected off my beautiful river
as I looked south.

Silent.

Steam rose out of my cup, condensing on my nose and
cheeks as I sipped the hot coffee.

Calm.

What had I missed? What could go wrong? I leaned back in the still morning and looked straight up at a pure sky. "Nothing," I said, "Nothing."

I drank the last of my coffee, pulled on my hiking boots, shouldered my pack and started walking, one last time, to Jesus Is My Redeemer Lane.

Part 1 CHAPTER 24

The music started when I left the house behind. These boots are made for walking … Really? Nancy Sinatra singing in my head as I went up to kill John and Scarlett Bradley. Where did this crap come from?

That morning I didn't cut across Baldy and into the trees. Walking through the woods in the dark, even woods I now knew very well could be a bad way to screw up a good plan. I just stayed in the middle of Baldy Road, walking steadily up the silent mountain.

At Jesus Is My Redeemer Lane I stopped, held very still. No birds singing. No dogs barking. It was a clear, thinkable time; a time of no doubt.

I could have turned and walked away right then. Just called Steve and gotten the package back and told him to go arrest the Bradleys for being child molesters, bear killers, and Tree Man murderers. Pick the crime you hate best.

I could have spent some more great time over at Ben's house with the dogs and the river and J.J. and Bobbi McGee.

Maybe if I went back home my wife would be there again. I could have plugged in the clock, crawled in bed and imagined being close to her for a little while … and gone completely, perfectly insane.

I went up the lane and rounded the blind curve.

There was a light on in the hall window upstairs. One of the Bradleys was in the stinking blue bathroom.

The light winked off. I could visualize John walking across the hall, bare gut hanging over his underwear as he slumped toward the bedroom where Scarlett was drooling into her pillow, unaware she only had a few minutes left to dream her twisted pink dreams.

My footfalls made a satisfying crunching sound in the dark. I had to pay attention. I had to avoid the potholes and the big rocks.

When I got to the concrete in front of the garage, the place was dead quiet. I took off my cap, stuck it in the pack and put on the headlamp. I replaced my boots with the sandal loafers and headed for the porch steps. The Beretta was hard against my hipbone. Son of a Bitch! I hadn't put a round in the chamber! I clamped my eyes shut in the dark. "Great killer Chip—going into a dark house to shoot a couple of psychopaths with an empty gun."

I reached in under my jacket; the holster strap came loose with a huge, metallic SNAP!

I froze, waiting for a light to come on or a door to open; nothing moved.

As I pulled the pistol, it got hung up in the net lining of my jacket. I was hopelessly tangled up, five feet from the Bradleys' front steps. Might as well have been handcuffed.

I padded to the weeds and grass at the end of the garage. No windows on that side of the house. I snapped on the red night vision. Fumbled open my jacket. The rear sight was snagged like a fishhook. I ripped it free, leaving a hole in the lining and a chunk of netting on the sight of the pistol. I laid the gun on top of a stack of old tires and wriggled out of the jacket.

I picked up the Beretta, pulled the nylon off the sight and gingerly pulled back the slide, easing it forward with a barely audible click. I had seen the brass of the cartridge gleam in the red light on its way into the pistol's chamber. I stuck the gun back in the holster and left the damn strap unsnapped.

"There. Did you forget anything else Chip?"

With the headlight back off, I sneaked across the concrete to the front steps, dropping the jacket and my pack. My feet were now cold and wet from the grass. The sandal loafers were quiet, not waterproof. I shivered from the chill—and the adrenalin.

I was quiet up the steps, but the porch groaned. In the soft 1:45 AM atmosphere it sounded like a tree falling. I'd never done this in the dark. Had it been this loud before?

At the front door I stopped for a listen. A train moved through Sandpoint. The screen door spring made its long yawning sound. The hook rattled. The doorknob made a click. God, things made a lot of noise when you tried to be quiet.

I stepped in. Did I hear fat footsteps above me? Was there a shotgun trained down the steps?

I relaxed my shoulders. Standing two feet inside the place, leaving the entry door hanging open, getting used to the different light. The place still smelled like Pine Sol and dead meat.

I had to be leaving tracks. It wouldn't matter. Quiet mattered.

My plan was unfolding in this familiar, horrible house, with my pounding heart as a backbeat.

Bum, bum, bum—another one bites the dust.

I pulled the gun out. My performance with the pistol and the lining of my jacket hadn't done much for my confidence. I fought the urge to check the chamber again. "The bullet is still in there. Don't stop!"

I went dead ahead three feet to the stairs. There was something dark four steps up; a black hole in the gloom. The hole moved. I caught a gleam off his eyes. I went up, stroked him under the chin. Purring erupted as he rolled over on his back and stretched across the step. I stepped over. He dug his front claws into my ankle, wrapped himself around and hung on as I dragged him up the step. Adolph was playing seriously. He moved up to my calf with his front claws, ripping big grooves out of my ankle with his back diggers.

Dancing around in wet loafers, teetering on the edge, I rapped him, clunk!, between the ears with the barrel of the Beretta. He dropped off, flipped to his feet, thundered down the steps, crashing into a dining room chair as he beat it around the corner on his way to the kitchen.

"What the hell was that?" It was Scarlett. "You hear that?"

"Yeah. You stay here. I'll go check it out."

Their bed was moving.

Seven more steps to the top. I spent a lifetime on every one of them ... Grandpa, Dad, Wife, Son—rats in the corn crib, nothing personal—John and Scarlett.

On the twelfth step their bed groaned again, a light spilled out of their room. I hit the top, broke across the hall, rushed through the door into the light. Not what I expected; Scarlett sitting up in bed pointing a gun at my head, John standing, bringing the shotgun up at me. Scarlett pulled her trigger. A bee buzzed past my ear. The stinking room filled with thunder and lightning.

I opened my eyes, trying to focus, trying to hear, trying to think—my plan gone.

John was across the bed, shotgun across his chest. His body pinning Scarlett's feet. Scarlett sagged, mouth open, staring at the bloody mess of her right hand, a black pistol in her lap.

The Beretta was hot in my hand. How many times had I fired?

John moaned and sat up, his hand pressed to his naked belly. The shotgun slid off onto the floor showing me a hole punched through its steel side.

"What the fuck?" John, dazed, looked from his gut up to me.

Scarlett found her voice, shrill screaming, a nail in my brain. I leveled the Beretta on her eyes.

"Shut up! Both of you." I was startled at the new sound of my voice.

Her mouth snapped shut—click! Her little pistol thudded onto the filthy carpeting as she wound the bedspread around her gushing hand. John looked back at his belly, still confused. No blood. My slug had traveled through the steel of his shot gun and barely bruised his fat. He shook his head trying to clear the cobwebs.

"Both of you look here, at me." I waggled my pistol.

"You shot my hand off you motherfucker!" Scarlett shrieked. "Who the fuck are you? Oh Jesus it hurts!"

It was all I could do not to snap off another shot and silence her hellish screech. No, I'd been given another chance. I was back in control. Follow my plan now to the end.

Cold, insane hate ripped across John's eyes. His feet touched the floor and he tensed.

"No! Don't move. Sit right there and listen. I came here to tell you something. This shooting wasn't part of my plan. It shouldn't have happened."

John slumped. Somewhere in his dim brain he knew we'd had a couple of brushes in the past few days, but he couldn't get it. "Who the hell are you? I haven't done anything to you." He glared at me, brain squirming, the memory just out of reach.

"You don't know me. But what you've done, you've done to everybody—not just me. I'm here to finish what Steve Albright started that night he beat the hell out of you in your driveway."

John went tense again, voice rising. "You don't know what you're talking about! That fuckin' cop attacked me for no reason! I could have sued him and the county and the state from here to Sunday! But I didn't. I just said let bygones be bygones." He pleaded and whined. "And they came and took my little girls away. The fuckers just took 'em for no reason!"

"Yeah, we did the right thing," Scarlett couldn't shut up. "We don't deserve to be treated like this. She cradled her ruined hand, lowered her tone. "Look, what do you want? We got a lot of money!"

"Shut up you stupid bitch!" John's voice low and menacing.

I was completely sure about what would come next. They were going to know.

"You both have it all wrong. I'm the one who's gonna do the right thing. I know who you are. Now I want you to know exactly who I am.

"I'm the guy who has seen three little girls so afraid and damaged that they may be past saving. I'm the guy whose best friend was punished while monsters like you went free. I'm the guy who will not let you get away with rape and murder, no matter what our fucked up system says or thinks. I'm here because killing you may help others see how wrong the world has gone ... and maybe they'll do something about it.

John's dull eyes suddenly flickered with comprehension. It all snapped into clarity like a lens being turned. "Oh."

I looked carefully into his face. Something there changed just before the bullet hit with its terrible result.

"AAEEEEEEEEEE!" Scarlett screamed, throwing the bedspread over her head as she keened. I pulled it off.

She stopped screaming ... and at last was quiet.

They were dead. I had done it. They'd known why. They'd known it was coming, and they knew it had been me, an impersonal, calm stranger killing them.

I didn't feel any way about it but right.

As horrible as the shots and the gore and the screaming had been, there wasn't even a tickle in the back of my head that I had made the wrong decision. Or that I had made the decision for the wrong reasons.

For something to live, something's got to die ...

I left the Beretta with its holster on the bed; done with it.

At the bottom of the stairs I touched the cat between the ears, "Good luck Adolph." I closed the Bradleys' door for the last time.

I put my boots and coat back on, grabbed my pack, and walked back down Jesus Is My Redeemer Lane humming a song I couldn't quite place.

Part 1 CHAPTER 25

Funny, I hadn't even thought about what would happen to my house and all my stuff. I just left it. It would be some work, but my sisters could split it up.

5:00 AM. I had a train to catch.

A person can be tracked with their cell phone. My plan was to stick mine on a train bound for Canada. Half a block from the train crossing at the west edge of town, I pulled into the parking lot of a metal fabrication company. It was small and this was Sandpoint, no video cameras or lights anywhere.

I grabbed a Ziploc and the duct tape then trotted down the tracks alongside a parked train. It sat rumbling, waiting for another train to pass so it could use the tracks for its journey on north.

I made sure my phone was on, stuck it in the Ziploc, and attached it up under the front edge of a lumber car with several strips of tape.

There were footsteps in the gravel on the other side of the train. I froze against the car, breathing hard in the darkness.

"Shhh," A voice hissed, "I thought I heard something over there."

I held my breath, gripping the roll of tape in my fist.

"Aw, you're just hearing things. They don't even care anymore if we do this shit, as long as we don't throw the cans on the ground," a young voice speaking in a hushed, overly-confident tone.

The odor of spray paint wafted toward me. I could hear muted giggling and the sound of the metal ball rattling inside a spray can.

Squatting down to look under the car, I saw three sets of legs, silhouetted by a distant security light. "You kids better get the hell out of here!"

"Holy shit …" The legs levitated and vaporized.

I couldn't stand it. I ran too.

I parked the Audi on the dark side of the gas station a block down from Skip's Pub.

Nobody was around and the kid behind the counter didn't know me. I used the john, got a block of ice for the cooler and a pack of Lucky Strikes. What the hell. They couldn't cut too much time off what I had left.

I wanted to be on the news. I had rid the world of some monsters who were eating into my life. I hoped others would find the courage to do something about their own monsters.

The media release I'd written the day before was waiting in my laptop.

For immediate release:

Local Man Kills Child Molesters

Authorities were contacted early today by a man identifying himself as Charles "Chip" Crandle of Sandpoint, Idaho.

Mr. Crandle, 60, reported that he had shot and killed John Bradley and his wife Scarlett Bradley of 101 Jesus Is My Redeemer Lane, Sandpoint, Idaho.

Mr. and Mrs. Bradley were guilty of prolonged and repeated sexual attacks on their children.

Mr. Crandle, having seen the result of this abuse on the children, and the hardship and personal pain experienced by the girls and their foster parents, shot the Bradleys at approximately 2:00 AM this morning.

Mr. Crandle stated, "I don't care if they were troubled, or victims of bad parents, or just doing what people on their evolutionary path do. We have to do something other than blab about it on TV, or sit and hope it doesn't happen to us or someone we know. Get your hands dirty folks, or your life is just fuel for someone else."

Mr. Crandle is unavailable for further comment.

About Chip Crandle:

Chip Crandle was born in Iowa in 1954. He has led an average life, sometimes making choices which others found baffling. He has served as a son, a father, a husband, a brother, a liar, a helper, a healer, a life saver, and a speaker of truth prior to taking on his new role as societal janitor.

Crandle's vision reflects the philosophy of Joseph Campbell; "to not accept without choice the condition of the world. To participate in life courageously and decently, in the way of nature, not in the way of personal rancor, disappointment, or revenge."

-END-

A little wordy, but I thought it would have the sensational effect I wanted. I sounded crazy, but crazy sells. And who but a crazy guy would kill somebody, send a confession and run away?

I would blast it out right away—I wanted maximum coverage. I also wanted to be across the state line as the noise started.

I parked at McDonalds and fired up my laptop, found the free WIFI, and I was on.

I opened the media list and sent my release to about a hundred media outlets all over the country, as well as the Bonner County Sheriff's department.

This thing should go viral in about thirty minutes.

The girl at the drive-through window said, "Have a nice day," as she handed me the bag and coffee.

"I already have." I chucked my $15.00 in change in the Ronald McDonald House drawer under her window, pulled out of the parking lot and headed east.

You deserve a break today, so get up and get away ...

◆   ◆   ◆

I had executed my plan. Things had come together.

One more goal to accomplish; I wasn't going to prison—I was going to Oklahoma.

OK-LA-HO-MA where the wind comes sweepin' down the plains! Who was that, Gordon McCray? Whoever it was, he was singing it in my ear.

I'd stay north until I got to North Dakota, then head down through South Dakota, Nebraska and Kansas; avoiding the interstates as much as possible. The country is prettier on the real highways, and I was hoping the state troopers would be less common too.

Fast wasn't as important as invisible. And I only had to be transparent for a few days.

The Audi was ideal. There was absolutely nothing that tied me to it. Ben and Jessica wouldn't be looking for it for another couple of weeks. By then Ben would be fighting with the insurance company about who was going to pay for the Audi's replacement. I felt kind of bad about that but it was *him* who gave me the idea in the first place. And I had left him something for his trouble.

I was relying on the movies I'd seen and the murder mystery books I'd read to avoid being spotted. Probably pretty naïve, but it was the best I had.

I was trying to blend—just an old guy in a nice car on an early camping trip. I'd fit in with the camping crowd because I *was* one of the camping crowd. It would work. Campgrounds were used to dealing in cash, and most of them didn't have the kind of registration that would be easy to track, especially the Mom-and-Pop spots I was looking for.

I wasn't sure how hard anyone would be looking for me. How could anybody in their right mind string me up for removing John and Scarlett Bradley?

I supposed there would be someone who figured they were the victims of bad parents, or the system (whatever the hell that was), who would be looking to make sure the rights of everyone, except the raped girls and the butchered bears, were protected. So I was being careful on my speed and fitting the average old-guy profile.

My phone was headed to Canada. I had nobody to talk to and nobody calling me.

I'd also gotten rid of my laptop. I didn't think it had any kind of GPS, but I didn't know for sure so I'd chucked it out the window just east of Sandpoint. It landed with a flat splash as I crept across the Pack River Bridge heading for Hope.

I had food, cigarettes and more money than I'd need. And, I didn't have a gun. I was no threat, hiding in plain sight, just tooling down the road.

I went across the border into Montana and was met by one of the new Welcome to Montana signs—big and blue with some mountains in the middle of it. No clever sayings or themes. Good choice Montana.

Big Sky Country stretched out around me like a dream, and Oklahoma, the land of twisters, was several states to the east and south. For some reason, I knew I'd find what I was looking for when I got there. I was sure of it. My trip would be the better part of two thousand miles. I would see some country, camp out under the stars, maybe meet some interesting people, and then fly away.

Part 2 CHAPTER 1

The highway was almost empty. Like someone had told people to stay home. I was alone with my thoughts and the vivid images and final smells of the Bradleys' bedroom. John had seemed relieved at the end. After the shot, he actually looked at me like he understood. No hard feelings. Scarlett had gotten quiet. They had to be in a better place now.

I'd said more to the Bradleys in thirty seconds than I'd said in sixty years to the important people in my life. Well, it was all history now.

About 10:00, several highways merged together with the interstate and the traffic picked up. After no sleep, and everything else, I was starting to flat-line. The Lucky Strikes were on the dash. I'd crank down the window, pep myself up with the wind, and a smoke, and some music. I stuck a cigarette in my mouth then realized I had nothing to light it with. I hadn't gotten any matches, and there was no lighter or even an ashtray in the car. I had plenty of fire in the camping gear, but no way to get to it without stopping. Well, shit.

Trailer for sale or rent, I can't light my cigarettes … So I drove on with Roger Miller, the wind in my face and an unlit Lucky Strike stuck to my lips, fighting weariness as the white lines streaked beneath me.

A car was coming up fast in my rearview mirror. It pulled out to pass. I looked over. There was John Bradley; no shirt, a cup of coffee in one hand and a burning cigarette held in the fingers of the other. He grinned at me through a haze of smoke, his eyes the color of the red bullseye on the Lucky Strike pack. In the back seat, Scarlett directed steaming coffee into an oversized white cup. There were two bullet holes in the center of her forehead and the coffee was gushing out of them. She said, "Hey Chip, don't let it keep you up all night."

My right tires were buzzing on rumble strips. A wall of red lights over my hood. I was coming up on the car in front of me impossibly fast. An old blue Taurus, its brake lights blazing. A kid's face, eyes like pie tins, looking at me out the rear window. Another car filling the lane next to it.

I jammed on the brakes, braced for the impact, howled to a stop six inches off the Taurus. My belt snapped me back hard against the seat. A car rolled calmly to a stop in the left lane, next to my door, an attractive young woman glaring at me through her window.

There was tobacco stuck to my tongue. The kid in the back seat of the Taurus pulled a Tootsie Pop out of his mouth, grinned around missing front teeth, tapped imaginary ashes off the end of the paper stick.

The car coming up in my rearview mirror had flashing blue lights.

The lights moved over and screamed past on the shoulder; a state trooper and an EMT booking east.

There was a line of vehicles stalled in front of me as far as I could see. The lanes were filling in behind me. Traffic on the west-bound side was crawling. People were walking around everywhere between the cars.

And I needed to piss; seriously.

A steer, white-faced and red all over, came trotting down the median. His eyes were rolled back in cow panic. Those people not already out of their vehicles jumped out, heads popping up over car tops like prairie dogs out of their holes. A sea of phones appeared on extended arms, as normally sane people jostled for position to take photos of a cow dropping green shit pies in a grass median just east of Missoula.

That was my chance to take a walk south into the ditch where I blissfully pissed behind some scrub brush. I was done and back before the steer-in-the-median frenzy had died down.

We waited. I bummed a match from the Taurus driver. Not a bad guy. He gave me the whole book. THE MINT BAR, barely legible on the fuzzy cover, but the fire still worked. He and I talked about nothing and smoked. His kid sat in the back seat, played a video game and play-smoked his Tootsie Pop stick.

The word was that a truck hauling cattle had overturned. Hard to guess how many bodies, and of what species, were scattered in the road. Were there blue blankets being put down on the concrete up ahead?

The bad news for me; there had to be a bunch of cops around. The good news; they had their hands full. I had to think their priority would be getting the jam moving again.

Then my smoking buddy asked the big question. "I see you're from Idaho. How about that guy killing those child molesters up there this morning?"

I smoked. What was my story? Why hadn't I thought about it? "Uh, no ... Haven't had the radio on. Listening to music. What's the deal with that?"

The number on my license plates loomed in my brain; 7B for Bonner County, of which Sandpoint was the county seat. Would matchbook man whip out his phone and have some cops down here in a couple of seconds while I stood by with my thumb up my ass and smoked?

"... Killed these bastards this morning; just a few hours ago then called the cops. They think he headed to Canada. Can you beat that?" the guy said. "Where you from in Idaho?"

A glaze of sour-smelling sweat broke out under my shirt.

Sirens started screaming. Flashing lights moved toward us over in the westbound lanes. The whoop, whoop, whoop deafening as one of the troopers, followed by the boxy EMT, flashed past. My heart beat rose to meet the tempo of the sirens.

There was a frenzy of activity on the highway-turned-parking lot. Doors started slamming and tailgates closed. A lot of cigarettes were stomped into the concrete.

"Nice talking to ya," the matchbook man turned and disappeared into his old car.

Slowly, ever so slowly, the traffic moved. I was just another car in the crowd and the troopers directing traffic around the overturned cattle truck didn't give me a second look.

It was 12:30; I was not as far east as I had expected to be. But my smokin' buddy *had* said something about the killer going to Canada.

♦ ♦ ♦

I was starting to feel thin. Like the wind could blow through me. And I was just about out of gas.

Checkerboard, Montana wasn't very big, but it had a gas station-convenience store right next to the highway with a bar in it. I figured I might as well fill the tank, get something to eat, have a coffee and then push on for another hundred miles or so. Five hundred was the magic number, not sure why, just seemed like a good distance to be away from the house on Jesus Is My Redeemer Lane.

I filled the Audi's tank and went inside with cash—I would never swipe a stinking credit card again.

At four in the afternoon the place was mostly empty. Two old cowboys were taking up one third of the stools; bottles of Bud in front of them and an ashtray full of butts between them.

"Hello, honey." If a pack of cigarettes could talk, it would have that voice. "You can pay me for the gas. Anything else you want? There is a cooler down past the end of the bar and some groceries on the shelves around the corner. The ice is outside and cold beer is back here, with me, where these no-goods cannot get to it!"

Wow, no contractions. "Thanks, I'll have a look around," I said.

I got coffee and little doughnuts. The cashier's look told me absolutely nothing. Coffee and doughnuts at 4:00 in the afternoon on a hot April day? OK by her, money in the till.

She laid a long, smoking cigarette on the edge of the counter. Red lipstick smeared the filter. "That will be seventy-four dollars and sixty cents please."

She enunciated perfectly, and there was a please on the end. I appreciated that.

"Here's eighty buc…er, dollars."

I slid four twenties across the counter. "Please buy my two friends here a beer. I don't have time to stop and have one with them, but I think that's my loss."

Slim and Lefty, who had been looking at me the whole time, broke out in ear-to-ear grins. Each had a face that demanded some storytelling; but five hundred miles was my goal and I was going to make that.

"Thanks buddy." Slim, a man who believed in the wisdom of just enough words.

"Yeah, thanks friend. We'll catch *you* next time." That Lefty; what a blabbermouth.

"Thank you sir, and please do come back," the smoky cashier said. "You seem to be a really nice fellow."

Oh my tattooed beauty, if you only knew.

There was a small TV just behind her, volume turned down, some kind of talking head with a line of words crawling across the screen below him.

I had a dizzying flash of a wanted man's face—my face—appearing on the screen. The two cowboys turned slowly from their free beers to look at me with narrowed eyes. Then they cast sidelong glances toward each other, and then at the cashier.

"It's him! It's Him! HE's HIM! "

The enunciator pulled a nasty little sawed off .410 shotgun, blinked her big green eyes at me, and blasted my spine in half.

"I got him boys."

Good as any end I guess.

But the TV just flashed silently on. My picture didn't show up. Nobody cared. The beer was cold. I was paying. And that was what counted right then.

The road goes on forever and the party never ends … Robert Earl's fiddle player sawed away, finishing the song as I hit the gas and headed east crossing and re-crossing the Musselshell River.

A hundred miles to go. I needed a place to sleep.

About an hour later, I spotted a faded, peeling sign; Fifty-eight miles to the ROUNDUP CAMPEROUNDUP. Under the words was a cartoon cowboy, bowlegged beneath a huge hat, leading his sway-backed trail-weary horse.

Fifty-eight miles; about another hour away. Looked like my kind of place.

The next sign for the CAMPEROUNDUP was at fifty miles, and thereafter every ten miles until I had the cottonwood trees of Roundup, Montana in view.

The signs had all looked the same, except the cowboy's horse steadily changed positions; finally winding up inside a tent with the cowboy standing outside. The horse's head and neck stuck out the tent door, his face turned to the highway with an insider's wink. Get it? The horse is in the tent and the cowboy is outside! Can you beat that? Clip clop, ha-ha.

Roundup was a nice town. The population sign said 1788. It had a river running through it and the Bull Mountains all around it; green, clean and pretty.

I checked in at the CAMPEROUNDUP office; $22.50 cash got you hot showers and shade trees by the river. The large guy behind the counter, Earl on his name-tag, was OK; one of those western guys who had a freezer full of elk all year long. He didn't even look at my registration card. That was good. I'd neglected to put any of the correct information on it.

◆　◆　◆

I was bent over next to the Audi, breaking up a bag of ice, when the State Trooper pulled in.

I stayed down, heard feet on gravel crunching toward me. Here came a Smokey Bear hat, a five-foot-two woman under it; cute, young, packing a Glock pistol, alone and in no hurry.

I dumped the ice around the beer in my cooler and snapped down the lid.

I wadded up the bag and tossed it in a high arching shot toward the trash can. It expanded like a parachute, fluttering to the ground five feet short.

"There's a fine for littering in Montana." The lady trooper, about ten feet away, a smile on her tanned face.

"Well I couldn't blame you," I said turning from my meager effort. "I oughta pay a fine for a shot like that." I scooped up the bag and gave it a slam dunk into the can. "There, I guess I can still make a layup."

"Yeah, thanks for that. Camping with Earl tonight?" she said.

"Who? No, I'm alone. Been on the road a couple of days." I'd been so cool with the trash shot, now I was rambling, heart pounding. The dull ache of fatigue was keeping me from thinking clearly. I re-upped the nervous sweat.

"Oh sorry, I meant Earl, the owner here. I supposed you had already met him since you had the bag of ice."

She stepped a little closer, checking me out, seeing if I'd been drinking … or maybe if my face matched the picture on the screen in her SUV? Had my picture gotten out already?

"Oh Earl! Sure. Sorry, it's been a long, hot day on the road. Yeah, I'm staying here with Earl." I was trying desperately to be just another gray-haired guy on a camping trip. "He fixed me up with spot 13, down by the river."

"The river's nice." She was close enough to get a good look and smell alcohol.

Thank God I hadn't popped a beer on the way in.

She gave me a look. I couldn't help but feel like she knew something; something she wasn't saying. "Well, I'm about done for today," she said looking at her wristwatch. "Just stopped by for a Drumstick out of Earl's freezer. You know the ice cream kind? Get yourself a shower and some rest—and drive carefully sir."

I guess my thoughts about her thoughts were just thoughts. "Thanks officer, I'll do that."

God I was weary. Things were starting to swim in front of my eyes, and it was so bloody hot and dusty out there. I put my butt against the hot fender of the Audi, afraid I might pass out.

"You OK?" She paused opening Earl's tragically dented aluminum door.

"Yeah, just fine. Ready to get the tent up and lay down, I guess. Thanks."

◆ ◆ ◆

Down by the river, parked right next to the little sign with the 13 on it, was a pair of beat-up Harley Davidsons. I could practically smell the oil and gas fumes coming off of them. The two guys I expected to see were there, taking their gear off the back of the old hogs. They glared at me as I rolled to a stop.

"Hi fellas." I gave them my best Midwestern, harmless accent. "Hot enough for you?"

"Yeah, plenty hot."

The shorter of the two fixed me with a fuck-with-me-and-get-stomped look and went back to unrolling a greasy-looking canvas pup tent in the middle of the camping space I had just paid for.

I was letting off the brake—just moving on made the most sense. I wasn't going to be there that long. It was hot. I was tired and hungry and I smelled bad. Just let it go.

"Uh, did you guys know you're in spot 13 ?" It was out of my mouth and out the window before I knew what had happened.

"The bigger one, the one with the blue gothic letters running down both arms, looked up and said, "No shit Sherlock? So fuckin' what?"

"So, have a good day." I smiled at the dull grey eyes, and the ink, and the stink and idled across the campground to spot 66, back by the office.

God I hate it when people meet my lowest expectations.

Spot 66 wasn't spot 13. It was fifty-three spaces different. It wasn't by the river. And it wasn't what I had paid for.

Compared to child molesting and murder, did the difference between spot 13 and 66 really matter? Yeah, it did. But I was too beat to think about it right then.

Over toward the river, at spot 13, blue smoke belched and the lovely sound of the river was drowned by the ear-busting roar of the engines. They left in a swirl of dust, giving me the bird on the way by, the blatting echoing all the way across Roundup.

See ya later boys …

I got everything organized for sleeping and eating. A group of swallows swooped and rolled over the campground and the river. It was that time of day when insects hatch, swim up and escape the water on new wings.

One of the little birds dipped low over me. It banked in and landed on the edge of my picnic table, not three feet away. I'd always considered the swallow a drab bird, but that night, up close I saw rich greens and blues, blacks and greys shimmering in the waning light.

Beautiful in flight and now more beautiful than I had known, it studied me closely, as a friend would. Had it been my wife, I would have expected a poignant question. The question didn't come. It dropped off the table, skimmed the ground, circled me twice then did a joyous loop and a roll and disappeared behind a cottonwood tree near spot 13.

Watching it go, I felt light ... ready to fly.

◆ ◆ ◆

It was just about dark. My steak had been superb, the beer ice cold. I sat, uncoiling. So far from where I'd begun.

The Harley Boys came back, headed for my spot. My spring wound back up a little.

They blasted up and down the lanes of the campground; dogs barked, babies cried, some fun.

A guy about my age, smoking a cigarette and watching the last light, leaned against the picnic table in *his* spot, looked at me and mouthed the words, "fucking assholes."

I nodded back.

He went into his motor home.

I got in my tent. I thought about John and Scarlett—my words, their last seconds. No trouble there; none at all. Then I was in clouds, flying through puffs of white sugar. I was under them, in them, above them. I flew with them and before long I couldn't tell where I ended and they began. It seemed weird at the time; why was I in sugar clouds?

Then it didn't matter and I flew and flew, faster and faster, and the stars came out and I could see it all and everything was just sweet and effortless.

◆ ◆ ◆

At 4:58 AM I poured myself a cup.

"Coffee ready?" It was my neighbor from the motor home. He sat smoking his first. His bug candle was lit, making undulating, spooky, Bradley-garage shadows.

"Sure is," I stage whispered back. "Want a cup?"

I got up and walked over with my coffee pot and a cigarette. "I don't know how to make less than a full pot, be a shame to waste it."

He smiled in the candle light, held out a travel mug. "Thanks, thanks a lot."

"Spare a match?" I said, always a great way to break the ice, braving lung cancer and emphysema together in the pure Montana air.

"You bet." The guy snapped a flame onto the end of my Lucky.

"Pete Reed," he said, holding out a big hand. I could hear movement inside Pete's motorhome. A light glowed on the other side of a curtained window.

"Roger Miller," I said. My neighbor was a strong guy. He gave me a good grip without trying to be impressive about it.

"Too bad about the neighbors," I said jabbing my cigarette in the direction of spot 13.

"Yes, it seems there are more of that kind around all the time." He tapped ashes into an empty soup can sitting on the table. "When did it become OK for that kind of crap to go on?" He stared at the end of his cigarette, not expecting an answer.

I let that slide for a couple of beats. The light was gaining on the dark.

"I don't think it is OK," I spoke in a low voice. "Too bad we've all become so afraid, don't you think?"

He looked up at me when I said that; took a drag and let the smoke out slowly. "Maybe we all aren't as scared as everybody thinks we are."

"Be good to do something about it … wouldn't it?" I sipped coffee.

"Got anything in mind?" he said.

Sometimes you just make a connection. He knew. I knew.

"I've always got something in mind." I grinned at him. "You know what I like in the morning? Coffee with neighbors; coffee with a lot of sugar. But the thing is, I don't have any with me—sugar that is."

"Oh, well I've always taken mine black, but Nancy, that's my wife, loves some sugar in her coffee." Pete Reed cast a look toward the glowing window of his motorhome where a silhouette moved.

He looked amused as hell, or maybe pumped up; more alive than just a few seconds ago. "I'm sure she'd be happy to loan you some." He got up, opened the motorhome's door. Said something I couldn't make out. He came back and shoved a half-full, five-pound bag of sugar across the table in my direction. "Think that'll do it?"

"Oughta work," I grinned. "So what does your wife think about sharing sugar with neighbors?"

"Oh one thing about Nancy, she is a generous person."

I took Nancy's sugar, dumped a good amount into the pot, swirled the contents. Light was leaking over the edge of the Bull Mountains.

Pete stood, snapped his fingers. "Wait a minute." He stuck his head in the motorhome again, returned with a plastic funnel.

We struck out in the greyness toward campsite 13.

As we got closer, we could hear loud snoring and a voice coming out of the canvas tent between the Musselshell and us.

"Dickey, Dickey, oh baby boy you are too sweet," said one of The Harley Boys. The snoring of the other continued unabated.

I choked back a giggle. Pete grimaced, bugging his eyes. Then a deep, deep chainsaw duet of snoring resonated from the tent.

The motorcycles leaned on kickstands. Pete unscrewed one of the gas tank lids, stuck the funnel in. I glugged about three cups in. The steam rising and the smell of the coffee and the gas mingled into a strange testosterone blend of go-juice.

Pete gagged on his own giggle, and screwed the cap back on while I opened the other bike's tank.

The snoring from the tent was steady.

He stabbed in the funnel and I emptied the rest of the coffee and sugar down the bike's gullet. It gurgled and bubbled up all the way to the top.

"Holy Shit!" we ran laughing back to his table and got there before our coffee had gone cold. We lit up, trying not to wake up the campground as we convulsed in glee.

"Think they'll have any clue who did that?" Pete sipped, smoked, snickered.

"Well they pissed off everybody in the campground, so they'd have to weed through about forty people to figure it out. I expect to be two hundred miles away by the time their hogs go belly up." I grinned back at Pete and extended my hand.

"Been fun," Pete said. You take care."

"Oh, that I will."

We probably hadn't made much difference, but some things just have to be done

◆   ◆   ◆

I stopped by the office on my way out of camp. Earl was there. He had just pushed the brew button. I looked at a clutch of breakfast sandwiches wrapped in foil, piled under a heat lamp. It all smelled good. I tried one of the foil hockey pucks.

"Hey Earl, not bad," I said. "I'll have a coffee too." I filled a cup and flipped him a hundred. "Been a pleasure staying here my friend. Keep the change."

His eyes shot side to side. A look I'd seen at the Conspiracy Theory table a thousand times.

"By the way … uh … the radio says it looks like that guy, who killed those two child molesters over in Idaho, may be headed this way." Earl's eyes went blink, blink, blink. That woman trooper you were talking to last night, Sammi Holt, she was talkin' about it too."

"No kidding? What's this guy supposed to look like?" I said it as casually as I could, fighting the urge to race out the door and see how long it would take the Audi to go from zero to a million.

"Older guy, I guess," Earl said. "Not like you … uh … have a safe trip. Stop back some time." Blink, blink, blink.

◆　◆　◆

The Smokey Bear hat still looked pretty good on Officer Holt as she came around the end of the CAMPERROUNDUP office. Her gun was snapped safe in the holster.

"Did you get some rest?" she said, left hand reaching up to the edge of my raised tailgate.

"Ah, yeah, I'm feeling like a million bucks today." I grabbed a bottle of water from my cooler, pushed down the lid. "Ready to hit the road."

"A good day to travel. You headed east?" Sammi had wonderful eyes, dark and deep.

"Yeah, I should be in Wisconsin in a couple of days."

"That sounds nice. I hear there were some bikers disturbing people in the camp last night. That true?"

She was so calm it made me jumpy. "Well, I saw them leave while I was cooking my supper. I went to bed. Didn't hear a thing until the birds started up this morning."

"Earl says they took your spot. That right?" Her arms went across her chest.

"Well, yeah, but I was so beat, and they were already setting up so you know, what the hell. I just found a different spot. No sense making a hassle over a little thing like that."

I pictured their fat asses dragging down the shoulder of Highway 12, hundred-degree heat cooking the half a brain they had between them.

"Sounds like you're a reasonable guy." She shifted her weight, pulled a pair of aviators out of her breast pocket. "Sometimes people aren't so reasonable and take things into their own hands when they shouldn't ... even if they're right."

She paused and said evenly, "I used to think about that a lot—while my daddy was hurting my little sister ..."

I stood bug-eyed next to my stolen car.

"If I were you," she said, "I'd think about setting up over in Wisconsin for a while." She put the aviators on, got in her car and went west.

Part 2 CHAPTER 2

In ten seconds I was in my car headed east. Trooper Sammi Holt loomed large in my mental rearview mirror. Her comment could not have been a cruel coincidence. I could not be imagining things. Somehow she had figured out who I was, but had reasons to look the other way.

What had I forgotten, or said, or done that led her to me so quickly? I hadn't seen a paper, been online, or watched a TV for more than a day. Was my face appearing on the news and America's Most Wanted?

Two people with holes in their heads seemed like another lifetime ago—not yesterday—and I was still at least a couple of days, and a lot of open territory, away from Oklahoma.

I figured I'd better stick to the local roads and away from the interstates. Trooper Holt had given me a break. I didn't think for a minute that I would be as lucky the next time.

I fight authority, authority always wins … John Mellencamp took me down the road fast. I headed east through a series of little cow towns: Delphia, Musselshell, Gregstone, Sumatra, Ingomar, and Vanada. I'm sure they all had fascinating stories behind their names. Towns always do if you can find the old-timer at the coffee shop and have the time to sit down with them. Like Lefty and Slim back at the Checkerboard Bar.

At Forsyth, I made a pit stop. I was about two hours from North Dakota. I would cross the line, turn south and skirt down along the border into South Dakota where I planned to spend the night in the Badlands.

Hardly any traffic going either way. I kept my speed just over the limit, like any good westerner, and crossed into North Dakota at about 8:00.

The sign said: North Dakota-Welcome to the West Region. It had a picture of Teddy Roosevelt on it. Bully! Not a bad sign.

I stopped in Marmarth for another cup of coffee, a pack of powdered sugar doughnuts and a few gallons of gas. I didn't want to have any chance of running low.

From Marmarth I headed straight south, thirty miles, and into South Dakota.

The sign there said: South Dakota: Great Faces, Great Places. A sappy line. There was a curvy illustration of the presidents carved on Mount Rushmore. The illustration would have been enough.

In the next three hours I saw one beat-up pickup going north and a power company cherry-picker truck headed south. About 11:00 I pulled into a tiny town in the Custer National Forest on the Little Missouri River. The sandblasted sign said: Camp Crook, POP 63.

The place looked dusty and harmless. I'd chance a quick stop and then I'd get on down the road.

I parked next to a line of cars at the Camp Crook Corner Bar and Café, got out and stretched the cramps out of my legs and back. A gasoline engine stuttered somewhere behind the low, white building; otherwise everything was quiet. I walked into what had to be the best café in town.

Not a soul in the place.

"Back here in the yard," a woman's big voice from behind the kitchen's pass-through order window. It was a window through which a few hundred miles of burgers, pancakes, and hot beef sandwiches had been slid by generations of short order cooks. A stainless steel wheel, with a green order slip, hung crookedly from a vertical shaft in the center of the window.

The woman's voice called again, "Come on back if you'd like; have some ice cream. Come on ahead through the kitchen."

Why I didn't leave right then I'll never know. Maybe I was ready for everything to stop, or maybe I was too tired to think straight. Whatever the reason, I couldn't resist her invitation. I bumped behind the end of the counter. The heart of the diner, its coffee maker, was cold. A silent ice machine drizzled water through a tube into a floor drain.

The spotless kitchen was a jumble of stainless steel pots and pans, cooking utensils, stacks of ironstone plates, and Pisa-towers of grey plastic tumblers. I went past the stainless-steel door of a walk-in freezer; not curious at all about what was in there.

Framed in the open back door was a group of maybe forty people, scattered at picnic tables under an ancient grove of cottonwoods. The Little Missouri flowed behind them perfectly.

I realized I was framed in the doorway; a life-sized wanted-for-murder-poster, with forty people staring at my face. Undoubtedly most of them had concealed weapons and were about to use them.

"Come on out and help us eat some of this before it all melts." It came from a round woman of indeterminate age. She sat at the end of a table, dressed in a tie-dyed Muu Muu. There was a toddler on her knee. The little girl's apple face was a fly-trap of sticky brown goo. Another kid, maybe seven years old, leaned against Muu Muu's big soft hip. Chocolate ice cream dripped down the front of his striped shirt and he grinned at me as he rooted more of the melting mess out of the soggy orange cone with his little pink tongue.

In the middle of Muu Muu's table sat a gaggle of brown cardboard containers. A tall thin man wearing a beat-up ball cap with a bucking horse on its front was scooping brown globs into a bowl.

The rest of the crowd was working on devouring their treats out of cones, bowls, plates, cups; and in one huge man's hands, a sauce pan and a long-handled serving spoon.

The tall guy grinned and held the bowl out to me. "Power's been off for a couple a days; might as well take a load off. Have some before it all runs out the bottom of the cans and the cats get it. Chocolate OK? We're out of everything else."

I couldn't argue with that. They hadn't fired at me yet, and if I ran now they'd be on to me. I took the bowl and sat.

"What happened to the power?" I said, digging into the melting mound. "I would think your walk-in freezer would keep stuff pretty cold for a long time, even without electricity."

"Yep," said the ice cream man. "It will, but we got the whole town's meat and other stuff in there right now. I got a generator keeping power to it, but it's not big enough to run more than the freezer."

Then I got the background on the power outage.

"Roger Stevens cut something big with his backhoe while working on the riprap along the river. It's a wonder he didn't end up like burned toast. Been a power company guy down there for a couple of days working on it, but being close to the water like that, I guess they have to do something special." He paused to wave at a couple of flies circling the ice cream containers. "Anyhow, it should come back on soon. This ice cream wouldn't fit after everybody else's stuff was in there, so we invited everyone over."

An impromptu ice cream social on a strangely hot spring day, with the better part of the population of Camp Crook; all of them, I was sure, trying to figure out where they'd seen me before.

"I'm Greg Shanks," I said, somehow bringing up the name of a college buddy I hadn't thought of in forty years. Rather than waiting for the where-are-you-headed question I said, "I'm taking some of the back roads; seeing the country." I hoped I hadn't stepped on any toes with the "back roads" comment.

I hadn't.

"Well, that's a refreshing way to see the country," said Muu Muu. "It's really special if you take your time and get off the pavement, huh? I'm Muu Muu Moss, and that tall drink of water with the ice cream scoop is my husband. Everybody calls him Judge."

I almost choked. Her name really was Muu Muu; it fit her just like the dress.

I recovered. "Hi Muu Muu ... Judge. Thanks for this," I said holding up my spoon. "It's really hitting the spot. Tell me, what's Camp Crook's claim to fame?"

A light danced across Muu Muu's eyes and she said, "Judge, run in and bring the Tipperary picture out here will ya? I think Greg here might enjoy knowing about all that."

I stifled a smile. I suspected that *running in* was something that Judge had not included in his repertoire for about sixty-five years.

"Sure thing, lovey," he gave Muu Muu a big smile and wink. Something pleasant passed unspoken between them. Judge laid down his scoop, took a swipe at the flies, and ambled off toward the back door of the café.

"He'll be back in a sec," Muu Muu said. She shifted the little girl from her knee to the table. The boy still clung to her hip, staring at me as kids will do when they encounter a stranger.

"Ardel!" Muu Muu spoke in a loud tone intended to be heard across the conversations at all the tables. "Ardel, this fella wants to hear the story of Tipperary."

I did? No ... I had no time for this ... but I couldn't just get up and run. So I nodded, grinned and waved at all the ice cream eaters who were now shifting and buzzing.

An ancient man, brown and furrowed, cowboy hat as much a part of him as his hands, rose from his seat. He moved toward me, as everyone at every table motioned and murmured, coming to a standstill where I could see the pearl snaps on his brown plaid shirt and the big rodeo buckle at his waist. The sharp crease down the front of his starched Wranglers ended on deep brown boots that pegged him to the ground.

The cowboy stood there, a living piece of the town's past, like the ancient cottonwood trees shimmering above it and the Little Missouri River running next to it. Ardel, the river and the trees; the oldest living things in Camp Crook, South Dakota.

He stuck out a gnarled hand and said, "Ardel Canutt."

"Greg Shanks," I said gripping his rough hand, my insides twisting, wondering why I wasn't still strapped in the Audi making miles.

He held onto my hand while studying my face. He seemed to make up his mind about something, stuck his thumbs in his pockets and looked toward the back door of the café.

I fully expected a big sheriff with a big hat and a big gun to step out. But no, it was Judge carrying a huge framed picture; its backside toward me, hanging wire bouncing against yellowed paper. It obscured all of him except his head and his legs below the knees. His face sprouted a big grin when he saw Ardel standing there at the end of my table. Judge propped the frame up against a table, went and sat beside his wife and whooped, "Let'er buck Ardel!"

The frame held a photograph of a dark horse, bucking a hapless cowboy off into the dirt of a rodeo arena. A brass plate screwed into the center of the frame's bottom said, "Tipperary, The King of the Outlaw Horses" Circa 1920.

I ate my last spoonful of ice cream and pushed my bowl aside; stuck, no way to escape. I took a long breath. What the hell, it was pretty nice there under those trees.

"Well young fella," (meaning me), said Ardel Canutt, "What you have before you is a photograph of the greatest bucking horse that ever lived." He stopped and looked up into the cottonwoods, emphasizing the serious nature of the story.

"For about twenty years, many a cowboy tried to ride him and many a cowboy ended up picking himself up out of the dirt or being hauled off on a stretcher while the crowds cheered. The horse's name was Tipperary, like the song the British Tommies sang during both Wars. It's a long way to Tipperary ..." Ardel's steady grey gaze bored into me and then swept across the entire group under the trees.

Nobody said anything, but they all looked pleased, settling in, and I joined them.

"The horse that would be known as Tipperary was born sometime in 1910 over in Montana on a ranch owned by Elmer Wichham, just a little west of where we're sitting right now. He was a dark bay; no white on him. He stood a little over fifteen hands high and had eyes that glowed red in the dark, like the devil playin' a guitar."

We all sat stone still. A passing breeze made the leaves of the cottonwoods chatter briefly before going limp. A guy behind me said in a low voice, "Devil playin' a guitar. Gol Dang I love that part." He was met with a round of shushs from the crowd.

"As is the custom in these parts," Ardel went on, "The horse ranged free until he was coming on his fourth summer. Then he was rounded up along with a big herd and corralled, waiting to be broke to saddle and rider. But the boys who took him in were in for a big surprise." Ardel took a deep breath and let it out in a huge stage whisper saying, "A REAL big surprise.

"When they closed the gate behind that horse, he didn't like it one bit, no sir! He laid back his ears and commenced to snortin', jumpin', fartin', blowin' snot, and tryin' to strike anything or anybody that got close to him!" Ardel was talking faster now, swinging his arms and swiveling his hips, like a rearing horse.

"The cowboys figured he'd bite their heads off if they got too close, and he was making all the rest of the herd nervous—their eyes showing white while they skittered around, knocking each other into the rails of the corral. The foreman had three of his best hands converge on the horse from different ways to throw their ropes on him. The first two got ropes around his head. Then he reared up and the third hand got one of Tipperary's legs, wrapped the rope around his knees, and brought him down hard, thrashing and screaming in the dirt. While those boys held him tight with their ropes, several others held him down. That was one pissed off pony let me tell you."

Ardel surveyed his audience; he had them transfixed. "It was no easy task, but they managed to get a halter on him. They tied it off short to a big Ponderosa log lying in the middle of that corral. They say that log was more than twenty feet long and three feet across; green, wet, and heavy as a locomotive.

"Then they went to supper, figuring a night tied up short would take some of the piss and vinegar out of that bay."

The crowd nodded and agreed. Being tied up short to a big log all night would take the piss and vinegar out of anybody.

"Well sir, after dark a thunderstorm came up, a big one with terrible thunderheads thousands of feet in the sky and lightening that lit up everything like the Fourth of July. The wind blew and the rain came sideways all through that terrible, long, loud night. Dogs howled and cattle got French-fried out on the banks of the Little Missouri right where they stood. Grown men hid under their beds; afraid the storm might take the roof right off their house and suck their little children up into the air!"

I looked over toward Muu Muu. She was taking in the story like it was the first time she'd ever heard it.

Ardel directed his yarn back to me, as if I were the only one there.

"And when the storm was over, and they came out the next morning to saddle and break that dark bay— the log, the horse and the whole shebang was gone—vanished! Like a bolt of lightning had carried 'em away!

"All the rest of those green horses were still there and the gate was still locked up tight with a big length of heavy log chain. The damnedest thing them cowboys had ever seen, and let me tell you son, it spooked 'em pretty good."

I realized I was sitting there with my mouth hanging open. I was more than half buying this; maybe because I wanted to, maybe because it was apparent the whole town believed it all.

"So the three boys who had roped him the day before, mounted up and rode out to find him. By noon, none of them had come back and everyone was getting pretty worried, what with the rain making the Little Missouri run up out of its banks.

"Just before sunset, four lathered up, riderless horses came jogging up to the corral. Three wore saddles, but the one leading 'em had no rig except a halter with a frayed lead rope on it. It was that wild bay horse the three riders had been out looking for.

"Not a one of those three cowboys, nor their bodies, was ever seen again. The story in the Harding County Tribune said that they were presumed drowned trying to cross the swollen Little Missouri River in search of a runaway horse. Those who knew 'em well said they'd never believe those experienced cowhands would have tried a stunt like that. No sir; they figured those boys had met their ends in a black and mystifying way, out there chasing that devil-eyed bay horse. Meanwhile ..."

I loved it. Ardel had said meanwhile.

"Back at the corral, the fellas got several loops on the wild bay and dragged him into the corral which, by the way, was over there." He pointed to somewhere on the other side of the café. "Between the livery barn and where the Old Camp Crook hotel once stood; both of which burned under mysterious circumstances in '22. But I'm not going to get into speculations about that at this time."

Apparently Ardel knew plenty about the dirty laundry of Camp Crook, but knew enough not to divulge it all in one fell swoop. He leaned toward me, delivering his words measured and sure.

"After about an hour of wrasling—two men with busted legs from kicks and another one missing the end of his nose from being bit—they forced the horse into a chute and cinched a saddle on 'em. A fella named Ed Marty, known by all present as a pretty good hand, climbed on.

"They say that damn horse's skin moved back and forth like wheat waving in the wind. He stood on his head and then sunfished so hard Ed Marty didn't know whether to clutch or spring; and he went down over the bay's shoulder—SPLAT in the dirt—after only three jumps, while the whole town stood by as witness."

A wave of a chuckles ran through the crowd as Ardel said, "SPLAT," taking the side of the hero horse whose picture sat against the picnic table in their midst.

"So them that cared gathered up the pieces of Ed Marty, arms and legs and head and trunk, and threw them all in a jumble on the billiard table over in the hotel. Then with the help of the doctor, they figured out more or less where each piece fit and patched that cowboy back together with barbwire, saddle strings, and pine tar."

Damn. Ardel was good.

"The doctor, Doc Latham was his name, poured himself a double shot of whiskey from a bottle standing on the bar and said, 'Well boys, here's to your health and God Damn a horse that won't be broke.' He threw back the shot, thumped his patient on the chest and left; slamming the cut glass door of the hotel behind him.

"Apparently Doc's thump got Ed's pump working again and he sat straight up in the middle of the billiard table and started singing, 'It's a Long Way to Tipperary'... And by God, that's what they named the bay horse that almost killed him."

Ardel paused and gazed around once again, taking in all the listeners. "I'm a little parched," he said, taking a handkerchief out of his back pocket and whisking it around the inside of his hat band, exposing a white forehead and slate-gray, wire-brush hair.

A pint bottle, half full, with a black cap and a black label, floated forward from the back table to Ardel. It rode on a wave of hands, the brown liquid in the bottle rolling back and forth as it bobbed up and down in the flowing human current of Camp Crook.

Canutt set his hat back in place, plucked the bottle from the last hand, spun off the top and took a long pull. "Ahh, much obliged," he uttered, replacing the cap and pocketing the bottle. "Now where was I?"

Someone said, "You jist got him named Ardel!" To which the crowd laughed and shifted about on their wooden seats.

"That's right. That's right. They named that outlaw horse Tipperary that very day."

He looked at me and grinned. "How you doin' young fella, still with me?"

I was a kid, listening to *my* grandpa tell a story ... I was with him more than I'd been with anybody in a long, long time. And I wouldn't have been anywhere else for the world.

Ardel saw that and beamed at me. "Now Elmer Wichham, the horse's owner, could see no good use for him so he sold him for forty dollars and a saddle to Doc Latham, the very same man who patched up Ed Marty.

"Both men figured they got the better end of the deal 'cause Elmer knew nobody would ever ride that crazy son of a bitch of a horse, and Doc, no fool he, was already lined up to sell a herd to some Frenchmen buying stock for their army. He figured he'd blend Tipperary in with his remuda. The Frogs would buy the whole lot and have the crazy devil out of the country before they discovered they'd been hoodwinked.

"But as Doc showed his buyers from France the horses, Tipperary broke from the herd and proceeded to run those Frogs out of the corral, biting one so bad they say he never did sit on a chair quite right again.

"They bought all the rest of the herd without culling a single one and skedaddled back to France, leaving Doc stuck with a horse he didn't care to have.

"For the first few days Tipperary was kept in an iron-barred stall over at the livery stable. The good doctor considered just shooting the horse and having it over with, but before he got it done some cowboy got a snootful and wanted to give Tipperary a try.

"So Doc says, 'sure you can ride him for a dollar,' figuring that would be the end of that. But the cowboy plunked down a silver dollar ... and Tipperary plunked him down in the corral in about ten seconds, breaking the boy's arm in the process.

"Doc figured this was a sure-fire way to keep a steady supply of paying patients coming in, so he kept Tipperary well fed and boarded and made a dollar a ride and some money on side bets … not to mention medical fees."

This brought out some chuckles from the crowd. Ardel fingered the bottle in his back pocket, but thought better of it and kept on with the storytelling.

"Then one day, Bob Paisley, a rancher out on the line, came along and said, 'I got a bronc buster that can take the starch out of any horse on four feet.' Doc Latham, being a wise and learned man, got that rancher all head up and said 'ain't nobody could ride Tipperary.'.

"That raised his dander so high Paisley bought Tipperary from Doc to prove his point. And he must have paid a pile of money, 'cause that night Doc Latham bought a round at the hotel bar; something never seen before or after in Camp Crook.

"Paisley's bronc buster tried for a month to break that horse to ride. After 30 days he wasn't any closer to having him broke than he was on day one. That boy up and disappeared the first of the next month after drawing his pay. The neighbors said he was the only hand they ever saw broke by a horse instead of the other way 'round!

"Didn't matter to Bob Paisley; he kept Tipperary, and that horse became quite an attraction.

"New fellas thinkin' they was as tough as a nickel steak kept showing up in Camp Crook to have their chance. During the next couple a years a hundred tried, each and all found themselves lying in the dirt or waking up on the billiard table over in the hotel.

"And with every try, Tipperary got a little wiser and a little tougher. They say he would stand on his hind legs, look around at you on his back and decide the best way to throw you off before he made his first jump. And to a man, the challengers all claimed the horse would laugh! It wasn't being thrown that cowboys hated most, it was that God-damned horse laugh."

I started to laugh, thinking this was the punch line, a pretty good one too; when I realized that the rest of the crowd was still listening with rapt attention.

Ardel knelt and picked a flat, round stone from the ground. He was gesturing toward me, holding it between his thumb and finger. "Remember son, once you're up in the air," He tossed the stone, spinning it in a high arc toward me, "You got nowhere to go but down!"

The crowd watched the stone reach its peak and tumble into my waiting hand. I was rewarded with applause from the entire town. Ardel grinned, motioning for silence.

"Bob Paisley started taking Tipperary to rodeos, where he offered five hundred dollars to anybody who could stay on with both feet in the stirrups, not changing hands on the reins, for a minute. He called him the Greatest Outlaw Horse, and by God nobody argued with him about it either.

"It was the damnedest thing you ever saw. That horse would get in a trailer and ride calm as a lead goat to a Rodeo, but when they went to clap a saddle on him his eyes would turn red as blood, fire would come out of his nostrils and fumes out of his tail-end like the smell of hell itself!

"Tipperary drew huge crowds and Paisley got ten-cents for everybody who came through the gate, plus five dollars from each cowboy who was fool enough to climb on. They say Bob made over two hundred thousand dollars putting Tipperary in the arena. And folks, that was a hell of a lot of money in those days!"

Shoot, I thought, it was a hell of a lot of money in these days.

Ardel's manner changed. He was bigger, there was something more in his voice. "The real capper is that my dad,

Yakima, stayed on Tipperary a couple of times in the twenties. Everyone knows this is true."

The crowd nodded. They knew it was true.

"Some say my dad is the only man to ever stay on Tipperary's back. Others say different. I can tell you for certain that it *was* a Canutt that stayed on him as long as anybody ever did.

"Tipperary bucked for his oats until he was twenty-two years old. Bob Paisley died pretty soon after that. Times were hard and money was scarce and there wasn't much use for a broken-down old bucking horse, but my dad and a bunch of the local cowboys and ranchers saved him; passing the hat to pay for his feed.

"Dad brought him home just before winter came roaring in, in '32." Ardel's grey eyes became distant. He wasn't just remembering, he was standing somewhere in the past.

"The day Tipperary came to live at our place, my dad said, 'Son, this horse isn't the worst outlaw horse that ever lived. No, by God, Tipperary wasn't a mean son of a bitch. And he wasn't mad at the cowboys he threw; he was only making a point. No one had ever asked his permission to get up on his back. The way that genius of a horse saw it, it was uncivilized and just plain rude. The horse got respect in the only way he could, by throwing 'em SPLAT in the dirt and laughing at 'em where they sat. Tipperary told me that himself,', my dad said."

The crowd under the trees held themselves as if in church, hearing about a miracle more real than wine-into-water.

"At ten years old, I was not at all surprised that my dad had gotten it straight from Tipperary's mouth because, like most of us Canutts, he could talk to horses and they could talk to him; at least the smartest ones could.

"So before Dad's rides, he and Tipperary talked it through. And by God, good manners paid off and Tipperary let my dad ride him to a standstill; not once, but twice. This led to a big payday, and Dad buying our ranch, and marrying my mom, and me and my sister being born, and pretty much everything fine that happened in our family from then on."

Ardel's voice was getting a little worn out. If my math was right, he was ninety-two years old.

"The winter of 1932 was the worst one anybody could, or still can, remember. Blizzards came roaring down from Canada. Cattle bunched up and froze along the fences. Antelope came into town to stand in the shelter of the hotel. The snow drifts got so high around the barns you couldn't tell where the ground ended and the roofs started.

"Most mornings my dad had to shovel a tunnel from the front door across the porch to get out into the yard so he could do chores.

"It was getting down to forty or fifty below zero, and when the wind howled it put so much snow up in your face you couldn't see the sky, or your feet, or even your gloved hand in front of your face.

"One day in December, my dad had scooped his way out to the barn where we had Tipperary, a couple other horses, and some bred cows sheltered. It was so cold that if you spit you'd hear it crackle in the air and hit the ground solid as a rock.

"Mom was busy upstairs with my sister who was only three years old. Having been trapped indoors for a couple of days, I was ready to get out. I figured I'd help Dad with the chores, so I bundled up and headed out toward the barn.

"The wind came up and I lost all track of up or down, east or west, north or south. The barn was only a hundred feet from the house, so I felt like I should be getting there, but when you can't see and you don't have any landmarks to navigate with, time doesn't mean much either. So I kept walking, sure I'd hit the barn soon. My hands were getting numb and the cold was stinging my eyes and my nose real bad. The wind was howling and the snow was hammering like gravel in a tin can against the scarf I had tied around my ears That damn barn had just picked itself up and walked away. It should have been RIGHT THERE but it wasn't. My heart was a beating drum, drowning out the wind as I realized I was lost and would never find the barn, or the house, or my dad or mom again. They wouldn't find me till the snow melted in May."

Ardel stared down at his boots. Hanging silently on every word, I honest-to-God felt a chill.

"Then a dark shadow moved toward me through that solid, screaming curtain of blowing ice. I could feel it more than see it. It came closer and a cushion of warm steamy air came up against my cheek and under my scarf and around my ears.

"I felt the velvet of his nose on my nose, that horse's warm breath waking up my numb face. I wrapped my stiff arms around his lowered neck and yelled in his ear, 'could you give me a ride?'. And sure as I'm standing here today, he swung me up on his back.

"I grabbed a handful of mane and hid my face on the lee side of his neck, clamping my eyes shut against the needles of snow. There was the slow up and down, side to side as he began to walk. I held on like fury 'cause the storm was doing its best to blow me off, hold me down, and freeze me stiff. It was like that damn storm was alive, and that horse and I were fightin' it together.

"How long we walked I do not know. It seemed like an eternity before I felt a change come up through his legs as he stepped onto the porch planking. Then came a long crack of light and my father's hands were pulling me inside.

"Getting out of that wind was the best thing I've ever felt before or since. Dad carried me across the room and set me down next to the woodstove. The relief of being out of that storm was quickly replaced by the realization that the horse was still out in the open. 'Wait, wait,' I cried. 'Don't leave him out there.'.

"My father thought I was out of my head with the cold. He towered over me, unsure whether to whack me a good one or hug me till I split. Mom was rubbing my hands and stripping off my boots to make sure I wasn't frost bit, all the while big tears were streaming down her face."

Ardel was far away; a boy inside a small ranch house, safe from the howling wind that had tried its best to kill him; desperate to save Tipperary.

"I wanted to go back out. Find Tipperary and get him safe inside. I told my folks, 'It was the horse. It was Tipperary. He got me back to the porch. We beat the God-damned storm. Didn't you see him? Bring him in or he'll freeze.'.

"My dad was stunned. 'Son that can't be,' he said. 'I found Tipperary dead, frozen against the lean-to of the barn this morning.'.

"I ran to the door and threw it open; nothing to be seen but snow blowin' sideways; not a trace of the horse who had carried me out of the blizzard."

I was squeezing the round stone hard into my palm, feeling Ardel's anguish over failing to save Tipperary.

"They say Tipperary died in 1932, during the worst blizzard of the worst winter ever. But you'll never hear me say that." He took off his copper-colored hat, mopped his white brow and clapped the Stetson back on.

"That damn storm went on for three more days and three more nights before it blew itself out, and it took Dad almost another day to dig through to the barn. I know because I helped haul the snow out as he cut his way through the packed drifts.

"Thing was, along the south wall of the barn, in the space between the big drift and the siding boards, where my dad expected to find the body of a dark bay horse, we found a halter and a lead rope tied up short to a Ponderosa log more than twenty feet long and three feet across; green, wet, and heavy as a locomotive."

Ardel paused. The sun streamed through the grey leaves of the cottonwoods, dappling his face.

"Tipperary was the smartest, greatest hell-fire bucking horse of all times. And though they say my father was the only one to ride Tipperary, I would beg to disagree." He reached into his back pocket, brought out the pint bottle and drank off the rest.

He was done.

We sat statue-still at the tables, trying to keep the fragile magic of the story alive in our silence.

When the spell broke, I stood, shook the brown gnarled hand of Ardel Canutt, storm survivor and storyteller; kissed Muu Muu on the cheek under the approving eyes of her Judge, and took one last look at the bucking figure of Tipperary, King of the Outlaw Horses.

In that space, there under those lofty trees with the Little Missouri River gliding in the background, *I* had lost all track of up or down, east or west, north or south. Without the usual landmarks, time and worry hadn't meant much either.

Ardel made me believe again.

Part 2 CHAPTER 3

Listening to Ardel's story, I felt as if I'd shed twenty years of desperation. My life was back on track. There was no way to be sure what lay up ahead other than to drive right into it. So I struck out down the tiny road toward Belle Fourche, South Dakota with a smooth flat stone riding in my pocket next to my poker chip.

Trooper Sammi Holt pushed into my thoughts. What had tipped her off to who I was? She had known I was the deliverer of justice to two evil people on Jesus Is My Redeemer Lane. But her history was in my favor. If it had been any other cop …

I pondered that as the road bumped along south. I snapped on the radio to a load of static that didn't change much as the seek function flipped numbers on the radio's screen; a couple of pauses at country western—uh-uh, not that desperate. A preacher got in a few quick words relating to Revelations and the imminent danger of burning in hell—nope. Somebody reading the news, "… unknowingly posted the picture on their Facebook page without knowing his identity."

Unknowingly, without knowing? … another genius on the radio. I was about to push the button again when the radio voice said, "Stuck in a traffic jam near Missoula, Montana, Chad Manning apparently snapped a photo of Charles "Chip" Crandle; the Idaho man suspected of killing alleged sex offenders, Scarlett and John Bradley."

I could see that damn cow running down the median dropping pies. I had needed to piss so bad.

"Chip Crandle is wanted by state and federal authorities in connection with the double murder. In a release sent to media outlets across the country, Mr. Crandle claimed the Bradley couple had sexually abused their daughters. In that release he stated ..." The guy quoted my release word-for-word and went to commercials.

Somebody had caught me pissing in the ditch in Montana. That kind of took the shine off hearing my words on the air and knowing that my message had gotten through.

I had wanted it to go viral, but now I realized social media had turned the other edge of the electronic sword toward me. I was being tracked by Facebook. A billion people knew my face.

The commercials ended and the talk-show host came back. "Hi everybody, Brian Birdsong here, we're talking to Chad Manning about the latest developments in the Idaho child molester murders. Manning took a picture of Chip Crandle yesterday morning as Crandle relived himself behind a bush in a ditch off I-90. Manning posted the photo of Crandle on his Facebook page with the caption—traffic jams can be a real pisser. Hi Chad, looks like you took a pretty important picture yesterday. What can you tell us about it?"

The voice of a not-so-bright young man came on. "Yeah, uh, hi Brian." Breathing ... then more breathing.

The host jumped in to save him, "Chad, can you tell us what happened?"

"It was, like, a real long time waiting, you know. And my buddy, Stuckey, he says, 'Look behind us Mano, that dude is gonna take a piss behind that bush.' So I whipped around and shot about ten pitch-urs. You couldn't really see nothing; just the dude's face."

"So you didn't know who this guy was?"

Chad "Mano" Manning replied, "Yeah, no, dude. I had no freaking idea the guy was a murderer or nothing. When I got home, I just put a couple of the shots up on my Facebook page, and got like a ton of likes. And then somebody posts a comment and says, 'hey bro, that looks like the dude on the news who shot those child molesters in Idaho.'. And then other people wrote stuff like; 'yeah dude, that's the guy. Better call the cops dude 'cause they're looking for this guy, even if he did kill a couple of creeps.'. Stuff like that, you know?"

"What did you do then?" asked Birdsong.

"So, I called 9-1-1 and they got me over to some cop and he logged onto my Facebook page and saw the pitch-ur. The cop got really juiced after he looked at my page."

I grabbed one of my smokes off the Audi's dash as the talk show host dug more facts out of Chad Manning's fertile brain.

"What did the police want to know?"

"Oh you know. Like, where did I see this dude? What was he driving? Which way was he going? Did I like, talk to him? Stuff like that."

"What was he driving? Did you see his car?" I was hoping Brian would get to that one.

"Naw, man it was like a freakin' parkin' lot out there. Like hot, and cows runnin' around, and people all over the place."

Chad didn't have much more to add, so Brian dumped him, "Thanks Chad, after a break we'll be on the talk-lines getting YOUR comments about the Idaho child molester murders."

A cheesy commercial for low, low, priced RVs came on.

Well, maybe old Chad didn't know my car, but considering I'd spent a bunch of time in the traffic jam smoking and joking, somebody must have put me in a black Audi Q7—thank God it was Sammi Holt who had found me first.

I passed a sign that said: Geographic Center of the United States, 7 Miles. The center of the country is way out in the middle of nowhere; the center, a place where people just don't live.

Two insurance and an E-cigarette commercial later, Brian Birdsong said, "Hi, we're back, talking about the Idaho child molester murders. We're on the line with Mindy from Chicago."

"Hi Brian, I just wanted to say I think they should give that guy a medal for killing those two monsters. I was the victim of a child molester and there is only one thing that should be done. That guy Crandle did it."

Wow. Mindy from Chicago had gotten my point.

"So let me get this right," Brian said in his not-quite-condescending manner. "You think he was justified in shooting two people in cold blood?"

"Somebody had to." Then Mindy from Chicago broke down in tears and hung up.

For the next forty-five minutes the callers sorted out about seventy-thirty in my favor. People did get it. They needed to get engaged in their own lives. I thought about calling in, but I didn't have a phone, and there sure as hell weren't any phones out where I was.

I tried another Lucky. It didn't taste good, but I smoked it down to my fingers, and kept the Audi rolling toward Belle Fourche at a hundred miles an hour, working out how I was going to ditch Ben's car.

Part 2 CHAPTER 4

I needed a different car, and unless something else occurred to me, I would have to steal it.

I wasn't a bad guy. I wasn't a car thief. I didn't know the first thing about stealing a car from some innocent stranger, nor did I want to.

Broad daylight in Belle Fourche, South Dakota. Not exactly a great time to be tooling around in an Audi with Idaho plates looking for a nice car to boost.

Maybe there was a better way.

♦   ♦   ♦

Funny how there is *always* someone in a McDonalds. I went through the door and smelled the grease and the fries and the burgers and the coffee. I was only halfway to the counter before I saw the exact person I was looking for.

A young guy in a booth; he had an Apple laptop and his eyes never left the screen. A bomb could have gone off in his shorts and he wouldn't have noticed it.

"Excuse me," I said. "How do you like your Mac?"

He looked up at me and I thought, shit he probably lives on Facebook! He's gonna know who I am and start screaming.

The kid didn't flinch. "Only way to go," he said, pushing his funky little glasses back up onto the bridge of his nose with a pudgy index finger, "PC's pretty much suck."

I had him. "My name's Greg Shanks," I said, staying with my latest alias. "I'd buy you a shake or something if you'd show me how to look up a couple of things online with your Mac. Would you be willing to do that?"

"Gee, uh, well, sure. What the heck." He was kind of a geek, but a nice enough kid. "What are you looking for?"

"Well, I'm new in town. My family won't be here for a while and my oldest son will need a car when he gets here. Don't suppose we could have a look on Craigslist?"

The kid's face lit up. "Awesome, I love to look around on Craigslist. What are you looking for? I'll log on."

"That would be super. What can I get you?" I said, motioning toward the counter.

"Uh, guess I'll have a Latte Grande, if that's all right." I could tell he was embarrassed to ask; small town kid with a Mac as his best friend.

I got him, his name turned out to be Donny, a Latte Grande, and a chocolate shake with a big order of fries for myself.

We started paging through the cars for sale. I wanted something less than five years old. It needed air and a big enough engine to cruise through the plains without sounding like a sewing machine, and it needed to have room for my camping gear.

Donny and I weeded the candidates down to three; all fit my criteria, all claimed to be in great running condition, and all had phone numbers attached to them so I could call right away.

I jotted down the names and phone numbers, sucked the last of my shake through the straw.

"Well Donny, thanks a million for helping me out and showing me your Mac."

"That was fun, ah, Greg. Good luck with your car hunt, and if you're around you can find me here most days." Donny's gaze flitted back to his screen.

♦ ♦ ♦

Mounted on the shady side of the SODAKGAS convenience store was a lonely pay phone. I grabbed all the spare change I'd been throwing in the cup holder of the Audi. The phone book was pretty thin. I quickly found what I was looking for. There were eleven self-storage facilities around town. I dropped change in the slot and dialed.

"Zorba's U-Store. We got room. This is Frank."

A couple minutes later, I had a time set up at Zorba's U-Store to finalize renting a storage unit from Frank.

Now if I could just come up with the right wheels. I dialed the first number, got a voice-mailbox, hung up and dialed the next number. No answer. I punched in the final number.

"Yello," a gravelly old voice croaked in my ear.

"Hello," I said. "Are you the person who has a pickup for sale?"

"Well," the voice was a bit clearer now; an elderly lady. "I did have, but I sold it this morning."

Shit. This wasn't working the way I wanted it to.

"But I do have another vehicle that I might sell." She had just made her mind up on that one.

"I see," I said. "What kind of vehicle is it?"

"Well, my husband just passed away two years ago, and I wasn't too sure I wanted to part with it." She cleared her throat. "It was our fun car, and I didn't have the heart to see it go. But I guess it's just silly to have it sitting there in the garage taking up space." She trailed off, losing her train of thought, then said, "It's a 1968 El Camino SS. Really beautiful and we took such good care of it."

Wow. This wasn't anything like what I'd been thinking about. The El Camino, a kind of strange hybrid between a pickup and a sports car; it had been one of those cars I'd always been fascinated with.

"That sounds interesting. What color is it?" Like I cared, but my brain was on overload and I didn't really know what else to say.

"It's a deep maroon with tan seats, a three-fifty, air, power windows, cruise control, four-speed with a Hurst Tee-Shifter and a posi-traction rear-end." She paused. "It has very low mileage. We were driving it in the Fourth of July parades before Evert died."

Huh, a little old lady from Pasadena right here in Belle Fourche, South Dakota.

Go granny, Go granny, Go granny, Go! Brian Wilson, so weird, get out of my head and I'll get back to business.

"How much are you asking for it?"

"I couldn't take a dime less than sixteen thousand." This said with force and conviction. There would be no haggling. She was selling something more than just a car. Not a lady who would be taken advantage of.

I looked at Ben's Audi gleaming like a lighted billboard—then at the seconds ticking off my watch—"OK, that sounds fair. Can I come and take a look at it in the next hour or so?"

"That would be fine. May I ask your name?" She was now all business.

"Greg Shanks. I'm moving here in a few weeks and I'm looking for a good car to drive in town so that my wife can use our other car for longer trips." I was rambling again.

"I've heard some pretty scary stories about people from Craigslist showing up and robbing you. But you sound like a nice man."

Now what is a guy supposed to say to that? "Well, I'm pretty harmless," I said (except of course when I'm shooting child molesters in the head). "I'm sixty years old, got gray hair. If we make a deal, would it be all right if I pay you in cash?"

"Well, uh, did you say you have sixteen thousand dollars in cash? I don't think I've ever seen sixteen thousand dollars in cash."

Oops.

"Yeah, I know that sounds kind of crazy, doesn't it? Actually we have a bit more than that. My mother just passed away a couple of weeks ago. This money was in her safe-deposit box. Kind of a surprise to find it, and well, we didn't want to have to pay taxes on it so we just kept it in cash. We were in the process of moving ..."

"Well I certainly understand that," she said with an edge creeping into her voice. "You work your whole life to put something away, or build a business, and the damn government comes along and takes it away from you. It's just a crying shame."

I had her.

She got back to business, "I live at 13 Westside Lane. That's just a couple of blocks east of the courthouse. It's a brick ranch with a two-car garage."

"I didn't get your name yet."

"I'm Max Gooby. Just ring the bell."

"OK, Max. See you in a little while."

I went into the store, found an envelope big enough to hold sixteen thousand dollars in cash.

I swung past Max Gooby's. The house and lawn were neat as a pin. There was a beautiful, maroon El Camino sitting in the drive. Max must have backed it out right after the call. I drove a few blocks and found a quiet out-of-the-way spot to park the Audi.

The sixteen thousand went into my big envelope. I'd been handling a lot of cash—a lot of cash. It was so satisfying handing over something real for something real in return; not swiping a damn piece of plastic through a slot. I felt like I had when I was twelve, buying a .22 for twenty dollars in ones and quarters.

It was shady most of the way, not an unpleasant walk back to Max's house. I could see the maroon gleam from a block away.

I rang the bell. Her weathered face looked up at me through the front door window. I took a step back and held up my hands, one holding the envelope.

Max gave me a smile and swung the door open. She was a small woman; wiry and probably looked a lot younger than she was. She had that bearing of someone who still got out and did what she wanted to do.

"Hello, I'm Greg Shanks," I said. "You must be Max." I had a good feeling about her.

"Maxine actually, but Max is what they call me." Her blue eyes darted toward the envelope. It bulged with the cash and she must have been imagining exactly what it would look like. She came out and we walked to her car together.

"Well there she is. Take a good look."

"It certainly is beautiful," I said. "Mind if I get in?"

"Guess that's what you're here for," she said. She swung open the driver's side door and I climbed in. Oh man, what I would have given for that car in high school.

"If you have any questions let me know," she was now talking about her baby. "Those are all original miles, sixty-two thousand. I know because I was in the shotgun seat for every last one of 'em. Evert and I had a ton of fun in that car and we treated her a lot like the kids we never had."

She took a couple of steps back and ran her parental gaze from bumper to bumper. "Only thing I know wrong with this car is a small dent in the inside edge of the bed over there."

I swiveled and looked through the slider window into the car's truck bed.

She walked back and put her finger over a small grey dent. "See that right there?" she touched the spot like she was petting a cat between the ears. "The day after we brought her home, Evert and I were doing some target shooting. We were sighting in the scope of our .22, leaning our elbows on the edge of the bed. I slipped one elbow off that edge over there, pulled the trigger and bang. It scared the daylights out of me and I thought Evert would be so mad. But he just grinned and put his finger on this spot, like I'm doing."

"Wow that must have been scary," I said "But he didn't raise a fuss?"

"Nope, he just laughed and said, 'Well honey, we don't have to worry about that first dent anymore.' and he left it there all this time as kind of a joke between the two of us. It's been that way since May of '68."

I walked back and had a look. The dent still had a gray spot in the middle of it where the slug had hit. Otherwise the car was perfect.

"Sounds like Evert was quite a guy," I said.

"Yep, he was," she gazed at something in the distance. "What say we take her out for a test drive, Greg?"

Max and I took a quick drive around the block and then went out onto the highway where she encouraged me to, "Wind'er up!"

The three-fifty had a deep throaty rumble that took me back to 1970. I wound 'er up, running through the gears. We hit a hundred, still had room to spare, and then backed down.

Max sat grinning. "She really is some kind of fun. So what do you think? Would you like to have her?"

I would have bought that car, at that moment, for whatever she asked, and thrown the Audi in as a bonus. "I sure would," was all I could think to say.

A tear rolled out of the corner of Max's eye as we turned into her driveway. "I'll get the paperwork," she said.

I pulled the cash out of the envelope to make sure she knew I was serious—serious and safe. She barely looked at the money as she smiled and wiped at her damp eyes.

About half an hour later I pulled out of the driveway with Max Gooby's El Camino. She went through her front door with sixteen thousand dollars of Tree Man's cash that the IRS would never know about.

I parked next to the Audi. There was nobody around. It took just a few minutes to transfer all my stuff to the El Camino; and another five to drive the Audi to within a couple of blocks of Zorba's U-Store.

I jogged to within half a block of Zorba's and slowed to a walk. I didn't want to be huffing and puffing when I arrived.

No fence, no lights, no cameras, and nobody in an office to check you in or out; small town storage for small town stuff—perfect.

There was a champagne-colored Coupe Deville sitting at the end of the first building. A guy, it had to be Frank, leaned against the front fender smoking a cigarette. He had a manila folder laying on the hood, along with a big round silver padlock, a huge wad of keys and a phone.

He flipped the cigarette into the gravel at his feet and extended his hand, "Frank Shannon." He was lanky and tall with sandy hair and bad teeth, big soft hands; probably played some high school basketball twenty-five years before. "Golly," he said. "It's a hot day to be on foot."

"Uh, yeah, I dropped my car off for service and just walked over, that's what I love about a small town," I said.

Frank nodded; a busy guy. "I've got your paperwork ready for a ten by twenty; hope back there in row D is OK." He pointed to a printed layout of the place lying on the hood of his Cadillac.

"That's great. I'm not particular about the location." I was tickled with the location. I could come and go from the facility without being seen from the street.

He pulled a contract out of his folder, laid it on the hood and spun it so I could have a look at it right side up. "It's unit D13, clean as a whistle."

I signed and gave Frank two month's rent, which went right in his wallet.

He walked me back and showed me the space. Then he padlocked the door and handled me the key. "Can I give you a lift someplace?"

"No thanks. It's a good day for a walk."

Twenty minutes later I took a last look at Ben's car sitting inside D13. I pulled the overhead down and snapped Frank's padlock back on the bolt. I hadn't seen anybody, and I was satisfied nobody had seen me.

Time to see what my new wheels could do.

Part 2 CHAPTER 5

In forty-five minutes the El Camino and I were well into the Black Hills; a big difference from the mountains of Idaho and the flat scrub of eastern Montana.

There was a VISIT WALL DRUG sign every mile.

I planned to cut south of Sturgis, catch Highway 44 in Rapid City, then take it on over to Scenic. Scenic, South Dakota, on the edge of the Badlands. You gotta love America's sense of irony. Even out in the heat and the dust and the drought and the Indian raids, the settlers had named a place Scenic.

Springsteen started: Badlands, you gotta live it every day … I wondered if Bruce Springsteen had ever been to *these* Badlands.

I kept the El Camino's speedometer needle locked a couple of miles above the speed limit as I approached Rapid City. I saw a state trooper and a local cop, busy, on their way somewhere. And I was in a new car, a car so obvious it made me invisible.

About an hour later, the rusty chalk teeth of the Badlands grinned at me across the horizon as I breezed into Scenic. A thread of a memory twirled up from somewhere. I had heard about it on CNN. A couple of years ago some church had bought the whole thing; zip code, post office, two bars, and whatever else there was to buy. They bought it from some old gal who had been a rodeo trick rider. Really, you couldn't make this stuff up.

I crossed into Badlands National Park, passed the White River Visitor's Center buildings, and turned west on National Park Road #2; looking right into the last of a huge sunset.

Just after crossing Wounded Knee Creek there was a wheel track heading north. I swung the El Camino over, bumping into the Pine Ridge Indian Reservation.

I imagine it looks a lot like the moon. Spires of whitish shale and rock loom all around you and it's a lesson in erosion. Fossils continually emerge as the place constantly disintegrates in South Dakota's weather extremes.

The track I'd picked was rough and hard to navigate in the failing light. Grass and brush in the middle scoured the underside of the car. Lights off, straining to see ahead, I crept along for another thirty minutes.

It got dark. Dark the way God had made it. No man-made light. No trace of the sun leaked over the ridges, and the stars were all there. The sky went all the way down to the ground.

It made me feel limitless, like I was a part of it all and all of it was a part of me at the same time. The moon hadn't risen and the heat was still radiating from the ground.

I'd have a beer, then start my little grill and cook a chop. I stood facing the El Camino, my elbows on its edge. The cracking pssst of the opening beer sounded like it could carry for miles. I tipped the bottle up, filling my dry mouth and throat.

"Got another one of those for me?"

If I'd been in a movie, I would have done a spit take and blown beer foam out of my nose. I managed to swallow and turned to find a short man in a round, wide-brimmed hat standing there in the track; his arms spread wide, palms up, showing he meant no harm.

His face was hidden under the wide hat, but the smile was there like a patch of snow on a dark rock at midnight. A hint of silver gleamed at his throat as he lowered his arms to his sides. He couldn't have been much more than five feet tall.

"Where on earth did you come from? You scared the living shit out of me."

The man laughed, a low melody spinning up from his belly. "Sorry about that. I figured you knew I was here. I saw you come down the road in that wonderful car and wondered what a white man was doing out here in the dark. Then I saw that I had been waiting for you. I thought maybe you had been traveling to see me—since you're looking for something important. Oh—and there's also the two people you killed to get here."

What was this guy talking about? I'm standing in the middle of the Badlands, in the dark, with some little Indian—I guess—who knows I killed the Bradleys? He sounded like an Indian, with that lilting kind of tone and inflection, and this was a reservation. I suppose Facebook even reaches out here. But how the hell did he know it was me?

My mouth went as dry as the roadbed. "Uh, I wasn't really looking for anybody, just ah, looking for a place to pitch my tent and look at the stars. Am I somewhere I'm not supposed to be?"

The little guy let out a Dalai Lama giggle. "Yes, I do believe you were looking for me. You just haven't stopped long enough to realize it. The beer looks good. Got one to spare?"

Not knowing what else to do, I sat my bottle on the El Camino and fished out a beer. I pried off the top and turned back. The guy was gone.

Holy shit, I'm losing it. I need to lie down and sleep. The past two days ripped through my head like a movie watched through a key-hole; it was all there, but the edges were cut off. Only part of my brain was registering it, while the other parts were trying to figure out what I should do next—and what was real.

"Over here."

Shit. He was back. The melodic voice came from somewhere on the other side of my truck. I heard a match scrape and a tiny blue-yellow glow danced. He said, "I moved back here. I thought maybe you and I could have a talk. And

I'd like to take a load off. There's a pretty nice spot over here where I have my chairs set up."

My toes had turned into rock and grown down into the moon-soil of the Badlands. I'd be just another eroding landform. The tourists would come take pictures of me and the coyotes would come by and pee on my stone legs. Old Rock Chip, standing out there in the Badlands with the wind and the rain and the snow wearing away at him until he'd just blow away.

He started humming—was that the Oscar Meyer Weiner song?

I picked up my beer, walked around the back of the car and moved off into the brush. I found him sitting in a folding camp chair, roasting a hot dog over a flaming can of Sterno set down into a hole in the ground.

"That beer will go great with this dog. Have a seat." He motioned with his hot dog, skewered on a coat hanger, toward another nylon camp chair on the opposite side of his fire.

I handed him his beer, took mine over to the offered chair, and lowered myself ungracefully but gratefully into it. I leaned back, took a gulp and looked up at the dome of stars.

This was the weirdest damn thing, but I felt at ease. Maybe pulling that trigger a couple of days ago had sent me into some sort of different reality; one that existed only for those who made that kind of life and death leap. Maybe this was how things REALLY were. I felt exactly right, exactly sure.

"Thanks," he said, and took a long gulp from the bottle. "Ahhhh. Sometimes everything comes together and the beer tastes just like you want it to, don't you think?" He sat the bottle down in the dirt beside his chair, reached inside a plastic bag and came up with a hotdog bun. Using the bun he gripped the sizzling hot dog and slid it off the end of the hanger.

"You want this one? I've got more."

I could see his eyes now in the fire light; dark and deep-set on either side of a wide nose, all under a prominent brow. His cheekbones were reflecting the flame, and he had a red kerchief around his neck with a silver slide on it. He wore a long, fringed shirt. His skinny old-man legs were covered by dark trousers, ending in well-worn work boots.

"Well sir, that's a good offer. I think I'll take you up on that," I said, reaching across the heat and light. He stretched and put the dog and bun into my hand.

"Ketchup?" he said.

"I'm trying," I said.

"I know you are," he grinned. "But what am I?"

OK, now I liked the guy; even if I was only imagining him.

I took a big bite. "I like mine plain and simple," I said.

"Good," he said. "That's the best way."

He took another swig of beer and gazed at his cooking dinner in a contented way while I finished off my dog and the last of my beer. "I wouldn't mind having another beer," I said, rising from the chair. "Shall I bring you one?"

"That would be fine." The little man turned the wiener slowly, browning it evenly. "Just one more though, and then we have some business to attend to."

I went to my cooler, grabbed the beers, and stuck the wrinkled cigarette pack in my shirt pocket. Wondered if the guy would still be there when I went back ... or would I wake up?

Still there.

I handed him a bottle; settled into my chair.

"Thanks very much, Chip Crandle," he said. "I have been thinking about you. I know who you are and from where you are traveling."

Nothing could surprise me. I was looking at the world now without judgment about anything. I let him finish eating before I asked him the obvious question. "OK, so what kind of hot dog was that? It had to be the best one I ever had."

"Good aren't they?" He sucked his teeth, getting the fresh bun unstuck. "I get them over in Rapid City from a Kosher Deli. Who knew there was a Rabbi in Rapid City? We tribal people gotta stick together; especially us spiritual leaders."

"No. You're making that up," I said. "I thought buffalo or rattlesnake or something. Kosher beef?"

"Yup, that's the deal," he said; sipped his beer. "So what are you really doing out here? It's kind of a long way to come to set up camp."

"Well, I think you somehow know the answer to that question," I said. "I'm not exactly sure why I came all the way out here. It's a bit like that movie where all those people travel out to Devil's Tower. They just found themselves going there."

I had a strange thought. "Hey, you're not some kind of alien are you?"

"Naw, I'm just a guy, like you, trying to figure out how it all works," he spoke in a very soothing voice.

"So, what's your name?"

"Jack Wilson," was his reply. "I've got a couple of other names too, but Jack works pretty well in all circles."

"And what are *you* doing out here Jack Wilson?" I asked.

"I'm going to a dance tonight; a dance that I've been looking forward to for some time." His fire sputtered. He picked up a small bundle of sticks and set the end on fire then dropped it into the fire pit and fed in a few larger sticks.

"I suspect it's getting late enough that nobody will bother us now," he said. "The tribe and the feds get a little cranky about people wandering around in this part of the park. It was used for bombing practice by the military—yours not mine— for about seventy years. There's a lot of unexploded stuff lying around, not to mention the graves, and the holy places, and the sacred objects. Bombs and ghosts, pretty interesting blend of flash and smoke, don't you think?" He chuckled.

He said all this as if he were asking directions to the corner gas station. It wasn't a big deal. It just was.

"This country has been a special place since time began for us. We still hang symbols from trees and carve images into rocks," he said. "Somebody thought it was special enough to make a national park out of it. I guess any person can feel it— if they stop long enough to consider their place in it all. The dance we're going to tonight is a part of that feeling."

Dance? We? Huh? ... I wasn't really tired anymore, in spite of having had such a long day. I reached in my shirt pocket for a smoke.

"Shall we smoke together?" Jack Wilson said as he eyed the crushed pack.

I moved from my chair and shook out the last Lucky, flattened and bent. Wilson deftly moved it to his smiling lips. I dug out the Mint Bar matchbook, lit the cigarette, tossed the match into the tiny fire.

"You know," he said, drawing in smoke with audible pleasure, "Smoking is a great thing when done in moderation and at special occasions when men are meeting to consider things that matter. It was only when it became a habit, rather than a ceremony of trust, that it turned into a killer of soul and body." He handed the cigarette over to me.

"I believe that's true," I said. "We lack courage; the courage to moderate and not make the good things ordinary." I took a drag and passed it back.

"Yes, and to be courageous enough to do what we know is right." He inhaled deeply, letting the smoke roll from his nostrils and form a wreath over his hat. "Isn't that what your trip has been all about?"

I had the feeling he was talking about more than just the past couple of days.

"Now that you mention it, I guess it has. I knew about courage a long time ago, but I lost it. I was a coward for so long I felt like I had no place in anything; almost like being dead I suppose. Took me almost fifty years to remember that it's worth whatever pain you have to go through to really live your life ... to do what you gotta do. If what I did was just plain wrong, would you tell me?"

"Why is it important that somebody else tell you that you're right?" He grinned in a wonderfully familiar way.

I suddenly felt the touch of Dad's hands holding me up next to the sky, and I grinned back. "Well, we all want to know we're doing the right thing, don't we?"

"Oh, I suspect we do." Jack took a last puff, exhaled and dropped what was left of the Lucky into the sputtering flame at his feet. "What do you say we go to a dance?"

Jack Wilson, with me in tow, set out through the scrub, leaving the embers of his fire to die out on their own. We climbed steadily up a steep slope, the loose shale of the ground breaking and crunching with every step. The heat bleeding up out of the rocks was making it a warm hike.

The moon peeked over the bench we were ascending; full, round and huge, changing the darkness to a labyrinth of long shadows that masked low spots and basketball-sized rocks in our path. We didn't speak. Making any noise beyond the scrape of our feet on the scree and the sound of our breathing seemed to be an affront to the night. The quiet was profound in my ears.

Jack had a purpose in his steps and I had to trust that he knew where he was going. I began to see that we were following a trail—not a beaten path like tourists make along river banks or canyon rims—but a whisper, a suggestion of a trail that followed the natural contours of the land. Deer and antelope, big cats and wise men would naturally take this path. They had for thousands of years. But they didn't wear it bare … keeping it a secret.

I could now see Jack clearly. His hat was a cliché for a turn-of-the-19th-century Indian. He had even jabbed a large feather into the silk hatband. Braids hung down his back from both sides of the hat. They were dark and almost waist length, with leather thong and ribbons woven in.

His shirt was not fabric, as it had first seemed next to his glistering little fire, but aged buckskin with figures and symbols painted over its entire surface. Fringe bounced along the shirt's sleeves and tails as he walked.

We crested a hill and far below us, down a little slit of a canyon, was the glow of a fire. Shadows moved around the fire in a circular pattern, casting images that were growing and shrinking on the walls. A shiver ran down through my guts.

Jack, standing on the edge of a steep drop-off, turned to me and said, "There's the dance; looks like we're just about on time."

This side was steeper and we traversed back and forth to keep from losing our footing in the loose layers of sediment. Our disturbance spooked an animal off to our right; something fairly big by the sound of it. It moved away, scattering debris that clattered and tumbled for several seconds before the night went silent again.

I lost track of time, but the moon was very high, directly overhead, and the shadows were about to reverse themselves. We had finally reached the bottom.

My feet felt raw from the long, steep climb. My legs burned. Jack seemed unfazed; as hard and tough as the Badlands. We rounded a corner and came blinking into the orange glow.

Not just shadow images in the distance now, the dancers were real. They moved around the fire in a circle. Bent at the knees they shuffled in single file, turning and pirouetting, their arms straight down at their sides, torsos ramrod straight, hands turned knuckles to the front.

I had expected to hear drums or music or singing or chanting. But they danced in a strange, serene silence; eyes closed, chins nodding up and down. Calmness washed across me. I looked toward Jack and found him staring back, studying something behind my eyes. Then he moved to join the dancers in their un-ending circle.

I realized then that I knew them. I recognized the face of each dancer as they came around. There was my grandfather, blue dungarees and a chambray shirt, a Camel cigarette between his fingers, a look of joy as he danced. The silence had gone. A piano played as Grandpa took the hand of the dancer next to him. It was my grandmother. And they did a line dance to the tune of Alley Cat.

Next came my father's parents who had never danced a lick in their lives. They were ripping it up as Chubby Checker belted out, Come on baby, let's do the twist …

And then my mom and dad were jitterbugging, Let's go to the hop!

And then them; Suzanne and him, my wife and my son, holding hands, smiling with beautiful faces, happy on strong legs; strolling to a deep saxophone. We saw each other, and I knew the end was good.

The circle continued and I saw all the people, now gone, I'd ever known; dancing and laughing and letting it all go as they moved and grooved around that fire in the bottom of a little canyon in Badlands National Park.

Aunts and uncles, fishing buddies, a school bus driver, preachers, the family doctor, co-workers, Eugene Triska, the guy from the gas station explosion, and Tree Man—yes Tree Man—all there, all happy, all dancing around a fire that would never burn out, in a circle that would never end.

And there they were; John and Scarlett Bradley. They were slim and trim, young and healthy, and floating on air as they danced to the Tennessee Waltz. They had light in their clear eyes, freed from whatever demons had stolen the life they had really meant to live. And there was something more in their eyes, gratitude.

I saw right there that death wasn't an end, but a sort of cosmic redo. Doing whatever gives you the most joy until the next better thing comes along.

A dancer stopped in front of me; Jack Wilson doing the Chicken Dance. He finished the wing flapping and beamed, "Well Chip, as they say on the rez, you don't have to quit dancing, you just have to quit dancing here. It's last call at the Ghost Dance Ball!"

He took off his hat, pulled the buckskin shirt off over his head and tossed it to me. He stood there, alone now in front of the fire, his shadow huge against the rock wall, in a black tee-shirt with the Swoosh and big white letters that said: Just Do It.

And I laughed when I saw him in spite of myself.

"That Ghost shirt's older'n dirt, but it's got a lot of wear left in it. It's yours now," he said. "It'll protect you from spitballs and bullets, keep you cool in the summer and warm in the winter. It has been known to grant a wish, cure the flu, and sweeten a sour disposition. But only love can break a heart and only love can mend it again ..." He clapped his hat back tight on his head and said, "We better head back, it's getting pretty late."

I looked down at the ancient leather shirt in my hands. Its touch like horse muzzle velvet, every square inch covered with human figures and cave painting animals, Greek letters and Egyptian hieroglyphics, quotes in Latin and Hebrew and Chinese and Sanskrit, musical notes and equations, bar codes and QR codes. Fastened among the figures were feathers, beads, jewels, sea shells, glass, and turquoise; the leather landscape moved and undulated.

It was like looking at the faces of the dancers as they moved around that fire. "I … I … I don't know what to say … why are you giving me this?" Stammering was starting to be my major form of communication.

"Well," Jack Wilson said, "Let's just say it's your turn."

We headed back out the way we had come in. This time I took the lead. It seemed a very long way back to where we had begun.

◆　◆　◆

I was lying in the back of the El Camino.

A young, dark-eyed, raven-haired lady in a Smokey Bear hat leaned on the edge of the truck bed, shaking her head in a school-marmish way, clucking her tongue at me. "If you people insist on sleeping out here, I will never understand why you can't let us know first," she said, a little bit pissed off and a little bit amused.

I was not stiff so much as rigid. Every muscle in my back, butt and legs hurt and my skin felt corrugated from the ridges in the metal floor on which I'd apparently been sleeping.

I had a strange petro-chemical taste in my mouth and there were four beer bottles lying loose around my feet. I thought about standing up and jumping out, but then decided I'd better take a quick inventory. Glad I did. Other than Jack

Wilson's Ghost shirt, I had nothing on; buck naked underneath.

"Am I in trouble?" I hoped I didn't sound too crazy.

"Depends on how good your story is," she said. "What's your tale there Tonto? Where'd you get that shirt?"

Shit.

"Uh. Well. Uh," I was back to my stammering self. "I just got here late last night and had to stop and sleep. I couldn't really go any farther and I just turned off the road and hit the sack. Didn't mean to break any rules or anything."

"Can I see your I.D.?"

Now I was awake. I never thought I'd get busted by some little woman park ranger for sleeping out under the stars, but it looked like this might be my undoing.

I'd heard that enforcement on reservations could be pretty creative. I imagined that could include scalping or being tied spread-eagle to a wagon wheel over a fire. For some reason, I remembered that the Indian women had cut off Custer's men's genitalia.

"Uh, sure it's locked up there in the car. I think." I was also wondering why these little dark-haired female officers seemed to find me.

"You *think*?" She was starting to sound less amused and more pissed off.

"Uh, well yeah. It was late and dark, you know. I'm sure I locked my billfold up there." I was trying like hell not to flash her as I got up. I couldn't imagine a good ending to that. I also had no idea where the keys were.

Then she did something unexpected. She stretched out her hand toward the fringe on my shirt. "That shirt," she said, "Seems like I've seen that before somewhere."

The fringe on the sleeve drifted over, all by itself, and brushed her hand. When it touched her, I could have sworn I saw some of the figures on the sleeve light up for an instant.

"Oh," she said. Her eyes changed, went soft. "No need to get up until you're ready." She walked over to her green Grand Cherokee, opened the door and said, "You have a nice day sir." Then she got in and drove away leaving me looking at her dust and disappearing taillights.

What the …?

Hit the road Jack …

About thirty seconds later, Ray Charles and I left Badlands National Park, leaving our own cloud of dust. I was wearing only the buckskin Ghost shirt, working the pedals with my bare feet, and heading for the Nebraska line like a scalded dog.

The keys had been hanging in the ignition, right where, I guessed, I had left them. My damp, filthy clothes and shoes were lying in a pile on the passenger-side floor.

I kept one eye on the road ahead, one eye on the speedometer, and both eyes on the rearview; fully expecting a bevy of police cars with screaming sirens and flashing lights to pop over a rise and unleash a torrent of bullets in my direction.

What had Jack said when he tossed me the shirt? "It's been known to sweeten a sour disposition and it'll protect you from spitballs and bullets." Huh.

The clock on the dash read 7:30 AM. Had time gone into a different mode? Maybe I didn't know what day it was. How long had I been asleep? How long had I been awake? How long was how long? Creepy.

Maybe I had PTSD or some other psychological acronym from shooting a couple of people in the head and leaving all my worldly possessions behind.

But I had on a really old, really funky smelling, psychedelic buckskin shirt, and *it* sure as hell felt real. So if *it* was real, how could the rest not be?

I snapped on the radio. Maybe I could get a handle on reality with some news of death and destruction in some far-off oil-producing country. Bombs and beheadings always seemed to make things pretty real.

The radio came to life and Fleetwood Mac came out singing: Seems like a dream, they got you hypnotized … The radio went dead. I got a chill. And all that air blowing up under my shirt wasn't helping either.

Then, the symbols and writing on the shirt seemed to glow and move around like words crawling across a TV screen. I jerked my bare foot off the gas pedal, pulled over on the shoulder.

The blacktop wasn't hot yet. It felt pretty good on my bare feet; rough and real. I stepped gingerly around the car onto the shoulder. The buckskin shirt came off over my head. I was waiting for something big to happen; like maybe it would call out to me or come alive, or maybe Jack Wilson would appear—POOF—beside me.

Nothing happened and the thing didn't look nearly as bright or alive as it had a minute ago. I opened the passenger door, draped the Ghost shirt over it.

Standing naked along the road, I hoped like hell I could take a spit bath and get into some clean clothes before somebody came down the road. With a pack of wet wipes I did my best to get the sweat and grime out of the nooks and crannies. Clean felt good.

I turned, stepped on something sharp, skidded on loose gravel and went down ass-over-tea-kettle in the ditch; my feet in the air and my dignity exposed to the South Dakota sunshine.

I lay in the ditch looking up at the blue sky and started to giggle. I couldn't stop. Tears ran down my face and into my ears and I just kept on until I was all done.

I took a deep breath. I was clean inside and out; ready to take on whatever I needed to take on.

Dressed in fresh clothes, I was stuffing my dirty stuff into my laundry bag when I saw the shirt I'd worn while killing the Bradleys. It had a dime-sized spot of blood on the cuff. I had a flash of John and Scarlett; first with holes in their foreheads, and then blissfully dancing around a fire in the Badlands.

Then Jack Wilson's Ghost shirt popped off the car door into the ditch. Still as death out there and the thing just jumped off all by itself. My first thought was to drive like hell, leave the shirt right there in the ditch. Then I heard Jack Wilson's singsong voice, "Let's just say it's your turn."

I had been called to the Badlands to get it. I couldn't just leave it there. I couldn't screw with that grand plan any more than I could let the Bradleys get away with raping little kids. I scooped up the Ghost shirt and zipped it inside my duffle bag. The bag went in the back, up against the cab. I got in the front and the El Camino went down the road.

Part 2 CHAPTER 6

Nebraska's welcome sign was a big green rectangle with a sun behind Chimney Rock; the landmark telling the pioneers that the Rocky Mountains were just over there—somewhere.

The sign said Welcome to Nebraska—The Good Life. An added sign on the bottom said, Home of Arbor Day ... Too much information.

This was big, empty country with a wide variety of hills and flats, buttes and open spaces without much but cattle and deer in them.

I went through a bunch of little towns; Ellsworth, Bingham, Ashby, Hyannis, and Whitman, all too small to have their own police.

I considered what may or may not have happened back in the Badlands and all the events that had gotten me there. The idea that I had entered a state of grace, or a new level of consciousness or something, by having actually done what I was meant to do, was even stronger. I was getting a view of things that had always been there. I just hadn't been capable of seeing them before.

Watching the lines on the road and the endless horizon, my mind wandered—flashes of moments. John and Scarlett, leather shirts and Lucky Strikes, Harley Davidsons, and ghosts who danced around a never-dying fire. Twisters moving across open spaces. Flying.

A coyote trotted into the road a hundred feet ahead of me, snapping me out of my daydream. I slowed the car and tapped the horn. The coyote meandered off onto the right shoulder and disappeared into a stand of scrubby cedar trees. I was about to accelerate when I thought I saw a pair of legs jutting out from under a cedar. Legs again!

I found myself making a U-turn, swinging past a sign that said DISMAL RIVER.

Creeping back north in the wrong lane, keeping my eyes peeled for oncoming traffic, I was about convinced I had been looking at shadows when something moved.

I stopped and called out, "Hey, do you need some help?"

A small, very dirty girl stepped from behind the brush, not ten feet from my front fender. She swayed in the ditch, a plastic bag on a drawstring dangled heavily from one clenched fist.

I choked back a gasp. The fear in her eyes was heartbreaking. They were brown and huge; one blackened and swollen. Her face was streaked with dirt and tear tracks, lips cracked and split. I imagined her hair to be blond, but it was so matted and dirty I couldn't be sure.

She hugged herself, exposing raw elbows. Her only clothing was a pair of grimy pink shorts, torn and stained, and a bloody tee-shirt. Both knees were scabbed and she shifted her weight back and forth on naked feet.

I put her somewhere around seven or eight years old; hard to tell through the dirt and the bruises.

She didn't make a sound. I had seen that look of terror before; from three other little girls in what felt like another life. The world, yet again, became a horrible place.

Afraid I might spook her, I shut off the Chevy, looked into her wounded face and asked softly, "Would you like a drink of water?"

I pulled the door handle. She jumped toward the brush. I slid out slowly. "It's OK. I'll get you a bottle of water. I won't get any closer." I was begging. Losing her would be the worst thing I could imagine.

She reminded me of the wild kittens on our farm. They'd let you get about so close, watching you with those scaredy-cat eyes, and then they'd dash away and disappear into unseen holes.

She leaned toward the cedar trees, rocking back and forth, the ratty bag hanging from her hand, ready to bolt if I made the wrong move.

"It's OK. I'll bet you're really thirsty." I wasn't sure she was even hearing me. She kept her eyes glued to my feet. Smart; I couldn't be any threat without first moving my feet in her direction.

"I've got water in the cooler. I'll get some for you."

I hated to take my eyes off of her, fearing when I turned back around she'd be gone. I took two bottles from the cooler and turned slowly. She was still there. Her eyes left my feet, looked at the bottles dripping water from the melted ice. A little patch of pink tongue appeared between her split lips.

"Here, this is for you." I rolled one of the bottles down into the ditch below me. "I won't move. Go ahead and get the water," I called softly.

She stood frozen to her spot, looking at the water lying in the grass fifteen feet away.

She took a halting step toward the bottle, every bit of her attention now focused on me. I sat down, stuck my legs out in front of me. She moved toward the bottle in the ditch, grabbed it and retreated to her original spot. She twisted off the cap and guzzled half the water. The stuff was so cold that her head had to be ringing, but she took a deep breath and drained the rest.

She looked at the bottle still in my hand. I stood and rolled it into the ditch next to the car. She would have to come farther to get it. I sat back down.

Was this a trap? She looked at the bottle; back at me. Thirst won out. She walked down the ditch, scooped up the bottle, twisted off the cap and drank.

I said, "I'll bet you're hungry too." I got up slowly. "If you stay right there, I'll get you something to eat."

She had been through some kind of hell and had been out here by herself for God knew how long. Tears stung my eyes as I moved back toward the red cooler.

I found an orange. "Will you take this from me? It's cool and good." I went behind the car and peeled it. I leaned across the tailgate and extended the fruit over the side toward her. "I'll stay back here and you can come get the orange."

Here she came. It hadn't taken long to make up her mind this time. She carefully reached out and took the fruit. She ate it down; juice dripping from her grimy face and fingers.

"I jumped out," she said. Her words split the air; coming out of nowhere.

"You jumped out of where?"

"The blue car. I jumped out when the men slowed down."

"What men?"

"The men who took me from the gas station," she said. "My mom was paying, and the man picked me up and put something over my mouth. Then I was in a big blue car going fast."

"Where was the gas station?" I said. "Do you know what town the gas station was in?"

"North Platte, where I live," she started to cry. "I want my mom. I want to go home."

She shuddered and sobbed, held her bag in front of her chest like a shield.

I walked around the car and squatted down to look in her eyes. "I will find your mom. You're going to go home really soon. I promise. My name's Chip. What's yours?"

"I'm not supposed to tell my name to strangers," she said with a glimmer of certainty. "My mom says so. She says, 'Maddie, make sure you know people and that I'm with you before you tell anybody your name!'. And that's what I do." Her tears had stopped.

"Well Maddie, that's a good rule," I smiled through my own hot tears. "How long ago did you jump out of the blue car?"

"Oh, I think it was yesterday, or the day before maybe." She drank the rest of her water and handed me the empty.

I tossed it into the car, reached in the cooler for a couple of Fig Newtons. She seemed to gain strength as I watched her eat. I looked at the ripped little feet on the gravel shoulder.

"Let's put something on your feet OK? I don't have any shoes to fit you, but how 'bout some socks at least?" I figured I could pull some of my heavy hiking socks way up on her legs.

"OK," she said.

I handed her a couple more cookies and then went to my duffle bag. Jack Wilson's rolled-up shirt was on top. I laid it on my camping gear as I dug out some balled-up grey socks.

She laid her bag down and separated the thick socks. They looked comically huge in her little hands. Standing on one foot, wavering back and forth, she managed to pull the first one on. It extended all the way up past her knee with the bump of the heel giving her calf a Popeye look. I had to grin. She got her toes in the second sock before she lost her balance and went down in slow motion onto her butt in the grass. She sat blinking for a beat and then laughed. Before I knew it, I was in the ditch laughing with abandon, harmonizing with the pure notes of a little girl's giggles.

She laid her hand on my shoulder. This close her plum-colored, swollen eye made me ache. The back of her shirt was a stiff mass of dry, brown blood.

"These socks feel lots better," she said, wiggling her toes.

"OK," I said. "So what do you say we take you home?"

"I wanna find my mom, but I'm not supposed to get inside cars with strangers. And you are a stranger."

She had me there. "You're right, you shouldn't get into cars with strangers, but I can't just leave you out here can I?"

And how was I going to get her home and keep with my stay-out-of-jail plan?

"Hmmm, do you think I could have another cookie?"

I went for the Newtons. The leather shirt had unrolled and was lying flat across the top of my camping gear in the hot sun. There was a nice little space behind the cab where my duffle bag had been stashed.

"Maddie, did you ever ride in the back of a truck? It's really fun to have the wind blowing in your hair. And I have a window in the back that opens so we could talk to each other."

"Really, I could ride in the back—all by myself?" She beamed through the dirt and the blood.

"Yep, and that wouldn't really be getting in a car with me. You'd still be outside, so I don't think your mom could get mad at you for that," I put on my best seven-year-old conspiratorial tone of voice. "You have to promise not to stand up once we got going."

"I PROMISE," she said solemnly. "Can I bring my stuff too?"

"What stuff Maddie?"

She held out her plastic bag; the strings taut with the weight inside. "Just this."

"What's in there?" I asked.

"My protection."

"OK …" this was creeping me out. What the hell did she have in there? "What is it?"

She reached inside the bag, pulled out a smooth, golf ball-sized, black stone. "There was a coyote watching me, so I got some good rocks to throw if he got too close. And I found the bag in the ditch. Can I bring 'em with me?"

I let out the breath I'd been holding. Don't know what I had expected, but some rocks would be the least of my worries. "Sure, kiddo, you can bring your protection."

"OK!" Maddie chirped.

I swung the little girl up into the spot vacated by my duffle, turned her around and looked at her back; stiff with blood. "Kiddo, I think we should get you cleaned up a little bit. Is your back really sore?"

"Yeah, my back hurts and my shirt feels crunchy," she pointed over her shoulder.

"I bet it does; but it doesn't look so bad," I lied. "Did that happen when you jumped out of the car?"

She got a far-away look in her eyes and the story tumbled out. "I was looking out the car window. It was rolled down. One of the bad men yelled, 'Look out for that coyote!' and then the car was shaking and there was a loud screechy noise and I went on out the window. When I looked up, the blue car was going away from me and I was in the road. I ran into the bushes to hide. The bad men turned around and came back. They got out and started walking, and they were saying bad words and yelling. After a long time a big truck came down the road and the bad men left. Then it got really quiet and I was all by myself. And then my back and feet started to sting real bad, and I couldn't see very well on this side." She laid her fingers under the swollen eye. "I laid down in the bushes and it got dark and I was scared, and I was crying. I fell asleep. When it got light, I woke up. The coyote came right by me. Then there you were Chip. There you were."

Getting it out had done something to her. Tears rolled out. She put her arms around my neck and sobbed. Unbelievably strong arms, almost choking me.

Then she leaned back to look into my face, determination in her eyes again. "Can you make my back feel better?"

We got to work. I gently wiped off her face with wet wipes. There were a lot of freckles under the grime. A cute, tom-boyish face emerged. I spent the next half hour dabbing water onto her shirt, trying to melt the blood and scabs that formed a gory wad from her shoulder blades down to the waistband of her shorts. She lifted her arms above her head and I gingerly peeled the shredded tee-shirt away from her skin. She braved it well with only a little flinching and air sucking through clenched teeth.

Her shoulders were deeply abraded, now oozing blood and fluid; bits of gravel and black grit in the wounds. Her elbows and arms were in the same shape. I worked gently cleaning her wounds.

"OK, kid. Off with the socks."

She pulled my grey socks off, exposing her poor damaged feet. This cleaning hurt worst of all. I dabbed salve on the wounds, then covered the whole mess with white cotton socks, followed again with the thick grey hikers.

I left her shorts alone. They were stained with blood, but it looked like her butt had escaped injury. I planned to let her clean up that area.

"We're about done."

"That's good," she said. "I tried real hard not to cry."

"I know you did. You were very brave." I found a clean white tee in my bag and laid it on the edge of the El Camino's bed. "Well kiddo, I guess we'll put one of my tee-shirts on you," I smiled. "Your, uh, bottom needs to be cleaned up some too."

"I can do it," she said, sensing my discomfort.

I gave her the wet wipes and the shirt and stepped away. I could hear her moving around, humming something the way little girls do.

The humming stopped. "There, all done."

My tee hung past her damaged knees, overlapping the tops of the socks. Except for the matted hair, the black eye and a few scratches, she could have been any cute little girl wearing her dad's clothes.

I picked up her plastic bag full of rocks, and plucked a small white flower growing near the shoulder of the road. "Here's a flower for a princess. And your bag too."

"Thanks Chip. I feel lots better."

I thought I might want to get her stuff to the authorities— DNA and all that— so I scooped up her bloody little rags and put them into a white garbage bag. My DNA was in there too, but somebody else could sort all that out. I was ready to put everything I had into getting Maddie home safe.

"Hey Chip, I want to wear this too. It's really pretty. Can I?" Jack Wilson's fringed leather shirt was in her hands.

"Absolutely, you can. It's your turn." The words just boiled out of my mouth like bats from a cave. I had not hesitated. Once they were out I wasn't even sure that I had said them; except that I heard them, and she had too. They seemed to flit around in the air above her head.

"Can you help me put it on?" She grinned, holding the shirt out to me.

The old buckskin was warm and soft when I took it. It sort of touched you back. Like holding hands in high school. Who was touching who?

The shirt almost slid on by itself. Her face and hands popped out—strange; it fit her better than it should have.

"You know, this is a magic shirt. Think that will be OK?" I said.

She loved it. She beamed as she turned and crouched to look at her reflection in the rear window; Maddie, the blonde Minnehaha of North Platte, Nebraska.

"Chip is this magic shirt mine now?" she asked, admiring her new look.

"For as long as you need it," I said.

She grinned and did a little I-gotta-go-dance. "I need to go to the bathroom now."

I swung her down, gave her some TP and she padded behind a bush in her new shirt.

"Hey Chip," she said. "Sorry, but I got your socks a little wet."

◆   ◆   ◆

In the distance, I heard the vehicle coming. I fired up the El Camino. Parked on the shoulder—facing the wrong way—a white-haired guy and a little kid. They were sure to stop if we didn't move.

Maddie came up the ditch and I lifted her back into her spot. "Sit down and hold tight Maddie, we're taking off."

A large vehicle came into view over a little rise. I jumped in and began a steady acceleration toward it. I'd go over the rise, wait a bit on the other side until they were far enough away, then make a U-turn back to the south; easy.

I looked back over my right shoulder. There was the top of Maddie's head. She seemed safe; sitting down, staying put. The wind was howling into my open window and out through the rear slider. The load in the back was flapping and finding its place again as we sped over dips and bumps.

The oncoming car, a blue SUV, got close fast; two wide guys in the front seat. The passenger was pointing and gesturing at something. The driver looked right into my face. They both had lighted cigarettes hanging out of their mouths and wore camouflage hunting caps. The driver's was jammed on backward.

I caught movement behind me. Maddie was standing, hair whipping, looking over the El Camino's top. I yelled toward the open rear window, "Maddie, please—sit—down!"

As the blue SUV got within ten feet of us, the world went into slow motion and high definition. The driver threw both hands in front of his face, knocking his cigarette away in a red shower of sparks. The passenger's eyes went huge and he screamed. The blue car's windshield exploded in a bursting spray of diamonds.

I had a glimpse in my side view of a blue streak heading through the ditch. My reflexes took over and time sped up. Maddie was still standing, looking back over our tailgate. The shirt had come alive, engulfing the little girl in pure energy.

"Sit down Maddie!" I yelled again.

She dropped to the floor; I got on the brakes, spun the wheel in a U-turn and raced back south.

We hit broken glass on the pavement where deep gashes down the embankment showed the blue SUV's path from the road. I pulled over and went to jump out. Seatbelt still fastened, I dangled there trying to work my way back into the seat; long seconds until the belt snapped open. A quick look in the back ... Maddie was gone.

My God! I ran to the center of the blacktop; nothing either way.

Black smoke rose from the brush. There! A tiny glowing figure moving quickly, disappearing then reappearing, weaving through the scrub toward the wreck.

"Maddie! Maddie! No! Get away from there!" She moved faster than possible, flashes of the shirt through breaks in the growth.

I ran, brambles and branches ripping at my face and clothes, stopping at a little clearing. The SUV lay upside down, rubber and oil fouling the air, a front wheel bent inward. A man rose and staggered. Somehow the camo cap still tight on his head.

A few feet to my right, Maddie darted from the brush into his path. His eyes popped white under the cap. "You!" he bellowed. His arm came up, blue and red tattoos from under a black sleeve. Something glinted. The sound of the shot filled everything. He fired again and again and again; the reports crushing together, echoing down the Dismal River Valley.

Impossibly, Maddie moved toward him—not falling. The Ghost shirt was alive with moving runes and symbols; vivid figures danced and cavorted around the leather.

Terror spread across the shooter's flat, stupid face. A golf ball-sized rock, black as coal, caught him just above the right eyebrow bouncing upward—the dull, wet thudding sound of the impact in stark contrast to his shots. The cap flipped back off his head as the stone spun away. He went down on his knees, arms at his sides, the barrel of his pistol stabbed into the ground. The second rock hit the left side of his forehead two seconds later, a perfect mirror image of the first. He fell, face down in a puff of white dust.

Birds sang …

Maddie vanished back into the brush.

"Maddie! Maddie!" I lurched, searching and calling. Gone again.

Maybe …

I tore through the scrub, up the embankment to the El Camino.

A little girl, wearing a big white tee-shirt, slumbered in the back of the car on my sleeping bag. She had a white flower clutched in one hand, her drawstring bag beside her.

"Maddie." Relief flooded through me. I touched her cheek gently; a curl of the lips, but she did not wake. A sleeping princess.

It couldn't be … but it was.

A dense mushroom of oily smoke grew from the clearing, towering over the river. Even way out there, somebody was bound to wonder. They'd be here soon.

I ran to the dead shooter, pocketed his gun and his camo cap, I dragged his body to the wreck, limp arms catching on roots and trees. I rolled and poked him into the broken-out passenger's side door.

The driver's dead eyes were open, staring up at the smoke-smeared sky. I snatched the greasy, sweat-stained cap lying next to his shoulder and backed away. A blast of hot air whumped past me as the gas from the SUV's tank caught and engulfed the wreck.

As I stepped up onto the road, the coyote ambled out. He paused, looking at me intently. In spite of the burning wreck, he was in no hurry. He was a beautiful light brown, like buckskin, and his eyes threw color. I gave him a salute. He smiled and meandered off into the scrub.

Maddie slept as we crossed the Dismal River. I slowed to a crawl and chucked the dead man's pistol into the water. The camo caps would go in the bag with Maddie's discarded clothes.

Maddie never woke the whole way to North Platte. I'd stopped twice to check on her. She'd barely moved a muscle.

In North Platte, parked at the Goodwill, it was time to wake her up.

Groggy, she didn't know where she was. "Hi Chip." She was still clutching the wilted, white flower. Looking down she exclaimed, "Hey! Where's my magic shirt?"

I'd been wondering that for the past two hours. "I'm not sure, but we'll look for it in a little bit."

She seemed OK, but there was something different about her. Her eye; the swelling was gone and the purple was gone. It was a cute, normal, little girl's brown eye.

"Maddie! Your eye! Your eye, it's all better!" I realized I was raising my voice and a couple of rotund old ladies getting out of a beat-up minivan looked over at me to see what the ruckus was about.

Maddie reached up to touch the eye, feeling the area around it with her slender little fingers.

The sleeve of the tee shirt slid down, exposing her elbow. The elbow was perfect; no scabs, no blood, no grit or gravel stuck in her skin. I grabbed the other sleeve and slid it up; same story, just a peach-colored arm.

I pulled off the socks; feet smooth as the day she was born. She sat wiggling her toes in the late afternoon sunshine; awake now, grinning like it was her birthday. Not a scratch on her …

"Maddie," I said, "can you tell me about what happened back at the wreck?"

She gave me a questioning squint. "What wreck, Chip?"

"The blue car, the men!" I said, trying to keep myself in control; the mini-van ladies still looking at us.

"What men?"

"What happened after you put on the magic shirt?" I asked.

Big brown eyes looked at me. "I was really warm; the shirt was soft and the air was fast. I fell asleep right away."

"You fell asleep right away?"

"Yeah, and I had good flying dreams about clouds until you just woke me up." She looked at me like I was out of my mind.

The Ghost shirt. I had told her it was magic, and it was.

♦ ♦ ♦

I didn't want to traipse her around in my tee-shirt. "Can you wait here in the car while I go inside and get you some clothes?"

"I'll be OK," she said. "I can take care of myself."

Yeah, I'd seen that. Doors locked, I left her in the car eating some string cheese and a flour tortilla, washing it all down with a root beer.

I came out of the Goodwill twenty minutes later with two bags of little girl clothes. I got in the El Camino and rolled down the windows.

A kid on a bike cruised by on Maddie's side. Gave her the once over. "Hey Maddie," he said.

"Hi Matthew," she said.

He shot a look at me and pedaled off, popping a wheelie as he went across the lot.

"You *know* that kid!!!?" I said it louder than I meant to.

Her bottom lip came out and tears welled up in her eyes. "Just our neighbor, Matthew," she said. "Did I do something wrong?"

"No. Oh Maddie, no you didn't do anything wrong. I'm sorry. I was just surprised. He's your neighbor?"

"Yeah, down the hill from us. He's kind of a blabber mouth."

Great.

My first reaction was to bust out of the Goodwill lot and go the opposite direction the kid had gone. He'd seen Maddie. He'd seen me and he'd seen the El Camino. Instead, I reminded myself to calm down; let things just fall into place, the way they always did when I didn't push.

See if there's something in there you can wear," I said, pointing to the bags.

She looked at the Goodwill bags. "I want the magic shirt," she pouted. "What happened to it?"

"I don't know Maddie. Maybe it's in the back. Maybe you wriggled out of it while you were asleep and it blew out."

"Nope. It *will* be back." She examined the clothes and wrinkled her nose at a pair of green shorts. "But, I'm not wearin' these."

Two minutes later, I stopped at a red light. I saw several police cruisers parked in front of a red brick, municipal-looking building—had to be the police station.

I went three blocks, turned onto a deserted industrial street and parked next to a weedy, cracked sidewalk shadowed by parked semi-trucks, chain-link and barbed wire.

"OK kiddo, time to change into some new clothes."

Maddie had selected a pair of white socks, some pink panties, a bright red tee-shirt, a pair of black shorts, and orange rubber shoes; very colorful.

"I'll get out while you change," I said.

"OK, but you'll be right back, right?"

"Yep, just have to get some stuff out of my bag in the back."

As I got out, Maddie's head and arms disappeared inside my tee-shirt. It looked like there were a couple of cats wrestling around in there.

The bicycle kid had gotten a good look at me. I needed a cap, maybe a new shirt. I walked around the car, got the duffle, balanced it on the El Camino's edge and pulled the zipper open. The world spun as figures danced around a fire inside the bag. Jack Wilson's Ghost shirt was making a dim light of its own. Not glowing exactly, more like energy coming off it.

I don't remember reaching into the bag, but I had the shirt in my hands. I stood transfixed, watching the figures dancing on it, savoring the feel of *it* holding *my* hand—and I knew exactly what to do.

Laying the shirt down, I zipped the bag closed and put it back. Maddie was still changing, wrestling inside my man-sized tee.

I heard footsteps behind me. Somebody leaned on the chain-link. "Hey, Chip Crandle."

I turned and saw a short man in a round black hat grinning at me from the shadow of a parked truck.

"Hello Jack," I murmured. "Where did you get off to last night?"

"Oh, I've been around," he kept grinning out from under his hat.

"Yeah, I guess you have," I said.

"Need anything?"

"Nope," I said. "I'm good. Seeing things better all the time."

"Yep." He gave me a little salute and walked off between the trucks and trailers.

As he disappeared I turned back to see Maddie stepping out of the car and into her orange rubber shoes.

"Chip, who were you talking to?"

"Just thinking out loud I guess …"

Maddie turned away, peering under a parked semi-trailer. She giggled and gave a little wave.

I picked up the beautiful, magical Ghost shirt, pulled it on and picked her up. Maddie laid her head on my shoulder and was instantly asleep again.

I drove back three blocks and parked while Maddie slumbered in her seat.

The shirt felt like it was part of me. No other way to describe it. Once inside it, I had no doubts. It was supremely peaceful. Everything was exactly right.

I took the receipt for the Goodwill clothes, turned it over on the console and wrote:

Hello. I'm Maddie, the missing girl. I am not harmed. I escaped from my abductors when they crashed their blue SUV near the Dismal River. They will not harm anyone again. I want to go home.

I realized I didn't know Maddie's last name. But I guess that really didn't matter. She didn't know mine either. In fact, she wouldn't remember ever knowing me at all.

I got out of the car, walked around to her side, picked up the sleeping child and the white garbage bag that held her bloody clothes and the caps I had taken from the dead men. On the dash I saw the wilted white flower. I tucked it carefully over her ear.

She was like a bit of fluff in my arms. The shirt was alive on me and I seemed to be expanding inside it. Nobody else on the street, I glided over the sidewalk.

The police station was dead quiet except for a young cop getting out of his black-and-white. He was facing the building; didn't see me coming. I brushed my arm against him; ghosts dancing.

"Hi," he said. "Can I help you?"

I handed him the note and the bag of clothes. Then I handed him Maddie; neck limp, blond hair pushed into a pile, the wilted flower peeking over her ear.

"Bye little princess, sweet dreams," I think I said that out loud.

"Take very, *very* good care of her," I said to the young officer. "Please sit here in your car with her for thirty minutes then take her, and the note, and the bag to your boss. Do not leave her with anybody else until her mother comes to take her home."

"Yes, that's what I'll do," he smiled and gently cradled Maddie up against his bulletproof vest with his big, weight-lifter's arm. "She'll be safe with me."

And I knew she was.

Part 2 CHAPTER 7

I felt just fine. You don't cry when you're sure.

The Ghost shirt came off like any other piece of clothing. The dancers were done. I rolled it up and zipped it back inside my duffle bag.

The confidence I'd felt at the police station hadn't come off with the shirt; it stayed with me all the way through town.

As I left North Platte, The Pretenders showed up; Chrissie Hynde's gritty staccato voice started my trip on the right notes: "Pains left behind me ..."

I still had some ground to cover, but my old fears and pains were steadily dropping out the back of the El Camino, breaking up on the asphalt and blowing away.

I was driving, flowing with the music. Not left, not right, but just right ... in the middle.

Outside McCook, the radio said the unseasonably hot weather was going to continue. It didn't have anything to say about a missing girl being found, or to be on the lookout for an old guy in a maroon 1968 El Camino. Maybe the kid on the bike wasn't such a blabber mouth after all. Or maybe the shirt had reached out to him too?

I imagined the scene at the police station. The young cop walking in carrying Maddie. He would be a hero. Then he would be the subject of intense scrutiny because he wouldn't have any answers, and neither would Maddie. It was sad to think she wouldn't remember me when she woke up. But that's the way it had to end.

The beehive of cops would begin buzzing, trying to sort it all out and make sense of it. And they would; but none of it would be what had really happened. They would want to get it off the books as quickly as possible. They'd check out the Dismal River area, figure out who the dead guys were and assign guilt to them. The caps I'd stuck in the bag with

Maddie's clothes would tie them to her abduction. It would make such a neat little package.

The Conspiracy Theorists Group, down at the North Platte version of Bevans Brothers coffee shop, would have a decade's worth of material to work with.

I pulled into a Shell station and topped off the tank; the spaces between towns would be getting bigger again. I resupplied my cooler and snacks. To my surprise, the Shell had Lucky Strikes. I grabbed a BIC and was set to go.

Next stop Kansas, the state in which I'd lost my virginity and gotten most of my college education forty years earlier. About forty-five miles later, I passed the blue welcome sign. It had a shooting star; I guess that's what it was anyway. I seemed to remember a sunflower on the Kansas welcome signs, but maybe it wasn't the Sunflower State anymore? Still; they'd kept it simple. Not a bad sign.

Kansas, the launching pad for the land of OZ, where all the characters figured out they'd always had what they needed.

I pulled over on the shoulder and opened up my atlas. About seventy miles south, Scott State Park looked like the ticket. I suspected that by 9:00 I could pitch my tent with little fuss, keep the car in the dark and leave in the morning before anybody knew I was there.

The sun was dropping to my right, golden and orange. Big, flat-bottomed clouds were forming, their tops growing into water towers above the plains as the sun lit them from below.

I felt as big as the clouds, and as fast as the car, and as open as the country spreading out all around me. I was doing the right thing. Suzanne would have been proud of me. God I felt good.

◆   ◆   ◆

It was dark when I passed through the gates of Scott State Park. There was a bevy of signs and notices on a roofed kiosk at the entrance. I rolled out of my seat and dug a flashlight out of my camp box.

"A startling oasis of natural springs, deep wooded canyons and craggy bluffs. And the site of the northernmost pueblo in the United States." Who knew? All I wanted was a hot shower and a place to pitch my tent without a lot of people noticing me.

I found the rules for camping. Here were the magic words I was looking for: Campers who arrive after hours must take the card to the office by 10:00 the following morning to register. Perfect.

I grabbed a park map, scanned it with my flashlight. The park had three modern shower buildings and a hundred primitive camp sites. Bing. Perfect again.

The shower building was where it was supposed to be. A big security light lit up the area around the building and a cloud of bugs was swarming around the bulb. As the car stopped vibrating and silence fell over me, weariness settled in my bones.

I grabbed all my toilet stuff and headed up the concrete walk. Two guys came through the door, on their way out. They looked familiar, but the light was kind of funky and I was dead-dog tired.

I nodded at them and said, "Evening guys. Hot enough for you?"

The bigger one, with the gothic letters tattooed up and down his forearms, stopped and glared at me. "What're you, some kind of fuckin' weather man?"

The short one added his insight, "Haw. Haw. Haw."

About that time, the biker clothes registered and my tired brain worked it out. I kept walking, hoping the Harley boys wouldn't remember me as the rightful owner of CAMPEROUNDUP's spot 13. And if they did, would they figure me for the early morning motorcycle barista? And what were they doing in a modern shower building in the middle of Kansas anyway? I stifled a laugh, no use pissing them off. But I found it all too funny for words.

The big guy grunted something to his road companion and they headed off through the parking lot into the darkness.

I waited until they were out of sight and went on in. The shower room was well lit with some kind of vapor lights mounted way up high on the ceiling trusses. There were four porcelain sinks, two toilet stalls and four showers. White plastic shower curtains hanging on galvanized pipes, between cinderblock partitions, gave some privacy to campers as they washed.

I went to the first shower and slid the damp plastic curtain aside. Somebody had left some shampoo. One damp stray white sock lay underneath the bench opposite the shower head.

I turned the handle and the water came out steaming. Yes! I had just set my stuff down on the bench and stripped down to my shorts when I caught movement at the door.

The big Harley boy stood glaring at me.

"What's up?" I said, considering my options, which were damn few.

He walked toward me, fists clenched, looking from side to side, stooping to look under the doors of the toilet stalls.

I unzipped my duffle and laid my hand on the Ghost shirt. The guy was almost on top of me. He bent forward, blowing sour breath just inches from my face.

"Hey dude, I think I left a fuckin' sock in here. Did you happen to see it?"

"Uh, yeah, yeah, there's one under the bench," I leaned down and fished the threadbare sock up out of the water and sand. "That the one you're looking for?"

"Yep, that's the one," He mumbled through his beard. "Fuckin' thing musta fell outta my bag."

I held it out gingerly; first because it had to be alive with all kinds of crud, and second because I thought he might just grab my wrist, break my hand off and stick it up my nose before he and his buddy, who had to be lurking outside, took me in the shower and gave me a jailhouse strip search with benefits.

"Thanks dude." He took the horrible rag in his bear paw, turned, and headed toward the door. He paused at the sinks, looked at himself in the mirror. "Do I know you from someplace? You kinda look familiar. You ever spend any time in Oklahoma City?"

I wasn't exactly sure what he meant by "spending time," but I hadn't spent *any* kind of time in Oklahoma City. "No, I sure haven't, but I get that all the time. I just have one of those faces."

"Huh," he said. "Yeah, I guess."

He checked his look in the mirror. Beautiful, he schlumphed out.

Threat gone, I got in the shower. The water was luxuriously hot. My chin on my chest, I let the stuff plastered to me like greasy diary pages of the past couple of days just run down the drain.

I stepped out clean—see-through—what-you-see-is-what-you-get clean.

I wrapped a towel around my waist and looked in the mirror. An old man stared out at me, but he looked content. Maybe for the first time in my life, I didn't ask myself who the hell I was and what the hell was I doing? I was OK. I was really OK.

After a shave, I dug down under the Ghost shirt to get some fresh clothes. It was just an old leather shirt now; nothing magic about it.

The El Camino took me to the most remote camping spot in the park, where I got set up. I pulled the top off the last of my original bottles of beer. I had bought it two days before I killed the Bradleys. The guy who paid for that beer was a different person living in a different world; both of which no longer existed.

A fantastic lightning show bloomed across the western horizon. I had read somewhere that a single electrical storm had enough power to light all the homes in the United States for a year. Watching that far-off display, I didn't doubt it.

I emptied my bottle then opened a beer from my new world. I drank it gratefully as the thunder rolled and the atmosphere thickened with moisture.

In my tent, I was gliding above the Great Plains. I was flying over a rainbow. And I thought, God, I'm in Kansas dreaming about flying over a rainbow … how hokey can you get?

Then stuff started swirling around and I was soaring amid all my worldly possessions. There was my house, the El Camino, the tent and all my camping gear up in the clouds. My Beretta, the one I'd used to get rid of John and Scarlett, came tumbling by. Then a fire pit, complete with a banked, flaming fire arrived and around it danced the ghosts and they saw me and the dance became more animated and they gyrated and threw their bodies into the motions with abandon. The music played and changed as it had in the Badlands, only this time two thick men in camo hunting caps brought up the rear, and they looked at me with peaceful eyes that conveyed what? Grace was the closest I could come to putting a word to it. Then hot dogs and packs of Lucky Strikes and powdered sugar doughnuts and bottles of beer. Then

Maddie, like a little princess floating in sugar clouds. None of them seemed to be going any place in particular, just flying through my dream.

Then Ben and Jessica, and all their girls soared high; high above it all in a formation like geese flying south, on their way somewhere, waving and smiling down at me.

Part 2 CHAPTER 8

The storm in the west never came into Kansas that night. I was glad. I hate putting away wet gear. As I was striking my camp site, there was a huge weather pattern moving into Oklahoma. It looked like Mother Nature and I were on the same wavelength.

The sun was just a glow in the east, a glow matched by the warm light coming out of the shower house windows. Walking up the concrete path, I heard a shower and singing. I thought about turning around, getting in my car and rolling south, but I was already out and ready to do my morning thing, so I kept on walking. The singer kept it up as I walked in.

"Just a closer walk with Thee …"

Outside the first shower, leaned up against the bench, was a large external frame backpack loaded with all the gizmos. It was bigger than Tree Man's; probably could have held three million bucks.

I chose a toilet stall, closed the door, shot the bolt and sat down. The voice in the shower continued the serenade, "I am weak, but Thou art strong …"

Then a horrible, high-pitched howling started— reverberating off the walls and the underside of the metal roof. As the guy sang louder, the howling got louder; until the doors on the toilet stalls vibrated against their stops and the windows rattled in their frames. An empty shaving cream can danced off a shelf, hit the floor and rolled—ker-lick, ker-lick, ker-lick—across the damp concrete, under the door of my stall, and came to rest against my toe. I flushed, and stepped out.

Except for the sound of the shower's spraying water, it all got pre-dawn quiet for a couple of beats. Then tremendous laughter erupted from behind the white plastic shower curtain as it waved out and in. A young man said, "How 'bout another?"

"Sure," a strange, gruff voice responded.

The singing started again, "I know a girl; she lives on the hill, if she won't do it her sister will ..."

The howling started again and the guy started laughing so hard I expected him to fall down and slide out under the curtain on a bed of bubbles.

As I took a step toward the sinks, a big, short-haired, red-and-white dog stuck its head around the curtain; water dripping from its ears and chin. I'd never seen a dog quite like it before; not exactly cute, but beautifully happy. It cocked its head and grinned at me.

"Hey there," I said.

Then a guy, maybe eighteen or nineteen years old, stuck his head out, water dripping from his ears and chin, and gave me a matching grin. "Hey," he said. "I didn't know anybody was up yet. Hope I didn't disturb you sir."

"Naw, I've been up a while," I said as I washed my hands. "You have some pretty interesting taste in music there my man."

The dog left the shower stall and began its post-shower ritual. The twisting and shaking started just behind his ears and worked its way back the length of his long tail, water pelting everything in a ten-foot radius.

"Well, they're the only two songs she knows," the kid said in what I'm sure was his most serious tone. "She loves a good shower almost as much as I do," he grabbed a towel that had been adroitly placed under the frame pack where it was shielded from the dog's shake-spray. "And that's saying something."

I thought of how good the shower felt last night and returned the kid's smile. "That is a very cool dog."

"Thanks," he said. "That's my pal, Sally."

I leaned over the sink to wash my face. Odd, I thought, I can't remember a kid that age using the word "pal" for a long time. And he had called me sir.

Putting his backside to me, he dried off and got dressed in teenage stuff. His hair was straight, not too long, and a reddish brown. He'd been in the sun and was tan. Maybe five foot ten, and slim. He looked like he could walk all day, and probably had been doing just that for a while.

The place was starting to smell like wet dog. I leaned over and wiped the fogged mirror with my hand. The face looking through the streaks looked happy enough, not nearly as old as it had the night before.

The dog's cold nose was suddenly thrust up between my legs from behind.

"Sally!" the kid yelled. "God, I'm so sorry sir. Sometimes she has the manners of a dog. SALLY! Will you just sit down and chill out!"

I had grabbed the sides of the sink and hoisted myself up on tiptoes just in time to avoid some serious male injury. "Sally, you just have a very aggressive way of saying good morning don't you?" I said, laughing.

Sally was now seated; tail wagging violently, looking out of the corners of her rolled eyes as the kid advanced on her with menace. The dog worked its magic. By the time the kid had walked the ten feet, he was out of the mood to mete out any discipline.

I held out my hand. "Hi, I'm Keith Crandle." There I went again! Why had I used my father's name?

The kid gave me a confused look, but his handshake was firm. Behind me, Sally whined just a single note.

"I'm Charlie ... Crandle," he said. "That doesn't happen very often. The name thing I mean; Keith was my dad's name." His face held a significant story when the name of both our fathers came out of his mouth.

"You spell your name with an A-L or L-E?" he said.

"It's L-E."

"Me too," he said.

I had not wanted to start a conversation with anybody, let alone someone with the same name. "Uh, I grew up back in Iowa," I said, thinking it wouldn't lead anywhere close to North Idaho.

"Iowa," the kid said. The dog was leaning on him so hard he had to readjust his footing so he wouldn't be pushed over. "My folks all came from California." He looked down at Sally. The dog was so in love with Charlie she was about ready to split.

Charlie stroked her spotted head lightly, "Where you headed?"

"Uh, well, uh, I'm heading to Oklahoma City. I've got relatives there." I wasn't thinking very fast yet and the kid's name had me distracted.

He broke out in another wide smile. "That's unbelievable. That's where I'm headed too. You don't suppose we're headed to see the same relatives do you?"

What happened to throwing the camp-site money in the box and high-tailing it for Oklahoma while it was still dark? I looked out the window and could see the top of the El Camino shining in the waking sunlight.

"Wouldn't that be something," I said.

"I'm going to stay with my aunt and uncle; my mom's brother. Oh, I guess they couldn't be related to you could they?"

"Not likely," I said, glad we didn't have to pursue that one any further.

Charlie kept talking. "I've been hitching for more than a week already, you know, seeing the country, keeping a diary. My dad always said the time he spent between high school and college, just seeing things, was the best time he ever spent.

He always said that ..." The kid trailed off and sorrow appeared in his eyes. Sally sensed it and groaned. He knelt down to touch noses with her. "Anyway, my dad always said I should take this time to get out on the road, so here I am."

"How long ago did you lose your dad?" I felt like he wanted to tell me.

"Oh, ah, last year. Yeah, sorry, I didn't mean to get into this. I, well, you have his same name and you even kind of look like him. He was older when I was born ... cancer."

"Sorry. Losing your dad is a tough thing. Mine died too young too. How 'bout your mom?" I said, forgetting that I was in a hurry to get going.

"Oh, Mom's great. I keep telling her she needs to start looking around. She's only fifty. I hope she won't stop living because my dad's gone. But it's only been a year so ..."

Sometimes things just gotta be said, and somebody's gotta be there to listen. I was OK with that. Then I had another one of those out-of-body experiences where I was sitting up on the roof trusses looking down, watching myself say something completely idiotic.

"So, what's your plan?" I said. "I can give you a ride all the way to Oklahoma City if Sally can ride in the back. I've only got two seats in my car."

Maybe two guys in a classic car would be a better cover than just one? I was having a separate conversation with myself trying to justify it all.

"Really?" he said, excited. "Oh, man, that would be so awesome; I'm about down to my last ten bucks."

We trooped out to the El Camino. Charlie made a big deal out of the old car while I showed him where I thought Sally and his gear might fit best. The campground was coming to life. A load of coffee and bacon was cooking; that wonderful, wonderful camp smell.

"You sure you want me along?" Charlie looked me straight in the eye and said this sincerely. He was a good kid.

"Absolutely, I can use the company and I'm going right to Oklahoma City anyway."

I walked back into the shower building to get my stuff. The face in the mirror grinned at me and said, "Oh, what the hell."

◆ ◆ ◆

"All set?" I asked, across the loaded back end.

Sally turned her head to look at me and said "Sure." She did. I swear it.

We made our way through the maze of one-way roads out toward the park's entrance. I dropped a twenty in the lock-box. We got up to speed on the two-lane, wind whipping through the open back window.

"You had your breakfast?" I asked.

"Oh, I had a couple of power bars, so I'm OK," Charlie said.

"Well, I'm not. I think it's half an hour to Garden City. I'll be up for coffee and something to eat by then."

Sally stuck her head in through the open slider. Charlie reached up and rubbed her nose. She closed her eyes and enjoyed the attention. "You lay down now girl," Charlie said. Her head disappeared below the window and Charlie slid it shut. It sealed up with a whooshing sound and the cab got a whole lot quieter.

I pulled the atlas from between my seat and the console and handed it to my new traveling companion. "I'd like to take the scenic route. You wanna plot us a course?"

"Sure," he said, taking it from me. "This is pretty old school. I didn't know they still made these, or did it come with the car?"

"You do know how to read a map, right?" I hoped I hadn't insulted the kid, but it occurred to me the paper map might be a new experience for him.

He gave me a look; maybe I was going to turn out to be an asshole, or maybe I was kidding him.

"I'd say we stay on 83, down through Garden City; and, let's see …" He flipped the Atlas pages again, finding the Oklahoma map. "Then we head east on 412 and angle down on 279 all the way there."

"Fine by me," I said. It didn't matter. It would all work out.

Charlie pulled a phone out of his pocket and was tapping the screen. A female voice with a British accent said, "Continue south on highway eighty-three for sixty-six miles."

"You do know how to follow a GPS, right?" he was looking straight ahead, smirking.

"Touché, "I said. The kid had only known me for about an hour and already was flipping me crap. "Call me a codger," I said, "but I still like to look at a real map, and read a real book."

"OK, you're a codger!" He didn't miss a beat.

This was going to be fun.

He looked up from the map, "I get what you're saying. I have a bunch of my dad's books. I like the real pages and the weight. Does that make sense?"

"Yes, it does," I said, new faith for the next generation growing the more we talked. "Something about the weight makes them seem less disposable."

His phone rang; the ringtone was classic Little Feat; those eleven notes from Dixie Chicken.

Charlie checked the screen; answered the phone, "Hi, Mom … Yeah having a blast …" His conversation faded and the tune took me over: If you'll be my Dixie chicken …

How could you not turn that up and push the accelerator down? I lost the thread of the song when I heard Charlie say, "Yeah Mom, his name is the same as Dad's."

The look on his face let me know *Mom* was taking a dim view of him sitting in some stranger's car.

"He's heading to Oklahoma City and is giving me a ride all the way."

He stopped. Apparently his mother was giving the mandatory, be-careful-young-man speech, because he looked at me and rolled his eyes. Then he said, "I always am Mom. Sally already gave him the nose test!" He shared a laugh with his mom. "OK," he said, wrapping it up, "Love you too."

"I'll bet your mom isn't as thrilled with your trip as your dad would have been," I said.

"You got that right." He looked out the window. "My mom's pretty incredible though."

Eighteen or nineteen and he had that figured out already. "I'll bet she is," I said. "I'll just bet she is."

We continued south, sailing the ocean of pivot-irrigated crops at seventy miles an hour. We talked about music—he appreciated all kinds; books—his dad had left him the complete set of Jack Aubrey Books and I did my best not to gush about that; dogs—Sally was a shelter puppy who had crawled in his backpack when his family went to look for the perfect dog; love—he had a steady girl in high school but they had gone their separate ways after his dad's death. We had just started talking about the relative strengths of digital versus vinyl when we hit the outskirts of Garden City.

That meant my favorite fast-food breakfast and coffee would be coming into view. Sure as death, taxes and the rising sun, the golden arches appeared on the horizon. About two minutes later, at the drive-thru menu, I asked Charlie, "So what'll it be for you?"

"I didn't hitch a ride with you for a free breakfast." Charlie opened the slider and put a hand on Sally.

"I think I asked you along. I've got some extra money I'm dying to spend," I said. He didn't know how true that was.

So we ordered.

Sally stuck her head through the opened slider. She was one of those calm dogs who understood a lot. She closed her eyes as Charlie rubbed her ear and worked down under her chin.

I pulled up to the window where a pleasant young lady in a jaunty brown cap took my twenty and handed me our stuff; followed by three Milk Bones.

The girl broke into a big smile and said, "What an awesome dog!" I think she would have liked to get to know the awesome dog's owner better, but we were pulling away.

I handed the whole load over to Charlie. "This thing has no cup holders at all?" he grimaced.

"Nope, we used to actually stop to eat and drink. And you know what; I'm not in that big of a hurry." I pulled into a parking spot by a couple of alfresco Mc-Tables. "Let's eat out here where we can enjoy our food and not end up wearing most of it. Maybe Sally needs to take a break before we get serious about putting on some miles."

After we ate, I worked on my coffee and Charlie took Sally to a grassy strip by the street. Successful, he picked up after her then took it, along with the rest of our trash, over to the bin and threw it all in.

That's when the Garden City cop pulled in right behind the El Camino.

The cop didn't look happy; probably been up all night fighting crime and just wanted to go home and have his wife rub his back. He had a little notebook in his left hand and was leaning his right on his holstered pistol. He glanced at the notebook, then looked right at me and said, "Is your name Crandle?"

I sat my coffee down and cleared my throat, which was hard because my heart was up next to my tonsils beating about six thousand times a minute.

Well I guess this was it. The magic had run out. I picked up the cup and took a sip of coffee to see if I could get my voice working.

The cop shifted his weight, his hand still resting on his pistol.

"Yes sir, it is. I'm Charlie Crandle."

But it wasn't me. It was Charlie, the other Charlie Crandle, who was talking. He and Sally had walked up behind me as the cop approached. I looked into my coffee cup. *It* couldn't see the confusion in my eyes.

"I thought that had to be you," the cop said. "I saw your dog and there couldn't be another one like it within a hundred miles of Scott State Park." He stood staring at Sally, mumbled something like, "Dead ringer … I'll be damned," then said to Charlie, "What's your dog's name?"

Charlie said, "Sally." And Sally looked up.

I sat stunned. I had been within a hair's breadth of throwing my hands up in the air and saying something brilliant like, "You got me," or "Well that's kind of a relief."

"My brother is the ranger over at Scott State Park," said the cop. Now he only looked tired, or maybe sad was a better guess. "He called me yesterday afternoon and said he'd seen this dog and he'd talked to you about her. Remember that?"

Charlie knew what it was all about. "Well, yeah. His name's uh, Ted, right?"

"That's right." The cop had gotten close enough that I could see his badge number, 422, and the brass name-tag with UDAHL engraved across it in big block letters.

I gulped more coffee.

The cop paused at the curb and looked down at me. "Are you two together?"

"Yeah," Charlie said easily. "This is Keith Crandle, no relation. He's giving us a ride to Oklahoma City."

"Hi, Keith," said the cop extending his meaty hand. "I'm Mike Udahl. Hope I'm not holding you up. This won't take too long, but it's kinda weird."

I shook his hand, hoping he didn't have some kind of cop radar that could detect my true identity. "Hi Officer Udahl. I'm in no hurry."

Charlie said, "What did you want to talk to me about Officer Udahl?"

"Well … awwww!" squeaked the cop. Sally had struck again. She'd worked her way behind the unsuspecting Udahl and only her ears were showing out from under his wide butt.

"Sally, damn it! God, I'm so sorry. She keeps doing that." Charlie was mortified.

Sally backed out, smiled and sat contentedly on the concrete, apparently having gotten whatever information she had wanted to extract.

Mike Udahl started to laugh. He must have needed a good one because the tears ran down his cheeks and he roared on so that Charlie and I couldn't help but join in.

"Well, I guess she just wants to be sure who's friendly and who isn't," he finally got out as he wiped his eyes. "Can I buy you guys a cup of coffee? I'm off duty now and I could use one myself. Then we can talk."

We told him that would be fine. He got up and moved his car into the space beside the El Camino and went inside.

"What the heck is this all about Charlie?" I said.

"Well, I'm not sure, but it's got to be something about Sally. His brother, the park ranger, was really interested in her. Said his nephew had a dog like her. He didn't say much more than that because he got a call and had to leave."

"I guess we'll find out in a minute," I said.

Officer Udahl came toward us with the coffees in a cardboard carrier. He sat at the table, took a deep breath, looked up under the Hamburgler umbrella and began his story.

"This is kinda tough ... and on the other hand it's kind of like some miracle you'd see in a movie." He looked at Charlie. "My son has leukemia, the worst kind of leukemia. I won't go into the details, but he's only six and he's in the hospital—probably for the last time."

Seeing this big cop, wearing a gun and a bullet-proof vest, with tears running down his face, I was overwhelmed by the depth of his love and despair as he faced something no father should have to face.

"Anyway," he wiped his eyes with the back of his hand. "My son, Toby, had a dog. Your dog Sally looks exactly like her. Not kind of like her—*exactly*."

"We got her two weeks after Toby was born. They were together every day and every night. We named her Sofie because she ate up an old sofa in our garage the first week we had her. Sofie and Toby were inseparable. They got in more trouble together, and we've had more fun with them than you can imagine." He paused and stared at the plastic lid on his coffee cup.

Charlie and I did the same. Sally snored in the shade of the table.

Mike Udahl continued, "A couple of years ago Toby started having his health issues. We've kept him at home as much as we could. Sofie always knew when Toby was having trouble before we did. She'd come and get my wife or me. Sofie has been the one thing that has brought him joy and comfort—and he's only six. He's only six ..."

When he repeated *he's only six*, I couldn't hold back the tears. They streamed out. Charlie looked stricken. Sally sat up;

put her head on his knee. His hand unconsciously stroked her neck.

"I'm not getting to the point here," Udahl said. "Last week things got worse for Toby and we had to take him to the hospital. We left Sofie in the house. Our next door neighbor was going to check on her. We didn't know how long we'd be gone."

"When we left, Sofie went crazy. She went through a screen and took off after us. She got hit half a block from our house by a truck. Our neighbor took care of her body ... and everything.

"The thing is; we haven't told Toby. I'm afraid it would kill him." He stopped; a father talking about the impending death of his son, desperate to do something.

"My brother called yesterday and told me about your dog. He went to talk to you this morning and you were gone. And then—this is the miracle part—I was driving by here and saw you and Sally walk out onto that grass. You had to be the guy. She had to be the dog ..."

Sally heard her name, got up and walked around the table to look at the big cop. She sensed his dismay and leaned against his tree-trunk thigh.

He let out a shuddering sigh. "You look just like Sofie. Yes you do." He spoke into her soft ear.

"So, what do you want us to do?" Charlie asked. "I'm just knocked flat by this whole thing. I mean, that you just happened to see us like that. It's weird. It had to happen. You were supposed to find us."

The cop nodded. "It seems like the closer I get to the end with Toby, the more this kind of stuff happens. He stopped and looked at both of us. "You think I'm crazy?"

"No," I said. "There's nothing crazy about it. Things arrange themselves. I've seen some stuff in the past few days that would make you ..." I thought better of saying more.

The cop grabbed a couple of napkins and wiped his eyes. "I want to borrow Sally for as long as Toby is, is … as long as Toby needs her. I'll pay you anything you ask." The big cop's pleading look was the saddest thing I've ever seen.

Udahl and I both turned our eyes to Charlie. Charlie Crandle, the owner of a smart, joyful dog that sang with him in the shower and now seemed to hold the one final hope for happiness for a terminally ill boy and his father.

"Well, that's, that's, uh. I dunno what else to say except, of course! You wouldn't owe me anything. I'm just so happy that you found us, and grateful that, uh we, Sally, can help your son." Charlie's eyes brimmed full and the tears ran down his tanned cheeks; a beautiful generous kid. He was actually going to give his dog to a stranger.

"What do you say Sally?" He said to the dog that was still leaning on Udahl. "You want to go with Officer Udahl? You want to go meet Toby?"

Sally gazed at Charlie, listening intently, then she threw up her chin and I swear she said it again, "Sure." The same word I'd heard come out of the shower stall and the back of my car that morning. Then she sat down beside Udahl and smiled again.

Udahl was dazed. Sometimes running after something is all you can see. But when you catch up to it and grab it, you don't exactly know what to do next.

"Please," said Udahl, "Call me Mike for Christ's sake. I'm sitting here bawling like a baby. You can at least call me by my first name."

"OK Mike. I want you to keep Sally as long as Toby needs her. I want only one thing from you."

"Anything," Mike had a rare kid in his presence and he knew it.

"Don't waste a minute of the time that Sally is with you. Not a minute, not a second." Charlie's eyes bored into the cop's. "You gotta promise me not to have any regrets at all."

Officer Mike Udahl stretched his big mitt across the table to Charlie. "I promise not to waste a single second of the time that Sally is with us. You have my word on that."

The kid and the cop gripped hands. I half expected the table to levitate and zoom around, with all four of us, over the golden arches.

Charlie looked at Sally and said, "Well girl, you better get used to being called Sofie."

We loaded Sally's stuff into Mike's car. There wasn't much; a couple pounds of dog food, a chewed-up Frisbee, and a fold-up nylon water bowl.

Charlie looked from Mike to Sally, and back again. "I'll have a talk with her and tell her to behave … And to knock off the cold-nose greeting stuff," he grinned.

"Uh, funny thing about that," Mike grinned back, "Sofie did the same thing."

We made an attempt at another laugh but things had gotten a little awkward.

Charlie knelt down to look into Sally's bright eyes. "You're going to be taking care of a different little boy now. I know you'll be really good at it, 'cause you already were. I'll see you girl."

"Here," Mike said as he handed something to Charlie. "That's a picture of Toby; took it a couple of weeks ago. I can never tell you what this means. What you're doing is pure good—pure good. Thank you."

Mike put Sally in the front passenger seat of his squad car. She sat, unconcerned, looking out at Charlie. The squad car backed out and pulled slowly away, turned onto the street and headed toward town.

"Bye Sally," Charlie said with one last tear. "Come on Keith. Let's go before I change my mind and run after them."

We clicked our seat belts.

"Hey Keith, take a look at this," Charlie said, handing me a wallet-sized photo; a little boy, completely bald, with a gap-toothed smile. He hugged the neck of a dog; Sally or Sofie? No way to tell.

"That was the most unselfish thing I have ever seen," I said, pulling out onto the highway. "You just scored about a gajillion Karma points. I've got a feeling Sally is going up a couple of levels too."

"She was already heading for Nirvana in my book," Charlie said through a sad smile. "I might have done myself some real harm if she hadn't been around during Dad's cancer. God, I wonder what my mom is going to say?"

"I feel like some music," I said. I wanted to think about gratitude, not loss. "What do you say?"

Charlie reached over and turned on the radio. Steve Winwood answered the call: "Think about it, there must be higher love …"

We tooled down across flat country, singing and talking. If he had any second thoughts about leaving his dog, Charlie didn't show it.

Part 2 CHAPTER 9

The sixty-seven miles to Liberal, the last town in Kansas, flew by.

As we hit town I said to Charlie, "I love that name, Liberal. Where else, but in this country, would somebody name a town for an attitude? The guy who lived here gave the settlers free water as they passed through on their way west. When the town got started they said he was *liberal* with the water, and that's what they named the town."

"Nah, really?" Charlie thought I might be making it up.

"True story," I said. "Google it if you want."

The car went quiet for a couple of miles. Charlie had discovered a Milk Bone in his pocket. He turned it over in his hand. "She was a little pup when we found her at the shelter. She's been with me for eleven years—more than half my life. A load of people on this trip seemed like they were giving *her* the ride and I was just part of the deal. I'm an incredibly charming guy ... But without Sally, I would have done a lot more walking."

I bit. "Yeah, I was trying to figure out a way to give Sally a ride and leave you singing in the shower, but you'd already seen me so I had to take you along."

He shook his head.

"Seriously ... how did you get her?"

"My dad and I had wanted to get a dog for a long time. We finally convinced Mom to go to the shelter and have a look for my seventh birthday. I'd watched the Iditarod on TV the week before and had it in my head that I had to have a Husky, so I ran into that shelter looking for the Husky section.

"There was this little dried-up guy sitting behind the counter. I said, 'Where's your Husky room?'. The guy said, 'What's a Husky room?'. And I said, 'You know, the room where you keep all the Huskies, when they're not pulling the sleds.'. My parents came in just in time to hear the guy say, 'Jeez kid, we ain't got no Huskies. I can't remember the last time we did. They can be pretty mean, you know. Got some Labs though.'.

"I was devastated. My dad put his hand on my shoulder and said to the guy, 'Maybe we should check just to be sure.'. We went into the back. I'll never forget how loud it was, walking through row after row of caged dogs, all hoping for a new home. There was this one puppy, all by itself, mostly white but with red spots and red ears. We locked eyes through the wire of the cage. I remember my dad saying, 'you want to hold that one?'

"I went into the room where you can visit with the dogs and took off my backpack. A red-haired lady, she looked like an elf, brought in the pup. She said, 'This little girl just came in.'. Well, that pup marched over, got behind me and stuck her nose up under my crotch; then proceeded to pull everything out of my pack and got inside like 'let's go!'. I forgot all about Huskies."

"Pretty great story, Charlie. So why'd you name her Sally?"

"My mom named her," he said, leaning his head back. "Since it was my birthday, Dad swung into a drive-thru and we all got burgers and stuff to go. We started to pull away from the drive-up window and the pup let out a terrific squeal. It scared the heck out of all of us. Dad slammed on the brakes and our drinks and fries and bags flew all over the place.

"Then this woman comes running out and practically dives down in front of our car. She popped up with this little kid in her arms and she's crying and the kid's crying ...

"I'll never forget the look on my mom's face. She said, 'Good Lord Keith, we almost ran over that little boy!'. Turned out the kid had wandered away while his mom was talking to someone. He'd worked his way around the building and gone across the drive-thru lane right in front of us. Dad couldn't see him at all. If Sally hadn't barked, we would have run over that little boy for sure. It was really quiet in the car during that ride home. The pup lay in my lap watching me like she knew me.

"When we got home, Mom picked her up and said, 'Puppy, you were our salvation today.'. And that was it. We always called her Sally, because her full name is kind of pretentious; Crandle's Salvation."

That put a chill up my back. "What are you going to tell your mom?"

"The whole story."

◆   ◆   ◆

The final sign:

Welcome to Oklahoma—NATIVE AMERICA. Really? What did that mean?

But, I was in the state I'd been aiming for. I could see forever. South of us, the sky was darkening. The clouds were promising—very promising.

I ran down my window and lit a Lucky.

The mood in the car got as dark as the storm front. Charlie glared at me. "You know lung cancer killed my dad!"

The cigarette suddenly tasted hot and stale; yesterday's ashtray in the back of my throat. "Is this about me smoking, or something else?"

He hadn't expected that. "I'm just not gonna let someone else I care about, kill himself. That's all!" Charlie was seething, feeling the kind of rage I knew something about.

I hadn't expected that. I tossed the cigarette out the window. "What do you mean, let someone else kill himself?"

"My dad; he OD'd on morphine when the cancer pain got too bad. He killed himself! It just wasn't fair. He didn't deserve to be so sick and in such pain … Mom didn't deserve to lose her husband ... And I didn't deserve to lose my dad. It's like I missed something—like I didn't do everything I should have. I should have stopped him."

"Charlie, don't blame yourself ..."

"This is crazy. I don't even know you—but I have this feeling—like we're family or something—and I'm damned if I'm going to watch you smoke and not say anything."

I had the same feeling about him, and I'd only known him for what, five hours? Didn't matter. He needed me to care enough to do the right thing—and he'd had the guts to tell me. I'd been there, feeling like I did nothing while all the people I loved had died. It had taken me all these years to figure out it wasn't up to me, and fairness had nothing to do with it.

"You're right Charlie, it wasn't fair. But your dad did what he thought was right for him—and there wasn't a damn thing you should have done about it."

He kept his face turned toward the window, silent.

"It wasn't up to you. Just like my father's, or my wife's or my son's deaths were not up to me." I was shaking. It was the first time I'd said it all out loud. I wasn't in control. It wasn't my fault. It had taken something terrible, like the Bradleys, to wake me up, make me live my life before it was too late.

I didn't want Charlie to repeat my mistake.

"Charlie, we all look back at what we did and didn't do, wishing we could make it better. I turned sixty a couple of months ago, wondering where my life had gone. I had to do something drastic to get it back.

"Don't fall into that trap. If your dad were here today, I know he'd be so proud of you he could just about fly—'cause I know I am.

"What you did back there with Mike Udahl was the most selfless thing I've ever seen anybody do; the best! Don't doubt yourself. You know what's right. Like you told Officer Udahl, no regrets."

Now I was the one choking up. It hadn't been exactly what I meant to say, but pretty close. I thought maybe I heard Jack Wilson chuckling somewhere, and my shakes disappeared.

Charlie kept silent. The Milk Bone was damp and gooey in his fist.

I drove on. Grandpa, Dad, Suzanne and my son, even the Bradleys, dancing around the fire, telling me it was alright.

A mile later I turned off, angling east and south on 270/412. The darkness of the sky was now solidly all around us. It was tangible, alive and independent of anything on earth.

The landscape got soft, losing its hard lines as the sky above demanded all my senses. The speed of the car became irrelevant under that living monster; impossible to tell if we were moving or merely holding in place as the purple-black walls stalked around us.

We traveled on, covered in our own thoughts. Glad to have said what we said, but still guys after all, trying to hide from each other inside the little space of the old car.

I turned the radio up, "This watch affects communities in Texas, Beaver, Harper, Woods, Woodward, Dewy, Ellis, and Major counties; including the towns of Woodward, Shattuck, Laverne, Elmwood, Mooreland, and Enid, until eight o'clock tonight. Conditions exist that could produce tornados."

Music came on. Not sure what it was; I had my own personal song going, Jim Morrison growling: Riders on the storm … Riders on the storm …

I looked over at Charlie. He gave me a crooked smile. "Looks like the weather's getting a little hairy out there." He was breaking the tension of our honesty with weather, the universal opener. "I've never seen anything like that. We don't get that evil-looking stuff in California."

A jagged ripple of lightening broke across the clouds miles to our right, showing the undersides of greenish billows stretching away toward the south and east. A wind gust pushed on the back end of the El Camino. Several tumble weeds broke out of the ditch and bumbled in a dusty herd over the road in front of us.

"I've always liked tumble weeds," I said. "Ever sing that song about 'em?"

"Sure." He sang, "Drifting along with the tumbling tumble weeds ... that's all the words I know though."

"That's all the words anybody knows." I laughed, glad to be back to talking.

The lightening continued way up high in the roiling clouds; now arching steadily in all directions. I followed them around through Charlie's window. Then in the rearview, constant flashes that looked almost blue.

It wasn't lightening.

◆   ◆   ◆

The cop was a long way behind us but gaining, dipping into hollows and reappearing. As the lights got closer I could see it was a convoy; three, maybe four of them.

"Wow," Charlie swiveled in his seat. "Looks like somebody's in trouble somewhere! They're really hauling ass!"

Time to get out of their way. I hit the brakes at a gravel road in the bottom of a dip, skidded off the pavement, tromped the gas and fishtailed down the road, throwing a cloud of dust. A blast of wind smacked us on the front fender, almost pushing us across the road on the loose gravel and blowing our dust cloud away along with another pack of tumble weeds and debris.

"What the hell are you doing?" Charlie gripped the dash with both hands, the seat belt digging into his shoulder.

"Just hold on!" I fought the wheel, yelling as I strained.

"Are you running from those cops?"

"I'll explain in a minute!" I cranked the wheel hard, clipping a mailbox as I whipped into an abandoned farmstead. Rusted farm implements huddled everywhere. We shot past a sagging clothes line, narrowly missing a low mound of earth and the scrub trees growing around its edges. Pounding and lunging, our gear crashing and flying; we halted behind the rotting barn. The old car rocked in the gale.

We listened to the wind, spiced now by the wail of sirens. Three cars, blue lights flashing, flew across a small visible section of Highway 270. They raced toward the storm and away from us.

"OK," I said. "I have a story to tell you. I am running from the cops," I looked him right in the eyes. "I killed two horrible people in Idaho three days ago. Maybe you heard about it?"

The look on Charlie Crandle's face was somewhere between astonishment and terror. "That was you?"

So he'd heard about it.

"You mean you shot those people? I can't believe it. You're not … I mean … you're just so …"

"Old and harmless?" I asked, grinning a little in spite of the situation. "They needed to be killed and I did it. No choice. I know the girls they hurt and the good folks who took them in. I'm done watching. Think about it. You understand."

He'd gone white. "Why did you come *here*?"

"I can't explain it Charlie. I just knew this was the place to come. I've met people all along the way that I was supposed to meet. You're one of them, and Sally, and Mike Udahl, and a bunch of others … you wouldn't believe it all if I told you."

Silence filled the car as we looked at each other. The wind had completely died. Sunlight seeped under the back edge of the storm and the old barn seemed to relax as it quit struggling to cling to its stone foundations.

"Do you think what I did was wrong?" I looked hard into his eyes. Charlie Crandle's answer mattered more to me than anything on earth or in heaven.

Charlie sucked in a deep breath; pushed it out. "No I don't," he said evenly. "In the few hours I've known you, I've told you stuff I've never told anybody else. And that whole thing with Sally … it was supposed to happen."

He was calm. "Keith, somehow I know you're doing what you should be doing," he murmured. "I think this may be the most important day of my life, and you're responsible for it."

"No Charlie, not me. You're responsible for it and what you get out of it is up to you."

Over on the highway two police cars, coming back toward us, ripped by; easily doing a hundred miles an hour. There had been three before.

The wall of clouds continued to gather, concentrating in front of us, lightening boiling inside. I'd seen this before, just before tornados came down.

Charlie said, "What are you gonna do now? You can't hide out behind a barn for the rest of your life."

"Charlie, I have to keep going," I said. "I can't take you where I'm headed."

"But we're in the middle of nowhere. You aren't gonna just leave me here in this storm?" He looked like he might be reconsidering my sanity.

"You've got your phone and I'll leave you all the food and gear. You got service, right?"

He pulled the phone from his jeans pocket, the bars were there; he set his mouth hard and nodded at me. "This doesn't make any sense. Why don't you just turn yourself in?" He stuffed the phone back in his pocket. "You'll get hurt if they have to chase you down. And we're gonna die if we stay here."

"No," I said. "That's not the way this will play out. Come on."

We hopped out into the tall grass. I looked for a second at the nasty crease and spoiled paint on the fender where I'd clipped the mailbox. Sorry Maxine. Two days and I'd already trashed the El Camino.

I grabbed my duffle bag and called to Charlie as the wind picked up again, "Put on your backpack. Come give me a hand with this cooler."

We set off through patches of head-high weeds and grass, lugging gear toward the house and the mound I'd seen next to it. It was slow going. We nearly went down twice before we reached the steps leading down into the doorway of the storm cellar. The heavy wooden door hung on hinges mounted in a stone wall. It had been well built, probably in the 1920s when electricity and refrigeration were only dreams; but twisters were always a nightmarish reality.

We dropped our gear and went down the four steps. With some persuasion the door opened to reveal a small room with shelves lining each side. Cobwebs hung predictably from every exposed surface. The floor and shelves were littered with junk. A string dangled from the ceiling leading up to the cellar's one modern addition, a porcelain light fixture, wiry filaments of a broken light bulb jutted from the socket.

"Looks pretty good," I said with a grin. "You'll like it here. All the amenities and the view is superb."

We looked back out the narrow doorway. The storm was immense. This one was growing faster and differently than my memories—uglier, more menacing.

"Yeah, this is great. Is the pool heated?" Charlie said; sarcasm in his tone and eyes. "Why don't I just come with you? We can share a cell; maybe sell a few black-market cigarettes to the other inmates."

I did like this kid. "Sorry guy, I'm taking this one by myself."

We made another trip back to the El Camino for more gear. I told him to take anything he wanted; he pretty much wanted it all. He took off for the cellar with everything he could carry. I stayed with the car for a minute, grabbed my duffel from the back and the manila envelope from under the seat.

In the cellar, Charlie had moved everything against the wall farthest from the door. Things were starting to buzz and flap in the wind outside.

I stood with my back to the door. "OK, one last thing. And this is not negotiable."

I handed him the manila envelope. "This is for you. It's mine. I earned it. And now I'm giving it to you. There's about thirty grand in there. Do something you want to do with it. You didn't do anything bad to get it. You didn't ask for it. It's purely a gift. Use it to some good end."

He laid it unopened next to a couple of broken jars on the dust-covered shelf and looked at me hard-eyed, with tears just underneath.

I took my watch off my left wrist. I reached in my right pocket; took out my pocket knife, my dad's blue poker chip, and a flat stone from the Little Missouri River.

"I want you to have these. The watch and the knife are mine. The chip was my dad's and the rock ... well I guess it's just a rock. Maybe you can build your own story around it."

Charlie reached out and accepted them. He stuck the rock in his left pocket, the knife and the chip in his right, strapped on my watch. Didn't say anything.

"Oh and one last thing, also not negotiable ..." I pulled Jack Wilson's shirt from my duffle bag, unrolling it and holding it up by the shoulders. It was holding on to me. The figures and the symbols danced again; Charlie's turn.

Charlie's mouth dropped open and the glow of the shirt lit up the inside of the dusty cellar. The sound of the storm faded away.

"You have to put this on. I won't even try to explain, but until this storm is over, or passes, or whatever happens in the next little while, you stay inside this shirt."

"Later, after the storm, call 9-1-1. When they come to pick you up, get close, shake their hands, and make sure the shirt touches them; touches them all. That's important. They'll take you anywhere you want to go. You'll know what to do."

His eyes were locked on the shirt. The dancing and the glow were a boiling caldron. He wasn't arguing.

"Charlie! You getting this?"

He looked up from the shirt. He was getting it … all of it. "Yeah," he whispered. "I got it. The shirt … it's …"

"That's not all. After that, keep the shirt safe inside your pack. Take it back to Mike Udahl and put it on his son. You can save him! Get this shirt on his son as soon as you can. Then you and Sally can leave. The Ghost shirt may want to go with you … You'll know. Then do something that scares the hell out of you." Like what I was saying didn't already fill that bill.

"OK, Keith."

I handed him the shirt. I felt it let go. He slid it on over his head and arms. The hem hit him just above the knees. The figures danced and undulated around his hips and over his chest.

"Actually, my name's not Keith." I couldn't bear leaving with any lies between us.

His eyes had changed. "Yeah, I know," he said. "No regrets Chip. No regrets."

I was not amazed by anything around that shirt anymore.

"You got it, Charlie Crandle. You got it!" I said. "I expect to see you again someday. Who knows, maybe sooner than we both think? Lock the door behind me the best you can. I gotta go, son."

He threw his arms around me for a couple of seconds and the shirt lit up the cellar like a beacon.

I turned from the light, and closed the old shelter's heavy door behind me. I heard Charlie slide the bolt, but the glow still surged out around the edges of the weathered doorframe. God, I hated to leave him, but it was the right thing. He had his own ground to cover; he didn't need me, and he wouldn't need the shirt very long to do it. I loved the kid; and it was almost as good as flying.

Part 2 CHAPTER 10

Battling the wind, I made it to the highway just as rain began to fall; huge crashing splats turned the red dust on my windshield into mud. The wipers streaked it into a pair of opaque arcs. I had to sit, waiting for the windshield to clear.

Coming up the gravel behind me, blue lights throbbing, was the third Highway Patrol car. He must have been driving the sections, maybe looking for me.

Screw the windshield. I stood on the gas pedal, shooting onto the highway toward the oncoming storm. The motor roared and the old car seemed relieved to be clearing its throat. In spite of the rain, the pavement didn't feel slick. I held on tight, concentrating on the road as it raced faster and faster at me through the streaked glass.

The blue lights swung out into my wake; headlights alternating, flashing left and right and coming fast. He was after *me*—no doubt now.

I kept the pedal down. The speedometer buried at one-twenty. The car wasn't done; still accelerating. It was terrifying and exhilarating. Considering what I was driving into, speeding didn't seem like much of a risk. No way the trooper would gain very quickly.

Rain swept across the road in a thick curtain, obliterating everything. Blind, I took my foot off the gas and felt for the center of the road, trying to stay on the pavement until I could see.

On my left, a blur of water streamed past, the green of the ditch getting closer. I pulled back to my right. The wheels found deep water. The car slewed and a huge spray came up over the hood. The wipers flapped uselessly, fighting their losing battle. The rear end of the El Camino swung left as the front tires dug into the unyielding rut of water. The water was slowing me. I nudged the wheel into the skid. "Come on!" The rear end came back. Gravel under the right front tire.

My windows blazed white, then blue. A shrieking siren pounded me as the cop shot by, close enough to touch. Then his blurred red tail lights filled the windshield and disappeared.

My wipers started to win. I could make out the road's edges. I touched the brakes; mistake! The water sent me skidding, spinning in slow motion. One, two revolutions? ... Three?

I stopped dead, right in the middle of Highway 270, listening to the rain on the roof, and my veins throbbing in my ears. Damn, that had been something.

I'd come to rest facing away from the storm. The cop sat below me, forty yards away. His car had gone through the ditch and sat in a field with its nose up in the air, high-centered on something big, lights still flashing.

Then the rain and the wind stopped again. The trooper got out and looked at me over the top of his car. He must have been a little dazed. He just stood there. As near as I could tell, he was not hurt.

He disappeared in darkness.

A black cloud enshrouded my car; rustling, brushing, flowing past. Black birds, thousands of them, rocked me side to side, like a gust, as they fled the storm. They were gone as fast as they arrived, a shoal of birds pulsating and vanishing into the distance. A black feather clinging to the rubber of a wiper blade was the only proof that it had happened at all.

I swiveled around to look out the back window. A wall of greenish-black rose from the horizon. Vast, it loomed over everything, thousands of feet up. It was cracked by lightening, and its surface boiled and slithered.

Then the funnel descended; grey-white, like the twisted sleeve of a dirty cotton shirt, slowly lowering a cuff toward the ground. It touched down. An eruption of dust and debris exploded and bloomed out around it.

Hail stones began to fall, golf balls clattering in the El Camino's steel bed. Through the dancing ice I watched the tornado destroy a building. It blew into a million bits that rose up to join the countless pieces of debris now swirling above the funnel.

The hail pounded harder, the noise of ice on metal deafening; I was inside a can beaten by a thousand hammers. The windshield had become a web of cracks and stars, the hood pocked and rippled with deep dents.

The hail petered out. Through the fractured glass, I looked toward the patrol car in the field. The cop popped back out. This time he had a rifle, and he was running toward me.

I wasn't waiting around to see what he wanted.

I spun the wheel and moved back toward the distant twister ... and what I had come to Oklahoma to do.

In my side-view I saw the cop reach the road with the rifle. Nothing came whistling through the back window. I kept on going.

The tornado seemed to be taunting me with space that I couldn't cover. Like mountains in the distance, it could have been a mile away, it could have been twenty. I leveled my speed off; forty-five felt like a hundred as I stuck my head out to get a clear look.

The cloud of debris had grown, and the pieces *in* the cloud had grown too. There was something huge and silver up there, lightening glinted off it; an old fashioned, small-town water tower; tank, roof, and legs intact, flying around inside the funnel. You couldn't have made it up.

Then the tower came down. It was a weird, home-grown missile; conical roof pointing at the earth, long legs pointing up; streaking down impossibly fast. It hit, no explosion, just gone.

After spitting out the tower, the tornado was working its way back and forth, north and south, across the road and back again.

It was waiting.

Up ahead sat an old straight truck with half its load of hay spread across the highway.

The road became a maze of eighty-pound bales, ditch-to-ditch for a hundred feet. I drove, zig-zagging, kicking up loose swirling hay, dodging bales until one lodged under the front bumper against the tire. Steering was impossible.

I skidded to a stop, jumped out into the wind and dug at the bale. The air filled with grit and hay and red dust. It stung my face, filled my eyes. The wind rocked the car as I cleared the bale away and climbed back in.

There on the passenger's headrest, sat a meadowlark, taking a nap, its grey feet locked into the upholstery as the wind blasting through the open window buffeted and pushed its feathers. It opened its eyes, black and shiny. Emotionless, it regarded me but made no move to leave.

I looked at my passenger, "Well birdy, might as well give it a try. I asked for it." The meadowlark didn't speak, just closed its eyes again and held on.

The funnel had grown wider, its taper gone. The cloud of junk up in orbit moved in a kind of slow-motion dance. There was no experience, or imagination, that would allow me to relate to water towers, brick buildings, semi-trucks, and mobile homes levitating and flying for miles.

As if to punctuate that thought, something massive crashed down on the asphalt fifty yards in front of the abandoned hay truck.

The road had sprouted a twisted pile of beams and pipes. A large square sign jutted up out of it; BUCKLE INN MOTEL. The fragile neon VACANCY sign, attached to its top edge, had somehow survived the flight.

A second later, a section of pink roof and a white wall of numbered doors came in for a landing behind me, shaking the ground and obliterating both lanes of the road.

I jerked the El Camino forward, my head out the window squinting against the junk in the air. I ran through the gears, accelerating toward the motel sign blocking my way.

Birdy was asleep. *Wake me when something exciting happens.*

The motel sign was fifteen feet tall. VACANCY growing and growing. My foot to the floor. I had not come all this way to be skewered by some damn neon sign!

Birdy and I hit the wreckage in a cloud of loose hay and steel. It blew away like match sticks.

"You have got to be shitting me." Pretty cool. No, fantastically cool. I had busted right through, scattering chunks of the BUCKLE INN as I went, the El Camino shuddering and gaining speed all the way.

Birdy was unimpressed.

I was rolling along now, the wind rocking us, the noise a beast in my ears; nothing between me and the storm except some empty highway.

It was tearing up a wide swatch of vacant green field, moving away.

Then, as if on cue, the storm looked back over its shoulder, threw its weight around and began a staggering walk back.

I forced myself to think only about how I would meet it when it came back to the road.

Here it came, slicing diagonally across the field … Coming for me.

The monstrous thing and I arrived at the same moment.

We got to know each other right away.

It was no longer a stranger at a respectful distance. Now it was in my face. Too close to see how the parts fit together. No edges, no funnel, no sides or top; just a hairy mass of dirty cotton candy that adhered itself quietly around the car, blotting out everything.

I was pressed back into the seat, pulled by gravity, as the nose of Max Gooby's wonderful car tilted smoothly upward.

I was up in the cloud.

Birdy woke and shook himself. He let go of the headrest and went past me, right out the open window.

I unbuckled, pushed out from under the wheel, and followed.

The last of my plan was accomplished.

Birdy floated along ahead of me. The car had fallen away, maybe seeking the road to which it was accustomed. We were going up. And it got lighter and lighter and I couldn't see anything below me—and there was no noise, no promises and no expectations. I put my arms out in front and flew into a black and white sky with my cape streaming out straight behind me.

Flying was easy. Effortless you might say.

EPILOGUE

STEVE ALBRIGHT – Idaho Fish and Game Officer

Chip's story hit North Idaho, and most of the country, with all the force he had wanted.

And then he vanished.

They tracked him through Montana and the Dakotas. He was connected by a few witnesses to a little girl in Nebraska; a girl that mysteriously turned up in a police station in North Platte.

Then they found his ID in a car that had been smashed flat by the strongest tornado in Oklahoma history. Funny thing, as devastating as that storm was, it hadn't killed anybody.

The smashed car had been owned by a little old lady in Belle Fourche, South Dakota. They found her, Maxine Gooby, 86 years old, sitting on her couch, smile on her face, dead from an aneurysm. She left no survivors and supposedly had a bunch of cash in her lap.

That was it. That's all I found out.

Chip was my friend. I'd learned a lot from him and he'd been the only guy I could really talk to. Don't think I ever told him that. I do miss him.

I could have stopped it all. But it wouldn't have been the right thing to do. Not for Chip, not for me, not for three little girls, not for anybody.

Had Chip really thought I wouldn't open that envelope until Monday? I promised I wouldn't, but sometimes the wrong thing is the right thing to do.

I saw Chip go into the Bradleys' house that night. I sat where I had so many times—saw the flashes and heard the shots and the screaming. Praying … letting Chip do what he had to do.

He walked right by me on his way home. He was humming something, but then Chip always had music coming out of him.

While *Chip's* disappearance was big news in Sandpoint, when chiropractor and Chinese herbalist Izzy Feldman went missing, it hardly caused a ripple. The Conspiracy Theorists down at Bevans Brothers insisted it was a cover-up of vast proportions. But nobody else gave it much thought. Izzy had been a weird one and maybe he'd just split. It happened all the time …

My family and I got to know Ben and Jessica Chandler better; and all their girls. Wonderful people. They had some tough times ahead, but then who doesn't?

Chip had made it all a little easier.

BEN CHANDLER – Financial Analyst

We arrived at the airport in Spokane expecting to see Chip waiting at the curb with our car and a big smile.

It was a Sunday; Mother's Day. The airport was nearly empty. I spotted Steve Albright, a guy I'd met but didn't know well, waiting at baggage claim as we made our way down the long corridor.

He gave me a slight wave and took me aside.

He filled me in about Chip's disappearance, what Chip had done before he left Sandpoint, and that our friend had vanished, without a trace, into thin air.

It had always been Chip's style to do things differently, but this I could never have predicted. He was the most even-tempered, under control person I knew.

He and I had talked about how the Bradleys deserved to die; sure. I'd even given Chip the combination to my gun safe so he could protect himself, and my house, while we were away. But down deep, I thought that was guy talk, you know,

BS. A guy says that kind of thing but never dreams of actually following through on it.

I never thought Chip was capable of killing anyone. Never.

I felt a lot of guilt and responsibility for what Chip had done. I thought back through our conversations. I'd said some hard things about the Bradleys. I wouldn't take them back, they were all true, but I most assuredly had not wanted Chip to act on my feelings.

I also couldn't help feeling this great relief and a sense of justice because he had killed them. Was that wrong?

Steve gave us a ride home in his Fish and Game Suburban. He had even brought along my trailer to haul our luggage. He dropped us off and promised to give me a call later to talk at length about the whole thing.

When our dogs came out to greet us, Finster wasn't with them. We were tired and upset anyway. Jess and the girls burst into tears. I went to look for him and did my crying while I checked on the rest of the animals. I had a feeling that Finster wasn't going to turn up.

And our Audi wasn't there. That didn't seem like Chip's style either. A lot of surprises that day.

I could tell that Chip had been in the house. He'd eaten the food we'd left and drank the beer I'd gotten especially for him. My phone was on the kitchen counter next to Chip's beer bottles. Jess's never did turn up. Funny, we hadn't even thought about the phones at that point.

I walked through the basement, hoped to find some clues about Finster. There weren't any.

I checked the gun safe. Chip had been in it. He probably thought he'd put it all back the way he found it, but there were some little differences.

Then I found the backpack stuffed under my desk. It was full of hundred-dollar bills. Close to two-and-a-half–million dollars. On top of the money was a handwritten letter.

> Ben,
>
> Welcome home. I expect you know most of the story by now. I can't tell you the whole thing, because I don't know how it's all going to end yet myself.
>
> I wanted you to know how much I admire you and Jess and what you are doing for all your girls. I wish I had half the generosity you two have.
>
> I wanted you to have the girls' "inheritance." The money came from some bad stuff the Bradleys were into. Keep it. Don't do something dumb like turn it in or tell the police. Nobody knows anything about it, and it certainly will go to good use with Beth and Mary and Dawn. Use it for them and for whatever you need for yourselves and your other girls.
>
> I hope what I've done doesn't put a shadow on them or you. If it does, I am sorry about that. They are very young. With time it will fade and you'll go on. I know things will be better for them.
>
> Talk to Steve Albright. He knew what the Bradleys were capable of. He'll help you. He's a man worth knowing.
>
> I'm sorry to tell you that Finster is gone. He was peacefully sleeping next to me and just never woke up. I buried him above the river near the huge cottonwood tree on the corner of your place. I know you'll miss him. But he decided to go and that's what dogs do. He was a dog worth knowing.
>
> J.J. and Bobbi did a great job of taking care of the animals. They're good kids.

As for me? Well, I had to do something that I knew was right. I did it because I wanted to, and I guess because I needed to. The only thing you had to do with it was that I got to do something for a couple of people I admire.

How many of us really get to do what we want in the end?

I'm lucky.

I doubt we will meet again, on this plane anyway. But I'd sure like to see you again on another one. Keep an eye out for me.

Chip

P.S.

Really sorry about the Audi. Have an IPA and think kind thoughts of me. Tell Jess I love her.

The next day I went into Sandpoint to pick up our mail being held at the Post Office. In with all the rest of the mail was a small padded envelope with a Belle Fourche, South Dakota postmark.

It held the Audi key, a smaller key, and a short handwritten note on a small square of paper with *Zorba's U-Store, We Got Room* printed across the top of it.

Ben,

Jess's Audi is locked in storage unit D13 at Zorba's U-Store in Belle Fourche, South Dakota.

Go get it. Try to get it without telling anybody. It will make your life easier. Just go get it soon or Frank, at Zorba's, will sell it!

On your way, stop by the Camp Crook Corner Bar and Café, in Camp Crook, SD. Ask for Judge and Muu Muu. Tell them Greg Shanks sent you. Ask them about

Tipperary, the King of the Outlaw Horses and Ardel Canutt. Meet Ardel if you can (take whiskey with you).

Then have an ice cream cone at one of the picnic tables out back under the cottonwood trees.

It's a trip worth taking.

Gotta fly,

Chip

Jess and I went and got "her" Audi.

Three months later we legally adopted our three new girls; Beth, Mary and Dawn *Chandler*.

We took Chip's advice and got to know Steve Albright and his family. In fact they have become close friends. People we value.

Chip was right. It has been a trip worth taking.

Acknowledgements

With deep appreciation to everyone who read, helped and encouraged. God knows I needed it all.

Especially; Sally, Morri, Ken and JoAnne, Kathy, Tom, Travis, Alan, Evans Bros (for the coffee), Lisa, Lynn, and Mom.

Kevin and Loni, your ability to give is unsurpassed.

And to everyone who believes life is magic if you'll let it be.

About the Author

Tim Martin lives in the Monarch Mountains outside Sandpoint, Idaho —about an hour's drive from Washington, or Montana, or Canada, and a long way from the Iowa farm where he grew up.

Tim relates well to dogs and cats, fly-fishermen, cold beer, hot coffee, dead spots in cell coverage, and people who care enough to listen after they ask a question.

On Death and Flying was inspired by real-life friends who adopted two abused children.

Tim continues to have a deep-seated belief that life is unexplainable magic and everything works pretty well when you don't try too hard. He is at work on his next novel.

Contact Tim: facebook.com/bytimmartin/

Made in the USA
Columbia, SC
07 February 2019